THE GIRL SHE WAS

Also by Rebecca Freeborn
Misconception
Hot Pursuit

THE GIRL SHE WAS

REBECCA FREEBORN

PANTERA
PRESS

PANTERA
PRESS

First published in 2020 by Pantera Press Pty Limited
www. PanteraPress.com

A Cataloguing-in-Publication entry for this book is available from the National Library of Australia.

ISBN 978-0-6485084-3-4 (Paperback)
ISBN 978-0-6485084-4-1 (eBook)

Cover Design: Christa Moffitt, Christabella Designs
Cover Images: Lyuba Burakova/Stocksy
Publisher: Lex Hirst
Editor: Lucy Bell
Proofreader: Alexandra Nahlous
Typesetting: Kirby Jones
Author Photo: Welcome to the Fold, wttf.com.au
Printed and bound in Australia by McPherson's Printing Group

The paper this book is printed on is certified against the Forest Stewardship Council® Standards. McPherson's Printing Group holds FSC® chain of custody certification SA-COC-005379. FSC® promotes environmentally responsible, socially beneficial and economically viable management of the world's forests.

*For all the fierce, funny, brilliant women
I've been fortunate to have in my life.*

A seventeen-year-old girl is just never, ever in her prime. Ever.

Hannah Gadsby

NOW

Layla Flynn was breaking up a fight when she got the message. Her two children grappled with each other in the bath, sloshing warm water over the rim and soaking Layla's shoes. She pulled Ella away from Louis, half-heartedly threatening, for the fifth time, to pull out the plug, then took her phone from her back pocket. On the screen, there was a notification from Facebook Messenger; a message from a woman whose name she'd never expected to see again.

I know what you did.

No preamble, no sign-off, just those five words.

An all-too-familiar unease glimmered deep inside her. It'd been twenty years since she'd left Glasswater Bay. She'd long ago stopped wondering whether anyone would find out what she'd done. It was in the past, and Layla didn't dwell on the past.

Louis filled his mouth with water and spat it in his sister's face, and within seconds they were splashing each other again, sending waves of water onto the bathroom floor. Layla pocketed the phone and lifted her son's squirming body out of the bath.

She'd ignore the message. No one could prove anything now.

THEN

Sweet sixteen and never been kissed. God, I was such a cliché. Except that I was seventeen, which made it even more pathetic.

Sitting here against the wall at the Glasswater Bay High School social, watching as half my classmates coupled up and began to sway awkwardly on the dance floor: a wallflower, Grandma would say. The blue, purple and white lights from the rotating disco ball overhead didn't reach the bench where I was, so I could sit in gloomy anonymity, the paper plate balanced on my lap littered with pastry crumbs. My gaze flicked irresistibly to my friend Shona, whose lips were locked with her new boyfriend's, their pelvises fused together, his hands clutching her bum.

Renee bumped into me as she plonked down on the bench beside me. 'Why don't they ever play decent music at these things?'

'If they played Magic Dirt or Regurgitator, I might actually enjoy a social for once,' I agreed. 'I don't know why we bother coming.'

'Well, for that.' Renee threw an arm out towards Shona and Daniel. 'Look at them. Practically dry-rooting.'

'They'll be rooting for real later on.' I laughed to cover up the sting of this fact. I'd had an unspoken and unrequited crush on Daniel for the last year. But considering I'd never done anything about it, let alone told my two best friends, I could hardly be angry with Shona for asking him to the social. So now she was pashing my one true love while I watched like a creepy weirdo in the darkness.

'We need to find *you* a guy,' Renee said. 'I bet you could hook up with anyone here. You look totally hot tonight.'

I glanced down at my black dress that I spent half my wages on last week. The bodice would've looked sexy on any of my classmates, but my almost-flat chest made me look like a twelve-year-old pretending to be a high-class escort. I was what was charmingly known as a 'late bloomer', confirmed by the lack of romantic interest throughout my high school years.

Renee was sweet to say so, but I knew how I really looked.

'It's not like we're inundated with options,' I said, ignoring the fact that none of the boys here even knew I was alive. 'Glasswater's a dive full of pigs and losers.'

Her eyes scanned the room. 'What about Sam? He's cute.'

I screwed up my nose. 'His idea of humour is telling the whole class how many times he wanked on the weekend.'

'OK, who else? I know, Rasheed! He's hot in a nerdy kind of way.'

'Rasheed's nice, but we've got nothing in common.'

'You're both brainiacs,' Renee pointed out. 'And you both like reading. Maybe he could *read your lips*.' She chuckled.

I couldn't help laughing. 'Thanks, but I think I'd rather wait for the right guy.'

Renee gave me a wry smile. 'Babe, you know I love you to death, but if I leave it up to you, you'll never make a move on anyone. Do you really want to start uni next year having never kissed a guy?' She glanced over her shoulder. 'Look, he's over there by himself. I'll go talk to him.'

'No, Renee, don't.' I tried to restrain my friend, but she'd already escaped, sidling between the gyrating couples until she reached Rasheed.

My face burned as she spoke to him. Rasheed was nice and all, and good looking too, with his golden skin and long-lashed dark eyes, but he was even more self-conscious than I was. I'd rarely seen him speak outside of being the first to answer all the teacher's questions in Biology. But Renee had a point about popping my kissing cherry before I finished school. The older I got, the more I felt like a giant loser. But doing it with Rasheed? No doubt he'd never kissed anyone either. He probably wouldn't even come over.

He was coming over.

Renee was clutching his hand and grinning at me in triumph as she delivered my prize. He looked embarrassed to the point of physical pain. I almost felt sorry for him, until I remembered that Renee had just told him I liked him and now I was about to be rejected by a guy I wasn't even interested in to begin with. Renee deposited him on the bench beside me.

'You kids have fun!' She winked at me. 'I'm going to get a Coke.'

Humiliation fizzed in my belly as she sashayed away. I darted a glance at Rasheed. 'Hey.'

'Hey.' He shifted uncomfortably, as if he was trying to move further away from me without being too obvious. We both stared straight ahead as the ballad ended and was replaced with an energetic Destiny's Child number. The guys peeled away from the dance floor in a wave while the girls whooped with glee and formed circles to shake their manes and wiggle their hips. I tried to think of something to say to Rasheed, but my mind was blank, and the longer we sat there, not talking, the more the discomfort swelled in my throat.

'Read any good books lately?' I finally managed to squeak.

'Sorry?' Rasheed leant closer to hear my voice over the music. His cologne smelt nice – spicy and woody. I repeated my question, and to my surprise his face lit up. 'Yeah, I've just finished *Assassin's Apprentice* by Robin Hobb – have you read it?'

'Sorry, I haven't heard of it.'

'It's an epic fantasy. Do you read much fantasy?'

'Uh, no, not really.' So much for having something in common.

We resumed our uneasy silence and stared out into the crowd. I spotted Renee gesturing at me from where she was dancing with Shona, giving me the *what are you waiting for?* signal. I frowned and shook my head at her. An early eighties song came on and there was a cry of joy from the dance floor. The night was almost over, and I wanted to be up there with my friends, dancing and having fun, but instead I was stuck here with Rasheed, vying for the position of Lord Mayor of Awkward Town.

Then Rasheed said something I couldn't make out, and as I moved closer to hear him better, he launched forwards and our teeth clashed. He drew back a little, mumbled an apology and then his mouth was on mine again. For a few seconds, I was frozen, then his tongue was in my mouth and I was trying to kiss him back, but our teeth kept knocking together and it was all very, well, *wet.* Was this really what I'd been waiting for all this time?

Just as I was wondering how I could politely break contact, there came the sound of whooping over the metallic synth-pop music. Rasheed drew away, smiling shyly. On the edge of the dance floor, Renee and Shona were clapping and cheering. My face flushed hot and I shuffled away from Rasheed, tugging my dress down over my thighs and wishing I could wipe my mouth. Renee swooped in and took my hand, pulling me to my feet.

'Come to the ladies with me.' She threw a smile over her shoulder at Rasheed as she led me towards the toilets. Shona fell in beside me.

As soon as the doors closed behind us, they both threw their arms around me and jumped up and down. I laughed. 'You guys are more excited about this than I am.'

'Layla Flynn, the tongue-wrestling champion!' Shona declared.

'So, how was it?' Renee asked as we turned to the mirror to reapply our lipstick.

'It was bloody gross,' I said. 'I can't believe you actually enjoy doing that.'

'Oh, I love kissing!' Renee enthused.

'It gets better.' Shona inspected her teeth in the mirror. 'It's like sex. The first time sucks, but the next time is better, and by the third you can't get enough.'

I stared down into the sink. Both my friends had lost their virginity when they were fifteen, and I was still going on about how yucky boys were. Renee bumped her elbow into me gently. 'You know what, Rasheed's probably just a crap kisser.'

'I guess it wasn't that bad,' I lied. 'I just don't really like him that way.'

'At least you've done it now,' Shona said. 'You'll be bonking before you know it.'

'Speaking of which,' Renee said, 'is bonking on *your* agenda tonight, Shona?'

'Well, Daniel's taking me to Bruiser's party after this, so we'll see what happens. But I have precautions!' Shona plucked a string of at least five condoms from her make-up case and unfurled them with a flick of her wrist.

They burst into giggles, and the ache in my belly grew. It's not as if I was anything more to Daniel than a cardboard cut-out beside my hot friends, but the idea that Shona was probably going to have sex with him in the back of his car tonight made me shrink inside a little.

Shona snapped her case closed. 'Let's go, bitches.'

The music had stopped and the lights were on when we emerged from the toilets. Students milled around in small groups, saying goodbye or finding out who was going to Bruiser's party. Shona made a beeline for Daniel, who was chatting with his mates, and Renee and I trailed behind her. Just as we reached them, Rasheed materialised, eyeing me nervously. He looked unsure what was expected of him.

Daniel nodded towards Renee, Rasheed and me. 'You guys coming to Bruiser's party? There'll be booze.'

Rasheed flushed. 'I can't, sorry, my mum is picking me up.' He stole a glance at me. 'See you at school on Monday, Layla?'

'Sure.' I tried not to show my relief that the whole encounter was over.

'I should go.' He began to back away. 'She'll be waiting out the front.'

Daniel snorted as Rasheed turned and hurried towards the exit. 'Can't keep Mummy waiting!' he said, loud enough that Rasheed must have heard him.

'Hey, don't be mean!' Shona elbowed him in the ribs. 'What about you guys? Coming to the party?'

'Absolutely,' Renee said.

I hesitated. I'd told my parents I'd stay at Renee's place for this very reason, but after the kiss, my mood had tanked. I didn't feel changed, or more mature, or different in any way. I was still the same geek I'd been before I bumped teeth with Rasheed.

'C'mon, Lay,' Shona said. 'We'll find you someone else to pash. Someone who's better at it than Rasheed.'

'I don't know—' I started, but I was cut short as Daniel let out a bellow of laughter.

'*You* pashed *Rasheed*? That's scraping the barrel, isn't it?'

I wasn't sure whether he was insulting me or Rasheed, or both of us, but suddenly Daniel didn't seem quite so attractive anymore. 'I think I might just go home.'

'No, come, please!' Renee took both my hands and gave them a little shake. 'It won't be the same without you. Have a few drinks and you'll be right.'

I squeezed her hands. 'I'm a bit over it tonight. Sorry.'

Shona gave Daniel a push. 'You didn't have to be such a dick about Rasheed.'

Daniel grabbed her hand and pulled her back to him, slinging his arm around her shoulders. His possessiveness both annoyed the crap out of me and made me feel small with envy.

'Fine.' He winked at me. 'If the lady doesn't want to go, then we'll give her a lift home.'

My annoyance dissipated and my estimation of Daniel went back up. 'Thanks. That'd be great.'

*

Renee and I squeezed into the back seat of Daniel's car with his two friends, me squashed against one window and Renee practically sitting in Vince's lap. No one bothered with seatbelts. As silvery beams from streetlights slid across our laps, I indulged the fantasy that Daniel secretly liked me and was only with Shona to get closer to me. It would explain his barbed comments to Rasheed, coupled with his offer of a lift home. And there was that wink before. Though his enthusiastic groping with Shona on the dance floor didn't exactly fit this theory. Then I caught a glimpse of my reflection in the window: the childish jut of my chin, my boring chestnut-brown hair, the dusting of freckles visible even in this light. I pressed my cheek against the cold glass. Of course he didn't like me; I was ridiculous.

When we stopped at Glasswater Bay's only set of traffic lights, Daniel started kissing Shona again. The lights turned green but they showed no sign of stopping. I went to nudge Renee, only to discover that she was similarly occupied with Vince, while Sam was too busy staring out of his own window to notice. Irritation rose within me.

'Hey!' I shouted, louder than I'd intended. 'The light's green.'

Shona broke away from Daniel with a laugh and he took off, the tyres squealing. Renee didn't even come up for air.

As I directed Daniel to my house, I realised that it wasn't going to parties or being Daniel's girlfriend that I wanted … I *wanted* to want it, but the truth was, what I really felt like doing was going home with my friends and talking all night like we used to do. Wearing our undies on the outside of our clothes and standing on Renee's parents' coffee table to mime Madonna songs. Talking about cute boys at school, safe in the knowledge that we'd never do anything about it.

My friends were leaving me behind, but I didn't want to catch up with them. I wanted to hold them back with me.

Renee finally came unstuck from Vince as we pulled up outside my house, her freshly applied lipstick kissed away, the pale skin around her mouth raw and red. There was an unfocused look in her eyes as she put her arm around my shoulder. 'Sure you don't want to come with us? It'll be fun.'

'Nah, I don't think so. Have a good night.' I swung open the door and got out onto the footpath. Daniel didn't even wait for me to get to the front door before he screeched away up the street.

Mum was sitting at the round table in the kitchen when I walked in, her hands clasped around a mug of tea. 'I thought you were staying at Renee's tonight?'

'Nah,' I said. 'They were going to a party, but I didn't feel like it.'

Her face brightened over the rim of her mug, and I could tell she was trying to mask her delight at how responsible I was. 'Do you want a cuppa?'

'Think I might go to bed,' I said.

'All right, sleep well.'

I went to my bedroom and threw myself onto my single bed with its pink quilt cover and girlish ruffles, cursing my stupid dumb immaturity and the stupid dumb boys in this stupid dumb town.

NOW

The moment Cameron got home from work, Layla forgot about the message. As always, his gaze sought out hers first, his soft brown eyes warm with affection. He kissed her, loosening his tie with one hand. It was this practice – this deliberate decision to check in with her first rather than focusing his attention straight on the kids – that kept the connection between them alive. It was one of the things she loved about him.

'How were they today?' he asked, kneeling down to let Louis and Ella hurl themselves at him.

'Oh, you know,' Layla said vaguely. 'Somewhere along the spectrum of sweet angel to chaos demon.'

Layla adored her children with a fierceness that surprised her, but sometimes the weight of their need was suffocating, especially on the days she was home with them. When she and Cam had decided to have kids, they'd planned to share the parenting equally, but despite their best intentions they'd fallen into traditional gender roles. When she'd returned from maternity leave to her job as a pharmacist the first time round, Cam had been earning more than she was, and there hadn't seemed much sense in him taking a pay cut to work part-time, especially when they'd planned to have another baby so soon. And then when she was ready to go back after having Ella, he'd just got a promotion and going part-time was out of the question. Over time, they'd grown accustomed to the extra money, and they'd stopped talking about when it would be Cam's turn to drop hours. She'd learnt to tame the hot flash of jealousy every time he donned his suit jacket and walked out the front door. But she couldn't quite shake the lingering suspicion that he was glad to escape to the refuge of his work … that he enjoyed playing the part of the overworked dad who wished he could spend more time with his kids.

Cam straightened, holding Louis upside down as he howled with glee. 'Did you eat your dinner tonight, champ?'

'No!' Louis crowed, his face turning red. 'It was yucky!'

Cam raised his eyebrows at Layla, and she shrugged. 'Apparently, spaghetti is the only decent food in the whole world. How was your day?'

'Busy. Oh, that reminds me, I ran into Nathan today. He's invited us over for a barbecue lunch next Saturday.'

'The kids are having their hair cut at two. I told you that, didn't I?' Layla tried not to show her exasperation. Cam was a brilliant commercial lawyer and senior associate in his firm, but outside of a professional setting he was a complete scatterbrain.

'Crap, I forgot, sorry. I can call tomorrow and see if we can make the appointments earlier?'

But Layla knew it'd disappear from his mind the second he got to work, and she'd end up doing it herself. She was the one who made all the appointments, who remembered when vaccinations were due, who thought about and organised Book Week costumes for child care, who had researched the local kindergartens for Louis next year. She didn't love these responsibilities, but she knew, with a sharp knock of horror, how much worse her life could've been.

That reminded her of the message, and she moved in close and put her arm around her husband's waist, drawing his warmth into her own body as if to convince herself that he was real, that she didn't have to be afraid. Cam looked down at her with a grin, but Louis was shrieking to be an aeroplane now, so Layla stepped away to make room for Cam to hoist him sideways and swing him around in mad circles. Ella jumped up and down, her eyes bright with excitement as she waited for her turn.

Layla knew they'd take forever to get to sleep now that Cam had revved them up, but it was so lovely to watch her beautiful man playing with their children. Besides, the one thing Cam committed to every night was getting the kids to bed. He read them books and tickled them and lay beside them in their beds until they drifted off to sleep, leaving Layla free to shake the day off her shoulders. She leant against the bench and smiled. She was so lucky.

'OK, kiddos, time for bed,' Cam announced. 'Say goodnight to Mummy.'

Layla swept them into her arms. Her patience, worn thin from the long day, softened into tenderness as their little arms tightened around her neck. She murmured endearments to them and kissed the sweet spot below their ears.

Cam took her hand and gave it a quick squeeze. 'Sit down and relax. Let's order takeaway for dinner.'

Layla was neither hungry nor satisfied after she'd eaten the kids' rejected meals earlier, but she said nothing as he flung a child over each shoulder and carried them up the hallway. She poured herself a glass of riesling and sat down on the couch with a grateful sigh. As soon as the kids' giggles softened to murmurs behind the closed bedroom door, she took out her phone and opened Messenger. The woman in the profile picture stared back at her from the little circle at the top of her list of messages. Jodie Telford. The mere sight of her name sent the tide of memories washing over Layla again. That year, the year she was seventeen, had changed her life. She had assumed the secret would remain locked inside her. Until tonight.

I know what you did.

Why would Jodie contact her now, after all these years? If she really knew what Layla had been responsible for, surely she would've done something about it twenty years ago? She must be bluffing. Layla was thirty-seven years old. She had a career, a family. She couldn't allow herself to be intimidated by empty words. Her thumb hovered over the 'delete' icon.

'What are you looking at?'

Layla gasped as Cam placed a hand on her shoulder.

'Nothing.' She locked the phone and dropped it in her lap, twisting to look up at her husband.

He raised his eyebrows. 'You were staring pretty intensely at nothing.'

She let out a nervous laugh. 'I was just zoning out. I'm really tired.'

'Messaging your secret boyfriend, were you?' He was smiling, but there was a strained look around his eyes that told her what the joke cost him.

'Ha! When would I find time for a secret boyfriend?'

His expression relaxed. 'Do you know where Ella's drink bottle is?'

She pointed at the bench. 'Up there. Do you need help?'

He squeezed her shoulder. 'Nah, you've spent all day with them; bedtime is my job. I'll leave you to your "zoning out".'

She let out her breath as he returned to Ella's room. She hadn't heard him come out, so she had no idea how long he'd been behind her, and how much he'd seen. She'd have to be more careful.

THEN

There were no customers in the cafe when I stepped out in my black jeans and shirt, my school uniform stuffed into my bag. Yumi stood behind the counter, lazily twisting the end of her long, black ponytail around her finger and staring off into the distance. I dumped my bag under the counter and nudged her arm, and her face lit up with her characteristic brilliant smile.

'Quiet afternoon?' I said.

She groaned. 'Dead. Lunch was busy, but I've only had a few takeaway coffees since two. At least the view's been good.' She indicated our boss and owner of the cafe, Scott, who was cleaning one of the tables, his black shirtsleeves rolled up above his elbows.

'Have his wife and kids been in today?' I darted her a cheeky look. Yumi had been lusting after Scott for ages – or at least since we'd both started working at the cafe last year.

'A girl can dream, can't she?'

I tied my black apron around my waist. 'As long as it's only dreaming.'

I would never admit as much to her, but I had a bit of a crush on Scott myself – I mean, who wouldn't? He was

17

super hot, with his sandy hair that flopped boyishly over his forehead, his clear blue eyes that crinkled at the corners when he smiled, and his honeyed skin. At twenty-eight, he was old enough to seem terribly grown up but still young enough to be cool. And he treated us like adults, which was more than I could say for most people in this town. He may have lived here his whole life, but at least he was making an effort to drag Glasswater Bay into the modern age; he'd opened the town's first proper cafe when he was in his early twenties. Everyone had assumed there'd be no appetite for flat whites, macchiatos and focaccias over the town's original tearooms, and the older generation had shaken their heads at Scott's arrogance, buying that huge floor space in the blind belief that it would be a success. But it was – with its close proximity to the beach, the cafe was a hit with tourists on weekends, and regularly frequented by locals. I'd be lying if I said I wasn't proud to be working at one of Glasswater Bay's few success stories. Besides, Scott made me feel good. He called me 'babe', and he touched my back when he passed behind me at the counter, and his eyes sparkled when he pulled on my hair in his good-natured way.

Yumi hung her apron on the hook next to the dishwasher. 'Well, I'd better be off. Gotta drive back to town tonight.'

'Big night out?'

'Big night of studying, more like, then back-to-back tutes for the rest of the week before I drive back here for the Friday-night shift.'

'I don't get why you keep living in Glasswater. As soon as I get into uni I'll be out of this shithole town.'

'I can't afford to live in Adelaide, and while I love my grandparents, I couldn't handle living with them more than a few nights a week. But once I finish uni and get a job, I'll move there. Until then, I'm stuck in Glasswater Bay and saving money while working in this place.'

'And perving on Scott.'

'Swings and roundabouts, girlfriend. See you Friday night.'

I watched as she crossed the floor of the cafe, her narrow waist above the smooth curve of her hips, pert butt in tight jeans, and for the thousandth time I wondered if I'd ever fill out my own jeans like that. She bumped fists with Scott, then stepped out onto the footpath and set off up the main street. Scott came over to the counter with his irresistible grin that always made me feel a little bit warm inside.

'Hey, you.' He tugged the end of my plait. 'Good day at school?'

'Fine,' I lied.

After the episode with Rasheed at the social, the last few days had been insufferable. The popular girls sneered at me with disdain, while the unpopular ones cast me envious glances whenever I walked by. And as for the boys, they ignored me altogether, which, let's face it, was nothing out of the ordinary. Except Rasheed, of course, who was too shy to do anything bolder than make brief eye contact across the classroom in Biology. My friends defended me fiercely, but it didn't stop me from feeling like a total loser. We'd always enjoyed the comfortable middle ranking at school, liked (or at least tolerated) by almost everyone, but the kiss had brought my previous under-the-radar existence out into the light, and not in a good way.

Scott lifted a tray of glasses onto the counter, the veins in his forearms standing out like cords. I allowed my mind (admittedly, not for the first time) to turn over what it might be like to kiss someone who knew what he was doing. Someone who had arms like those. If kissing happened the way it did in my head, maybe I'd actually enjoy it.

Scott looked up then and caught me watching him. He raised an eyebrow as if he'd read my thoughts. A warm flush of embarrassment – and something else, something a lot more pleasurable – spread in my chest and worked its way down low. I ducked my head to hide my face, which I knew from experience would have turned a vivid shade of magenta.

There'd always been something about Scott's raw male presence that intoxicated me, especially in comparison with my classmates. Of course, the classroom environment didn't exactly help, but still. This felt different; the space between us had a physical presence all of its own, pressing up against me as if daring me to push back. Or maybe it was all in my imagination.

The door of the cafe swung open and three girls from school swept in on a gale of giggles. This was the downside of working in the only cafe in Glasswater Bay – everyone who came in knew who I was and where I lived and who my parents were and what year I was in at school and which uni course I was going to apply for when I finished Year Twelve. Anonymity was not an option. When the girls noticed me behind the counter, they exchanged glances and giggled again. Katrina was one of the only girls at school who'd ever given me any trouble, and the other two were her hangers-on who followed her lead in everything.

'Hi, Layla,' trilled Katrina, tossing her sleek blonde hair over her shoulder.

'Hey,' I mumbled.

'Three lattes, please,' she said, and the other two laughed again as if she'd made a hilarious joke.

'I'll make them,' Scott said. 'You catch up with your friends.'

I started to protest, but he was already behind the coffee machine.

'So, Layla,' Katrina said slyly. 'You had a pretty good time at the social last week.'

'Yeah, how *is* Rasheed?' one of the other girls said.

Katrina held my gaze, her pale eyes like ice chips. 'I hear it was your first kiss.'

'Ooooh!' chorused the other two, and my face flushed hot once again.

'Rasheed Geekface wouldn't have been *my* first choice,' Katrina went on. 'But I guess beggars can't be choosers, can they?'

In my peripheral vision, I saw Scott glance over at me, and the heat in my face intensified. 'Seven fifty, thanks.'

Katrina handed over a ten-dollar note, and I shoved her change at her without meeting her eyes.

'Why don't you girls sit down?' Scott said. 'I'll bring your coffees over in a minute.'

Katrina looked at Scott as if noticing him for the first time, and a slow smile spread across her face. 'That'd be great, thanks,' she said silkily.

She strutted across the room to one of the dark wooden tables near the window, which offered a sliver of a view of the bay. The other girls followed.

Scott sidled across to stand beside me. 'Guess they're not your friends, then?'

'Not so much.'

We watched as they took turns whispering and shrieking with laughter.

'They remind me of seagulls,' Scott said. 'Squawking away like that. Sometimes I forget you're just a schoolkid … you're so much more mature than this lot.'

I ducked down and opened the door of the dishwasher to hide my smile. He thought I was mature. Katrina's teasing suddenly meant nothing to me.

It was only as I watched Katrina batting her lashes and tilting her head to the side like a demented canary as Scott delivered their coffees that I remembered he'd overheard that I'd only just kissed someone for the first time. My smile dissolved as his words rang in my ears.

You're just a schoolkid.

NOW

Layla was already running late for work on Saturday morning, and had nearly finished her toast when Cam held the phone out to her and mouthed *your mother*. He gave a wry smile.

Her mother always called on the landline, so Layla couldn't even put her on speaker and rush out the door. She almost asked Cam to take a message, but she knew the conversation would be quick, efficient; the bare essentials. That was the way it'd been since, well, pretty much since they'd left Glasswater Bay.

'Hi, Mum.'

'How are you, Layla?'

'Running late for work, actually. What's up?'

'Oh, sorry, I keep forgetting you work on Saturdays.' There was a hint of relief in her voice. No need for small talk. 'This will just take a minute. I was wondering if you had plans with your father for Christmas?'

'No, he's going to Sydney this year with Petra.' Layla pondered how easy it was these days to speak the name of her father's second wife. She'd spent years hating him for his weakness, for not being able to make it work with her mother. Hating herself too, of course, for her own hand in it. But over time, resentment had mellowed into resignation. Understanding, even.

'Oh, lovely,' her mother said with feigned brightness. 'What about Cam's mother?'

'I think she wants to do dinner.' There was no need to consider Cam's father. He hadn't been in the picture for years. 'Why?'

'I've been speaking to Zach and he wants to bring Caitlin around on Christmas Day.' Her voice took on a genuinely cheerful tone. 'She's the first girl he's been serious enough about to bring home. I thought it might be nice if we all got together for lunch.'

A faint bitterness prickled Layla's tongue. It didn't matter how accomplished she was, how beautiful her children were, how she had built her life up from emptiness to fulfilment, Zach was always the favourite. Sweet, uncomplicated, good-natured Zach, who'd never had a serious girlfriend, who jumped from casual job to casual job, who moved from one rental to the next whenever his lease expired, who'd never set down any roots. But who'd also never made any terrible mistakes.

'Layla?'

'Sorry. Yes, that sounds good.'

'How's everything at home?' There was a hint of concern in her mother's voice that Layla hadn't heard in a long time, and for a second, she contemplated telling her about the message. The girl she was needed someone to tell her everything was going to be all right, to take over and smooth down the fear and doubt with a firm yet gentle hand.

But she swallowed down the urge. That girl, and the mum who'd been there for her when she'd needed her most, had to remain in the past. For both their sakes.

'I'm fine,' she said. 'I just really need to get to work.'

*

The shopping centre car park was packed with Christmas shoppers and it took Layla forever to find a park. She'd taken her coffee in the car to save time, but once she'd touched up her lipstick in the rear-view mirror, she was still ten minutes late. The only thing she hated more than being late for work was appearing in public without her perfectly applied mask in place. She got out of the car and hurried across the car park, her heels clacking over the baking bitumen, the crushed stones within sparkling in the morning sunlight like tiny jewels. The glass doors slid open, and she was hit with a fresh blast of cool air. As she entered the mall, she glanced briefly, as always, at her reflection in the window, cringing, as always, at her gait and the tilt of her head.

Layla worked every second Saturday at the pharmacy in the shopping mall opposite Coles. Most of the time, she savoured the sweet freedom of walking out the door and leaving Cameron to entertain the kids for the day. But after the conversation with her mother, she was rattled and wished she could've remained home with her family, let the cheerful chaos of the household drown out her doubts. No matter how carefully she'd papered over her memories, everything now seemed to be pulling at the edges of the layers.

Before she even reached the counter, Layla spied the distinctive stoop of Allan Johnson's shoulders. Normally, she would groan internally at the prospect of dealing with him again, but this morning she grasped at the chance to transform herself into cool, professional Layla who took refuge in rules and laws.

Christine, the owner of the pharmacy, spoke in a low tone as she handed Layla the prescription behind the dispensing counter. 'He's been to a GP out in Salisbury this time.'

This wasn't the first time Mr Johnson had come in with an ill-gotten prescription for oxycodone. He was casting an increasingly wider net over the doctors and pharmacists of Adelaide to get the drug sooner than his usual two-month allowance. Layla knew he suffered from a rare autoimmune illness and was afflicted by chronic pain, which only made it harder for her to continually tell him she couldn't give him the relief he craved in ever stronger doses. She sighed as she wrote down the name of the GP so she could call next week to warn her about him. 'I'll talk to him,' she said to Christine.

The older man raised his gaze to Layla's as she sat in the chair beside him. His face, grizzled beyond his years, drooped even further. 'Let me guess, you can't give it to me today?'

'I'm so sorry, Mr Johnson, but you know I can't give you more pills,' she said gently.

'But I ran out two days ago.' He looked close to tears. 'The pills are the only thing that keep me going. Some days I wish I could die.' His voice cracked a little on the last word.

Layla's whole body tightened. She'd heard those words before, from him and some of her other customers, and they always took her back to the way she had felt in the weeks and months after she'd left Glasswater Bay ... except that her pain hadn't been the kind she could medicate with

26

painkillers. That feeling still lived inside her, lurking in wait. She squeezed her hands together so her voice would come out steady. 'I wish I could help you, but these drugs aren't good for you to take long-term.'

His face sagged into a half-smile. 'It's OK, love. I know you're just doin' your job. If I could just have me script back, I'll be out of your hair.'

Layla raised her eyebrows at him.

'I know, I know,' he relented. 'You can't give it back. I'll see you next time.'

Layla helped him to his feet and watched as he hobbled out the door, leaning heavily on his walking stick.

'Poor guy,' Christine said as Layla joined her behind the counter. 'You know he's only in his sixties? And his life is ruined.'

Layla would usually remind Christine that chronic illness didn't mean a person's life was over; one of the things she loved about her job was helping people live their lives to the fullest. But ever since she'd got that message, all she could think about were the lives she'd ruined all those years ago. And despite her determination to close that chapter, it was all starting to come back in technicolour detail.

THEN

Friday nights at the cafe were always frantic. The Rusty Anchor across the street was the only pub in Glasswater Bay, and notorious for its cheerfully terrible food, so the after-work crowd always spilled over the road to the cafe when they needed to soak up the week's worth of booze they'd just consumed.

Yumi and I zoomed between tables, taking orders with a side of sleaze from the more inebriated clientele. By the time Scott sent the chef home at ten o'clock, my feet were killing me and there were still no signs of the cafe emptying.

'Laaaylaaa,' sang a bloke from one of the nearby tables. His mates guffawed as he warbled the rest of the verse from the Eric Clapton song.

I rolled my eyes. 'Never heard that one before, Matty.'

'Wouldn't mind gettin' you on your knees,' he muttered under his breath.

I flushed as I cleared the empty West End Draught bottles from the table. Matty Cartwright was one of Glasswater Bay's two sparkies, but he got most of the local work on account of being from one of the town's oldest families. He was doing pretty well for a guy in his twenties and, as a result, thought the sun shone out of his arse. Everyone thought he was a harmless larrikin, but he still gave me the creeps. As I was walking away, his hand shot out and clenched one of my buttocks, strong fingers digging in as he pinched hard. The shock of the act bolted straight to my heart. The empty bottle I'd tucked under my arm slipped out and clanged on the floor, then rolled across the wooden floorboards with a slow rumble.

Matty and his mates started laughing again, and the gazes of other customers prickled my skin. Fright and humiliation channelled into fury, and I rounded on him and hissed, 'Don't touch me!'

'Aw, c'mon,' he drawled. 'I'm just havin' a bit of fun. Can't you take a compliment?'

I bent to retrieve the bottle from under the table, my face burning, then retreated to the safety of the counter as he and his mates started up their stupid singing again.

'What happened?' Scott asked. 'Was he giving you a hard time?'

'He fucking groped me.' To my horror, tears rose in my eyes and I swiped at them.

Scott gave an exasperated sigh and turned back to the register, and my embarrassment deepened. Since I'd worked in the cafe, I'd seen Yumi brush off similar encounters with barely a grimace, but the men usually left me alone. I used to wish for such a problem; to be attractive enough that guys couldn't keep their hands off me, and now someone had finally considered my body worthy of touching and I'd totally overreacted. Scott probably thought I was a childish idiot.

But then he marched over to the table with the bill, slapped it down and plucked the half-drunk beer bottle out of Matty's hand. 'Pay your bill and get out.' He pointed to the door.

'What the fuck?' Matty said. 'I just paid for that beer.'

'Actually, you didn't. I've taken it off your bill. Now pay and leave.'

'Who do you think you are?' Matty stood up, his face red with anger, and his chair clattered over. 'My money not good enough for you, mate?'

Scott got up in Matty's face and stabbed a finger in his chest. 'If you come into my cafe and grope my staff, you're not welcome here.'

There was a tense moment as the two men glared at each other, and just as it looked like Matty might punch Scott in the face, one of his mates handed Scott two fifty-dollar notes and gave Matty a shove towards the door.

'C'mon, mate, let it go.'

They stumbled out the door, Matty still swearing to himself, and it clanged closed behind them. Yumi and I watched Scott as he calmly righted the chair and began to clear the table.

'My hero,' Yumi murmured.

Most of the rowdy tables went quiet after that, and soon the patrons started to leave. A couple of them gave Scott affectionate slaps on the back as they left, but none of them said a word to me.

I was all mixed up inside. While I was grateful to Scott for sticking up for me, I still had to live in the same town as Matty and everyone else who had witnessed the confrontation I'd caused. I shouldn't have been so sensitive. Should've taken it as a compliment, as Matty himself had said.

Yumi yawned as she wiped down tables, erasing wet rings from beer bottles and brushing off crumbs.

'You go home, Yumi,' Scott called from across the room. 'You look exhausted. Layla and I will finish up here.'

I tried to hide my annoyance as Yumi took off her apron and waved goodbye. She got an early minute while I was stuck here cleaning up?

Scott balanced the till while I finished cleaning off the tables and stacked the dishwasher. We didn't speak, and I ached with misery at the thought that he might be disappointed in me. It was only as we stepped out into the chill of the night and Scott locked the door behind us that I dared to speak. 'I'm sorry about earlier. With Matty.'

He turned to face me. 'What are you apologising for? Matty's a dickhead and everyone knows it. I went to school with him and he was a dickhead then too.'

'I shouldn't have made such a big deal out of it.'

'Christ, Layla. You're a bloody teenager. No one has the right to treat you like that.'

There was that warm feeling again. 'Well, thanks for having my back.'

One side of his mouth twitched upwards in a crooked smile. 'Anytime, babe. You let me know if he ever pulls that shit again.'

A frisson of pleasure tingled down my spine. 'Careful. I might start thinking there are decent guys in this town after all.'

The crinkles appeared around his eyes as he gave a low chuckle. 'I don't know about that.'

'No, I guess all the good ones are already taken.' I gave him an arch smile, then looked away to hide my embarrassment, studying the row of gum trees that lined the median strip in the centre of the street. Typical that I would finally get up the courage to flirt with the most unavailable person possible.

He laughed again. 'Well, you found one, didn't you? Rasheed, wasn't it? The Khan boy?'

I hoped the street lighting was dim enough that he wouldn't see the colour creep up my neck and into my face. 'No, that was … no. There's nothing happening there.'

Scott appraised me for a moment. A light breeze sifted through my ponytail, carrying the salty tang of the sea. Finally, he broke our mutual gaze and glanced up the main street. 'Your car nearby?'

'Just up there.' I pointed to my red Laser hatch, glinting under a streetlight twenty metres up the road.

'I'll walk you.'

We strolled up the street together until we reached my car, then I turned to face him, suddenly awkward. I'd spent countless hours in his company, but we'd never been alone together outside the cafe. It felt different. More intimate. The white noise of the waves crashing on the beach in the distance was the only sound as our eyes met again. 'Well, thanks again.'

He reached out and hooked a bit of loose hair behind my ear, and as he did, his fingers brushed my cheek. 'Goodnight, Layla.'

Shock zapped through me, both because he'd touched me and at the current of electricity that sizzled under my skin. I tore my gaze away from his to open the car door. ''Night.'

As I buckled my seatbelt and started the engine, I watched Scott striding away up the street, his hands in his pockets. I touched my face where his fingers had grazed my skin.

On the drive home, his words ran on an endless loop in my mind.

Anytime, babe.

You're a bloody teenager.

Anytime, babe.

You're a bloody teenager.

I hadn't imagined that jolt of electricity, I was sure of it. Had he felt it too? Or worse, had he noticed my reaction and was on his way home to join his wife in bed and laugh about the kid at work who had a crush on him?

My heart sped even faster at the thought of seeing him at work the next day.

NOW

Layla kept her eyes averted from the mirror as she stepped out of the shower and towelled herself dry. Most days, she set her alarm early and got up before Cam, before the children, so she could set her armour firmly in place; apply the layers that cushioned her from the world. But first, she let the towel drop to the floor and steeled herself to look in the mirror.

First, her face. Her nose, which always looked slightly too broad. The clusters of tiny pimples that congregated around her temples the week before her period started. The translucent grey shadows beneath her eyes. The way the skin of her cheeks had become looser, saggier over the years.

Then her gaze dropped to her breasts. Pathetically small, as they'd always been, but after breastfeeding two children they'd lost their perkiness and drooped downwards. Her stomach, crisscrossed with pearlescent stretch marks, had never regained its tone and was white and dimpled. The swell of her hips, covered with the extra padding that hadn't gone away after her pregnancies.

She clenched her stomach against the wave of hatred. It hurt. Every time, it hurt. She'd tried so hard to maintain the figure of her youth, but each year added new imperfections to her body, new lines, new flesh, and now this was what she was. She slipped on the satin dressing gown that hung from the bathroom door and tied it around her waist, concealing her detestable body.

Her make-up bag was already open on the bathroom bench. She moisturised her face, then applied the primer with the first two fingers of both hands. Then she took up her brush and applied an even coat of foundation over her face and down her neck. Concealer followed to hide the dark smudges beneath her eyes, then highlighter along her cheekbones, chin and between her eyebrows. Contour powder along the sides of her nose and under her cheekbones. Blush on her cheeks. Two shades of eyeshadow, perfectly blended. Eyeliner, hugging her lash line. Mascara. An eyebrow pencil. Finally, she coloured in her lips with a creamy natural rose lipstick.

The woman who stared back at her looked familiar. Presentable. Adequate, at least. She breathed more easily as she packed her tools back in her bag.

There was a light knock on the door and Cam stepped in. His arms encircled her from behind and there was a hint of mischievous amusement in his eyes as he slid a hand inside her gown.

She smiled at his reflection. 'I need to get dressed for work.'

'I know.' His other hand pulled the bow of her gown free and he slipped it off one shoulder. 'But you need to take this off to get dressed.'

The open gown exposed the spongy white flesh of her stomach and panic leapt inside Layla. She gathered it around her again and stepped out of his reach. 'I need to get ready. Sorry.'

'I'm not trying to start anything.' There was hurt in his eyes, as there always was when she hid her body from him. 'I just feel like I never see you anymore. You know I'm more attracted to you now than when we met?'

She laughed. 'Yeah, right!'

'It's true.' He put his arms around her waist, and she stood on her tiptoes to kiss him.

'Well, thanks for saying so.'

'I'm not just saying so. I love the way you look. I always have.'

Layla buried her head in his chest and hugged him tight. There was no way he could be happy with the body she'd just seen in the mirror; her whole life, men had told her all the things that were wrong with it. But she knew he wanted her to feel good about herself, and she loved him for that.

Every now and then, a Facebook memory would pop up from some party or another she'd been to in her twenties. She'd be drunk, of course, clinging onto some random she'd met that night whom she'd ended up going home with for bad sex in the hope of drowning out the dark undercurrent that had always drifted along at the bottom of her mind. Every time she saw these photos she was shocked at how thin she'd been, how shiny those moments from her youth seemed now. She remembered the unhappiness that had pervaded her life back then, and knew how much better things were these days. But still, the photos were a bludgeon on her floundering self-esteem. How could she not have appreciated what she'd looked like when she was young? How could she not have known that she'd never look that good again? And, worse, how could she have let herself get like this in the first place?

At least Cam seemed willing to put up with her, even if just for the sake of their relationship. For now, anyway. He was the best thing that had ever happened to Layla, and she couldn't take him for granted. She raised her head to kiss him again.

He pushed her hair back from her face and smiled. 'You are a very sexy woman, Layla Flynn.' He bent to kiss her neck, his hand running over her shoulder, down her waist and hip, in between her thighs. His fingers found her, and the breath escaped her lips. 'Is this OK?' he asked.

'It's very OK.' Her breathing quickened as he stroked her lightly. A warmth spread through her body, sparking, crackling, ready to ignite.

Then came the unmistakeable thunder of four small feet running up the hallway, and the warm feeling dissolved.

'Bloody cockblockers!' Layla gasped, resting her forehead against Cam's chest.

He chuckled. 'I could go and put the TV on and come back?'

She groaned. 'I'd better get ready for work. But thanks.'

He kissed her cheek, and Layla retied her robe as he opened the bathroom door to two tousled heads and fresh smiles.

'Mummy! Mummy! Louis is a poo head!' Ella crowed.

'Ella is a poo-bum wee face!' Louis retaliated.

'I AM NOT!' she screamed back at him, her face turning pink. Within seconds, they were shoving each other and bellowing.

'Breakfast time!' Cam shouted over them, taking their hands and marching them out of the ensuite as Layla turned back to the mirror to reapply her smudged lipstick.

*

Layla raised one hand to shade her eyes from the final rays of the sun as it set over Nathan and Mei's backyard. She hadn't realised it had got so late – it was already past the kids' bedtime, but Louis was still tearing around the backyard with the other two kids. Ella was happily ensconced on Cam's lap.

The wine had made Layla's limbs pleasantly heavy.

'Top-up?' Mei said, the bottle of wine in her hand.

Layla and Cam exchanged glances. 'Go ahead,' he said. 'I can drive.'

She flashed him a grateful smile and held out her glass.

It had been more than a week since Jodie's message, and her fear had begun to ebb away with each day. And it had been such a lovely afternoon with their friends; the sensational pork ribs Nathan had cooked on the Weber, the wine, the conversation, the mild summer day. Even the kids had behaved themselves. She brushed Ella's soft cheek with the back of her hand.

'She's almost asleep,' she said to Cam.

He kissed the top of their daughter's head. 'We may as well stay a bit longer, then.'

'Hey, Mum?' yelled Hunter, Nathan and Mei's eldest son. 'Can we go and play inside?'

'Of course you can,' Mei called back. 'Just make sure you look after Louis, OK?'

'Yeah, you'd better keep an eye on him. He's got a destructive streak in him; I don't know where he gets it from,' Cam joked.

Layla almost dropped her wineglass. Bright fear leapt inside her at the memory of the destruction she'd once caused. 'What year will your two be in at school next year?' she blurted out to Mei.

'Hunter's going into Year Three and Hugo will be in Year One,' Mei said. 'I can't believe how quickly it's gone. Louis will be at school before you know it.'

Layla took a deep breath, felt her composure returning. 'I'm already emotional about him starting kindy. I'll be crying and drinking in the car after dropping him off.'

'Speaking of drinking in cars,' Nathan said. 'Did I ever tell you guys about the time I almost ran over my dad when I was sixteen?'

'What? No!' Mei spluttered.

'Yeah, I was sitting in my car in the driveway sneaking a beer when Dad came out of the house. I panicked and went to take off, but I forgot to put the car in reverse and I ploughed straight into him instead.'

Mei clapped her hand over her mouth. 'Oh my god!'

'He was fine,' Nathan said. 'Well, mostly. The car knocked him over, but he only got a few bruises. He was pretty furious though.'

'Guess you were in trouble after that?' Cam said.

'Yeah, I was grounded for a month,' Nathan said.

Mei gave him a push. 'I can't believe you never told me about that!'

'I'd almost forgotten about it.' Nathan looked at each of them in turn. 'What about you guys? Did you ever do anything catastrophically stupid when you were teenagers?'

Layla hid her expression behind her wineglass. She'd never told Cam about what she'd done, and she certainly wasn't going to let that secret out now, here, in front of their friends, with her daughter sleeping sweetly on her husband's lap. She didn't want anyone to know the kind of person she'd been back then.

'I went through a shoplifting phase,' Mei said with a self-conscious laugh. 'I used to go to this lingerie shop and put on four bras underneath my T-shirt, then I'd pay for one on the way out. No one suspected a thing.'

'My wife the criminal,' Nathan said.

'My parents found my stash one day though,' Mei said. 'They made me take all of them back to the shop and admit what I'd done. It was *humiliating*. But I never stole again after that.'

'Don't you love how parents always make you face up to your mistakes?' Cam said.

Shame sprouted inside Layla. *Her* mother had done the very opposite.

'I spent a night in the police lock-up,' Cam went on. 'Drunk and disorderly. They called my mum and she told them to leave me there for the night.'

Layla grinned. 'I can't imagine your mum doing that!'

'She wanted to teach me a lesson, I guess,' Cam said. 'And it worked. I never let myself get in that state again.'

'What about you, Layla?' Mei said. 'You're always so calm and in control. You must have some teenage fuck-ups to make us feel better about our poor choices?'

Layla let out a nervous laugh. 'Oh, you know, just the usual. Underage drinking at parties, that sort of thing.'

'Come on,' Nathan said. 'You gotta give us more than that.'

'No, really,' Layla insisted. 'I've got nothing interesting to tell.'

'Really?' Mei sounded disappointed. 'No one's *that* vanilla.'

Cam put his hand on Layla's knee. 'Everyone knows vanilla is the best flavour. I'll take vanilla any day over a chocolate-fudge explosion with whipped cream and sprinkles and deep, dark secrets.'

'I think you're losing control of your metaphor, Cam,' Mei said.

They all laughed, but heat was rising in Layla's cheeks, expanding inside her, threatening to set her on fire. Cam liked her as he thought she was: pure, predictable. In control. Early in their relationship, he'd made it clear he didn't want to know about her previous sexual partners. No judgement, of course: what was in the past was in the past; he just didn't need to know the details. At the time, she'd been only too happy to comply, but now this streak of puritanism bothered her. If he knew what she was really like, the terrible mistakes she'd made as a teenager – mistakes far worse than stealing lingerie, or getting drunk and spending the night in jail – he wouldn't want anything to do with her. She'd lose this fragile, beautiful life they'd built together. She stood up and set her wineglass down on the table. 'I'm going to check on Louis.'

She blinked back the tears she refused to let fall as she entered the house. Just when she'd begun to feel on an even keel again, yet another reminder of her past rolled in, a dark storm cloud shadowing the perfect summer afternoon.

Louis was in the lounge room watching a Disney movie with the two older boys. He jumped up when he noticed her.

'Mummy, I want to go home.'

She gathered him into her arms and held him tight to guard against the alarm that Cam's words had triggered in her. 'OK, sweetie, let's go tell Daddy it's time to go.'

Before Daddy works out that Mummy isn't the person he thinks she is.

THEN

I was exhausted when I rocked up to the cafe for my shift the next day. I had tossed and turned all night, the bed sheet twisting around my body as I wrestled with the cacophony of feelings that were crashing around inside me after the incident with Matty and then the buzz I'd felt when Scott had touched my face.

Yumi wouldn't be in until five, so it was just me waiting tables while Scott took orders and made coffees. Something had changed inside me after that moment on the street last night. Just looking at Scott brought back the same rush of excitement, desire and panic.

After a couple of hours of avoiding eye contact with him, he called me over to the counter during a quiet spell.

'What's up?' I tried to sound nonchalant.

'You seem kind of spaced out today,' he said. 'Are you OK?'

'Yeah, fine.' I flashed him a quick smile.

'You're not still thinking about last night, are you?'

'What?' I glanced up at him, alarmed at the idea that he could see right through me to my silly infatuation.

'With Matty,' he prompted.

43

'Oh. Nah, 'course not!' I studied my fingernails. 'I just didn't get much sleep last night.'

'Me either.'

I felt his gaze on me and I raised my eyes reluctantly to his. We stared at one another and a strange, fizzing kind of anticipation began inside me, delicious but scarily intense. Then the bell tinkled over the cafe door and I broke his gaze with a rush of relief as Renee and Shona came in.

''Sup, Lay?' Renee said.

'Hey!' I moved over to the counter. 'What are you up to?'

'Daniel and Vince are going surfing at Tor Beach, so we're going down to watch,' Shona said. 'Thought we'd grab some coffees on the way.'

'Two flat whites?'

'I'll make them,' Scott said, moving over to the coffee machine.

'What time do you finish?' Renee said. 'Wanna come with us?'

'Not until five. Sorry.' I only half meant it. The only things the boys in Glasswater Bay were interested in were surfing and football, and both bored the crap out of me. Sport wasn't my thing, and I looked like a prepubescent greyhound in a bikini, so the beach wasn't exactly my natural habitat either. But I really wanted to talk to my friends. I'd never told them about my silly crush on Scott, sure that the vibe I'd sometimes suspected was between us was all in my head, but after last night it'd taken on a more significant sheen. I needed someone more experienced to help me dissect all these weird feelings. 'Do you guys want to come around to mine tonight? We could listen to music, order pizza?'

Shona scratched the back of her neck. 'Daniel reckons there's gonna be a party on the beach later. Come down when your shift's finished and get crazy with us, biatch.'

'Yeah, come!' Renee said eagerly. 'There'll be a bonfire, and the guys are bringing drinks.'

I looked from one of them to the other. 'But you guys will be off pashing your boyfriends all night and I'll be left by myself looking like a loser.'

'No, you won't!' Renee said indignantly. 'We wouldn't abandon you.'

I raised my eyebrows at her.

'There'll be heaps of guys there,' Shona said. 'Not just from school either. I'm gonna make it my mission to get you laid tonight.'

Normally I'd laugh off Shona's ludicrous overstatements, but Scott was standing a few metres away, and after last night I hated that he might think she was serious. 'That's OK,' I said quickly. 'Reckon I'll have a quiet night in.'

Scott set their coffees down on the counter. 'There you go, ladies.'

'Are you sure?' Renee said. 'Feels like we haven't caught up outside school in ages, other than the social.'

I rang up their order and took their coins. 'We've got Spiderbait next Friday night. That'll be fun.'

'Yeah, I can't wait!' Shona said. 'Do you mind if Daniel comes with us? He loves Spiderbait too.'

That stung a little. I'd rearranged my shifts so I could have a rare Friday night off to spend with my friends, sharing our love of music. But if Daniel came, then Vince would probably come as well, and once again I'd be a fifth wheel.

'Of course,' I said. 'Have fun tonight.'

45

They said goodbye and left the cafe, and I turned away and busied myself wiping down the already clean counter.

'I forgot how harsh teenagers can be,' came Scott's voice from beside me.

I threw the cloth down on the counter. 'You don't have to keep reminding me that I'm just a kid!'

He raised his hands in defence. 'Hey, I don't think that at all.'

My hot burst of anger shrivelled into embarrassment. Way to show my maturity by spitting the dummy at my boss. 'Sorry,' I said to the counter.

'All I meant was, that wasn't cool, inviting their boyfriends along to your thing. I'd be pissed off too.'

'I'm not pissed off,' I said. 'It's only normal that they want to spend time with their boyfriends. Not that I'd know, given I've never had one myself.' I threw him what I hoped was a jokey, self-deprecating kind of smile, but the pity in his eyes made my insides shrink. 'Might take my break now if that's OK?'

Without waiting for an answer, I turned and went through the doors into the kitchen. Dave, the chef, was wiping down the stainless-steel bench, his work finished for the next few hours until he came back later for the dinner service. He looked up at me with his friendly smile. 'I'm out of here. See you at five.'

I gave him a wave and continued through the kitchen, the lunch room and into the bathroom. I stared at my reflection, at the pimple on the side of my too-broad nose, the extra button I'd left open on my black shirt, hoping that – what? That Scott would notice and think I was hot? That the attraction I'd felt last night had somehow dissolved his wife and kids into nothingness? That there was any part of me worthy of desire?

I did the button back up and splashed water on my face.

Scott was in the kitchen when I walked in, leaning against the bench, his arms crossed in front of him. My eyes slid away from his. 'Back in ten.'

Just before I reached the door, Scott reached out and his hand caught my waist. I turned to look at him, and without a word he pulled me back to him. I flowed like liquid into his arms. He lowered his face to mine, and as our lips came together, it was the most natural thing in the world to hook my arms around his neck and open my mouth to his. Our tongues met, but it wasn't gross like it had been with Rasheed: it was like silk, like being drunk, like being suspended in a sizzling bubble of perfection. His breath was hot; his hands clutched my waist, fingers pressing into the soft spots in the small of my back.

Then the bell over the cafe door filtered through the spell and we parted with a breathless smile. Scott went out into the cafe, the kitchen door swinging closed behind him and muffling his voice as he greeted the customers. His tone sounded normal, as if nothing at all had happened.

But something *had* happened … I was lightheaded, my heart racing a hundred miles an hour, my body still humming from his touch, my face tingling from his stubble. I pressed my fingers to my lips. It was without a doubt the most romantic, dramatic, exciting thing that had ever happened to me. Nothing would be the same after this.

*

I should've felt guilty. I knew it was wrong. But when I relived the kiss in my head that afternoon, over and over again, there was only exhilaration.

Scott made no mention of it for the rest of my shift, and by the time Yumi and the other casual, Jacinta, showed up for the evening shift, the cafe was buzzing and he was busy. He waved goodbye to me from across the cafe floor as I left.

It felt as if the whole thing had been in my head.

But my body knew what'd happened. Every time I looked at him, I felt that same rush of longing that'd started up last night when he'd touched my face outside the cafe, the same exquisite ache in my lower belly. I could still feel his hands on me, and I kept touching the tender spots where his fingers had pressed in; proof that it had been real. It was as if he'd branded me. I could never go back to the nervous schoolgirl who'd swapped saliva with Rasheed. And I sure as hell didn't want to.

Instead of going home to face my normal life again, I got in my car and drove up to The Knob. Situated on the clifftops just out of town and overlooking Glasswater Bay's most popular surfing beach, Tor Lookout was colloquially referred to as The Knob for its giant, phallic granite outcropping that reared over the cliff's edge. Some of the more adventurous boys (and plenty of drunk men) had climbed to the very top, and by some miracle none had yet tumbled to their deaths on the rocks below. The ebbs and flows of life in Glasswater Bay were marked by the number of times the more conservative residents had petitioned the council to fence off The Knob for public safety, only to be thwarted by the larger group, which was made up of the apathetic, the anti-nanny-state and the anti-more-expenses-driving-up-our-rates cohorts.

And so, The Knob remained accessible to all but accessed only by teenagers either getting wasted or getting it on. The council had installed a couple of picnic tables in a half-hearted attempt to make the area more family friendly, but the danger combined with the relentless wind kept most people away.

It was still too early in the evening for parkers or dope smokers, so when I pulled up in the car park overlooking the sea, there was no one else there. I killed the engine and took off my seatbelt, scanning the beach below for signs of my friends and their boyfriends. But the beachgoers were nothing more than stick figures against the white sand, the surfers disembodied heads bobbing on the water until they rose onto their boards to ride the waves into shore. I was torn between the desire to talk to my friends about what had happened that afternoon and the tingling satisfaction of hugging the secret close to my chest. I couldn't tell anyone about it anyway. At least not until I'd talked it over with Scott. And no doubt he considered the whole thing a giant mistake. But the way he'd looked at me ...

I opened the car door and stepped out into the wind. The sun sat atop the horizon, fat and orange and drunk with sleep. I crossed my arms over my chest. The day had held the languid warmth of lingering autumn, but the cold had crashed in as soon as the sun started to go down. The wind tore at my ponytail, pulling tendrils of hair loose that whipped wildly around my head.

Laughter from the group on the beach below wafted up through the roar of the wind. Earlier in the day, the sounds would've stabbed at me, made me simultaneously jealous and angry with myself at all the things I wasn't. But now I was full to the brim with a serenity I'd never known before. My school friends seemed like the immature ones now, sucking face with boys when I knew what it was to be in the arms of a man. I smiled and hugged myself tighter. Now it felt like I was leaving them behind.

I stood on the clifftop, bracing myself against the wind, until the sun had disappeared and the bonfire on the beach was just a soft glow against the twilight gloom.

NOW

It was always with a strange mixture of euphoria and loss that Layla and Cam walked out of the house and left the kids in the capable hands of Layla's mother.

Once a month, Angela came over to their house to babysit so Layla and Cam could go out for dinner and reconnect. At first, their conversation had felt forced, and they'd spoken of little else than the children, but now Layla looked forward to their monthly date nights in the same way she used to look forward to holidays and birthdays.

When she'd been pregnant with Louis, Layla had foolishly proclaimed to anyone who would listen that she wouldn't let the baby get in the way of their social life. Her friends with children had laughed at her, but Layla had seen plenty of parents eating out with their babies, so she knew it could be done. Of course, she hadn't counted on not having the kind of baby who sat happily in a pram staring at his hands for two hours.

'We never went out when you kids were little,' Layla's mother had told her after yet another disastrous attempt at going out had resulted in taking it in turns to walk a crying Louis around the restaurant in between wolfing down their meals.

'That's because there was nowhere to go in Glasswater other than the dodgy Rusty Anchor,' Layla had retorted, trying to hold back the tears of powerless frustration that had always seemed to be there back then.

'Well, it may not seem like it now, but this chapter in your life will pass in the blink of an eye. Believe me.' Angela abruptly turned away from her, and Layla knew she was angry at this reminder of their home town, how happy their family had been before Layla had ruined everything.

But her mum had been right, of course. Now Ella was two and a half, things were becoming easier. And Layla was beginning to feel like herself again.

'I thought we were never going to get away,' she said as they got in the car. 'My mum loves you.'

Cam laughed. 'All the mums love me.'

Layla raised her eyebrows. 'All of them?'

'Well, mine anyway.' He threw her a grin.

Layla nudged him teasingly. 'I think it's cute.'

He glanced away from the road at her for a second. 'I know you're not really close to Angela, but I get the feeling she wants to spend more time with you.'

Layla shrugged, looking out of the window. How could she possibly explain that her mother had once done something no mother should ever have to do for her daughter? How the secret they had to share had stretched their relationship so far apart over the years that they could barely make eye contact anymore?

'Maybe you should, I don't know, go out for lunch with her sometime,' Cam went on. 'Without the kids. I think she'd appreciate it.'

Layla fiddled with the air vents, turning them away from her face. The idea of being alone with her mum without Cam or the kids as a buffer, especially after that message, set her teeth on edge. 'We don't have that kind of relationship.'

'But she must be lonely,' he persisted. 'I know my mum never got over being on her own after Dad left.' His jaw tightened, as it did whenever he spoke about his father, and Layla once again shrank under the secret she'd kept from him.

*

The second message came the following morning.

Louis and Ella had just piled into bed with them, giggling hysterically. It was early, the sun barely risen, and the children were so delicious, still soft and pliant and warm from sleep. These precious, perfect moments didn't come with the regularity she'd anticipated when she'd fallen pregnant with Louis, so when they did, Layla suspended herself within them. She knew that the kids would soon be wrestling or pinching one another, or that one of their heads would collide with hers, and she didn't want to waste this moment. She pulled her son's body closer and buried her face in his hair, breathing in his warm, bready scent.

Cam climbed out of bed, hoisted Ella over his head and flew her around like an aeroplane as she shrieked with excitement. Right on cue, Louis wriggled out of Layla's arms. 'I wanna turn! Daddy, do it to me!'

'No, me!' Ella bellowed.

Layla sighed and rolled away from them as Cam began to explain for the hundredth time that Santa wouldn't bring them any presents next week if they didn't behave themselves. When she picked up her phone from the bedside table, the words on the screen sent shock waves through her:

Thought you got away with it, didn't you?

Her fragile contentment shattered into pieces around her. After her hurried exit from Glasswater Bay, she hadn't spoken about Scott to anyone – especially not Cam – and eventually the silence became a habit. She'd been a silly girl playing at being a woman, and the whole episode was better off remaining in the past. She'd trained herself not to think about him too much, a cringe of shame only occasionally seeping through the cracks in the walls she'd built around her memories.

And guilt, of course. The guilt had crushed her; forgetting had been mandatory or she wouldn't have been able to get through uni, let alone have a normal life. Although, given the string of disastrous relationships she'd pinged between in her twenties, maybe it had already been too late for normal.

'Who are you messaging now?' Cam plonked back down on the bed beside her.

Layla locked the phone and put it back on the bedside table. 'No one.' She rolled over, and together they tickled the children until tears streamed down their faces and delighted cackles banished the dread that had begun to leach into her again.

*

When Cam took the kids out to the playground after breakfast, she opened Messenger. For a long time, she studied the two messages, separated only by the dates they'd been sent.

I know what you did.

Thought you got away with it, didn't you?

Fingers trembling, she clicked on Jodie's name and was taken to her Facebook page. She'd been assuming – hoping – that it would be locked down, but her profile was public … Every status update, every photo, every link she'd shared was there for the world to see.

Layla enlarged the profile picture. Jodie was still attractive – same dark hair and high cheekbones, same blue eyes, same even white smile. Only a few lines around her lips and eyes gave away the time that had passed. She must be, what, forty-eight? Forty-nine? It was absurd to think that Layla had once considered her washed up at twenty-eight, when she herself was now in her late thirties. Forty-eight seemed shockingly young, especially for one whose life had been ruined before she turned thirty. Layla closed the photo and scrolled down her profile page. The first post was an ultrasound picture, shadowy black and grey.

So proud to announce that I'm going to be a grandma!!! the caption read. *My first baby is having her first baby!! Best Christmas present ever!!!!!*

Layla bit her lip. She clicked through to the photos and scrolled down the thumbnails, looking without seeing. Most of the photos were of Jodie's children, now adults themselves. In some, Jodie stood between them, her arms around their waists, eyes shining bright with pride. Occasionally, there was a series of photos from a family barbecue, but the face Layla was seeking was never in any of them.

She closed the app and locked her phone.

THEN

At home, I wondered whether Mum and Dad or my brother, Zach, noticed anything different about me; how irrevocably changed I was after kissing Scott; how he had become part of my DNA. And at school, I wondered if the boys would now see me as a potential girlfriend rather than the geeky quiet girl they'd never noticed.

But everyone treated me the same as they always had. Even Scott. Over the following week, he didn't mention the kiss at all, and we never found ourselves alone together during any of my shifts. In fact, he sent me home early instead of Yumi.

It hurt. Maybe he blamed me. Maybe he thought that I'd made a move on him. I'd relived the kiss in my head over and over again and I'd been so sure he'd been the one to initiate it, but maybe I was wrong. Had he told his wife? Was she going to come into the cafe and claw my eyes out? Or maybe I just hadn't been good at it. The idea that he was ignoring me, not because we'd done the wrong thing, but because I'd been so obviously inexperienced, seemed somehow worse.

I got into the habit of driving past his house on my way to school, knowing he would be inside, having breakfast, getting ready to go and open the cafe. He lived on King Street, one block from the beach. The briny scent of seaweed would float in my open window on the chilly morning breeze as I cruised by, the rising sun bouncing off the perpetual silvery sheen of salt that covered the windows of all the houses this close to the sea. One morning he was outside, hose in one hand, coffee cup in the other, watering the bed of geraniums with their red, fleshy flowers and woody stems. I panicked, pressing down on the accelerator and speeding away, hoping he hadn't recognised my car. He didn't mention anything at work that afternoon, but then, he'd hardly been talking to me anyway.

It was confusing, to see him and be close to him almost every day while pretending that nothing had happened. My uncertainty was a serpent, twisting and writhing in my guts until I no longer knew what I wanted. I needed to study, to keep my grades up so I'd get into uni next year, but whenever I got my textbooks out at home, all I could think about were Scott's arms, Scott's lips, Scott's smile. It was pathetic. I was pathetic.

*

Excitement zipped around inside Daniel's car as we drove towards Victor Harbor on Friday night. There was nothing quite like the anticipation of going to a gig, and even Daniel tagging along with us couldn't dampen my enthusiasm. It was funny to think that only a couple of weeks ago I'd had a crush on him. After kissing Scott, he seemed insubstantial, like part of him was missing. It was hard now to pinpoint what I'd seen in him in the first place.

'I can't believe Vince didn't want to see Spiderbait,' Renee grumbled from beside me.

Daniel chuckled, his eyes lifting to the rear-view mirror to look at her. 'Acca Dacca is more Vince's style.'

Renee snorted. 'Then I think this relationship is doomed.' But she was smiling, like maybe that wouldn't be such a bad thing.

The Crown Hotel was heaving when we got there. It was an all-ages show, and we watched enviously as the adults in the line were fitted with wristbands so they could buy alcohol.

'Wish we had fake IDs,' Shona said.

The support band had just started when we finally made it inside, but other than a few groupies who were moshing enthusiastically in front of the stage, most of the patrons were still at the bar getting drinks.

'Let's get up the front now,' Daniel said.

'But this band is shit,' Shona said. 'And I wanna get a Coke.'

'But if we get a good position now, we'll be able to see everything when Spiderbait come on,' Daniel said.

'How about Daniel and I go get a spot while you guys get us some drinks?' Renee suggested.

Daniel smiled at her and let go of Shona's hand. 'Good idea. Let's go.'

Shona raised her eyebrows at me as we waited at the bar for our drinks. 'Was that weird?'

I glanced over my shoulder at Renee and Daniel, who were both laughing, then shrugged at Shona. 'They're just saving our spots.'

'Daniel's gonna dump me, I just know it,' Shona said.

'What? Why would you think that?'

'He's barely looked at me all night.' Her eyes were suddenly bright. 'Sorry. I'm such an idiot.'

I slung an arm around her shoulders. 'You're not an idiot! You're just imagining things. He had his hand on your leg the whole way here.'

'Yeah, you're right.' She swiped the back of her wrist across her eyes. 'I'll probably get my period tomorrow and then we'll know why I was being such a weirdo.'

The bartender set our Cokes down on the bar and we each took two of the plastic cups. 'Come on,' I said. 'Let's get over there so your boyfriend can provide a human barricade against that lot.' I gestured with my cup at the groupies near the stage, one of whom was attempting to crowd-surf on a group of four other guys.

*

By the time Spiderbait came on stage, the crowd had thickened around us. It was a living, liquid thing, pressing in around me like a swirling river, buffeting me from side to side. I surrendered to it, allowing my body to become one with it as it flowed back and forth in time to the band's glam-rock sound. Renee, Shona and I all had our arms around each other as we jumped around and screamed the lyrics at the tops of our lungs. And when the final song finished in an explosion of flashing lights and reverberating bass, we all grinned at each other, our breathing heavy, faces flushed with elation.

'Reckon they'll do a second encore?' Daniel said from behind us.

'Doesn't look like it.' Renee indicated the huge speaker at the end of the stage. 'They've put the music back on.'

Shona snuggled up to Daniel and stood on her toes to kiss him.

I fanned my sweaty face with both hands. 'I need water.'

'Me too,' Renee said.

Leaning against the bar, sipping water, Renee and I watched Shona and Daniel pashing near the stage. 'I think Vince is going to break up with me,' Renee said in a flat voice.

'Not you too! Shona said the same thing about Daniel earlier.'

'Really?' Her face changed, and she glanced over at them again. 'Doesn't seem like it at the moment.'

Seeing Shona locked in Daniel's embrace, I remembered how it'd felt to have Scott's arms around me, his mouth on mine. And now he hardly even spoke to me.

'We've got absolutely nothing in common,' Renee went on. 'And he never wants to hang out. All he's interested in is sex ... which would be OK if he was actually, you know, good at it.'

I laughed. 'So why don't you dump him?'

She looked at me. 'Because then I'd have no one.'

'What, like me?' I tried to keep my voice light, but my expression must have betrayed my hurt, because she bumped me with her shoulder.

'God, I wish I was more like you, Layla. You're so smart and independent, and here I am crying over some dipshit who doesn't even care about me. You don't need a boyfriend to make you feel good about yourself.'

We watched Shona and Daniel in glum silence. If only Renee knew how insecure I really was. My secret bulged inside me. It would feel so good to be able to talk about it, to share it with my friend. 'If I tell you something, do you promise not to say anything to anyone? Not even Shona?'

Now I had her attention. 'Of course. What's the thing?'

'I've done something bad.'

'Bad bad or boy bad?' Renee's blue eyes twinkled.

I grimaced. 'Both.'

'Well, don't hold out on me now! Did you root Rasheed or something?'

'No!' I laughed. 'No, I … I kissed my boss.'

Renee's eyes bugged out of her head. 'What? Your boss, as in Scott Telford?'

I nodded.

She frowned. 'But Lay … isn't he *married*?'

I nodded again. 'That's why you can't tell anyone. We didn't plan it, it just … happened.'

'He *is* good looking.' She screwed up her nose. 'But don't you think he's kind of … old?'

'He's only twenty-eight, Renee.'

'That's old! So, how was it?'

'It was amazing. I see what you guys meant about kissing now.'

Renee shook her head in wonder. 'You really got back on the horse after the Rasheed disaster, didn't you?'

She caught my eye and we both giggled.

'So, what now?' she said after a while.

'I don't know.' The brief warmth of sharing the experience with my friend dissipated back into nothing. 'He hasn't even spoken to me since then.'

Renee studied me, her expression serious. 'But you want to do it again, don't you?'

I hesitated. No matter how conflicted I'd felt over the past week, the one thing I knew for sure was that I wanted to kiss him again. But what kind of person would that make me if I said it out loud? 'I've never felt this way before,' I said instead.

Shona and Daniel had disentangled from each other and were heading over to us, holding hands.

'You know you can't, Lay.' The crease was still there between Renee's eyes. 'He's got *kids*.'

'I know,' I said. 'It won't happen again.'

NOW

The kids were on the edge of hysteria by the time they arrived at Layla's mother's place for Christmas lunch. Layla and Cam had been up until midnight the previous evening, wrapping presents in silvery paper and stuffing them into Christmas stockings and leaving the spoils under the tree. It was the first year both children had been old enough to understand Christmas, and the morning had felt as magical to Layla as her own childhood Christmases. But the children's excitement had quickly turned to tears and tantrums as they fought over their presents, and Layla was relieved to transfer them to a different environment, where there were other people to distract them.

Angela knelt down to sweep the children into her arms. 'Merry Christmas, my little angels!'

Louis wriggled out of his grandmother's arms and charged up the hallway towards the living room. 'Uncle Zach!' he bellowed.

Layla exchanged a smile with Cam. It was cute to see how Louis idolised Layla's younger brother, and Zach was always good value, playing with both the kids long beyond the time most people would've tired of it. Ella took off after

Louis, leaving the adults alone together. Angela gave Layla a brief hug, then reached out to squeeze Cam's arm. 'Merry Christmas, you two.'

'Same to you, Angela,' Cam said.

They followed the kids into the living room. An anaemic-looking Christmas tree stood in a corner of the room, swamped by thick tinsel and blinking with multi-coloured lights, and with a jolt Layla recognised it as the tree from her own childhood. Had it been here every year and she just hadn't noticed it until those messages had pried open the door to her past? Brightly wrapped presents were piled beneath the tree. Muted Christmas carols played from the stereo.

Louis and Ella were sitting either side of Zach on the couch, both talking to him at once at the top of their lungs.

'I got a skateboard for Christmas!' Louis yelled.

'Cool!' Zach said. 'I'll have to teach you a few moves. I was a keen skateboarder back in the day.'

Ella shoved her wrist, which was bristling with colourful plastic bracelets, under Zach's nose. 'Look what Santa got *me*.'

Zach took her wrist and studied the bracelets. 'Santa has seriously good taste.' He looked up and gave Layla and Cam a cheerful wave. 'Hey, Cam, hey, sis. Merry Christmas.'

Cam and Zach shook hands then struck up a conversation.

'Sounds like those two did pretty well this year,' Angela said.

Layla grimaced. 'By the time we left home, Louis said he hated skateboards and he was never going to use it. Then they fought over those bracelets and broke one, and Ella screamed until she threw up. So yeah, merry bloody Christmas.'

Cam glanced back at them. 'I think we could all use a drink, Angela. Why don't you two go and open a bottle of wine while Zach and I entertain the kids?'

Layla glared at her husband for his obvious attempt to throw her into her mother's company, but he'd already turned back to Zach and didn't notice.

Angela looked quickly at Layla, then away again. 'Come on, then.'

There was a moment of uneasy silence when they reached the kitchen before a sudden realisation gave Layla something to say. 'Hey, where's Caitlin? Isn't this whole thing for her?'

'Well, it was actually so we could spend time together as a family, Layla,' Angela said tartly.

'Sorry,' Layla said, feeling remarkably like a teenager. 'I didn't mean it like—'

'They broke up last week,' Angela interrupted. 'Your brother has rubbish timing.'

'You seem more upset about it than he does,' Layla said.

Angela got a bottle out of the fridge. 'I liked her. She was good for him.'

She looked more comfortable now, and that made Layla relax a little too. She shrugged. 'Zach doesn't know a good thing when he's got it.'

Her mother twisted the cap off the bottle of white wine and poured two glasses. 'He's got to settle down one day.' She pushed a glass across the bench, and Layla couldn't help smiling.

'Not drinking out of a box today?'

'There's nothing wrong with cask wine.' Angela waved a finger at her. 'City snob.'

'You've lived in the city as long as I have, Mum.'

But this comment was a reminder of the reason they'd moved to the city in the first place, and the brief camaraderie between them dissolved. Layla sipped her wine as her mother bustled around the kitchen. Zach, Cam, the kids, work – whenever they diverted from these safe topics, things became awkward between them. And now, watching her mother slicing the avocados and getting the pink prawns and thousand-island dressing out of the fridge reminded her so acutely of the Christmas Days of her childhood that she had to swallow down the lump of nostalgia that rose in her throat. If not for her, her family might never have fractured in the first place. And maybe her dad would still be here with them, rather than opening presents and laughing with someone else's family in Sydney.

'Any chance the kids will eat a prawn cocktail?' Angela asked.

Layla snorted. 'They don't eat anything.'

'It doesn't last forever, you know.'

'Feels like it sometimes.'

'You were a little terror when you were their age.' Her mum's face softened into a wistful smile. 'But by the time you started school you were an angel. Your father and I were so proud of you. So smart and so focused.'

Layla pressed her lips together and looked away. Whenever she thought about what she'd put her parents through, shame stamped down on her. 'I wasn't smart all the time,' she said in a low voice.

Angela's hands paused in their prawn-cocktail assembly. She didn't look up at Layla when she spoke. 'It doesn't matter now.'

The tension stretched between them. Layla had the urge to escape back to her family, but how could she ignore the enormous sacrifice her mother had once made for her? 'That doesn't take back what I did.'

'That whole episode is well and truly in the past.' Angela's voice was strained.

A flurry of emotion overwhelmed Layla, and she rested her elbows on the bench and buried her face in her hands. After a moment, her mother's hand landed on her shoulder. 'Layla, what's wrong? Why are you bringing this up now?'

After leaving Glasswater Bay, they'd never spoken about what she'd done, but ever since Layla had got that first message, she'd found it harder and harder to push her memories into the background. It had opened the floodgates, and she wasn't sure if it was going to be possible to stuff everything back in.

'Do you get lonely?' she asked through her hands.

'What do you mean?'

'Since Dad left. Are you lonely, by yourself?'

'Layla.' Angela gave her shoulders a little shake. 'Please tell me what's wrong.'

Finally, Layla met her mother's eyes. 'I got a message. From Jodie Telford. She knows what I did.'

Angela's face blanched. 'But how?'

'I don't know.'

'What does she want?'

'I have no idea—'

'Mummy!' Ella raced into the kitchen and wrapped her arms around one of Layla's legs. There was a smear of chocolate on her cheek. 'Wanna cuddle.'

Layla picked her up and sat her on the edge of the bench, and Ella hugged her around the neck, blonde curls tickling Layla's face. 'Your uncle has been spoiling you again, hasn't he?' Layla scrubbed at the chocolate with a thumb. Her eyes met her mother's over Ella's head, but there was no more time to talk, because now Zach was in the kitchen too.

'Guilty,' he said with a rueful smile.

Then Cam came in behind him and put his arm around Layla's waist, inhaling the smell of roast chicken from the oven. 'Smells delicious, Angela.'

'It's almost ready,' she said. 'And entree is done. Everyone ready to eat?'

Layla didn't get another moment alone with her mother for the rest of the afternoon as everyone pulled Christmas crackers, read out the terrible jokes, stuffed themselves full of food and covered the living-room floor in a sea of torn wrapping paper. So when they left a few hours later, juggling dozens of presents, she still hadn't had the chance to discuss the problem of the messages.

THEN

'Help me make the coffees, Layla?' Scott said on Saturday night as Yumi cleaned the empty tables. It was half an hour before closing and there was one table of patrons left; a group of elderly tourists who were travelling around the coast of Australia. When they'd first come in, we'd assumed they'd have a quiet dinner and leave early, but they'd been here for hours, chatting animatedly and catching up on travel stories.

I joined Scott behind the coffee machine. This was the closest we'd been in a week and I'd been going crazy, over-analysing everything to the point of paralysis before forcing myself to accept that the kiss would never be repeated. But now, as I frothed the milk for the coffees, I was hyper-aware of his presence. The fine hairs on my skin sprang up as he leant across me to grab another cup and his arm brushed against mine.

He glanced at me with a half-smile. 'Sorry.'

'No problem.' I smiled back, and there it was again, that little shot of electricity that made me feel invincible yet defenceless.

We finished the coffees and I took them out to the group. 'Thanks, dear,' one woman said as I placed her coffee in front of her. 'This is such a lovely town; so quaint! I wish we could stay for another few days.'

'You probably wouldn't love it so much if you had to live here,' I said as I collected the used cups.

She chuckled. 'Oh, I remember what it was like to grow up in a small town. But my home town was nowhere near as pretty as this.'

'That beautiful bay!' exclaimed the woman beside her. 'It reminds me of San Sebastian. Have you ever been there, love? It's in Spain.'

'I've never been overseas,' I admitted. 'But my friends and I are going to backpack around Europe someday.' I smiled at the thought of the dreams we'd once had back when we'd first started high school.

'Good on you, dear.'

'Can I get you anything else?'

'Just the bill, please.'

*

When the group finally left, the silence was like an animal crouching in the shadows.

'Want me to balance the till?' I asked Scott.

'Sure, thanks, Layla.' His hand touched my back, feather-light. It was just for a second, but it was enough to set my heart flapping against my chest.

He stood beside me as I counted up the cash and reconciled it against the sales, and gradually we drew closer together until his arm was pressed against mine. He wore no cologne; there was just the faintly earthy smell of his sweat overlaid with the synthetic pine scent of deodorant. A man's smell.

I breathed it in, trying to concentrate on the money, but I kept losing count and having to start over. I swore and Scott glanced down at me with an amused smile. 'You all right?'

I grinned at him. 'Pretty great, actually.'

'I'm outta here.' Yumi materialised behind the counter and whipped off her apron. 'You OK to finish up?'

'Sure,' I said, but now that I was faced with being alone with Scott again, nervousness rushed in. What had I been thinking, flirting with him like that? This thing was too big for me; I needed to get out of the situation now before I got myself in too deep.

As soon as I'd finished balancing the till, I took off my apron and hung it on the hook, then went out to the kitchen to get my bag. But just as I was reaching for the doorhandle, the door swung open and hit me right on the nose. 'Ow!'

'Oh shit, Layla, I'm sorry!' Scott was clutching my shoulders as I hunched over, hand over my nose. 'Are you OK?'

'Bloody hell.' My words were muffled through my hand.

'I didn't break your nose, did I?'

The throbbing was already subsiding, leaving a fizzing sensation in its place. I was pretty sure my nose wasn't broken, but the look of genuine concern on Scott's face was unexpectedly pleasing. I pulled my hand away and glanced at my fingers. 'No blood. I think I'm going to live.'

His face relaxed into a relieved smile. 'Sorry, I shouldn't have rushed in here so quickly.'

'No harm done. Well, maybe a little bit of harm. But I'm all good.'

He dropped one of his hands away from me, but the other one lingered on my shoulder. Our eyes locked, and his gaze darkened. I held my breath as his fingers crept up to the nape of my neck. Goosebumps rose on my skin. Then he splayed his hand on the back of my neck and pulled me towards him. Heat suffused me as he lowered his face to mine. He kissed me harder this time, his tongue exploring my mouth, stubble scraping my face. He dropped his lips to my throat and a zing spiralled down my back as his teeth grazed my skin. I ran my hands over his shoulders, my fingers tracing the muscles through the fabric of his shirt. Then he broke away from me abruptly and backed up until he was against the door.

'God, Layla, we can't do this.' He ran a hand through his hair, his eyes wild.

Shame filtered in around the warm glow that had started up inside me. 'Sorry.'

'I thought I could ...' His face was anguished. 'I've tried to stay away from you, but ...'

'Do you want me to quit?' I said in a small voice.

'No! I don't expect you to do yourself out of a job. Fuck.' He went over to a chair in the corner of the room and collapsed into it. 'I don't know what to do.'

He dropped his head into his hands. I kept expecting him to take charge, but now he looked like the teenager, waiting for me to come up with the solution. 'You're married,' I said.

He looked up at me. 'Yeah.'

'That means something. Doesn't it?' I wasn't sure what I wanted his answer to be, all I knew was that I needed to confront the situation head-on, no matter how much it hurt.

Scott heaved a sigh. 'Don't get married young, Layla. It'll ruin your life.'

I waited.

'We were together in high school. Then we were on and off for a couple of years, but it always seemed inevitable that we'd end up together, you know?' I didn't, but I let him go on. 'We got bored, so we got married, thinking that would change everything. Built a house. I bought this cafe. Then Jodie got pregnant and that was it. Life sentence.'

I didn't want to know, but I asked the question anyway. 'Do you still love her?'

He sighed again. 'We're like housemates. We talk about the kids, and about when the bills are due, and when we've run out of milk. There's no excitement anymore. It's just … it's really fucking boring. I thought my life was going to be more than this.'

'You didn't answer my question.'

He looked frustrated. 'There is no answer, Layla. Love is a lie. It tells us stories that aren't true.'

I didn't want to believe his words, but he looked so sad that I felt a strange tenderness towards him. 'Tell me what you want me to do.'

He beckoned to me. 'Can you come over here?'

I knew I shouldn't, but now he held me by a thread, tugging me towards him. I approached tentatively, knowing and not knowing what was going to happen. He patted his knee, and after a moment of hesitation I sat down sideways on his lap.

'No. Like this.' He stood me up again and turned me to face him, then guided me forwards until my legs straddled his. His hands rested on my hips, the heat of them burning through my jeans. For a few seconds, I entertained the thought of withdrawing, of leaving before things went too far, but then he pulled me down onto his lap and we were kissing again. Doubt nudged at me, but there was no room left for that internal voice now, not when his hands were running up and down my back, not when his tongue was tracing the contours of mine, not when my whole body was coming alive. Scott clutched my buttocks and pulled me against him, and I took in a sharp breath as his erection pressed into my groin. A delicious sense of anticipation began to balloon inside me.

'Oh god, Layla, I want you so much,' he breathed in my ear.

He took my hand and moved it down his chest, down his belly, pressed it against the bulge in his jeans. The pleasurable feelings faded into uncertainty. I didn't know what to do, so I rubbed my hand against him and he let out a long groan. It was only when he began fumbling with his belt that my sense of control disintegrated. Anxiety flooded me and I snatched my hand away and got to my feet. 'Sorry, I … I can't. I'm not ready for this. Sorry.'

Scott's eyes refocused and he stood up too. 'No, I'm sorry. I didn't mean to push you.'

The butterflies in my stomach coupled with embarrassment at my crippling inexperience, leaving me brimming with doubt and poised for flight. 'I should go.'

He was still breathing heavily. 'I want you to know that I won't push you into anything. If you just want to kiss, we'll just kiss.'

The implications of this both thrilled me and sent a wave of trepidation crashing over me. 'Are we really going to do this?'

He rested his hands on my waist. 'I can't stop thinking about you, Layla. How can it be wrong when it feels this right?'

The logical part of my brain knew his words were clichéd, rehearsed. If Renee and I heard them in a movie, we'd laugh and cross our hands over our hearts and pretend to swoon. But somehow, with my skin still sizzling, I felt their truth deep inside me. They caught up all my tumultuous feelings and swirled them around into a potent cocktail that left me drunk on the possibilities.

Scott kissed me gently, his lips lingering on mine. 'Can we just see where this takes us?'

I nodded breathlessly.

NOW

Layla's body was still buzzing when she woke in the early hours of the morning. It had been years since she'd dreamt about Scott, and the pleasant warmth in her belly grappled with her shame. She stretched out her limbs, enjoying the coolness of the sheets against her bare skin. Her fingers drifted down her belly and she allowed her thoughts to turn back to those early days with Scott, when her body had first begun to awaken.

She hadn't known anything, and she'd let him take charge. It had all been new and exciting, and she'd felt sexy for the first time in her young life – but there'd been a heavy dose of fear there too. Fear of what she didn't know. Fear of being found out. Fear of losing him. Fear of the power contained within her body; power that, with hindsight, had always been an illusion.

She rolled onto her side and reached out to Cam, trailing her fingers over his chest. He stirred and, barely awake, took her into his arms. She redirected the feelings in her body towards her husband, kissing his chest, her hand seeking him out, guiding him to her. The sex was good. It was always good. If someone had told her back in her twenties that one day she'd have sex approximately one night a week, in the same positions and in the same marital bed, she would've scoffed at the mechanical dullness of it.

But it wasn't dull. It wasn't mechanical. There was comfort in the familiarity of him, in the gradually softening contours of his body as they aged together, at the certainty that he would make her come, at the warm glow that followed. If only she'd known then what she knew now – that she would only begin to feel comfortable seeking out her own pleasure once she had matured. If only she could learn to feel comfortable in her maturing body. As long as the lights were off, she could enjoy her husband's touch without the self-consciousness that engulfed her when he could see all her imperfections.

They came together and she collapsed over him, his arms tightening around her. 'Sorry I woke you up,' she said.

He laughed. '*Never* apologise for that.'

'Well, thanks. It was good. You're good.' She raised her head to kiss him. 'I love you.'

'Hmm, we might have to do this more often if this is how you repay me.'

'I mean it, Cam.' Sudden tears stung behind her eyes. 'If it weren't for you, I don't know where I would've ended up.'

He shifted beneath her. 'What do you mean?'

She bit her lip. She couldn't tell him, not after what had happened with his own father. And she didn't want him to know about the series of destructive relationships that littered her past, and how far she'd already disappeared inside herself when he walked into the pharmacy that day. How brittle she had been then. How empty. How close to giving up. He had made some lame joke, and she'd laughed, and it was only after he left that she'd realised she couldn't remember the last time she'd laughed spontaneously at anything. He'd come back the next day on the pretence of asking her a question about the antibiotics she'd given him, and then, just before he left, he'd asked her out for coffee. He'd looked at her like she was someone, and she'd felt seen for the first time in years, immediately imagining being looked at like that for years to come. She'd never imagined that about anyone else before. But to articulate all of that now would be too weighty, too loaded. It would upset the balance she'd so carefully curated.

'Nothing, I'm just glad I found you, that's all,' she said.

She got up to go to the bathroom, and when she slid back into the bed, Cam was asleep and snoring lightly. She lay on her back for a while, staring up into the darkness, then reached for her phone.

At first, she'd tried to banish the messages from her mind, but now she found herself looking at Jodie's Facebook profile every day. It had become an addiction that she couldn't seem to break. Yesterday, Jodie had posted a new album with the description: *Christmas Day 2019. Love my family!! xxx*

Layla began to scroll through the photos. Jodie's kids had inherited her good looks, with the same dark hair and high cheekbones. She followed the tags to their profiles and plunged down the rabbit hole.

The eldest, Claire, shared her mother's lack of concern for online security. She was married, pregnant, living in Victor Harbor with her husband. It seemed like she spent a lot of time in the garden, having regular lunches with her mother, shopping for baby clothes, and catching up for girls' nights with her old school friends, who were already starting families of their own.

What was it about people who stayed in country towns settling down and having kids so early? Was it boredom? Lack of better options? A kind of Stockholm syndrome, where they believed it was safer to stay than to experience something different? The idea suffocated her. She would've been out of Glasswater Bay at the first available opportunity, even without everything else.

She returned to Jodie's post and clicked on her son's profile.

Bradley was more security conscious than his sister and kept his account locked down, but Layla was able to view his profile photos as he'd changed them over the years. He'd joined Facebook when he was fifteen, and she watched as teenage acne and braces gave way to a chiselled face and sensuous lips. His most recent photo included a young blonde woman with a bright Instagram-worthy smile. His location was listed as Adelaide. At least one of them had got out.

Once again, Layla went back to Jodie's profile and scrolled through the rest of the photos from Christmas Day. They'd obviously had a big family do: most of the photos were from the backyard Layla had never seen, and included a parade of at least twenty different people. Then two familiar figures leapt out at her from one of the photos and she gripped the phone more tightly. She'd known they were family, of course, but this reminder of the connection between what she'd done and what she'd lost was visceral, as if her skin was being sheared from her bones. She stared hard at one of the faces, once so familiar but now the face of a stranger.

*

Cam's arms encircled her from behind as she buttered the kids' toast. She inhaled his fresh shower scent.

'I can't stop thinking about this morning,' he murmured in her ear. 'I could get used to waking up like that.'

She turned her head to kiss him. 'One day we're going to get sprung by one of them.' She nodded at Louis and Ella, who sat up at the breakfast bar, fidgeting as they waited for their toast.

'Then we might have to put a lock on the door.'

She laughed, pushing the brightly coloured plastic plates across the bench to the children. 'What are you going to do with them today?'

'Dunno. Playground. Play cafe if it gets too hot. Coffee?'

'Thanks.'

Both Cam's work and the children's childcare centre shut down over the Christmas and new year period, but Layla still had to go to work.

Her phone pinged on the bench in front of her and she reached for it as Cam turned towards the coffee machine.

Does your husband know what you did, Layla?

Layla clapped her hand over her mouth, clamping down on the fear that was trying to leap out. All this time she had been stalking Jodie, she'd never considered the possibility that Jodie might be doing her own research. But how had she known Layla was married? Layla kept her Facebook profile under lock and key; neither Cam nor the kids were in any of her profile photos, and she didn't use any other kind of social media. A seed of panic lodged in her chest and began to radiate outwards, her breathing becoming shallow and fast. Did Jodie know where she lived? Was she watching her house, her husband, her children?

Maybe it wasn't too late to tell Cam about Scott, to make the first move before Jodie did. But even the idea of his disappointment was too painful. Early in their relationship he'd told her, his voice wobbling with emotion, how his father had walked out on his family when he was a child. An affair with his secretary – so clichéd, so seedy. They'd been doing it on his desk one night when Cam's mother had walked in on them, holding a beef casserole in a Tupperware container for his dinner because he'd told her he was working late. 'The casserole ended up on that bitch's peroxided head,' Cam had said, 'and she deserved much worse after she ripped my family apart.' Layla had flinched at his uncharacteristically harsh words, had felt them as keenly as if they'd been directed at her. And as she rubbed Cam's back and kissed away his tears, she'd realised that he could never know the truth about her.

What would he think if he knew what she had destroyed? How would his face change if she told him about what she'd done, the regrets that had haunted her for years, that she'd buried until Jodie had wrenched them from the earth?

Cam turned to hand her a coffee mug, then frowned when he saw her face. He glanced down at the phone in her hand. 'Are you OK?'

She threw him a quick smile and put her phone in her pocket. 'Just daydreaming. I'd better finish getting ready for work.'

Louis got down from the stool and came around to the other side of the bench, holding up his arms for a hug. Layla crouched down so he could put his arms around her neck. 'Can I kiss your eyes?' he asked solemnly.

She closed her eyelids obediently for him to land light kisses on. Louis was a whirlwind of energy, creating chaos everywhere he went, but when he was like this, the sweet perfection of him squeezed her heart. She hugged him tight. 'Be good for Daddy today, OK?'

*

Cam brought the kids out the front to wave goodbye to her as she pulled out of the driveway. A wave of love swept over her, and she swallowed her fear. Whatever Jodie's reason for contacting her now, she had to shut this down. She couldn't risk losing everything that was important to her. As soon as she turned the corner, she pulled over, opened up the message again and tapped out a reply.

What do you want from me?

THEN

It was really happening.

It was intoxicating, carrying around this delicious secret, the memory of sitting astride him … The two days the cafe was closed seemed an age as I waited for my next shift on Tuesday. While I was apart from Scott, it was easy to forget my uncertainty and doubt, to remember only the way it had felt to be wanted, to yearn to do it again. I tried to study, but my mind kept wandering back to our last encounter, questioning where it was leading us.

I wasn't so innocent that I didn't know he'd eventually want to have sex. For a moment, when I'd felt him hard beneath his jeans, for me, I'd wanted that too, and the realisation had been shocking. But the line we would cross if we did, not to mention losing my virginity when I'd only just kissed someone for the first time, filled me with anxiety. It couldn't happen. And anyway, Scott had said he was happy just to kiss.

By the time Tuesday came around, I was so tied up with anticipation that I felt like I was going to burst. As soon as the school bell rang, I ran down to the road below the school oval where I'd parked my car and jumped in. Renee waved at me from outside the school fence, but I pretended I didn't see her and continued past the school, excitement building within me as I sped up Bay Road, past the park with the rotunda, and turned right onto the main street.

''Sup, bitch?' Yumi said as I threw open the door and set the bell clanging. 'You're certainly in a hurry to get to work.'

'Nice to see you too,' I retorted. I threw a smile at Scott, who was standing behind the counter. 'Hey, Scott.'

'Hey, Layla.'

I loved the way he smiled as he said my name, the way his tongue was visible as it flicked to the roof of his mouth with each syllable. A look passed between us, and I felt it must be obvious to the whole world. I looked away, flustered. 'Just gonna get changed.'

I went through the kitchen, greeting Dave on the way, and out to the staff bathroom. I was about to enter one of the cubicles when the door swung open again and Scott was there. My schoolbag thudded to the floor as he guided me into a cubicle, trapping us in the small space. He pushed me up against the wall and kissed me. I put my arms around his neck and closed my eyes, shivering as he tugged my shirt out from where it was tucked into my skirt and his hands found my bare skin.

At last he pulled away from me, his eyes gleaming in the gloomy half-light.

My mouth twitched into a smile. 'Sir, I think you've got the wrong bathroom.'

'Oh, no I don't.' He tugged at the hem of my checked woollen skirt. 'I like this. Very sexy.'

I pushed at his chest playfully. 'I didn't know you harboured schoolgirl fantasies.'

His face fell. 'Don't say that. I'm not like that.'

'Hey, sorry.' I touched his chest again. 'I was just kidding.'

He smiled again, his hand moving slowly up my bare leg. 'Anyway, you're no girl. You're a woman.'

No one had ever called me a woman before. I liked the way it made me feel, and so when he walked two fingers up under my skirt, holding my gaze, I didn't stop his hand. I sucked in a breath as he brushed his fingers across my underwear. Then there was a noise from outside the bathroom and he was gone. The door sighed closed, my hammering heart the only indication he'd been there at all.

*

I worked every night that week.

When it was quiet, after Dave had gone home, Scott would close the cafe early and we'd end up in the kitchen. And every night his hands wandered a little further, his kisses became a little more demanding, until I'd break away, my heart juddering, and tell him I needed to go home and study. He always retreated as soon as I asked him to, but I couldn't help wondering how much longer that would be enough for him. Every day I'd talk myself into giving him what he wanted, but then when it came to the moment, everything would start to feel out of control, and I'd lose my nerve and shut him down again.

One night after he tried to take my shirt off and I stepped away, his normally easy smile was stretched and thin with desperation. 'I'm not sure if I can do this anymore, Layla.'

My stomach dropped. 'Did I do something wrong?'

He gave a rough laugh. 'No, god, no. That's just the problem. I want more of you all the time, and it's so hard to hold back.'

I'd known this would happen eventually, but it was still a sharp blow. I clasped my hands together in front of me to stop them from shaking. 'I'm sorry. I know I'm not very good, but I've never done any of this before. I'm not ready for … that.'

He cupped my face in his hands. His eyes were soft. 'I don't want to have sex with you, Layla. I just want to be close to you.'

I nodded. 'That's what I want too.'

'Jodie won't even let me touch her anymore,' he said. 'All I think about is you, and there's this … pressure inside me.'

He looked wretched. And I had the power to help him. 'What do you want me to do?'

He fingered the top button of my shirt. 'I just want to look at you. I won't touch you, if you don't want me to.'

I hesitated. I could say no. I could walk out of here and get in my car and go home and pretend to focus on my textbooks. But I knew if I did that, all I'd be able to think about was whether I'd blown it by not giving him this one small thing. It wasn't that much to ask. My friends had done far more than letting someone look at their breasts. I started to unbutton my shirt as Scott collapsed into a chair, his hand already moving down to his pants. He unzipped himself and I instinctively looked away.

'It's OK, Layla,' he said, his voice husky. 'You can watch.'

I didn't really want to, but I didn't want him to think I was a prude either, so I dragged my gaze back to him. It looked different to what I'd expected; dark, angry, urgent.

I slipped my shirt off my shoulders and Scott let out a low moan. He reached out his free hand to stroke one of my breasts, and I fought the urge to move away. This had already gone further than he'd promised. But his eyes were glazed over with desire as he stared at my breasts and my lacy black bra, and what would he think of me now if I pulled the pin and put my shirt back on?

'Can you kiss me?' he pleaded.

He pulled me into his lap and fondled me harder, slipping his hand inside my bra before I had the chance to slow things down. I gasped as his thumb flicked over my nipple. All my instincts screamed at me to retreat, but his other hand was moving so fast that his whole lap juddered, and there was nothing I could do to stop this now. His mouth was open wide as he kissed me, like he was trying to swallow me whole. 'Layla, you're so beautiful. Can you help me?'

Before I realised what was happening, he'd taken my hand and put it on his penis, then closed his own around it, pumping it up and down vigorously. It seemed like it would never end, but then he cried out and semen spurted out of him. Some landed on his jeans, but he didn't seem to notice. He let out a long groan and rested his head against my shoulder.

'Thank you, Layla. You're amazing. Thank you.'

I remained frozen, still shocked at what had just happened. After a minute, he released my hand and looked into my eyes. The hard-edged urgency had gone from his face now; he looked like himself again, and so pathetically grateful that it was hard to believe he'd just pushed me beyond my comfort level. In any case, I'd let it happen; it wasn't like he'd forced himself on me. He kissed me again, his lips soft, hands gentle on the bare skin of my back.

'You've made me very happy tonight, Layla. It wasn't too much for you, was it?'

His expression was so earnest that all I could say was, 'Of course not.'

NOW

Layla checked her phone compulsively, waiting for a response from Jodie. She'd instantly regretted sending the message, engaging with her, but she couldn't live with this anxiety any longer, with not knowing what Jodie intended to do.

It was a quiet day in the pharmacy, and she hid in the back of the dispensary, taking her phone out every few minutes to check for a new message. She knew Jodie had read it. The little circle of her profile picture had bobbed up beside the message not long after Layla had sent it. What was she doing now? Deciding how she was going to destroy Layla? Or maybe – Layla grabbed the slim hope with both hands – maybe she'd only ever wanted to rattle her, and now that she'd got what she wanted, she'd give up and leave her alone.

In her lunchbreak, Layla went out into the shopping mall and bought a baguette she didn't feel like eating from one of the cafes. She wandered listlessly up and down the mall, taking the occasional bite. For a while, she shadowed a small group of teenage girls, the nostalgia swelling within her as they chattered and shrieked with excitement about boyfriends and the New Year's Eve party they were going to.

It didn't matter how much time had passed since she, Renee and Shona had fallen out, seeing other young women and girls together like this always gave her a pang of bitter regret. Childhood friendships drifted apart all the time, she knew that, but it had been different with the three of them. They'd all had different personalities, and emotions had been larger than life back then. They'd disagreed vigorously, fought often, loved each other in the fierce and unrestrained way that teenage girls did. But in among that, there'd always been something real and solid between them.

Until Layla had taken a sledgehammer to their friendship and smashed it to pieces.

For years, she'd tried to put them back together, and sometimes it had seemed like it was going to work, but things had never been the same after she'd left Glasswater Bay. She'd never been able to undo the damage. Their fractured friendship had limped along until they'd finished uni and then Shona had gone to London and Renee had returned to Glasswater Bay, and now their relationship was confined to Facebook, where the occasional like on a photo had taken the place of real engagement.

Layla had made new friends over the years, but no friendship had ever come near what she'd shared with Renee and Shona. Losing them was one of the greatest sorrows of her life; more so, in many ways, than what she'd done to Jodie's family.

As if summoned by her thoughts, the message came.

I want you to understand what you did to us. Meet me for a coffee.

Layla slumped onto a vacant bench seat and lay the barely touched baguette in her lap. She'd lived with the guilt all this time; the last thing she wanted was to see the consequences of what she'd done. It was in the past. And if Jodie actually had any proof, she would've done something about it then, not waited twenty years.

No way, she typed back. *Don't contact me again.*

Her phone began to ring and Layla jumped so violently that the baguette fell from her lap onto the tiled floor of the mall. Jodie was trying to call her through Messenger. She rejected the call with shaking fingers and switched off her phone. She could ride this out; Jodie would get bored and soon it would all fade into the background again, leaving Layla to get on with her life. She bent to pick up the baguette, stood up and dropped it into the bin beside the bench. Then she went back to work, her belly hollow with worry.

*

Layla's body was already buzzing with anticipation as she and Cam walked into the Governor Hindmarsh Hotel on New Year's Eve. Despite her love of music in her youth, she hadn't been to a gig in years, and she'd been overjoyed on Christmas morning when Cam had surprised her with tickets to see Magic Dirt and The Superjesus.

'I haven't been to the Gov in years!' she shouted over the crowd. 'We should get a good spot in front of the stage now.'

'You don't actually want to go up the front, do you?' Cam looked surprised.

'Of course I do! Magic Dirt is one of my favourite bands, and I haven't seen them in fifteen years.'

'But if we stay over here, we'll have a good view *and* access to the bar. Best of both worlds.'

Layla laughed as she gazed around the room at the vintage photos of musicians hanging on the walls, the lamps that curved over the bar, the clumps of people chatting in groups, beers in hands. 'God, I love this place. I used to spend most of my weekends between here and the Adelaide Uni bar. The music scene was so good back then.'

'Lucky for you, all these nineties bands are touring again,' Cam said. 'They must all be having midlife crises.'

Layla slapped at his chest. 'It was the noughties, thanks very much! And you don't have to keep reminding me that I'm older than you.'

They reached the bar and he pulled his wallet out of his back pocket. 'Wine?'

'Nope, it has to be beer. It's practically mandatory.'

He ordered their drinks then turned back to her. 'I can't believe that once upon a time while you were going to gigs and drinking beer, I was getting drunk at the Law Ball.'

'Ugh, the Law Ball!' Layla laughed. 'I went to one of those one year with this guy, and—' She stopped abruptly, not wanting to explain how the night had ended. The guy fucking her against the wall down the side of the venue. Leaving her there, the ball gown she'd borrowed from her housemate ripped and spattered with his spilt beer.

'And what?' Cam raised his eyebrows.

Layla laughed to dispel the heavy feeling that the memory had brought back. 'Oh, you know what they were like. Lots of drunk girls in pretty dresses, guys swilling beer and beating their chests in their fancy suits.'

He handed her a beer. 'Hey, I never beat my chest.'

'Bet you picked up plenty of girls though.'

He stared across the room. 'I didn't play the field, if that's what you're asking.'

'It's not.' Layla frowned.

'I've never been interested in girls who are like that.'

'Like what?'

He took a gulp of his beer, but didn't respond.

Layla stared at the side of his face, at the line of his jaw that was vibrating with tension, and hot indignation flared inside her. 'I was talking about you, not other women,' she said when he remained silent.

He threw her a bitter glance. 'I don't ask about your past, so don't ask about mine. It's irrelevant to who we are now.'

Layla regretted starting an argument that was so close to her own fears. She was trying to think of something to say to bring back the light mood that had been between them only minutes ago when there was a roar from the crowd and her gaze turned to the stage as the band came out.

The lead singer, Adalita, greeted the crowd in her sheath dress and combat boots, her black hair rippling down her back, and they launched into the first song. The bass thumped inside Layla's chest like a magnified heart and her foot tapped with barely contained energy. Then, when the fuzzy opening chords of 'Vulcanella' sent a shot of adrenalin straight to her heart, and when the lyrics began to cascade from Adalita in a sultry stream of consciousness, she handed her drink to Cam and drifted away into the crowd, allowing it to jostle her along until she reached the front, where a group of women made room for her in front of the stage. There, she lost herself in the music and the memories of old times.

It was only when the band had finished and she was heading back over to Cam that she saw a familiar figure in the crowd. Just the back of her head, but the sight of red hair made her heart lurch. Could it really be her? With no thought as to what she was going to do or say, she changed direction and began to follow the woman. It was no surprise, really, that she would be here tonight too. She'd almost reached her when the woman paused to greet a man who'd just emerged from the bathroom, and Layla came to an abrupt halt. The man's eyes swept over the room and rested for a split second on Layla, then she whirled around and pushed back through the crowd, her heart beating fast. She wasn't prepared for that confrontation.

Cam gave her a quizzical look when she reached him. 'Where were you going?'

'Thought I saw someone I knew.' But the idea that she might run into them again made her stomach flutter with panic. 'Do you mind if we go home?'

He grimaced. 'Listen, I'm sorry about what I said before. I didn't mean to upset you. We don't have to leave if you don't want to. It's nice to see you having fun. You've seemed so distracted lately.'

'What?' She was too busy looking around the room for Renee to focus on his words. 'Oh, it's fine. Don't worry about it.' She glanced over her shoulder again. 'I'm just a bit tired, that's all. It'd be good to get an early night.'

Cam drained the last of his beer. 'OK, we can go if you want, but I thought you really wanted to see The Superjesus.'

Layla gazed wistfully back to the stage, where The Superjesus would soon appear. She did want to see them, but the euphoria she'd felt only minutes ago had dissipated at the sight of Renee's husband. She'd been on the verge of approaching her old friend, but she couldn't do it – not with him there. She wasn't ready to face him.

She turned back to Cam with a strained smile. 'Think I'm getting too old for this stuff.'

He grinned and put an arm around her shoulders. 'Let's go home, then, old lady.'

She kept her head down as they left the Gov, her heart heavy with regret.

THEN

After a few days, the episode in the kitchen didn't seem like such a big deal. It wouldn't have been fair to continue pushing him away when he wasn't getting any affection at home. What harm was there in me giving him what he needed? It wasn't like we'd had sex. He'd said himself that wasn't what he wanted. I was lucky, really, that he was satisfied with that. Nevertheless, the thought of what might be coming next made me nervous.

And so, it was almost a relief when Renee burst into tears during lunchbreak on Friday and I could turn my attention to someone else's problems. Shona and I sat down on either side of her and each put an arm around her.

'What's wrong?' Shona asked.

'It's fucking Vince!' she cried. 'We were waiting for pizza last night and Katrina walked into the shop. They talked for a few minutes and I didn't think anything of it, but then later we were eating the pizza in his car and he told me to go easy. I laughed it off, but then he said, "Do you think Katrina looks the way she does from eating four slices of pizza?" And he still expected me to have sex with him afterwards!'

'Fucking prick!' I said savagely. 'How dare he treat you like that?'

'Please tell me you didn't actually *have* sex with him after that,' Shona said.

'Well, I thought he was going to dump me, didn't I?' Renee wailed.

'I'm going to stab him in the dick with a fork,' Shona declared. 'As if you're not a thousand times better than Katrina.'

'A million times better,' I said.

'A trillion times,' Shona said.

'A squillion,' I said.

'That's not a real number.' Renee rested her head on my shoulder. 'I love you guys. I don't know what I'd do without you.'

'Let's catch up tonight,' Shona said. 'You guys stay at my place and we'll listen to loud chick rock and bitch about idiot boys.'

*

But when I asked Scott that night if I could finish my shift a bit early, he looked so disappointed that I immediately regretted my decision.

'I was really looking forward to seeing you tonight,' he said.

'Me too,' I said in a low voice. 'But it's just one night. We'll see each other again tomorrow morning, and I'll make sure I get in nice and early.'

'I had a surprise for you tonight, but that's OK. I guess it can wait.'

'Oh, I'm sorry. I didn't realise.'

A group came into the cafe and we were forced to halt our conversation until they were seated at a table and I'd taken their orders, and then Jacinta always seemed too close for us to talk for most of the evening.

Finally, when my shift was almost over, Jacinta took the food orders out to Dave in the kitchen and I sidled up to Scott again. 'I'm sorry about tonight, but Renee needs me. She's worried her boyfriend's about to dump her.'

He smiled down at me. 'I told you, it's fine. Though it seems a bit hypocritical that she goes AWOL as soon as she gets a boyfriend, but then expects you to drop everything for her.'

'She's my friend,' I said. 'She'd be there for me if I needed her.'

'Of course, I get it. Friends are important.'

'Well, thanks for understanding.'

'You don't have to thank me for acknowledging that you've got your own life outside this place.' He looked up as the bell over the door jingled. 'Here's your friend now. She doesn't look too heartbroken to me.'

Renee and Shona waltzed into the cafe, grins on their faces. 'We beat 'em to it,' Renee announced.

'What do you mean?' I said.

'I told Daniel what Vince said about Katrina,' Shona said. 'He said I was overreacting, can you believe it?'

'So that was it,' Renee said. '*We* dumped *them.*'

'Wow,' I said, genuinely impressed. 'Good on you.'

'I'm done with boys,' Shona said. 'Let's go to the Anchor and find some real men at the front bar.'

I felt Scott's eyes on me and my face went hot. I took off my apron and grabbed my bag. 'We're not going to get into the front bar, Shona. Everyone in Glasswater knows we're underage.'

'Well, what are we gonna do, then?' Shona said. 'I'm so bored I could die.'

'I can't wait to get out of this town,' Renee said. 'I bet there'll be way more decent guys in Adelaide.'

I hoisted my bag onto my shoulder. 'See you tomorrow morning,' I said to Scott, smiling in a way that I hoped conveyed how much I was looking forward to it.

'Let's go down to the Esplanade,' Shona said when we were outside.

'It's bloody freezing,' I complained, crossing my arms. 'Why don't we just go straight to your place?'

'Because then we wouldn't be able to drink these.' Renee pulled a sixpack of Bacardi Breezers out of her bag.

'Nice! Where'd you get them?'

'Daniel's sister bought them for us,' Shona said. 'She's nineteen. Luckily she got 'em *before* I dumped her brother's lousy arse!'

We laughed. It seemed like a long time since I'd hung out with my friends with no boys around, and it felt good to laugh with them again. Renee pulled a drink out of the cardboard casing and handed one to me, and I twisted off the top and took a drink. Sweet enough to mask the flavour of the alcohol, just the way I liked it. Renee and Shona opened theirs and we continued to stroll down the main street. The wind picked up as we drew closer to the Esplanade, throwing itself into our faces. It tasted of salt.

We found a bench overlooking the water and sat down together, swigging from our bottles and gazing into the darkness. Renee and Shona talked a bit about school and their grades and applying for uni next year, and I realised I'd barely done any study in the last week. Mid-year exams were coming up soon, and I needed top-notch grades if I was going to get into pharmacy next year; there was no way I wanted to repeat Year Twelve. It was as if I'd been walking around in a dream world ever since Scott had kissed me. It had been less than two weeks, but it already felt like I'd embarked on a new life.

By the time we finished our drinks, we were all shivering violently, so we got up and headed back, second drinks already in hand. The main street was deserted; the streetlights created pools of yellow light, the few trees throwing long shadows across the road. The statue of Benjamin Andrews, the town's founder, towered over us, and we sat down on its platform. I was halfway through my second drink already and there was a pleasant warmth in my belly. My mind skipped along, flying free. I felt strong, euphoric. This was what I should be doing: blowing off steam with my friends like a normal teenager.

I stood up and tipped my head back to gaze up into Benjamin's bronze face with its perpetual glower. He didn't look friendly, but then historical authority figures never seemed to. 'Why are there never any statues of women? It's not like women haven't done more extraordinary things than founding a shithole town like this.'

Shona pointed a finger at me. 'Structural inequality. We have to be so much better than them at everything just for them to throw us a cookie, and meanwhile, this dipshit gets a gig for doing bloody nothing.'

Renee raised her arms to the sky in mock prayer. 'One day we too will have statues erected in our names when we … I dunno, apply mascara, or something equally impressive.'

'I'd rather have something else erected in my name,' Shona spluttered.

We all giggled.

Shona leapt to her feet. 'Girl power!' she bellowed, and hurled her empty bottle against the statue.

Renee and I gasped with shocked laughter. Then Renee followed suit, smashing her bottle against poor old Benjamin, and after a moment I did the same. The sound was piercing in the silence of the street, but it was liberating too. I felt invincible. The shattered glass littered the base of the statue, glinting in the streetlights.

'Fuck men,' Renee said decisively when our laughter had died down. 'We should all become lesbians.'

'The problem,' Shona said, slinging an arm over Renee's shoulder, 'is that I like dick too much to give it up.'

'Cheers to that, girlfriend.' They high-fived.

'So, Layla,' Renee said with a grin. 'What's the deal with your situation?'

Shona's head shot up. 'Situation? Layla has a situation?'

'Renee,' I hissed. 'You weren't supposed to say anything.'

Renee shrugged. 'What's the big deal? You said you were going to shut it down.'

Shona was watching me, practically gagging to find out my secret, and now I was pretty pissed and my tongue felt loose. I had a *situation*, and it was nice to feel like a sexual being for once rather than the virgin sidekick. 'Well, speaking of dick ...'

Renee and Shona both shrieked with delight. We started walking back towards my car as I told them about the after-work kitchen sessions with Scott. And in the telling, somehow the fear I'd felt last night was dispelled and the encounter seemed hot and passionate rather than scary and out of control. I even started wishing I'd blown off my friends and stayed back at work instead.

'Far out, Lay, that's full on,' Shona said when I finished.

'I know,' I said. 'It's amazing. He's amazing.'

'What are you going to do?' Renee said. 'I mean, he's married.'

'I'm aware, Renee.'

'Are you going to root him?' Shona asked.

I flushed. 'No. I don't know. I don't think so. He said he doesn't want to have sex.'

'Yeah, on account of being *married*,' Renee said darkly.

Shona stopped and put her hands on my shoulders. 'Babe, it's only been two weeks and you've already given him a hand job. You're young and hot, and he's a dude. Of *course* he wants to have sex.'

I turned this knowledge over in my mind, the knowledge that all this was leading to something, had always been leading to it – knowledge that deep down I had already known to be true. By denying the possibility to myself, I hadn't allowed my own desires to come to the fore, but now I pictured it, really pictured it. Being in bed with him, not just letting him do things to me, but wanting him to. Doing things to him; private things that my mind had always instinctively shrunk from. A surge of carnal lust took hold of my hips, swirling inside me like a wild animal. I shook my head, inexplicably ashamed and afraid of the images that paraded through my mind; all the things I wanted and yet didn't want.

I broke away from Shona and continued walking. 'It's not like that. I've got it under control.'

We reached my car and I leant against the bonnet. The warm feeling inside me had dissipated, leaving me melancholy. I thought about the way Scott's lips felt when he kissed me, the assured firmness of his hands on my body. How disappointed he'd looked earlier when I'd told him I couldn't stay back at work with him. He wanted me. I'd never felt wanted before, and I'd gone and rejected him for my friends who didn't seem the least bit unhappy about their newly single status. The longing hollowed me out.

'How the hell are we going to get to Shona's place?' I said into the silence. 'None of us are in any state to drive.'

'I'll drive you,' said a familiar voice.

The three of us jumped as Scott materialised on the footpath. Adrenalin pumped through my body. Had he heard me bragging about our exploits like a silly schoolgirl?

Shona pressed her hand to her chest. 'Fuck, you scared the shit out of me. I didn't even see you there.'

He smiled. 'I just finished up and was on my way back to my car. Do you want me to drive you girls to Shona's place?'

'That's OK, we can walk.' Renee's voice was cool. 'It's not far.'

'I can't let you walk by yourselves at night,' he said smoothly. 'It's not safe. I'll drive you in Layla's car, then I'll walk back here.'

'Thanks, Scott,' I said, without looking at Renee and Shona. 'That'd be great.'

I handed him the keys and we all got in, Scott and I in the front and Renee and Shona in the back. I looked at the time on the dashboard of my car: 10.45. Suspicion prickled at my neck. The cafe closed at 10 pm; it rarely took longer than twenty minutes to clean up and balance the till. Had he been waiting out here, listening in on our conversation?

'You girls have been drinking, haven't you?' Scott said.

'Um ...' Shona said nervously.

Scott threw an easy grin over his shoulder. 'Don't worry, I won't tell. God, I was getting wasted when I was a lot younger than you.'

'Nothing else to do in this fucking town,' Renee muttered.

I directed Scott off the main road and down the side streets to Shona's place. He killed the engine and handed my keys back to me. Renee and Shona got out, but Scott made no move to follow suit. I wound down my window. 'You guys go in,' I said to my friends. 'I'll be there in a sec.'

We watched as they went up to the front door and Shona let them in. When the door had closed behind them, I felt Scott's eyes on me. 'Why did you tell them about us, Layla?'

My face went hot. So he *had* heard. 'I'm sorry, I didn't mean to. It just slipped out. Don't worry, they won't tell anyone.'

There was a wounded expression on his face. 'Do you really think I'm only interested in you because I want to get in your pants?'

'No, of course I don't!' I protested.

'This isn't a game to me, Layla. I wouldn't be risking my marriage to be with you if I didn't care about you.'

I realised how immature it'd been, telling my friends about the things we'd done together. And now he was looking like he regretted doing those things. 'I'm sorry, I shouldn't have told them. I just can't stop thinking about last night, and—'

He gave a low groan and lunged towards me, taking my face in his hands and kissing me. I closed my eyes and melted into him. I thought again about the scenes I'd pictured earlier and that same almost unbearable ache gripped me, made me want to touch him everywhere at once. I ran my hands over his shoulders, down his chest, up under his shirt, kissing him hard, deep, the way he had kissed me last night. His skin was hot, his stomach taut and hard. I moved my hand down, slipped my fingers down the front of his jeans, but he groaned again and sat back.

'We can't do this here, it's too risky.' He nodded towards the dark house. 'And I'm pretty sure your friends are watching us through the curtains.'

I tried to catch my breath, embarrassed by my impulsiveness. 'I should probably go in.'

'Yeah.' He ran both hands through his hair. 'And I'd better get back to my car. Hopefully I don't run into anyone on the way, considering the state you've left me in.' He pointed at his groin with a wry grin.

'Sorry.' I felt my face reddening and hoped it was too dark in the car for him to notice.

'This is what you do to me, Layla. God, as soon as you mentioned last night I felt like I was going to explode.'

'Sorry,' I said again. 'I'll make it up to you, I promise.'

He raised his eyebrows. 'Oh yeah? Got any plans tomorrow night?'

'Well no, but I'm working the morning shift tomorrow.'

'I've got another idea. Meet me up at The Knob at ten thirty.'

'I don't know if I can get out that late …' His face began to drop. 'OK. OK, I'll work something out. I'll see you there.'

'Great.'

We both got out of the car. 'Thanks for the lift.'

'No problem.' He raised a hand in farewell before walking away up the footpath. I lingered for a moment, watching him, then headed for Shona's front door.

NOW

Jodie didn't fade into the background like Layla had hoped. In fact, the calls started coming more frequently, and Layla worried that Cam would notice. She rejected each of the calls, and then the messages began again.

I'm not going to let you get away with this.

I want you to face up to what you did.

You don't deserve a nice, normal life after you ruined ours.

Meet me for coffee or I'll tell your husband what you did.

Layla deleted the Messenger app off her phone, and for a few days, there was nothing. Then one night, they were sitting in front of the TV eating dinner after the kids were in bed. Layla got up to put their plates on the bench, and when she returned to the couch, Cam was looking at his phone and frowning.

'What is it?' she said.

'I just got a friend request on Facebook from some random woman. Jodie Telford. It says on her profile that she's from Glasswater Bay – isn't that where you grew up?'

Layla's heart began to beat faster. 'Yeah.'

'Do you know her?' He tilted the screen towards her.

Layla pretended to study Jodie's profile picture for a minute, everything inside her jangling in fear. 'I've never seen her before. She must have moved there after I left.'

'Huh. Weird. Guess I'll just reject it, then?'

Layla smiled so the scream couldn't leap out. 'Unless you want to be friends with a random woman from a country town? She looks a bit old for you though, honey.'

Cam laughed then kissed her. 'I've got everything I need right here.'

When he withdrew, she pulled him back to her and kissed him again. She wanted to absorb him, exercise her claim over him, stamp a brand on him so no matter what Jodie did, she could never ruin what was between them.

When Layla had first started seeing Cam, she'd known straightaway that he was different from the other men she'd been involved with. He'd asked her questions about herself, and actually listened to her answers rather than just waiting impatiently for his turn to speak. He'd been interested in knowing who she was. But the sex had been a surprise. She would never have guessed that this quiet, kind, unassuming man would be so proficient, so thorough in bed. After they'd spent weeks getting to know one another – the longest Layla had ever been with anyone before sleeping with them – the chemistry between them had been off the charts. And though time, and the advent of children, meant that sex had become far less frequent, their enthusiasm for one another had rarely wavered. And now, with the danger that Jodie represented still fresh in Layla's mind, her anxiety channelled into desire, and she pulled him on top of her and kissed him harder.

Cam looked down at her, eyes shining. 'Well, I wasn't expecting *this*.'

'Are you complaining?'

'Not on your life!' His breath quickened as she pulled his shirt over his head and pushed her hips into his. 'Should we go to the bedroom?'

'No. I want you to go down on me.'

'Here?'

'Now. Please.'

He gave her a crooked smile. 'Yes, ma'am.'

He dropped to his knees before her and removed her jeans, and Layla leant against the back of the couch with a sigh. When he was touching her, tasting her, bringing her to the brink with the patient, methodical skill that he'd perfected over the years, Layla was able to forget that all the lights were on in the living room, exposing the dimpled flesh of her hips and thighs. And when, at last, her body shook beneath his hands, she didn't rush to cover up, but pulled him back to her, giving him everything she had.

*

Later, when they'd gone to bed and Cam's breathing had deepened into sleep, Layla reinstalled Messenger. There was a new message from Jodie.

I know where he works. Meet me or I'll find another way to contact him.

Layla's breath was ragged. All the wild sex in the world wasn't going to save her relationship if Cam found out about this from a stranger. She typed a response.

One meeting, then it's over. Then you leave me alone.

*

Cam's face registered first surprise, then confusion when Layla told him she was going to Glasswater Bay on Sunday.

'Why do you want to go back there? I thought you hated that place.'

'I did. But my old school friend Renee wants to catch up. Do you remember Renee? She came to our wedding?'

Cam squinted, as if trying to see into the past. 'Vaguely. Red hair?'

'That's the one.'

'I didn't even know you were still friends with her. She seemed kind of distant at the wedding.'

Layla's heart quailed a little at the memory. Although Renee lived in Glasswater with her husband and her twin sons, she'd come alone to the wedding. They'd barely spoken, and she'd left early without even saying goodbye.

'I'm not really. But she wanted to catch up for old time's sake.' Her skin crawled as she laid on the extra layer of lies. How many more layers would she have to add before this was over? The brief glimpse of Renee on New Year's Eve had given her the idea for the perfect excuse to visit her old town. Then she could go back to her normal life and leave the past in the past, where it belonged.

'Why don't we all go for the drive? Make a day of it.' Cam looked animated.

Layla forced herself to sound calm even as her body buzzed with panic. 'Nah, you'll be bored out of your brains. There's nothing to do there, and Renee and I will probably just end up walking around the town reminiscing about all the parties we got drunk at.'

'That doesn't matter,' Cam said. 'I'll take the kids to the beach or something while you and Renee catch up. It'll be nice to see where Mummy grew up, won't it, kids?'

Desperation rose in Layla's throat. 'Actually, I'd rather go by myself if that's OK? I'm feeling a bit burnt out and I'd like a bit of time alone.'

'Oh. OK, sure.' Cam looked concerned. 'What's got you so burnt out?'

She waved a hand in the air in a vague gesture. 'Oh, nothing really. I just need some time to myself. You don't mind, do you?'

'Of course not.' But there was a frown on his face as he turned away.

THEN

I agonised over what to wear to meet Scott at The Knob. He'd only ever really seen me in my school uniform or the black shirt I wore at the cafe. I wanted to be sexy for him, but there was nothing I felt sexy in. And anyway, I'd look ridiculous if I dressed up when we were probably just going to sit in the car in the dark and kiss. And I didn't want to send the wrong message ... although to be honest, I wasn't exactly sure what message I did want to send him. I'd told him last night that I'd make it up to him, for leaving him wanting like that, and I'd been keen at the time to take things further. But now, twenty-four hours later, not knowing what he was going to expect made me more anxious than ever.

My stomach churned as I tried on outfits only to discard them on my bed. Too slutty. Too girlish. Too modest. Too fancy. Too casual.

Finally, when it was 10.20, I threw on jeans and a T-shirt and grabbed my keys. He wanted to see me, not a different version of me. The only change I made was to brush out my long hair rather than tying it back in a ponytail or plaiting it like I usually did for school or work. *Please don't let him be disappointed*, I thought as I said goodbye to my parents. *Please don't let him think I didn't make an effort for him.*

'Tell Renee we said hello,' Mum said when I passed her and Dad on the way out.

'Feels like we never see her anymore,' I heard Dad say.

'She's a teenager, that's the way it works,' came Mum's voice as I closed the front door behind me.

It was a cold night and I shivered as I got into my car and started the engine. I was so nervous I could hardly change the gears as I headed out of town and up the hill to the lookout. Part of me hoped there would be other cars parked there too, something that would prevent our rendezvous from happening, but the small car park was empty. The long grass in the moonlit expanse leading up to The Knob ruffled in the wind. I turned off the engine and stared back at the road, shivering both with cold and anticipation.

My heart knocked painfully against my chest as a set of headlights wound their way up the road, and then Scott's car turned into the car park and came to a stop at the other end. I got out of my car, arms crossed over my chest against the cold wind, and walked towards his car. Scott reached over and opened the passenger door.

'Hi,' I said as I slid in.

He smiled. 'It's good to see you, Layla. I've been looking forward to this all day.'

My chin quivered as I smiled back at him. 'Me too.'

He reached out and touched my hair. 'You're not scared, are you? I'm not going to push you into anything you don't want to do.'

But you already did, a voice whispered in my head. 'I know,' my real voice said.

'I love your hair down like this.' He twisted a lock of it around his finger. My scalp tingled as he moved his hand further into my hair. 'Can you come closer?'

I leant towards him and he kissed me, his tongue light against mine. I tried to relax, but I was so nervous that my feet were dancing over the floor of the car like a manic marionette. Slowly, he moved further over the console, reaching across me and lifting the lever beside the seat. The seat slammed down and suddenly I was lying on my back. I let out a shocked laugh.

Scott smiled at me. 'Sorry about that.'

He clambered awkwardly over the console until he was suspended over me, his knees either side of mine. He gave a laugh. 'It's been a *long* time since I've done this.'

'I'm not …' I put a hand on his chest. 'I'm not ready to have sex.'

'I know.' He caressed my face. 'Tonight is for you, Layla. That's the surprise. Whatever you want me to do, I'll do it.'

I took in a ragged breath. 'Can we just kiss for a while?'

'Of course.' He smoothed my hair back from my face. 'I love kissing you.'

He was gentle, undemanding. His weight gradually settled on me, bit by bit, his erection hard against my leg. My breathing became heavier as his hands moved over my body. When I opened my eyes for a second, I saw the car windows had fogged up from our breath, obscuring the outside world. His mouth moved down to my neck, biting lightly. It stung a little, but it felt good too, and my hips involuntarily rose to meet his. He moaned.

'I want to make you come so hard,' he murmured in my ear. 'Tell me. Tell me what you want me to do.'

'I … I don't know,' I stammered. 'I don't know what to do.'

He raised his head. His eyes were heavy-lidded, as if he'd just woken up. 'Do you trust me, Layla?'

I nodded.

He lifted up my T-shirt and I raised my head so he could slip it off, then he dropped his head to kiss my breasts. He reached behind me and unhooked my bra, and I let him pull it down over my arms. He tossed it on the driver's seat and sat back to look at me. His gaze made me feel exposed and vulnerable, and I had to resist the urge to cover myself. 'You have a beautiful body, Layla,' he said.

'Sorry they're not very big.' The words squeaked out of me before I could prevent them.

'It's only stupid schoolboys who are into big tits. You should see what Jodie's look like now, all saggy and stretched.' He shuddered. 'This is what I'm into.' He traced his finger down my chest and around one of my nipples. 'You're perfect.'

I didn't like being compared to his wife, but I couldn't focus on that now because he was taking my nipple between his thumb and forefinger and rolling it gently, and a small sound escaped my lips. He started kissing me again, moving his hand slowly down my stomach. Anticipation joined with apprehension, building inside me as he unbuttoned my jeans and pulled down the zip. I tried to sit up, and he stopped.

'It's OK, Layla. I just want to touch you, OK? Just touching, that's all.'

I nodded again and lay back, raising my hips so he could pull down my jeans. To my relief, he left my underwear in place. For a moment he just looked at me, his eyes running up and down my body as if he didn't know where to look next. Then he began to move his finger in a light circle on my stomach. He watched my face as he moved lower, over the top of my underwear, rubbing lightly and moving down. At first it almost tickled, but he gradually increased the pressure until it started to feel good, and then it started to feel bloody amazing. I was breathing hard now as a warm, fuzzy sensation began to radiate outwards from his fingers. Then he yanked down my underwear and there was no longer anything separating us. I arched against his hand and he slipped a finger inside me and I cried out and he was watching me with a look of wonder, like he'd never seen anything like it.

Then he was lying on top of me again and he was kissing me, and I hadn't even noticed that his pants were down until his erection was butting between my legs. Fear, strong and sharp.

I pushed against his chest. 'Scott, stop. Please, can you stop?'

He thrust against me one more time, then withdrew, gasping. 'See what you do to me, Layla? This is how much I want you.'

Despite what he'd said earlier, I could tell he was disappointed. My obvious pleasure must have made him think I wanted to go the whole way, and once again I'd failed to live up to his expectations. 'I'm sorry.'

He was still panting. 'I need to come.' He took my hand in his and guided it down, then kneaded my breasts as he thrust himself into my hand. He was rough, and it kind of hurt, but maybe if I got it over with quickly he'd be soft and affectionate again, he'd look at me like he worshipped me again. My wrist was burning with the effort when he let out a long groan and came on my stomach.

And finally, the intensity was gone and his face went slack. He opened up the console and took out a couple of tissues, then wiped my stomach. 'Was that good?'

I didn't say anything. I had no answer for what had just happened. I'd enjoyed it when he was touching me, but the way it had ended had left me shaken and turned off. But maybe that's just the way it always was. Maybe I was naive.

'You had an orgasm, so you must have enjoyed it.' He shoved the soggy tissues on the floor then began trailing his fingers languidly over my skin.

Had I had an orgasm? Surely I would've known if I had, but I was also deeply inexperienced. He would probably know better than I did what that feeling had been.

'It was incredible seeing you like that, Layla. I loved doing that for you. Did you like it?'

I wished he'd stop talking. I wished he'd stop touching me. I wanted to go home, but it seemed like this debrief was a mandatory part of the process.

'It was nice,' I offered.

He squeezed down beside me, his arm across me. 'This isn't the most romantic place. We should get a hotel room one night, out of town. Then we'll have plenty of room to stretch out and plenty of time to try other things.'

My limbs were heavy, my mind thick with uncertainty. 'Scott.'

He didn't answer.

'Scott. I don't think I want to have sex. Not for a long time anyway.'

He raised his head to look at me. 'Who said anything about sex? We're just having a bit of fun, that's all. We're not doing any harm.'

'But you ...' I hesitated. If I said it out loud, that he'd tried to push himself on me after I'd told him I wasn't ready, it would sound like an accusation, and there would be no going back after that. He might be angry at me. He might not want to see me anymore.

'But I what?'

'Nothing. This probably sounds lame to you, but when I have sex, I want it to be with someone who cares about me. I want there to be ... love.'

He raised himself on one elbow. 'You think I don't care about you?'

'It's not that, but ...' I floundered, unable to articulate what I was feeling. 'It doesn't feel right. Not when you're married.'

Scott sighed. 'I know it's not ideal. But I don't love my wife anymore. I haven't loved her for a long time.'

'But you did once. Didn't you? You might think I'm just a schoolkid, but surely she doesn't deserve this?'

'I don't think you're just a schoolkid, Layla.' Scott touched my face. 'And I don't *want* to hurt Jodie. But the problem is, I think I'm falling in love with someone else.'

I stared at him blankly for a second, before the full realisation of what he was telling me swept me up and carried me away on a tide of euphoria. The uncomfortable end to our encounter paled in comparison with the significance of this moment.

He loved me. He *loved* me. He loved *me*.

This changed everything.

NOW

Layla woke to Cam shaking her shoulder.

'Layla. Wake up.'

She rolled over and opened her eyes. Their bedroom was still dark. 'What's going on? What time is it?'

'Three thirty. Ella's sick. I don't know what's wrong with her.'

Layla blinked a few times and realised Cam was holding Ella in his arms. She sat straight up and switched on the lamp on her bedside table. Her daughter was limp in her husband's arms, her blonde head resting against his shoulder. She was breathing heavily, each of her breaths punctuated with a grunt on the exhale. 'Lay her down on the bed,' Layla said, getting to her feet to make room.

Cam did as she requested. Ella's head lolled to the side, a damp curl falling over her face. She'd had a cold for the last few days and had seemed to be recovering, but now her forehead was burning hot. She coughed and it came out as a harsh bark, a sound incongruent to such a small being.

'Oh Christ, what's wrong with her?' Cam's voice shook with fear. 'Should I call the health line?'

'It's croup.' Layla lifted up Ella's nightie and watched her breathe. Her stomach retracted sharply under her ribs whenever she breathed in. 'She's got intercostal recession.'

'What's that?'

'It means her airways are blocked. She needs to go to the hospital.'

Layla hurriedly dressed in the clothes she'd worn yesterday. Cam looked helpless as he watched her throw a spare change of clothes in her bag and go into the bathroom to get her toothbrush. 'What can I do?'

'I'll take her. You stay here with Louis. I'll let you know what happens.'

'But ... but you were going to see Renee today.'

She paused to look at him. 'This is serious, Cam.'

He looked really scared now. 'Is she ... is she going to be OK?'

Layla forced herself to breathe, to be strong for him and for Ella, even though her own fear had wrapped its fingers around her throat and was squeezing tight. 'She'll be OK, but I need to get her to hospital now.'

*

Despite the hour, a long line snaked its way out from the window where the triage nurse stood. Layla swore under her breath. Ella was a dead weight in her arms. Occasionally, a barking cough would erupt from her, causing other parents to cast startled looks her way, but otherwise she lay silent against Layla's chest.

Layla felt calmer now that she was here, but the panic still lurked beneath the surface. She knew that once she'd explained Ella's symptoms to the triage nurse, they'd be whisked straight through the double doors and into emergency. The other children who sat around the room, with their broken arms and split lips, could be waiting here for hours before they were seen, but respiratory trouble was high risk. Still, she knew she had to wait calmly in this line to be assessed, even though everything inside her was screaming to push past them all and demand to be seen immediately.

Finally, they reached the front of the line. She knew doctors and nurses liked dealing with people like her, who had strong medical knowledge, who knew how to navigate the system. She saw the relief that crossed their carefully composed features, the recognition that lit up their eyes: *You're one of us.* They were ushered through the doors and shown to a bed, where a different nurse examined Ella and attached an oxygen monitor to one of her fingers. Layla answered all the same questions again and offered extra information about Ella's symptoms and medical history.

'Are you a doctor?' the nurse asked.

'Pharmacist.' Layla couldn't help a little current of pride at being able to give this answer. While her job sometimes seemed dull and repetitive, she'd always been proud to be part of this industry, proud that when something went wrong, she was ruled by knowledge rather than emotion.

Nevertheless, her heart tugged as Ella woke up and started to cry. She hugged her daughter tightly to her body as the doctor arrived and she answered the same questions for the third time.

'I think Ella has a viral-induced wheeze,' the doctor said. 'Her oxygen sats are quite low, so what we'll do is give her some prednisolone to open her airways, then we'll give her three doses of Ventolin over the next hour. If she doesn't respond as well as she should, we'll have to admit you and monitor her overnight and tomorrow.'

Layla held Ella still as the nurse squirted the steroid medication into her mouth with a plastic syringe. Her daughter screwed up her face and writhed in Layla's arms, wailing. She cowered as the nurse approached with the Ventolin puffer and the clear plastic spacer, and Layla had to pin Ella's arms to her sides and hold her with more force than she'd ever used against her as the nurse pressed the mask over her mouth and administered six puffs of Ventolin.

Ella's eyes gazed up into Layla's, pleading with her to make it stop. Her terrified expression hacked through Layla's composure and she choked back a sob. It was times like this, seeing her daughter's fear and need, that her love for her children seemed too big, too sharp, too fragile; the very idea of losing them too much to bear. It was like a wound that never quite healed.

'Good girl,' the nurse said when she was finished. Layla wasn't sure whether she was referring to Ella or to her. She gave Layla a little pat on the arm. 'Try to get some rest. I'll be back in twenty minutes for her next dose.'

Ella turned to Layla and put her arms around her neck. Her breathing was no longer laboured and wheezy. Layla spoke softly to her, and after a while her little body grew heavy as she fell back to sleep.

With her free hand, Layla got her phone out of her pocket and sent a text to Cam to let him know what was happening. He replied immediately; she could almost taste the relief in his words. Now that the danger was out of the way, she allowed her own relief to wash over her. Ella was going to be fine. Bringing her to hospital had been the right decision.

But underneath her concern for Ella lay a river of worry about what Jodie would do now that Layla wouldn't be able to go to Glasswater Bay after all.

*

By morning, Ella had brightened considerably. She ate the breakfast that was brought for her and chattered away to Layla, the nurses and the doctor when she came to check on her. After the long night, Layla was suddenly conscious that this was the first time in years she'd been out of the house without make-up. The glances from the hospital staff were a thousand tiny ants swarming over her naked face. She busied herself with fussing over Ella and avoided looking at her reflection in the bathroom mirror.

Cam dropped Louis at his mother's house and came in to see them, armed with all Ella's favourite picture books. He hugged their daughter so tightly that she gave a little squeal. 'Sorry, sweetie,' he said, his eyes damp. 'I'm so glad you're OK.'

'Silly Daddy,' Ella said.

Cam reached out to rub Layla's arm. 'How are you?'

She gave him a smile. 'Pretty tired. I didn't get much sleep. But she's OK; that's all that matters.'

'Sorry you didn't get to see your friend today,' he said.

Layla shrugged. 'It doesn't matter. It's kind of a relief, to be honest.'

'Still, you should try to reschedule the visit. She seemed so keen to catch up with you.'

That reminded Layla that she still hadn't messaged Jodie to tell her she wouldn't be coming, but now the doctor came into the room on her morning round. Layla and Cam watched as she listened to Ella's chest and tickled her to make her laugh.

'She's doing really well,' the doctor said. 'We'll have to keep her here until she can go three hours between doses of Ventolin, but I anticipate we'll be able to discharge her this afternoon.'

Once the doctor had left the room, Cam pulled Ella into his lap to read her a book. 'I can take over here if you still want to go to Glasswater Bay today?' he suggested to Layla. 'I'm sure Mum would be happy to have Louis for the rest of the day, and I can pick him up when we get out of here.'

Layla watched as Ella opened the book and started to flick through it, murmuring to herself. 'I don't want to leave while she's still unwell.'

'Go home and get some sleep, then,' he urged. 'You look exhausted.'

'I look washed out and revolting, you mean,' Layla said.

'No, I don't mean that at all.'

'Sorry,' Layla said. 'You're right. I'll go home and have a shower, then I'll pick up Louis.'

He took her hand. 'Thanks for taking over like that last night. I would've been a mess.'

They shared a smile. Layla gave Ella a hug, then said goodbye to them and left, grateful to escape the clinical smell of the hospital now that she knew Ella would be OK. When she reached the car, she pulled out her phone and sent a message to Jodie explaining what had happened. The reply came back before she'd even started the engine.

I don't want your excuses. You make sure you're here, or I'm telling your husband.

Rage burned in Layla's throat.

You want to drag up my past to a man who's worried to death because his daughter's in hospital, you go for it. I'm done, she replied, then pulled out onto the road without waiting for a reply.

By the time she got home, Jodie had messaged her back.

I'm still living your past while you're playing happy families. I'll let it go for now, but I'm not dropping this.

THEN

I floated through the next few days. I didn't study. I barely ate.

Scott loved me.

So that's what this weird, volatile swing of emotions had been about over the last two weeks. That's what love was. It was big, and scary, and confusing, and it hurt. All the movies told me so. But it was exhilarating too.

He loved me.

I ignored the warning voice in the back of my head, the whisper of Scott's words back at the start of all this: *Love is a lie.*

When I returned to work on Tuesday after school, he didn't bring up his feelings again. In fact, we didn't really speak at all. But as soon as he closed the cafe, he led me out to the kitchen and started kissing me and unbuttoning my shirt straightaway.

The same thing happened on Wednesday night, and Thursday. He didn't try anything more than what we'd already done, and my lingering anxiety competed with my desire to make him happy, to be worthy of his love.

'You've been working a lot lately,' Mum commented when I got home one night, my face still flushed.

'It's been busy at the cafe,' I said.

'Well, I hope it's not interfering with your study. Your future is more important than an after-school job.'

I muttered a vague reassurance on my way to my bedroom.

At school, Shona constantly pumped me for information about Scott, and while I'd promised not to talk to my friends about him anymore, I couldn't help telling her everything. Renee always seemed to find some excuse to walk away whenever the topic came up, but Shona thought it was all terribly exciting, and it was comforting to paper over my own doubts with her enthusiasm.

I was on for the first shift at the cafe on Saturday morning, so I got there an hour early. Things went further with Scott than ever before, and I pretended to like it more than I did so he'd know how much I cared about him. When he started pushing my head downwards, I'd never been so relieved to be interrupted by Dave's key in the cafe door so I could rush out to the front counter, pulling my dishevelled hair back into a ponytail.

All morning, Scott found excuses to get close to me, to dance his fingers across my buttocks when we were behind the coffee machine, to brush his arm against my breast as he passed me. 'Meet me up at The Knob again tonight,' he whispered in my ear when I was unstacking the dishwasher. 'We can finish what we started this morning.'

Nervous energy skittered in my belly. I kept my head in the dishwasher as I answered. 'I'm not sure if I can. My parents are getting weird about how much I'm going out lately—'

'Oh, hi, honey.'

I looked up, startled, to find Scott was already on the other side of the counter, scooping up a little boy into his arms. I watched, dread rising in my belly, as he hugged his son to his body, as he bent down to cup his daughter's face in his hand, as he kissed his beautiful wife on the cheek. This morning I'd let this man do things to my body that no one else had, but this … I'd compartmentalised this aspect of his life in my brain, kept it separate from the things we did together. While he had been becoming my everything, I hadn't let myself consider the possibility that *they* were his everything and I was just the distraction.

Jodie stepped up to the counter and flashed her radiant smile at me. 'Hi, Layla. How's school?'

'Good, thanks,' I managed to force past the lump in my throat. 'What can I get you?'

Her brilliant blue eyes ran up and down the menu. 'I don't know why I bother looking; my husband hasn't changed this menu in two years. I'll have the focaccia with chicken and avocado, and two serves of the nuggets for the kids.' She gave me a conspiratorial smile. 'You know, before I had kids I swore I'd never order chicken nuggets. It's amazing how quickly you sacrifice your principles when they eat nothing but white bread and pasta for two years straight.'

My smile stretched tight across my face.

'You eating with us, hon?' she threw at Scott.

'Sure, babe. I'll have the ragu, thanks, Layla.' He didn't even look at me.

'And two flat whites, thanks.'

I numbly wrote down her order and took it out to Dave in the kitchen.

Scott and Jodie sat at a table near the window. The children were noisy but well behaved. Scott doted on them. He had genial conversation with his wife. He didn't look

127

at me once. I couldn't stop staring at them. They were the perfect picture of a happy family; I'd never been more aware of my own youth and immaturity.

Yumi came in for her shift and followed my gaze to the family at the table. 'Checking out my competition?'

I snorted. 'In your dreams.'

'They *are* pretty good dreams.' She nudged me. 'What's with you? Bad morning?'

I thought about Scott's lips on my collarbone. I thought about his fingers unhooking my bra. I thought about his hand on the top of my head, pressing down. Maybe if I wasn't always holding back, maybe if I gave him what he needed like a normal person, maybe he'd want to sit at a table like that with me, in the open.

'They're such a good-looking couple,' Yumi said. 'And those kids! They almost make my ovaries explode. She's so gorgeous, isn't she?'

I followed her gaze to Jodie, who was laughing at something Claire had said, her head tipped back, her teeth shining white. Everything about her demeanour said, *this is all mine.*

'Sure, if you like looking frumpy and old.' I turned away, ignoring Yumi's surprised glance. Compared to Jodie, I was a stupid kid who didn't know how to satisfy a man. I could never compete with her.

*

When the family had finished eating, they all got up from their table. Scott knelt in front of the kids and hugged them both. When he straightened, he put an arm around

Jodie's waist and they kissed briefly. Acid stirred in my stomach.

'Bye, handsome,' Jodie said. 'Let's go, kids.'

Scott came back over to the counter. I couldn't look at him. 'Going for my break,' I mumbled, taking off my apron and hanging it on the hook.

The autumn wind bit into me as I stepped out of the cafe onto the main street, but it was a welcome relief from the hot shame that had swathed me as I'd watched Scott kiss his wife. That hadn't looked like a dead relationship. She hadn't looked like the kind of woman who wouldn't let him touch her.

I pushed aside the heavy plastic straps in the doorway of Keen's Deli. I'd been coming here since I was a little kid, and it had barely changed over the years. Despite the chill outside, the place always smelled inexplicably of summer. Or maybe the smell was a byproduct of the memory of leaning over the edge of the ice-cream freezer to reach the last Bubble O'Bill, sand from the beach still between the toes of my bare feet suspended above the grimy black-and-white-chequered lino floor. I was gripped by a sudden longing for those simpler days, before I'd become self-conscious about the way I looked, before I'd started hating this town, before I'd got involved with a man I couldn't have.

'What can I get you, Layla?' Bob Keen gave me his characteristic grandpa smile, leaning his elbows on the counter. His comb-over had grown thinner and greyer over the years, but his kindly eyes hadn't changed since he'd slipped in free cobbers with my mixed lollies when I was six.

'Pastie with sauce, thanks, Bob.'

'You OK, love?' He eyed me over the counter as he plunged the spout of the sauce bottle into my pastie and squeezed until the sauce bloomed out of the hole.

I forced a smile. 'Just tired.'

'You teenagers need to get to bed earlier, then you won't be so tired.' He wagged a finger at me before sliding the pastie into a brown paper bag and handing it to me. I paid him and was about to walk out when he said, 'Wait a minute, love. Here you go.' He held out his hand, in which there was a single cobber.

'Thanks, Bob.' I took it from him, fighting the urge to cry.

'You have a nice day, all right?'

I popped the cobber into my mouth as I left the deli, and the chocolate on the outside began to melt away, exposing the hard, chewy caramel underneath. There was a small park just before the Esplanade, with a single picnic table in the middle of the square of grass. No one else was there. Bitter wind whipped in from the beach and stung my face as I sat down at the table.

I'd just chewed the last of the caramel and started on my pastie when there was a voice by my left shoulder. 'Mind if I join you?'

'You've already had lunch, haven't you?' I couldn't keep the bitterness from my tone.

He sat down opposite me. 'Sorry about that. I didn't know they were coming in.'

'Really? You didn't discuss it together before you got out of bed this morning?' I hated the petulance in my voice, but it had taken over and I couldn't control it.

'Layla,' he said evenly.

'I know, *grow up, Layla, you're being childish, Layla,*' I parroted.

'I'm sorry; I know it was weird. Let me make it up to you tonight.'

I put down my pastie on the table. 'I don't think I can do this anymore. It's not right.'

He smirked. 'Didn't see you complaining when I had two fingers inside you this morning.'

'Is this a joke to you?' I stared at him, astounded at and hurt by his flippancy. 'This is wrong, Scott. We're doing the wrong thing.'

'I know.' His voice was gentler now. 'But I can't help how I feel about you, Layla. I lie awake every night thinking about you.'

I wanted to believe him, wanted everything to be different. His gaze was steady, his blue eyes soft. He looked stripped back, as if he'd revealed his true self to me and was waiting to see whether I'd accept or discard him. He reached across the table and closed his hand over mine.

'But it's OK if you don't feel the same way.' He gave my hand a gentle squeeze, then stood up. 'I'll leave you to finish your lunch.'

He turned and walked away. I watched him go, the ache in my chest getting bigger and bigger until I was sure it would swallow me whole.

NOW

There were no new messages from Jodie, and Layla convinced herself that she'd changed her mind and let her off the hook. Ella's health scare combined with the spectre of seeing Jodie again had made Layla more appreciative of how fortunate she really was. She hugged her children more often, kissed her husband more, and started thinking about planning a family holiday for later in the year.

Then one evening, when she was cooking dinner for the kids, she opened Facebook to discover that Renee had tagged her in a post.

Curious, she followed the notification. A moment later, the wooden spoon she was holding clattered to the floor as a photo filled her screen. It was from the hotel restaurant where they'd had dinner before the school formal. Six or seven of her classmates sat on one side of a long table, but she only had eyes for Renee, Shona and herself. Their heads were close, arms around each other, eyes bright with the excitement of the evening. Tears spilled onto Layla's cheeks. After the way that night had ended, she had never got any of the photos, so this was the first one she'd seen in twenty years.

They were beautiful. Even her. And so, so young. Too young to be playing grown-up games with someone else's husband.

She zoomed in on the photo so the three of them filled the screen. It was a photo of a photo so the quality wasn't great, the glossiness enhanced by the light that had fallen onto it while whoever it was had taken this picture. She studied their vivid smiles, their bright lipstick, could almost feel the softness of Renee's hair trailing over her arm as she rested her head on Layla's shoulder.

'Mummy, why are you crying?' Louis tugged at her hand, his big blue eyes searching her face.

Layla swiped the tears away from her cheeks. 'Oh, I'm not really crying, sweet. Just remembering some old friends. Want to see a photo of me when I was young?'

Louis nodded vigorously, and Layla crouched beside him and held out the phone. He studied it in silence. 'Your hair looks cool.'

Layla laughed and kissed the top of his head.

He wrinkled his nose. 'What's that funny smell?'

'Oh crap!' She leapt up and inspected the chicken strips she'd been frying. They were blackened on one side and the burnt smell was already filling the room. She switched off the gas and regarded the ruins of the meal. Now she'd have to make something else, and it was already six thirty.

'Crap!' Louis cried with glee.

'CRAP!' Ella bellowed from the couch.

Once she'd cleaned up the mess and got a pot of water on to make pasta, Layla went back to look at the photo again. At first, she'd assumed Renee herself had posted it, but now she saw that the post was from someone else: a classmate who had probably married, changed her last name and become a stranger to Layla.

Was going through some old photos today and found this one from the formal dinner. Good times!

She scrolled down to look at the comments. They were mostly tags of the other people in the photo, including Renee and Shona, along with a few exclamations of wonder and commentary on how old fashioned their dresses looked now. Then there was another comment from the original poster:

Anyone still know Layla Flynn? I'm not friends with her on FB so can't tag her.

By some miracle, no one had commented on the disgrace she'd made of herself later that night, but down near the bottom, Renee had tagged her: *Layla Flynn.* Just the two words of her name, no direct engagement. Not that she could blame her, considering how Layla's actions had destroyed their friendship that night. As she liked the comment with a trembling finger, she noticed another comment from Shona:

OMG, we were BABIES!!

Layla clutched the phone. Shona had been in London for fifteen years: it was unlikely she'd come back to Australia now. But Renee was still here, and somehow it felt like she'd been handed another chance to revive their friendship. She opened Messenger and started typing out a message to Renee before she had a chance to change her mind.

Hi, Renee. Thanks for tagging me in that photo — it brought back a lot of memories ... some bad ones, but some pretty good ones too. I've been thinking about you a bit lately — I think maybe I saw you at the Magic Dirt gig on New Year's Eve? Anyway, I was wondering if you'd be interested in catching up sometime ... Maybe we could have lunch the next time you're in Adelaide?

I know it's been a long time, but it'd be great to see you again. Love, Layla xx

She paused for a moment, then went back and changed 'love' to 'cheers'. Then, right before she sent it, she changed it back again.

Renee saw the message a few minutes later, and Layla waited, feverish, holding her phone in one hand while she dropped pasta into the boiling water with the other.

But there was still no reply when she served up the steaming pasta to the kids. There was still nothing when Cam got home, when Louis and Ella were splashing around in the bath, when Cam was reading to them in bed, when she had finished stacking the dishwasher and turned it on.

And when she went to bed later that night, Renee still hadn't replied.

THEN

I only got two shifts the following week, and both times Scott sent me home early. He barely made eye contact with me. We were never alone together.

I missed him. School days were dull without the anticipation of seeing him after the bell rang, and when I did see him, he always seemed to be on the opposite side of the cafe. I wondered if I'd made a huge mistake by ending things.

Renee and Shona were pleased that I'd broken it off. They begged me to let them set me up with one of the boys at school. But when Rasheed, after a month of silence, finally approached me to ask me out, the comparison between my first fumbling encounter with him and Scott's assured, experienced hands was too great.

'If I can't be with Scott, I don't want to be with anyone,' I said to Renee.

'We just want you to be happy because we love you,' Renee said.

'Well, you guys are single,' I said glumly. 'Let's be single and miserable together.'

And so I let Rasheed down gently and went off to work on Friday after school. I was on until close and had hoped to snatch some time alone with Scott, but he said he'd finish up and sent Yumi and me home at the same time.

Yumi glanced at me when we reached the footpath outside. 'You OK, Layla? You seem a bit down lately.'

'I'm fine.' I tried to look reassuring. 'Just stressed about school. You know how it is.'

'If it's any consolation, uni is way easier. Hang in there, girlfriend. It doesn't last forever.'

She got into her car and tooted her horn as she drove away, and I continued up the footpath to my car. It was parked away from the streetlights and as I got closer, I noticed a shadowy figure leaning against it. My heart contracted as I recognised him. He was alone; there was no sign of his dickhead mates who usually flanked him. And he'd already seen me, so it was too late to turn around. His mouth spread wide in a grin.

'Laaaylaaa,' he sang softly as I approached.

'Piss off, Matty,' I said.

'Well, that's not very friendly, is it?'

I clenched my teeth. 'I'm not in the mood. Get off my car. I've had a shitty week and I want to go home.'

He pushed off from my car and stepped towards me. 'I think I know a way to take your mind off your shitty week, darlin'.'

Panic leapt in my throat. I turned to run, but he'd already reached me. He grabbed my arm and yanked me back, wrapping his arm around my middle like a vice. The other hand fondled my breast roughly. A deep, primal fear gripped me and I drove my elbow back into his ribs. The air escaped his lungs with a sour puff of stale beer. His arm loosened for a fraction of a second, but it was enough for me to twist around and bring my knee up into his groin.

'You fucken little *bitch*!' he yelled, but I'd already broken away from him and was sprinting back towards the cafe.

It was dark inside and the front door was locked. I fumbled in my bag for my key, but my hands were shaking too much, so I gave up and banged on the glass with both fists. If I was too late, if Scott had already left …

Then his head was silhouetted against the light from the kitchen, and he rushed over and unlocked the door. I flew in with a sob.

'Layla, what happened?' There was a furrow between his eyes as he gazed over my head onto the street.

'Matty! He was waiting at my car!' I got out between gasps.

Scott stepped past me and ran up the footpath a short way, then turned and went the other way. I waited behind the door, still trembling.

'No sign of him,' he said when he came back. 'He must've taken off. Did he hurt you?'

I shook my head. 'He groped me, but I kneed him in the nuts.'

Scott chuckled. 'You little ripper!'

I tried to laugh, but a sob came out instead. Scott pulled me into his arms, drawing my head against his chest, and I wrapped my arms around his middle. He held me so tightly I could hardly breathe, but I clung to him until my shaking had subsided. It was only when he released me that I realised we were still standing in the front of the cafe for passers-by to see, if they looked closely enough. Without a word, I followed him into the kitchen.

'Do you want me to take you to the police station?' Scott asked.

I shook my head. 'No, I think I should just go home.'

The frown was still there between his eyes. 'We can't let that fucker get away with this.'

'There were no witnesses. He'll say I'm making it up.'

'I'll tell them I saw it from the cafe and he ran off when I came out to help you.'

'Matty's brother's a cop. They'll protect him.'

Scott's jaw worked. 'I hate to say it, but you're probably right.'

The depth of my helplessness weighed on me, and I collapsed into a chair. 'I hate this town.'

Scott knelt on the floor in front of me and pushed the hair back from my face. 'It's not all bad, is it?'

I moved my hand up to his and clasped it. 'Not all of it.'

We stared at each other for a long moment. 'I've missed you,' he said.

'Me too.'

Scott gave my hand a squeeze. 'I love you, Layla. I've tried to fight it, but it just keeps getting stronger.'

Elation blossomed inside me, but I pushed it down under the misery of our hopeless situation. 'What are we going to do?'

Scott put a hand on my cheek. 'I want to be with you, but the time's not right for us yet. I'll understand if this is too much for you to deal with … if you want to stop.'

'I don't want to stop.' I rested my forehead against his. 'I never want to stop.'

NOW

Louis wriggled away from Layla as she tried to wrestle him into a pair of shorts. Giggling, he started running away, the shorts still tangled around his ankles, and in a shock twist that Layla could never have seen coming, he tripped over and fell face first onto the floor. He looked up at her for a second of horrified silence, then gave a long, high-pitched cry. Layla gathered him into her arms.

'I need a bandaid!' he wailed, pointing to his arm.

Layla made a show of checking him over. 'No blood. I don't think we're going to have to amputate.'

Louis pushed her hands away, his face already contorting, signalling the start of a lengthy tantrum. '*I NEED A BANDAID!*'

'You don't need a bandaid, Louis; it won't do anything.' Sometimes Layla wondered why she didn't just give him the bandaid, but she had a stubborn streak and she was buggered if she was going to let a four-year-old get the better of her.

Louis roared at her, his words almost unintelligible now, and Layla released him and stepped away. She'd learnt long ago that when he was like this, it was too late to bring him back with cuddles and calm reasoning. They just had to ride it out until the meltdown was over.

'Silly Louis,' Ella said helpfully.

'*No!*' Louis screamed, whirling around and shoving his sister. Ella fell onto her bottom and started crying too. She clambered to her feet, ran over to Layla and threw herself into her arms. Layla hugged her tight.

Louis had been such a lovely toddler, always wanting to be close to her, even when she was desperate for space. But as soon as he'd turned three, he'd transformed into this emotional, angry child who had tantrums at the drop of a hat. She'd assumed he'd grow out of it quickly, but he was four and a half now and there were no signs of the behaviour going away. In the endless cycle of positivity and gloom, Layla frequently wondered whether he had ADHD, or ASD, or one of the other alphabet combinations, but then he'd be funny and cute and sweet and she'd decide she was overreacting, trying to diagnose her perfectly normal child as an excuse for her own poor parenting. Maybe his behaviour was a reaction to her own anxiety – or worse – maybe he'd inherited the emotional weakness that hid inside her.

She glanced at the clock on the wall. She'd been trying to get them ready to leave the house for an hour, and somehow hadn't made any progress. At times like these, she longed for professional, efficient Layla, the one who only seemed to be present at work these days. That Layla would have had them dressed and out of the door with military precision, but this version of her was powerless against the might of her tiny tyrant children.

She was dressing Ella, Louis still wailing in the background, when she heard the distinctive *ping* of Messenger. Anxiety clamped her belly. She hadn't heard from Jodie again, but the dread continued to lurk beneath the surface.

But when she dared to look at her phone, she felt a little glimmer of excitement at the sight of Renee's name. After she'd sent that message a few days ago, she'd assumed her old friend had no interest in contacting her. She'd been disappointed, but she'd understood. There were some wrongs that could never be righted. She opened the new message.

Hey, Layla, sorry I didn't get back to you the other day, have been flat out. Yeah, we thought we saw you at Magic Dirt, but then you disappeared. How good was that gig? I think I'm still a little bit in love with Adalita. I'd like to see you again. I know you'd probably rather gouge out your own eyes than come back here, but our twenty-year school reunion is in a couple of weeks. I've attached the invite here. Shona's back from London for a few weeks and she's coming too. You could stay with me if you wanted? Cheers, Renee.

Layla opened the image in the message. The invitation had a black background with fireworks and streamers. *Y2K didn't finish the world, but we finished school!!* proclaimed the invitation in pink-and-yellow Comic Sans. *Let's get together again to reminiss about the old times and catch up on what we've all been up too since we graduated!*

'Can't even bloody spell,' Layla muttered.

But her breathing had become tight, strained. She'd been so careful to shut out the memories of the way school had ended, but now her old town seemed to be stalking her, all the negative experiences converging on her at once, cornering her. She couldn't go back. Especially not now.

Louis's screaming had subsided to a high-pitched keening. Layla could withstand the screaming and the roaring, but this persistent whine was a crowbar edging into her brain, levering it open and spilling out all her accomplishments, leaving only the raw edges of her imperfect motherhood. Her sanity stretched taut.

'Louis, will you cut it out!' she yelled.

Her son looked up at her in shocked silence, then his face crumpled and he started wailing again.

'For fuck's *sake*!' Layla said under her breath.

'Fuck*sake*!' said Ella immediately.

Layla led Louis over to the couch and sat down, pulling him into her lap and holding him until his sobs became hitching breaths. Once again, she'd fucked up, made things worse instead of comforting him like a real mother – a good mother – would. Why was she so bad at this? Why did everyone else seem to be able to bring up their kids without losing themselves, without this constant self-doubt? And it only seemed to be getting worse lately. Her children didn't deserve to pay for her mistakes. She hugged her son tighter and murmured into his hair.

*

Later, when the kids were sitting on the floor, clicking Lego together with only the occasional mild squabble, Layla opened the invitation to the school reunion again. It was still ridiculous. But suddenly, she longed for the days when having a family was only theoretical, before she and Cam had created this life that was simultaneously more and less than she'd hoped for; she yearned for the fierce, joyful, complicated friendships of her adolescence.

It would be intolerable. It would be embarrassing, and cringeworthy, and it would bring up all sorts of memories.

But it would give her a chance to make amends with Renee, to laugh with Shona again, to maybe, just maybe, revive their friendship.

I'll think about it, she typed back to Renee.

*

When Cam got home, Layla was cooking dinner, a glass of wine in one hand. Louis and Ella sat on the floor under the dining table, eating from a bag of corn chips and playing a game only the two of them understood. They both jumped up and ran over to Cam, yelling, 'Daddy! Daddy!'

Louis screeched an unintelligible song, jumping from side to side like a deranged monkey. Ella hugged her father's leg, gazed up at him and proclaimed, 'Fuck*SAKE*!'

Cam raised his eyebrows at Layla as he struggled not to laugh. 'That kind of day?'

Layla gestured at her wineglass. 'They broke me.'

Now he laughed, his eyes crinkling at the corners. 'Do you want to go out for a while and I'll feed them and get them ready for bed?'

'Nah, I'm too knackered to go anywhere now. Drink?'

'Thanks.'

She poured him a glass of wine. 'So, you're not going to believe this, but I'm actually thinking of going to my twenty-year high school reunion.'

'What?' Cam laughed.

'Renee messaged me about it today and it made me kind of nostalgic for my high school days. God knows why; I spent the whole time I was there dreaming about getting out.'

'Twenty years.' Cam shook his head with mock wonder.

'You're getting on a bit. I might have to trade you in for a younger model.'

'Look how funny you think you are.' But underneath Layla's laugh, the ever-present fear raised its head. She was only two years older than Cam, but surely it was only a matter of time before he worked out that he could do so much better.

Cam came around to her side of the bench and put his arms around her. 'I guess I'm not quite up to a midlife crisis yet. Maybe in a few years I'll find myself a hot, nubile young thing in the prime of her youth.'

Layla broke away from him abruptly. 'No girl is in her prime when she's seventeen!' she snapped.

'Who said anything about seventeen?' Cam looked confused. 'I was just joking.'

Layla took a gulp of her wine. 'Sorry if I don't find it funny for a grown man to take advantage of a teenager.'

Cam's mouth fell open. 'I said *nothing* about teenagers. What are you attacking me for? It was just a stupid joke.'

Layla took a deep breath in an attempt to slow the flurry of panic inside her. 'Yeah. Yeah, I know. Sorry, it's been a rough day.'

She reached out for him again, but he turned away, his face still stormy. 'Why don't you go and have a shower?'

'I'm sorry, Cam,' she said, but he didn't acknowledge her, just turned his attention to the kids as if she hadn't spoken at all.

*

As she stood under the shower, eyes closed against the spray, she berated herself. Despite her own insecurities about her appearance, she'd never really thought that Cam might cheat on her. She didn't believe he would, not after what his father had done. But could she really blame him if he did, after she'd just bitten his head off for no reason? Could she really blame him when he had to come home to this disgusting body every night?

And wouldn't it be karma, considering she'd never been punished for what she'd done?

THEN

I watched Shona as she doodled lazily on her sketchpad. She'd chosen art as an elective largely due to the teacher's lax standards. Miss Grainger was around fifty and a full-on hippie, with masses of curly blonde hair, long velvet skirts and a perpetually dreamy look on her face. I always had a free period at the same time as Shona's art class, and Miss Grainger never seemed to mind me wandering in and chatting with Shona. She also let the boys bring in hip-hop CDs to play on the stereo, the explicit lyrics floating right over her head. There was a constant debate between the students over whether she really was as innocent as she seemed or whether she was playing us all for fools.

'Hey, Miss Grainger?' Katrina called from the other side of the classroom.

'Yes, Katrina?'

'Do you think a head job is rude?' she said slyly.

Miss Grainger's face turned pink as she searched for a suitable response. 'I think you should concentrate on your artwork and stop asking irrelevant questions.'

Katrina and her minions giggled, and there were sniggers from around the classroom.

'She *so* doesn't know what a head job is,' Shona said.

I rested my chin on my hands. 'Have you ever … you know?'

Shona glanced up at me. 'Gone down? Yeah, I did with Daniel a few times.'

'Was it gross?'

'I didn't love it,' Shona admitted. 'But he did, which kind of made it sexy, I guess. Why, is Scott putting the pressure on?'

I looked away, blushing. 'Not really.'

Things had been getting hotter and heavier with Scott ever since we'd resumed our post-work sessions a few weeks ago, and the hand on the top of my head was becoming more insistent. He always backed off when I asked him to, but I could tell he was getting impatient. And so I'd make him come, all the while wondering when he was going to tire of waiting for me, and I'd leave the cafe hating myself for not being able to give him what he wanted.

'So you haven't had sex yet?' Shona asked.

'No. And we're not going to. Not while he's still married.'

But the possibility was there all the time, weighing on me. When we were apart, I thought about it constantly, conjuring up the perfect situation where there would be no fear, no pain, and that little thrill of arousal would buzz through my entire body. But when we were together, everything felt out of my control, and there was this kernel of me – just a tiny one – that felt threatened. Sex was supposed to be natural, but in the moment, nothing we did made me feel like I wanted it. And that made me panic that he would think I was frigid, so I let him do more than I was comfortable with, which made me feel even less like taking things further.

Shona was watching me closely, her usual flippant expression replaced with a serious one. 'So he's going to leave her, then?'

'I … yeah, he will eventually. When the time is right.' More and more, I found myself using Scott's words to my friends as a way of convincing myself that he meant them. Shona was still looking at me, but I couldn't maintain eye contact and false bravado at the same time, so I let my gaze drop to the table.

When Scott had told me he loved me, I'd assumed it would only be a matter of time before he separated from his wife and moved out. But he didn't seem to want to discuss those specifics, and I'd been too scared of losing him to push him on it. And to be honest, I wasn't sure if I was ready to face up to the reality of the situation myself … what I'd tell my parents, what everyone would think of me for breaking up a family. It felt safer this way, convincing myself that we weren't hurting anyone, that we hadn't committed the ultimate betrayal because we hadn't had sex.

'Do you think I should?' I asked when she didn't say anything.

'Babe, I'm the last one to judge you about sex stuff,' Shona said, 'but this isn't the same as popping your cherry with your high school boyfriend. Imagine if his wife found out.'

I stared at my hands. I imagined it all the time.

Shona nudged me. 'Whatever you do, make sure you tell me about it, OK? I want to live vicariously through your hot affair.'

We laughed, and I perked up a bit.

Affair. I was having an affair. It did sound quite exciting when she put it like that.

*

Scott's mouth was on my neck, his breath coming in short gasps. 'I want to be inside you so badly.'

The usual nervousness returned, and I broke away from him.

Scott groaned. 'God, I want you so much. Why do you keep pushing me away?'

'I'm sorry. I want you too, but I'm not—'

'You're not ready,' he interrupted. There was a smile on his face that didn't quite reach his eyes. 'I know, I know. I'm trying to be patient, but you don't know how hard it is for me to stop when you get me going like this.'

'I'm sorry,' I said again. 'Let me help you.'

I reached for him, but he stepped back. 'It's not enough, Layla. It's like torture, having to hold back like this.'

'But …' My voice shook. 'But you said touching me was enough.'

'And you said you'd have sex with me if I loved you!' The words exploded out of him, and I stared at him in shock. He'd never raised his voice at me before.

'That's not what I …' I stopped. Had I said that? Maybe not in so many words, but I couldn't blame him for coming to that conclusion. He was twenty-eight years old; he wasn't going to be content with my inexpert fumbling forever.

'I do everything I can to pleasure you, Layla, and all I get in return is hand jobs.' He ran a hand through his hair, his eyes desperate. 'Do you understand how frustrating this is for me?'

I hung my head. 'I'm sorry I'm so bad at this.'

There was a moment of silence, then he clasped my face in his hands and guided my gaze back to his. 'You're not bad at anything.' His expression was softer now. 'I didn't set out to fall in love with you, Layla, but here we are.'

I could never resist him when he was looking at me like this, with his heart in his eyes. I kissed him, let his tongue stroke mine, let his fingers tangle in my hair. If only it could always be like this, tender, gentle, then maybe I could see myself going the whole way.

He drew back and pushed my hair away from my face. 'Making love is the most beautiful way to express our feelings. I want to show you how amazing it can be.' A wistful smile touched his lips. 'But if you don't feel the same way about me, well … it hurts, Layla, but I can let you go.'

Desperate panic gripped me; that I'd lose him, that I'd go back to being alone. 'I do! I do feel the same way.'

'You love me?'

'Yes, I love you. I love you so much.'

'Show me,' he breathed. 'Show me how much you love me.'

He pushed down gently on my shoulders. The fear rose inside me again, suffocating, choking, but I wrestled it down and dropped to my knees. I didn't want to do this, I didn't feel ready for it. But I couldn't lose him, because who in the world would love me then?

NOW

When they'd ordered their meals, Layla sat back in her chair. 'I've been hanging out for this all week.'

Cam clinked his glass against hers. 'Cheers to date night.'

Layla took a sip of her wine. Things had been tense between them ever since she'd snapped at him the other night. But now her husband was smiling at her the way he always did, and maybe this was what they needed, to get away from the house for a few hours.

'Apparently, Louis bit one of the other kids at child care today,' Layla said. 'Left teeth marks on his arm.'

Cam shook his head. 'He's a rough little bugger sometimes.'

'He's been out of control lately, but I don't know if his behaviour is normal or if there's some other issue.'

Cam stared out across the restaurant. 'I'm sure it's normal.'

It wasn't the first time Layla had brought up the subject, but Cam always got defensive, as if she was blaming him for Louis's challenging behaviour, and this in turn frustrated her. 'But how would we know? He's our first. Maybe we should get him assessed.'

His gaze flicked back to her. 'Assessed for what?'

'I don't know. But all the literature says that early intervention is best for kids who need a bit of extra help.'

Cam made a casual gesture with his hand. 'Bugger the literature. He's a normal, rowdy kid. There's nothing wrong with him.'

'It's not about there being something wrong with him.' Layla set her wineglass down on the table. 'Why can't you understand that?'

'What I can't understand is why you'd want to stick a label on our child.'

'Jesus, Cam, I'm not trying to put a label on him! I just want to give him the best start.'

The waiter approached their table, and there was a tense moment as he placed their entrees before them. He disappeared and Layla and Cam ate and drank their wine in silence for a few minutes, staring into their meals rather than making eye contact. Finally, Cam reached across the table and took her hand. 'Sorry. I know you want what's best for him.'

She squeezed his hand. 'I'm just worried about him, that's all.'

'I know, me too. Why don't we see how he goes when he starts kindy? I bet he'll leap ahead then.'

'I guess so.' Layla twirled her wineglass by the stem.

'Anyway, I thought we weren't going to talk about the kids tonight? This dinner is for us.'

She smiled at him. 'You're right. No more kid talk.'

The silence stretched out again. Sometimes Layla worried that they'd lost the ability to talk about anything that didn't revolve around their children. By the time they got the kids to bed, she just wanted to flop onto the couch and stare at the

TV for a few hours. Then when they finally had these few hours a month to themselves, there seemed to be nothing to say. One day the kids wouldn't be around anymore; would there be anything left of them by then?

'How's work?' She clutched at a conversation.

'Busy. Boring,' Cam said absently. 'Oh, I keep forgetting to tell you. I got a message today from that woman who tried to friend me on Facebook a few weeks ago. Jodie something.'

Layla's throat constricted, and for a second she couldn't breathe, let alone speak. 'Which woman? What was the message?'

'Hold on.' He unlocked his phone and tapped the screen. 'Here.'

Layla tried to stop her fingers from trembling as she took the phone from him and stared at the screen.

Has your wife told you what she got up to when she was in high school?

She read and re-read the message, trying to work out what on earth she was going to say. 'What the hell?' she finally got out, manipulating her face into what she hoped was a confused expression. 'That's just weird.'

'I know. Especially since you don't even know her.'

Layla felt lightheaded, and she threw back a mouthful of wine.

'I thought maybe it had something to do with your school reunion,' Cam went on. 'Except that she's obviously older than you.'

Layla leapt on this. 'Actually, yeah. I think maybe she works for the school and is helping to organise it. Come to think of it, Renee mentioned something about a naughty list. They're giving out awards or something. Bit childish if you ask me.' The words tumbled out of her mouth.

Cam raised his eyebrows. 'You don't seem like the type who got into trouble at school. Star student, weren't you?'

She blushed and took another sip from her glass. 'Something like that.'

'Should I reply to her?'

Layla almost choked on her mouthful of wine in her rush to answer. 'No, don't. She shouldn't be contacting you.'

'If you say so.' He took his phone back and locked it.

Layla avoided his gaze by picking up her own phone. 'I wonder whether Mum's got the kids to bed yet.'

Cam waved a finger at her. 'No kid talk, remember?'

*

When they got home, Layla's mum was flicking through the TV channels.

'How was your dinner?' she said brightly.

'Great,' Layla said. 'How were the kids?'

Angela gave a dismissive gesture. 'Angels, as always. Got both of them down by seven thirty.'

Layla gave a frustrated sigh. 'Why do they always behave for you? We struggle to get them to bed by eight.'

'Grandparents have special powers.'

Cam laughed. 'It's called chocolate, right?'

Angela pointed a finger at him. 'Bingo.'

'So, Angela,' Cam said, 'Layla's twenty-year high school reunion is coming up soon.'

'Oh yeah?' Her mum's eyes flicked to Layla's briefly.

'Yeah, they're putting together a list of all the bad things the students got up to. Got any dirt on Layla?'

'Pfft, Layla was top of her class. She never did *anything* bad. You're not actually going to go, are you?' Her eyes sought out Layla's again, and Layla turned away.

'I'm not sure. Shona's back from London, and Renee's going. I haven't seen them for years.'

A tense moment passed before Angela switched off the TV and reached for her handbag. 'Well, I'd better get going and let you two get to bed.'

'I'll see you out,' Layla said.

Her mum turned to face her when they reached the doorstep, a crease between her eyebrows. 'Does this have anything to do with Jodie Telford?'

Layla glanced over her shoulder to make sure Cam wasn't in earshot. 'She asked me to go to Glasswater to talk to her, but then Ella got sick and I fobbed her off. Now she's sent Cam a message telling him to ask me what I got up to in high school. I let him think it had something to do with the reunion.'

The look on her mother's face reminded Layla of the day she'd told her what she'd done. 'Do you know what she wants?'

'No.' Layla wrung her hands. 'She just said she wants me to know what she's been through. She's threatening to tell Cam.'

Her mum put a hand on her shoulder. 'Why don't you just tell him yourself?'

'I can't.' The very idea made Layla's stomach lurch. 'What would he think of me?'

'It's not good to have secrets in a marriage, Layla. I can tell you that from experience.'

Guilt washed over Layla again, and she dropped her head into her hands. 'I'm sorry I forced you to keep it all from Dad. I know it's my fault that he left.'

'Oh, it's not your fault, Layla. It was my choice not to tell him, and I'd do it again.'

Layla looked up at her. 'But if it wasn't for me you'd probably still be together. I'm sorry.'

Her mum gave her a grim smile. 'Keeping that secret wasn't the only reason your father and I split up. There'd been distance between us for years before that. The problems were already there, but we didn't try to address them until it was too late. Don't leave it until it's too late to tell Cam. It'll be better coming from you than from some stranger.'

It had been so long since she'd connected with her mother. If only it didn't always happen when she was consumed with fear. She wanted her mum to take control, as she'd done all those years ago; make the bad things go away. But Layla was no longer a teenager.

'I can't, Mum. I've already lied to him. I told him I didn't know her.'

She smiled gently. 'Cam loves you. He'll understand.'

'I don't know.'

'Are you really going to your school reunion?'

Layla hesitated. 'I don't want to, but now that I've made up this stupid story I feel like I have to. And I do want to catch up with Renee. I've got a lot to make up for.'

'How *did* you two fall out anyway? You were inseparable all through school.'

Layla closed her eyes for a moment, remembering the stricken look on Renee's face, remembering her words: *I never thought you'd do something like this to me.* She swallowed.

'I did something that really hurt her. We never recovered after that.'

Her mum moved forward as if to hug her, then stopped and touched her on the arm instead. 'Whatever you did when you were seventeen, it shouldn't matter anymore.'

They said goodbye and Layla went back inside. Maybe her mother was right. Maybe it didn't matter anymore. Maybe it wasn't too late.

She was cleaning her teeth when Cam came into the ensuite, looking sheepish. 'I know you said not to, but I just replied to that Jodie woman.'

Layla went hot and cold all over. She bent over to hide her face as she spat toothpaste into the sink and rinsed her toothbrush. 'What did you say?' she asked with forced casualness.

'Ah, it's a secret.' He tapped the side of his nose.

'What did you say to her, Cam?' Her voice came out sharper than she'd intended.

Cam looked taken aback. 'I asked her if it was something to do with the reunion, that's all.' He gave her a wry grin. 'Why, do you have a skeleton in your closet that I don't know about?'

'I asked you to ignore her.' Layla's hands prickled with pins and needles and she clenched her fists. 'She's a troublemaker.'

'I thought you didn't know her?'

Layla's composure shattered. 'I don't, Cam, Jesus! Will you just let it go?'

He stared at her, his eyes hard. 'What's going on with you lately? What are you so touchy about?'

'I'm not touchy, I just don't need the Spanish Inquisition because I don't want you to message some random woman.'

'And I don't need you attacking me every five minutes.' His face was turning red now. 'I don't think I've done anything wrong, but if I have, just fucking tell me what it is, because I'm sick of this.'

He waited for a few seconds, but Layla was frozen to the spot and couldn't respond. He whirled around and left the bathroom, slamming the door behind him. Layla knew she should follow him, try to apologise, but the panic was fluttering madly inside her, throwing itself against her rib cage, trying to escape, and she couldn't let it out, not now, not when she still didn't know what Jodie's intentions were.

She got the facial wipes out of the cabinet and slowly and painstakingly began to remove her make-up, stripping back her mask until there was no longer anything to hide her imperfections. Then she washed her face thoroughly and crept out into the bedroom, bracing herself to tackle the situation with Cam. But the room was dark and silent. She knew he was still awake by the rigid way he held his body as she slid into bed beside him.

She rolled away from him, staring into the darkness.

THEN

'Come to The Knob with me tomorrow night,' Scott said as I was pulling on my jeans for my Thursday-afternoon shift. He'd snuck into the toilet stall with me and my heart was still pitter-pattering after what his hands had been doing to my body.

'I can't,' I said. 'I'm going away with my family for the whole weekend.'

Tomorrow was Good Friday and the cafe would be closed for the next four days. It would be the longest we'd been apart since we'd started this thing, and there was already an ache in my guts at the thought of not seeing him for so long.

'That's a shame,' he murmured, grabbing the waistband of my jeans and pulling me back to him. 'I'm going to miss you.' He put his hand down the front of my jeans and I moaned a little as his fingers found me again. 'Are you sure you can't get out of it?'

'It's Easter, Scott,' I said breathlessly. 'Surely you've got family stuff on too?'

'My in-laws are staying with us. I'd do anything to get away from the house for a while.'

My head fell back. 'You're going to make it very difficult for me to concentrate on work, you know.'

'I'm counting on it.' He grinned. 'Speaking of which, I'd better get back out there. Wait here.'

He withdrew his hand and opened the door a crack before disappearing. I leant against the door and sighed, my body still buzzing. After another minute, I followed him out.

It was a quiet evening and Scott talked about closing the cafe early. I took the garbage out while he balanced the till.

The main street was deserted when I slipped down the side alley to the dumpster the cafe shared with the surrounding businesses. I stood on my toes, hoisted the bag over my head and hurled it into the bin. It was only as I was turning back, brushing my hands on my jeans, that I saw the figure silhouetted against the entrance to the alley. My guts turned to water as he began to walk towards me.

'You didn't think you were gonna get away with that little stunt you pulled the other week, did you?' Matty drawled.

I backed away until I was up against the dumpster. There was no way out. 'Scott's expecting me back inside.'

'Anyone ever told you you'd look prettier with a dick in your mouth? You know how the song goes, Laaaylaaa.'

He'd almost reached me now, and I was paralysed with fear. I couldn't force my limbs to move no matter how hard I tried. 'Get away from me! I'll scream!'

He laughed, sending a gust of sour alcohol breath into my face. 'Everything's closed. I could do whatever I fucken wanted to you right now, and there's no one around to hear.'

Then there were running footsteps from behind him and someone yanked him away from me and slammed him against the brick wall. Fear of a different kind rose within me as Scott's hand closed around Matty's throat.

'You touch her again and I'll kill you,' he growled.

'I was just muckin' around, mate,' Matty said, his voice muffled. 'The bitch kicked me in the balls; I was just havin' a bit of fun with her, scaring her a bit, y'know?'

'Jesus, Matty, I know you're an arsehole,' Scott's voice was dangerously low, 'but she's a fucking kid.'

'What can I say, mate, I dig virgins. Had a taste for them ever since I fucked yours in high school.'

Scott drew back his fist and slammed it into Matty's nose with a sickening thud. Scott's face was unrecognisable, ugly in its rage. I'd never seen him like this before. 'Scott, don't!' I cried, but neither of them took any notice of me.

'I don't care how close you are to the cops,' Scott said, 'if I hear you've done anything like this again, I'm gonna fucking destroy you.'

Matty gave a wet chuckle. 'You've been wanting to do this ever since I moved in on your girlfriend, haven't you?' His eyes changed for a second; there was a sudden vulnerability to his expression that I hadn't seen on him before. Then it was gone again, and his sly smile returned. 'Tell me, *mate*, were you ever able to live up to my performance, or were you only ever her sloppy seconds?'

Scott gave a guttural roar and punched him again. 'Go home, Layla!' he yelled over his shoulder.

I didn't hesitate, running past them down the alley and onto the main street. Their grunts and the thud of fists on flesh followed me to my car. My whole body shook as I stabbed my key in the ignition and started the engine.

*

I sat in the car outside my house for a long time, trying to calm down. There was no way I could tell my parents what had happened or they'd completely freak out. They'd insist on going to the cops, and there was no way Matty's brother and his colleagues would believe me over Glasswater Bay's golden boy. I knew how things worked in this town. I'd end up being the one on trial, the one who was vilified and made out to be a slut. I couldn't do that to my parents. I couldn't do that to Scott, who would be dragged into it all with me.

And as for Scott, the sudden change in him had been shocking. I'd felt the violence in his eyes, in his body, as a physical thing. It'd frightened me, even though I'd been the one he was defending. There'd been no satisfaction in watching him beat the shit out of Matty … it'd been chilling.

I got out of the car and walked slowly up the path to the house. Mum was at the table, nursing a cup of tea and reading a magazine. 'How was work?' she asked as I went to the fridge to get the bottle of Coke.

'It was OK.' I took a swig from the bottle and sat down at the dining table with her.

'Don't drink out of the bottle, please, Layla, you're not a street urchin.'

I pulled a face behind her back as I got up again to get a glass.

'Looking forward to Renmark?'

I made a noncommittal sound. Every Easter since I was a little kid, we'd gone to stay at the river shack my grandparents owned in Renmark. There was nothing to do there other than swim in the chocolate-milk river or go yabbying with Dad, but we always had a good time. Part of me *was* looking forward to it, even though I knew I'd be bored out of my brain and desperate even to get home to Glasswater by the end of the weekend. After the encounter with Matty, the idea of returning to childhood traditions was comforting, even if it had been years since Zach and I had been interested in swimming in autumn or sitting on the riverbank for hours waiting to pull up yabby nets. But going away right after Scott had just done his best to break Matty's face didn't feel right either.

'Hey, Mum,' I said, my head still in the fridge as I replaced the Coke bottle. 'Would you and Dad mind if I stayed home this weekend?'

'But it's Easter,' Mum said after a pause. 'We always go away for Easter.'

'I know.' I turned to face her. 'But I've got exams coming up next term. I thought it could be an opportunity for me to knuckle down and study while the house is empty.'

'There's nothing stopping you from studying at the shack. This is our family time, Layla.'

I sighed. 'I'm sick of going to the shack every year. It's boring and there's nothing to do.'

'You just said you needed to study, so you won't need to worry about finding anything to do. How about you give it a chance?'

'And how about you stop busting my balls!' I exploded in frustration.

'Layla!'

'Well, sorry, but you're the one who's always going on at me about how important my education is, and now you expect me to cram myself into the tiny shack and try to concentrate while Zach annoys me.'

Mum looked up at me, her face a little sad. 'I don't want you to be by yourself over Easter.'

I rolled my eyes. 'I'm seventeen, Mum, not twelve.'

'Less attitude, please. You may be seventeen, but that's no excuse to be rude.'

I sat back down at the table opposite her. 'Sorry. I didn't want to tell you, but I've been struggling a bit at school. I really need this time to catch up, get back on track.'

Mum sighed. 'I'd really like you to come, but I don't want you to fall behind either. If your heart is set on spending the weekend studying, I won't stop you.'

'Thanks, Mum.'

She looked wistful. 'My little girl is growing up.'

She rose to wash her cup in the sink before going to bed, and I remained at the table, nervous about the plan I'd set in motion. I wasn't a little girl anymore. Scott had saved me twice now. I owed him.

NOW

The kids' bickering had graduated to poking and pinching, and Layla's anxiety had reached tipping point by the time she lined up the trolley at the checkout. They were seated side by side in the front of the trolley and it hadn't taken long for the novelty of helping her choose the groceries to wear off.

'Stop fighting or we're not going to Grandma's place,' she said for the twentieth time, but she may as well have been talking to her handbag. Louis shoved Ella with his shoulder and she retaliated by grabbing a fistful of his hair in a death grip. He started yowling.

Layla continued to unload the groceries onto the conveyer belt, outwardly calm while everything inside her was screaming to get out of there, to abandon the week's worth of food (and maybe her children too) and run.

'What's this?' broke in a gruff voice from behind them, and Louis and Ella abruptly went silent, staring at the man and woman who had joined the queue. The man had snatched a packet of chocolate biscuits from the woman and was holding it up in front of her face. 'What are you buying this shit for?'

The woman couldn't have been much more than twenty-two; slim and pretty, dark hair and smoky eyes. She tittered nervously. 'I just thought they'd be nice.' The unnaturally high pitch of her voice made Layla's stomach contract.

'Until you get fat and ugly and then you'll be stuffing your face with them every day.' He spat the words at her with such contempt that the woman flinched.

But she pasted on her bright smile again and sidled up to him, clinging to his arm. 'Don't be like that, honey. I only have one or two a week.'

He looked down at her, his lip curling. 'You want to turn into a fat slut, you go ahead. But don't expect me to stick around.'

The woman's face coloured. Layla had the urge to grab her, to pull her away from him, tell her to run now while she still had the chance, before he swallowed all her self-esteem and she was stuck in his cage forever. It didn't seem like so long ago that Layla had been that person, placing all of her value in other people's opinions of her, staying in relationships with men who treated her badly, gulping down compliments to keep her going through the neglect, knowing the day would come when she would no longer be fuckable and then she'd be worth nothing.

The man stared across the supermarket, his face still stormy. Layla knew his type: older, dominant, less attractive so he had to take her down a peg every day until all her self-worth was gone. She knew that if she tried to intervene, it would only make things worse for the woman later, and yet she remembered what it had been like to be in public with a man like this. The way people's eyes slid away, the way no one was willing to really see what was happening.

She remembered how alone she had felt. Checking that the man was still looking away, she made eye contact with the woman. *Are you OK?* she mouthed. The woman's eyes darted away, then she gave an almost imperceptible nod. But Layla knew she wasn't OK, knew that when she went home with this man, he would punish her in some way, maybe with his words, maybe with his fists. Maybe with unwanted sex. She knew all this from experience, knew that it was the words that left the deepest scars.

The cashier called out her total, and Layla realised her shopping was already packed in the bags and waiting at the end of the checkout. She got out her credit card and moved over to pay. The children were still miraculously silent, perhaps unnerved by the chilling atmosphere the couple's presence had cast over everyone around them. Layla lifted the bags into the trolley and began to push it towards the exit. When she turned once to look back, the woman was placing the packet of Tim Tams on top of the chewing gum on the shelf beside her.

*

Layla was still feeling uneasy when she and the kids arrived at Cam's mother's house for their fortnightly visit. The arrangement suited all of them: it gave the kids an afternoon of being spoilt, Cam's mother, Ruth, got some much-needed company, and Layla got the chance to drink a whole cup of tea before it went cold.

'Hello, my darlings!' cried Ruth as she bent to hug both children at the door. 'Would you like a milkshake?' The kids nodded vigorously and ran off towards the kitchen. Ruth gave Layla a brief hug. 'How are you, love?'

'I'm good, Ruth, thank you.' Layla liked her mother-in-law. She was a kind, generous woman who doted on her son and grandchildren, and she treated Layla with a warmth that had been missing between her own mother and her since she'd been a teenager. It was an uncomplicated relationship, and she looked forward to their visits.

But while Ruth made the kids' milkshakes and put the kettle on for tea, it was clear from the way she kept glancing at Layla that there was something she wanted to talk about. Once the kids were seated at the dining table with their drinks, she made eye contact with Layla across the bench.

'Is everything all right with you, love?' she asked gently.

'Of course!' Layla dunked her tea bag in her cup a little too energetically, and a bit of the tea slopped over the rim. Avoiding her mother-in-law's eyes, she moved the cup aside and wiped away the brown ring with a washcloth.

'Cameron told me you two had been having some problems.'

Layla looked up. 'He did?' She knew Cam was close to his mother, and she'd always suspected he talked to her about their marriage on occasion, but the thought of him telling her that they had problems – real, tangible problems – made her feel chastised, as if she were a child.

'Oh, don't worry,' Ruth said. 'He's not going to do anything drastic. He's just worried about you. And I wanted to see if there was anything wrong.'

'There's nothing wrong,' Layla said carefully. 'I've been a bit stressed lately, that's all.'

'OK. OK, good.' Ruth looked relieved. 'Cameron is a sensitive man. He was only thirteen when his father left, and it affected him quite badly.'

169

'I know.'

'Did he ever tell you he got a warning from the police after he started stalking the other woman?'

'What? No.' Layla put down her cup and stared at Ruth.

'It didn't last for long, and he didn't do anything serious. He followed her home from work a few times ... I think to see whether his father was staying with her, but of course it didn't look good. It wasn't until he graffitied a certain dirty word on her car that she called the police.'

The image of her own car windscreen, shaving cream slashed across it, flashed into Layla's mind. How could she not have known this about the man she'd married? But then, she'd kept her own share of secrets from him. This gave her an even deeper insight into her husband's feelings about infidelity, and all the more reason to make sure her secrets remained hidden forever. 'What happened after that?'

'He stopped harassing the woman and started shutting himself in his bedroom for hours at a time. I think the police visit frightened the bejeezus out of him. And so it should have.' Ruth smiled. 'But I'm not telling you this to shame him. I'm telling you because that whole episode with his father left its mark on him. It was a terrible shock for him to realise how ugly people could be.' Layla shrank beneath her own ugliness, but Ruth didn't seem to notice. 'As he grew up, he was determined to not become his father. And he's succeeded, with you. But now you're having ... difficulties ... I guess he's worried you're going to abandon him like his father did.'

Layla felt a tremor of annoyance. 'I've got no plans to abandon him.'

'I'm not attacking you, Layla.' Her eyes were soft. 'But he's my son, and he deserves to be happy … as do you.'

'Are you saying he's not happy with me?' Layla's voice shook.

Ruth gave her a gentle smile. 'I'd never seen him happier than when he met you. And I think you feel the same. I'm saying that it'd be a shame to let that go because you're having trouble communicating with each other.'

Layla was silent. Things had been tense between Cam and her ever since she'd got that first message from Jodie, but she hadn't realised the effect it'd had on him. She hadn't realised that he thought their marriage was in trouble.

Ruth reached across the bench and placed her hand over Layla's. 'You can fix this together.'

THEN

The doorbell rang and my belly swooped. Now that this was actually happening, I was no longer sure I wanted to go through with it. But Scott had been so excited when I'd told him I'd have the house to myself for the whole weekend. I couldn't back out now, not when he'd already been so patient.

It wasn't that big a deal anyway. My friends had been having sex for two years. It was immature, being scared like this. Once I got it over with, everything would be easier.

I opened the front door and Scott stepped inside quickly, looking over his shoulder in case anyone was walking by. But the street was dark.

'Did you have any trouble getting away?' I asked when I'd closed the door.

'I said I was going to my mate's place,' he said.

We stared at each other for a second. He was holding a bottle of Jim Beam and I gestured to it. 'That's different.'

His face went pink. 'God, I just realised how dodgy this looks. You don't have to have any if you don't want … I thought it might relax you a bit. Or me.' He laughed self-consciously.

'I've got some Coke,' I said.

We both went quiet again. Then he put down the bottle on the hallway table and stepped in close to me. We kissed for a bit, my back against the door, until we were both breathing fast, our hands under each other's shirts. When we came up for air, he had a look of anticipation on his face that set off my trepidation all over again.

'How about that drink?' I said.

We went to the kitchen and I got two tumblers and the Coke. He poured us both drinks and we sat down at the round table and sipped at them. I didn't like Beam; the treacly maltiness was too overpowering, the sweetness of the Coke not enough to offset the sharpness. But I was already so on edge, and maybe it would help still my anxiety.

'I'm so glad you invited me over, Layla,' Scott said.

'I'm sorry about calling your house. I wasn't sure how else to get in contact with you.'

'That's OK. It was lucky Jodie didn't answer.'

'Sorry.'

He smiled at me. 'Don't apologise, Layla. I'm happy to be here with you.'

I looked into my drink. 'I didn't thank you for what you did last night. With Matty.'

'I wasn't going to let that arsehole get away with scaring you like that.'

'How did you explain this?' I nodded at his knuckles, which were bruised and scabbed.

He closed his left hand over his right fist. 'I told Jodie I got in a fight with him.'

'She wasn't upset?'

'Oh, I didn't tell her about you. Matty and I have a history. She understands.'

I stiffened. That rage I'd witnessed, that I'd thought had risen from his instinct to protect me … it'd never been about me. The realisation was crushing. 'It was her, wasn't it?'

He gave me a questioning look. 'What was her?'

'What Matty said about your girlfriend … that was Jodie?'

'Yeah.' His jaw tightened. There was that violence in his eyes again, so incongruous in his normally amiable face.

'Oh.' I stared hard at the wood-grain surface of the dining table, hoping my hurt didn't show on my face. If he didn't love her anymore, why had he been so eager to defend her honour? And if he *did* still love her, why was he here with me?

Then his finger was under my chin, tilting my face up to look into his. 'That's all in the past now. It was you I was worried about.'

And there was that look again, the warmth in his eyes that told me how much I meant to him, and all my doubts dissolved. 'Well, like I said, I'm grateful.' I hesitated and clutched my glass tight between both hands. 'And I want to show you how grateful I am.'

'Layla, I didn't beat up Matty so you'd sleep with me. I want you to want to.'

'I do.' I held his gaze. 'I do want to.'

He reached for me and pulled me into his lap. His mouth was cold and tasted of bourbon. His hands were urgent on my body. 'Should we go to your room?'

I swallowed down my fear and stood up, took his hand and led him to my bedroom. I'd changed the pink ruffly quilt cover for a plainer yellow-and-white-chequered one, but my face still went hot when Scott laughed.

'A single bed.' He shook his head. 'You're so mature it's easy to forget this is the room you grew up in.'

'Sorry.'

'Layla.' He put his arms around me. 'Stop apologising. I'm here to be with you. I wouldn't care if we had to do it on a rug on the floor.' He kissed me again. 'Can I take your clothes off?'

I nodded, lifting my arms so he could pull my T-shirt over my head. He took off his own and threw it on the edge of my bed. Despite all our encounters up until now, this was the first time I'd seen him without a shirt. I ran my hands over his muscled shoulders and down his back. He unbuttoned my jeans and pushed them down with my underwear, and I kicked them off my ankles. Then his were off too and we stood facing one another, naked together for the first time. He was gorgeous, with his trapezoid shoulders narrowing down to his waist, the bulge of his biceps, the light dusting of hair on his chest, just enough to look manly but not enough to be off-putting.

'You're so beautiful, Layla.' His eyes traversed my body, and this time I didn't shrink away. His desire for me was intoxicating.

'So are you.'

'God, look at you.' He ran a hand down my waist to my hip. 'You're perfect. There's nothing in the world sexier than a woman in her prime.'

We kissed again, our naked bodies pressed together. It felt different with nothing between us. My nerve endings felt alive. Together we moved backwards until we were lying on my bed.

'We're going to take it slowly, OK?' he said. 'As slow as you need.'

I nodded, grateful that he wasn't going to push me. The bed was so narrow that we had to lie pressed up against each other. His body felt amazing against mine. He kissed my neck and my shoulders, then moved down to my breasts, unhurried, his breath hot against my skin, his hand already between my legs, stroking lightly. He took his time, pausing every now and then to look at me with a half-smile. My body began to feel soft, warm, like it was melting. At last he was lying on top of me, his weight deliciously heavy, and there was no fear anymore, no voice whispering to me to flee. I was ready to give myself to him.

'I love you, Layla,' he said. 'I love you so much.'

'I love you too.'

He traced a finger down the side of my face. 'Are you ready?'

I nodded breathlessly. 'Do you have a condom?'

A flicker of something – irritation or impatience – crossed his face. 'I don't like using condoms. I can't feel anything with them on, and they don't usually fit me anyway. I won't come inside you, I promise.'

My certainty faltered. 'But … but what about STDs?'

His expression turned hard and he sat up, legs over the edge of the bed, facing away from me. 'I've been married for the last eight years, Layla, where do you think I would've picked up an STD? Jesus.'

My body felt cold now that we were no longer in contact. I started to think I'd made a mistake, bringing up the condom thing this late, and now I'd forced him to think about his wife when this should've been about us. 'I'm sorry, I didn't mean it like that.'

'So you think I sleep around, is that it?' He threw an accusing look over his shoulder. 'You think this doesn't mean anything to me?'

'No! Of course not. I'm sorry.' I tugged at his shoulder. 'It's OK, we don't need to use a condom. It's fine.'

But he wouldn't turn around, and I started to panic. The softness I'd felt had drained out of my body, but I couldn't lose him, not now.

'Scott, please. I want you. Please come back to me.'

He swung his legs onto the bed and lay on top of me again. But there was a change in him. He felt heavier than before, and that hardness hadn't left his face. It reminded me of how he'd looked when he had Matty around the throat, as if he was punishing me for what I'd said. It frightened me a little, but I couldn't back out on him, not when we'd come this close. My body felt less pliant; I was no longer ready for him. I wished he'd slow down, bring me back to where I'd been before, but he was already between my legs, pushing, pushing. He held my shoulders down, his face red with the effort, or with impatience, I couldn't tell. Little by little, he began to edge inside me. It hurt, but I could handle it because his expression was changing now, his anger dissolving into something else as he moaned in pleasure.

'Oh, Layla, you feel so good.'

He tipped his head back and thrust hard into me, and the sudden, searing pain made me cry out. But he didn't seem to notice, his fingers digging into my shoulders, pinning me to the bed. I couldn't move, and the pain kept getting worse. I pushed at his chest. 'Scott, stop! It hurts, please stop!'

But he held onto me tighter, pushing me down into the bed, his pace getting faster and faster. 'Try to relax, it won't hurt for long.'

Fear flashed through me as I realised he wasn't going to get off, he wasn't going to stop.

And then, just as I thought it was never going to end, it did start to hurt less, and then less. It wasn't exactly good, but it wasn't too bad either. Scott gave a long groan, grimaced, then pulled out of me and came on my chest. He reached over and plucked a couple of tissues out of the box on my bedside table and wiped my chest. There was a tender smile on his face.

'That was amazing,' he said. 'I'm sorry I hurt you.'

I felt small as I looked up at him. 'I asked you to stop.'

He looked confused. 'But you said you were ready. You said you wanted it.'

'I thought we were going to take it slow.' My chin quivered. 'It really hurt.'

'I know.' He lay down beside me and pulled me close. 'But you don't know how hard it is for me to stop once I get going … You felt so amazing. And I did it for you, really. If I'd stopped then, it would've hurt again the next time.'

I was silent. He was acting like that had all been for my benefit, but the look on his face when he'd held me down had said otherwise. The tender spots on my shoulders said otherwise. But his words reminded me that I wasn't a virgin anymore. There would be no more first time. The relief was absolute, and my feelings towards him softened. Maybe he was right. Maybe it had been better to get it over with.

He smoothed my hair back from my face. 'It'll be so much better next time, you'll see. I can't wait until it feels as good for you as it does for me.'

'Me too.'

'You're mine now, Layla.' He hugged me close to him. 'You're *mine*.'

His words gave me a perverse thrill and I lifted my head to kiss him.

We lay in silence for a few more minutes, then Scott propped himself up on one elbow. 'I'd better get going.'

'Oh. Already?' I couldn't hide my hurt. I'd known what was going to happen when he came here, but I'd assumed he'd stick around for a bit afterwards.

'Sorry, I wish I could stay, but if I lie here with you much longer I'm going to fall asleep.' He touched my face. 'Can I come and see you again on Sunday? Jodie and her parents are taking the kids to the park for the Easter egg hunt, so I'll have a couple of hours free in the afternoon.'

A heavy blanket of guilt settled over me. I didn't like to hear the lies he told his family so we could be together. It made it too real; the bubble that surrounded us too fragile to hold. But then, hadn't we just crossed the ultimate line? Maybe I needed to know the details of what he had to do for us to be together.

'OK,' I said. 'Only if you can get away.'

'For you, anything.' He sat up. 'Don't get up. I'll see myself out.'

I watched as he dressed and put on his shoes. He smiled and came over to kiss me again. 'I'll see you on Sunday.'

After he'd left, I sat up. There were spots of blood on the quilt. The sight of them filled me with a crushing sense of shame. I felt hollowed out, vacant, insubstantial. Worthless. I stripped off the quilt cover and left it to soak in a bucket of water in the laundry, then got in the shower. Desolation swelled inside me. I'd just lost my virginity to the man I loved, but I'd never felt so empty.

NOW

When the Me Too movement had soared across the world a few years ago, it had brought up a lot of memories that Layla had forgotten about, or buried deep inside herself. As she read countless stories from women who had been sexually harassed or assaulted, she felt raw, as if each had happened to her. And in a way, they had: the catcalls, the gropes in pubs and nightclubs, the men who had exposed themselves to her on public transport, the guys who had tried to get her drunk at parties when she'd been at uni. The casual sense of entitlement to her body that had sometimes made her scared to risk their reaction if she rejected their advances. The near misses with Matty, accompanied by the guilt of not reporting the incidents. The uncertainty because nothing serious had actually happened. The terrible thought that he might have gone on to assault other women or girls. The things she'd always accepted as part of being a woman had been laid bare, each leaving its mark on her, like motherhood had left the silvery marks that striped her belly and hips.

But even then, she'd still hesitated to put a label on that first time with Scott. Her mind shied away from the word. She'd consented to the sex, had encouraged it even. But she'd asked him to stop – *she'd asked him to stop* – and he'd held her down and kept going. And she'd continued to justify it to herself, even after things had started getting ugly between them. But now she realised she had only ever been a conquest to him, someone to be possessed, claimed, controlled. And she'd let him do it, like the naive child she'd been. The more she thought about it, the angrier she became, both with herself and with him.

So when Jodie messaged her again to tell her she knew about the reunion and that she expected her to come and talk to her, for the first time, Layla was tempted. Suddenly, she *wanted* to talk to Jodie about him, to apologise for the hurt she'd caused, to explain what he'd done to her … what he'd done to both of them. But if Jodie wasn't bluffing – if she really did know what Layla had done – it could ruin Layla's life, tear her family apart. Her marriage already felt stretched and weak, and after her conversation with Cam's mother, the risk seemed too great. If Cam knew what she'd done, he'd want nothing more to do with her.

She sent a message to Renee telling her that she was sorry, but she had something else on that night and wouldn't be able to make it to the reunion after all. She'd been looking forward to catching up again, but maybe they could all have dinner together in Adelaide sometime before Shona went back to London.

Forget it, Renee wrote back. *I knew you wouldn't come.*

Pain twisted inside her. She hadn't realised how much she'd been counting on the chance to reconnect with her old friend. It was like losing her anew, like the moment when Renee had told her she never wanted to speak to her again.

She wrote and deleted several different responses, but they all sounded like weak excuses. She read her previous message from Renee's perspective, and she saw how it looked: like she had better things to do. Like she didn't care at all. She had the urge to tell Renee the real reason she couldn't go, but that hadn't been what caused their friendship to stretch so far in the first place that it had never snapped back into place. She didn't know if she could ever make up for *that*. Instead she wrote, *I'm sorry, Renee,* and closed Messenger, not expecting to hear from her again.

THEN

I spent all of Easter Saturday studying in an attempt to allay my guilt over lying to my parents. I hadn't been exaggerating when I'd told them I was struggling at school. Ever since I'd got involved with Scott, I'd been neglecting my school work and skipping classes, and my grades had been suffering as a result. And if I didn't nail my mid-year exams next term, I'd be pushing shit uphill for the rest of the year to get into uni.

On Saturday night I invited Renee and Shona over and, with Shona's *Reality Bites* DVD playing in the background, I filled them in on my first sexual experience. Renee was initially shocked that I'd gone through with it, but even she couldn't help hanging on to every word while Shona pushed me for details. I told them everything ... well, not quite everything. I left out the fact that we hadn't used a condom, and that I'd asked him to stop halfway through and he hadn't. I wanted to ask them whether that weird, bereft feeling I'd had afterwards was normal, but I knew, instinctively, that it wasn't something I should share.

We drank the rest of the Jim Beam that Scott had left on the kitchen table. It still tasted gross, but it seemed funnier when I was drinking it with my friends. We all got rip-roaringly drunk and Renee loosened up and stopped looking at me like I'd killed a puppy. I put a Killing Heidi album on and we danced around the living room, giggling wildly. I felt older, gloriously liberated of my virginity. I felt fantastic.

Renee slung an arm around both of our shoulders. 'I love you guys,' she slurred.

'I love you too, man,' I yelled.

'D'you reckon we'll still be doing this when we're thirty?' Shona picked up the bottle of Beam and took a swig, then screwed up her face in disgust. 'Ugh!'

'Pffft!' Renee spluttered. 'We'll be old and boring and responsible by then.'

'All the more reason to live it up now,' I said.

Shona laughed. 'We'll all have hot husbands by then, anyway, so we'll be too busy rooting them to get pissed.'

Renee's smile soured. 'Oh, but Layla's got a hot husband already,' she muttered darkly. 'Only problem is that he's someone else's.'

I threw her arm off me. 'Can you give it a rest, Renee? You've been pushing me to have sex for the last two years and the second I do it, all you can do is judge me.'

'Well, I never expected you to do it with someone else's husband, did I?' she shot back. 'You've done the wrong thing. You know that, right?'

I grabbed the bottle from Shona and took a gulp, but the liquid was like fire in my throat and I coughed roughly. 'Can't you be happy for me? I know it's not perfect, but I love him. We're just waiting until we can be together properly.'

'Oh, you're so fucking naive, Layla!' Renee cried. 'If you'd ever watched a single episode of Oprah you'd know that married men never leave their wives. He's just using you up and then he'll spit you out.'

Before I could prevent it, doubt began to creep in. He'd come over for sex last night and had left almost as soon as it was over. Maybe that would be it now that he'd got what he wanted. But he said he was coming back tomorrow. It wasn't going to be like Renee said. I jutted out my chin. 'It's different with him. He loves me.'

She snorted. 'Can you tell her she's insane, Shona?'

Shona was looking from one of us to the other, as if watching a tennis match. She swayed a little on her feet. 'I have to spew.'

She rushed off towards the bathroom. Renee and I tried to keep glaring at each other, but the room seemed to be tilting and I was having trouble remembering what we'd been arguing about. Her mouth twitched at the corners. Mine started smiling against my will. Then 'Mascara' came on the stereo, and we were dancing again, our arms around each other, singing our heads off over the sound of Shona's retching from the bathroom.

*

My head was still woolly when I let Scott in the next afternoon. He was wearing a leather jacket over a white T-shirt, and his James Dean vibe was a balm for my hangover. Renee and Shona had only left an hour ago, eyes still bloodshot, clutching their bellies and moaning.

Scott raised his eyebrows. 'Big night?'

'You could say that. The girls stayed over last night. We drank the rest of your Beam. Sorry.'

He laughed. 'That's OK, as long as you enjoyed it.'

'It tasted like shit, actually. But we had a good time. A bit too good, really.'

He smiled, and his eyes crinkled in that way I could never resist. 'Sometimes I miss the days of getting slaughtered with my mates every weekend. But I don't miss the hangovers. I can go if you're not feeling well?'

'No! Stay. Come here.' I pulled him to me. We kissed all the way up the hallway and into my bedroom. 'Sorry, I didn't ask if you wanted anything. Do you want anything?'

'Actually, yes I do. I want this.' He started tugging at my clothes.

He'd been right: it was much better this time. I wasn't as self-conscious or afraid, and I felt more confident in my skin. It wasn't exactly *good*, and the whole thing was over before I could really get into it, but Scott's obvious enjoyment made the experience worthwhile. He held me in his arms afterwards.

'I wish I could spend the whole weekend here with you,' he said. 'Cook you dinner, walk around naked, make love to you every hour on the hour.'

I smiled at the warmth in his words. This was real. Renee was wrong about him. 'I'd like that.'

'Was it better for you this time?' He sounded anxious. 'It didn't hurt again, did it?'

'It did a little bit at first, but then it got better. It was nice.'

'This is only the beginning.' He kissed my bare shoulder. 'I'm going to show you how good it can be.'

I stroked the fine hair of his arm. The empty feeling that had followed our first time had dissipated. I felt languid, lying in the arms of my lover, talking about what we'd do if we had all the time in the world together. What we *would* do when we could be out in the open.

'Tell me about your kids,' I said.

He didn't answer straightaway. 'Why do you want to know?'

'I want to know everything about you.'

His arms stiffened around me. 'We don't get much time together, Layla. Could we keep this to just us? I don't want to mix things up.'

'OK, if you want.' I fingered the raised veins on his forearm. 'It's just that they're important to you. You love them. They'll always be in your life, and maybe one day I will be too. So I want to know about them.'

He raised his head to look at me. 'You *are* in my life. You know that, don't you?'

I hesitated. 'Well, there's this. But it's not exactly a relationship, is it? We can't go grocery shopping together, or go out for dinner, or hold hands on the street.'

'Layla. I love you. I want to be with you. But we need to take this one step at a time. For now, I need to keep my two lives separate. Can you live with that?'

A pinprick of doubt punctured my serenity. I wanted to ask him what the next step was, when he was planning to leave his wife, but it was so warm and dreamy in his arms that I didn't want to ruin the moment.

'Yeah. Of course. Of course I can.'

He bent his head and we kissed, slowly, languorously. Shyly, I let my hands wander over his body and cup his buttocks, and his breathing quickened. 'You're so sexy, Layla. I can't believe you've made me want to go again already.'

'Really?'

He grinned. 'Really.'

We went on kissing, and over the sound of our heavy breathing, I registered the faint crunch of gravel that sounded very much like it was coming from my driveway.

'Shit!' I sat up.

'What's wrong?'

'I think my parents are home!'

We stared at each other in blind panic, then both leapt from the bed. Scott began to throw his clothes back on. 'What are we going to do?'

I wrapped my dressing gown around me as the key slotted into the front door with a metallic crunch. 'Come out the back. Quick.'

He picked up his shoes and followed me out to the laundry, his eyes wide. I let him out the door. 'Stay here a minute, then go down the side path to the front. They'll come out to the living room looking for me, so they won't see you leave.'

'Layla! Are you here?' came Mum's voice from the hallway.

'Out here!' I called.

Scott had already disappeared down the side of the house. I shut the door and came out of the laundry just in time to see my parents and Zach. I could feel Scott all over me, his hands, his smell, and horror gripped me at the idea they might be able to work it out.

'Why are you home so early?' My voice was too shrill.

'Didn't you get our message this morning? Zach was sick, so we decided to come home a day early.'

'Uh, no … Renee and Shona stayed over last night and we slept in. I didn't hear the phone and I haven't checked the machine.'

Mum looked quizzically at my dressing gown. 'Have you only just got out of bed?'

'I had a nap. I was about to get in the shower.'

'What on *earth*?' came Dad's voice from the kitchen and dread thudded into me. He'd seen Scott passing the window. Scott had left something here. We'd been found out.

'What?' chorused Mum and Zach.

I followed them into the kitchen, heart in my throat, and followed my family's gaze to the glasses, sticky with syrupy Coke and clouded with fingerprints, and the empty bottle I'd forgotten to clean up last night.

'What's this, young lady?' Dad's voice was stern. 'Did you have a party last night?'

'*Layla!*' said Mum. 'No wonder you were still in bed. You told me you were going to spend the whole weekend studying!'

'I have been!' I gestured to the papers and textbooks that still covered the kitchen table.

'Then where did the alcohol come from?'

'Renee brought it.'

'Where did *she* get it from?'

'I didn't ask.'

Mum shook her head. 'Very irresponsible of her parents to let her have access to alcohol. I've half a mind to ring them and—'

'No!' I thought fast. 'There was only like two centimetres left in the bottle. We hardly drank anything, really. And it was just the three of us.'

'We're not stupid, Layla,' Dad said. 'We know that teenagers are going to try alcohol, but I'd rather you did it when we were around. You're usually so responsible.'

I nodded. 'OK. Sorry, Dad.'

'You'll be eighteen soon enough, and then you can do it legally,' Mum added. 'There's no rush.'

'Yep, OK. I might go have that shower now.'

My stupid brother followed me up the hallway to my bedroom. At thirteen years old, Zach was pretty much the most annoying person in the world, always hounding me to get out of the bathroom, telling me that no amount of make-up could ever make me look good. It was a wonder I hadn't throttled him yet. 'Alco, alco, alco,' he sang.

'Bugger off, idiot.'

'Can't believe you left out the evidence,' he jeered from the doorway.

'Well, I didn't know you'd be such a pansy you'd have to come home early, did I? You don't look too sick now, by the way.'

He laughed. 'I wasn't sick, I was bored out of my brain.'

'You pretended to be sick so you could leave the shack?'

'Yep. And it was worth it to see you get sprung like that.' He grinned. 'Bet you got pissed after like two sips.'

'Get lost, Zach.'

'Captain Comeback strikes again!' Then his gaze switched to something behind me. 'Hey, cool jacket. Whose is it?'

Shock juddered in my chest as I followed his gaze to Scott's leather jacket draped over the end of my bed. My mind stumbled over itself to find a way out. 'Oh, that. Renee wore it here last night. Think she nicked it from her brother. She must've forgotten to take it home. I'll give it back to her later.'

Faint surprise filtered through my panic at the lie that had tumbled from my lips. When had lying become so easy for me?

'Whatever.' He rolled his eyes and continued up the hallway to his own bedroom.

My heart was still beating hard as I stuffed the jacket into the back of my wardrobe and went to the bathroom to wash Scott off me.

*

Scott looked sheepish when I handed his jacket over at the start of my next shift.

'Sorry about that. I was so focused on getting out of there before your dad saw me that I forgot all about it.'

'It's my mum you have to be worried about, believe me,' I said. 'Luckily, I found it before they did.'

He touched me lightly on the waist. 'I've been thinking about you nonstop since Sunday.'

I blushed a little. 'Me too.'

I'd assumed the lack of an available bed would limit our encounters, but Scott had a solution for every problem. He started keeping a swag in the storeroom, and he'd spread it out on the floor of the kitchen so we'd have something to lie on. Sometimes, if he couldn't wait that long, we'd do it against the wall as soon as he'd locked the cafe doors. Sometimes we went up to The Knob after work.

But while the sex was mostly nice, it was never amazing, and I never came close to that melting, fizzing feeling he'd given me the first time he'd touched me. I was often left with a lingering sense of disappointment and the feeling that Scott was getting a lot more out of the arrangement than I was. Was this really all there was to it, or was I just not very good at it?

'Did you come?' he'd ask afterwards, every time, and look increasingly despondent when, every time, I said, 'I don't think so.' It wasn't his fault I couldn't get there. He didn't deserve to take that on as his responsibility, and so after a while I started answering yes instead, and then, so I wouldn't have to lie to him, I started faking it. It was awkward the first time, but he totally fell for it, and the look in his eyes encouraged me to do it again the next time, and the next. A small part of me wondered why making him feel good was more important than my own pleasure, but I pushed the thought aside. His home life was difficult, unloving. He needed to feel desirable, and I could do that for him in this one small way. It was so easy.

I became bolder. I'd steal kisses from him in the lunch room; trail a finger over his groin when we were both behind the coffee machine. He couldn't get enough of it. I felt powerful. Sexy.

Jodie occasionally came into the cafe, sometimes with the kids, sometimes on her own. I felt sorry for her now. She'd lost her husband and she didn't even know it, all because she didn't know how to love him right. I was nice to her, almost to the point of excess. Even Scott told me I should tone it down a bit in case she got suspicious. But I couldn't help it. Their marriage was over and the sooner she realised it, the better. It wasn't fair for her to keep thinking they had a future together when Scott and I were in love. She was as polite and friendly to me as she'd always been, but every now and then I'd catch her looking at me shrewdly, and I'd quickly look away.

It was then that I would feel ashamed at the thought of what it would do to her when they split up and she found out about me. I tried to imagine what I'd say to her – if indeed we'd ever speak again – but there was nothing. I couldn't think about that reality now, I could only enjoy this moment while it lasted. It was exciting. I carried the secret around with me at school, pitying my classmates' ordinary lives. I stopped giving a shit about what anyone thought of me, and out of the blue, some of the boys started showing interest in me.

'Jason hasn't stopped staring at you,' Renee hissed to me in home class one day.

I glanced over at Jason Stott and he looked away before I could catch his eye. 'Whatever.'

'What do you mean, whatever?' Renee seemed outraged. 'He's one of the hottest guys at school!'

As I watched Jason, he looked up again and flashed me a half-grin that I might've found cute a few months back. 'He's all right, I guess, but he's not really my type.'

Renee stared down at her desk. 'I take it this means you're still doing it with Scott?'

I glanced at her. She'd stopped asking about him since that night at my house, and I'd stopped volunteering information. 'Do you really want to know?'

'Not really. Kind of.'

'Yeah, we're still doing it.' My stubborn streak reared up, urging me to make out that it was better than it really was. 'And it's mind-blowing … being with someone who knows what he's doing.'

She threw a bitter look at me. 'So, when's he going to leave his wife?'

I had no answer to this. I hadn't broached the subject again with Scott, but he'd told me he wanted to be with me. He'd told me he loved me. That was good enough for me. It was enough to hold onto, for now.

'Thought so,' she muttered, and I scowled at her.

NOW

The pharmacy was quiet when the girl came in. She couldn't have been more than sixteen, and Layla could tell she was nervous by the way her hands kept twisting, together and apart, together and apart. When she approached the counter, Layla gave her what she hoped was an encouraging smile. 'Can I help you?'

'I need …' The girl's eyes darted around the room, down at the counter, over Layla's shoulder. 'Can I get the morning-after pill without a prescription?' Her words weren't much more than a whisper, but they thumped Layla hard in the chest. She had to collect herself, to do her job and help this girl.

'Yes, there are two types of emergency contraception, and you don't need a prescription for one of them.'

'Oh good. Good.' The words rushed out of her.

An elderly woman approached the counter with her prescription held out in front of her, and the girl looked as if she might jump out of her skin. Her haunted eyes found Layla's at last, and Layla beckoned her down the other end of the counter. Christine's bright conversation with the older woman almost drowned out the girl's timid voice as she spoke again.

'I'll get that one, then, please.'

'Of course,' Layla said. 'Wait here, I'll get it for you.'

Layla escaped behind the wall of medication, her hands shaking as she found what she needed. She'd dispensed the morning-after pill hundreds of times before, but there was something about this girl that reminded her so much of herself once upon a time. It was like looking at a ghost. She gave herself a little shake and returned to her customer.

'What's your name?' she asked as she scanned the box and slipped it straight into a paper bag. The girl started nervously, and Layla rushed to reassure her. 'It's not required. I'd just like to call you by your name.'

Her chin quivered. She couldn't take her eyes off the package. 'Amber.'

'OK, Amber, when did the intercourse occur?'

'It was last night.' Her eyes widened. 'It's not too late, is it? My parents … I couldn't get here any earlier.'

'The pill is usually effective for at least three days after intercourse, so it should be fine.'

Amber's voice wobbled. 'Will it make me feel sick?'

'You may experience some nausea or cramping, as well as breast soreness, headaches or dizziness, but it shouldn't last long. I do recommend that you see your GP in a couple of weeks to make sure there's no pregnancy and to discuss regular contraception and screening for possible STIs.'

'I can't!' She looked appalled at the suggestion. 'My parents go to that doctor.'

Layla smiled gently. 'Your doctor is bound by confidentiality. They won't be able to reveal anything to your parents.'

'I know, but ...' Amber's eyes slid away from Layla's. 'I don't have a boyfriend. I don't need regular contraception. It was a ... one-off situation.'

There was something about the girl's body language that set off alarm bells in Layla. 'Did you consent to the sex?'

'I ... yes. Yes, I did, it just ... It was my first time. It wasn't what I was expecting, that's all.'

Layla didn't usually touch her customers – she didn't usually touch anyone outside of her family – but now she reached out and took Amber's hand. 'First experiences can be disappointing and confusing. It's OK to feel strange or sad about it, but if there was any question of coercion or force, you can get help. And you can always withdraw consent, no matter how far it's gone.'

Amber nodded, biting her lip. 'I know. I'm OK, really.'

Layla tried unsuccessfully to catch her gaze. 'Are you sure?'

'Yep.' Her tone was stronger now that she was so close to escaping. 'How much is it?'

Layla watched Amber's face as she rang up the bill and took her money. She'd done all she could to help, but she still felt a strange tug – something close to grief – as the girl left the store, head down, and she wasn't sure whether it was for Amber or for the teenager she'd once been.

*

Layla worked late and Cam had picked up the kids. He was at the stove making dinner when she got home, his back to her. He didn't turn around as she threw her handbag on the bench and greeted Louis and Ella. 'Good day?' he said absently.

It seemed like he was getting further away from her every day, and she didn't know what to do to bring him back. 'Actually, it wasn't great.'

Now he turned to look at her. 'What happened?'

Layla tried to smile, but her mouth tugged sideways. She told Cam about the teenager who'd come in, and the feeling she'd had that the sex wasn't consensual. 'I can't stop thinking about her,' she finished.

Cam turned off the stove and faced her. 'What did you say to her?'

'I told her she could get help if she needed it, but she brushed me off. I keep wondering if I should've pressed her further, encouraged her to go to the police.'

'You did all you could,' Cam said. 'It's not your job to be her counsellor.'

Indignation flared in Layla. 'It's not about doing my job, it's about being human! What's wrong with caring about what happened to someone?'

Cam's face began to harden again, but then tears sprang to Layla's eyes, and he moved towards her and put his hands on her waist. 'You're right. Sorry.'

Layla looked up at him, eyes wide. 'What if she was raped and all I did was pussyfoot around the issue?'

'Hey, it's OK.' Cam took her into his arms. 'She might've been telling the truth, and even if she wasn't, you can't drag it out of her.'

She hugged him around the middle, fighting the sobs that were rising in her chest. 'There was something about her that reminded me of myself when I was that age,' she said into his chest. 'I was too young to deal with that.'

Cam stepped back abruptly. 'Deal with what? What do you mean?'

Layla shook her head frantically. 'She. I meant she.'

But Cam's brows were still knitted together. He wasn't going to let it go this time. 'Layla, did something happen to you when you were a teenager?'

For a second – just a second – she entertained the idea of telling him everything. It'd be a relief to get it out in the open. But she couldn't tell him that part without telling him about the affair, and after what his mother had told her, she couldn't bear to think of his disappointment when he realised what she was really like.

'No! I'm just tired and feeling weird about that girl. Ignore me.'

'Is this something to do with the reunion thing? You've been acting strangely ever since I got that message.'

Layla withdrew from him and turned to face the bench. 'I'm not even going to the reunion. It's stupid. Glasswater Bay is the last place I want to go.' She willed him not to push her on it.

'Layla, please. Tell me what's wrong.'

She whirled around to face him. 'Can you get off my back? I said there's nothing wrong.'

He stepped away from her, shaking his head bitterly. 'I know there's something going on here. I don't understand why you won't tell me. I'm your *husband*.'

Layla was on the verge of lashing out at him when she noticed the children's stares. 'You're my husband, but you don't own me, Cam,' she said through clenched teeth. 'And I'm fine.'

He glanced once at the children, then turned away. 'No, you're not,' he muttered as he left the room.

'What's wrong, Mummy?' Louis was staring at her.

'Nothing, sweetie,' she said brightly, swallowing hard to push down the fear that kept climbing and climbing inside her.

THEN

Scott talked about taking me away for a weekend, and I became enthralled with the idea. Hiring a shack up the coast; walking hand in hand along the beach, watching the sun go down over the water, having all that time together to talk, to plan our future rather than just tearing each other's clothes off. Maybe I'd even cook for him, show him I was capable of satisfying him in more places than just the bedroom.

But after a while, he went quiet on the topic. I was disappointed, but I couldn't ask too much of him. He was already risking so much. For now, I was content with what we had, even if our encounters seemed to be getting shorter, more abrupt. He said Jodie was getting suspicious, so he needed to get straight home afterwards. But he wouldn't – couldn't – forgo our time together completely. I had too much power over him for that. It was intoxicating, seeing how I could transform him, the way his eyes darkened from the things I did with my body. Sometimes all I'd have to do is give him a certain kind of look from across the cafe and he'd be an animal when we were alone at the end of the night. Sometimes he was a little rough, but it was only because I turned him on so much. Later, I'd treasure the marks he left on me, the occasional bruises on my shoulders or grazes on my knees, as brands of his desire for me.

But I could never fully banish my paranoia: if Jodie really was getting suspicious, why was he racing home to reassure her instead of ripping off the bandaid and telling her it was over? Since we'd started sleeping together, he hadn't told me he loved me with quite the same regularity, and I worried he was already becoming bored with me. Was I too vanilla, not adventurous enough? Maybe if I gave him more, he'd see that I was deserving of him.

But no matter what I did, he became increasingly distant. One night in the kitchen, he seemed more distracted than usual. For once, he didn't get straight up from the swag and start pulling on his clothes, but lay beside me for a long time. He barely seemed to hear my words when I tried to make conversation. After a period of silence, I snuggled into him and rested my head on his chest, but he rolled away from me and sat up. Dismay welled inside me. 'Have I done something wrong?'

He gave a heavy sigh and got to his feet, then sat down in the chair against the wall, head in his hands. 'I don't know about this, Layla. I just don't know anymore.'

No. No. No. This couldn't be happening.

'What do you mean?'

He raised his head and gestured wildly. 'What do you think I mean? I'm sleeping with a fucking teenager! The guilt is killing me.'

I was suddenly aware of how immature I must look, curled up naked on the swag. My inadequate breasts; the burgeoning pimple on the side of my nose; my childish plait hanging over my shoulder. Of course I could never be enough for him. 'Are you saying you want to end it?'

He looked away. 'I don't know. Well, I know what I *should* do, but I don't have the guts for it.'

Desperation clawed at me. He hadn't specified exactly what he *should* do, but from the way he avoided my eyes, I had a feeling I knew the answer. I had to do something. I went to him and sat on his lap, my legs straddling his, and took his face in my hands.

'I love you, Scott,' I whispered. 'I can't let you go. I'll do anything.'

His arms tightened around me and I kissed him, watching his eyes as they sank closed. I moved his hands up to my breasts, and as he grew hard again beneath me, I lowered myself slowly onto him and moved forward so he was deep inside me. We'd never tried this position before, and it felt incredible. I had complete control over the intensity and the pace, and almost at once I felt a swelling inside me, a balloon of anticipation that expanded and expanded until I thought I would explode.

Then Scott began lifting me off him as if to change position, and the feeling started to dissipate.

'No!' I cried. 'Stay there. That feels so good.' I rocked harder and it came back, a fizzing warmth like there was a fountain bubbling inside me.

'Layla, stop! I'm going to come!'

But I couldn't stop, not when it felt like this. I bent my head to kiss him again, digging my fingernails in his back. There was no way I was going to interrupt this feeling, not when I had waited for it for so long. I straightened and arched my back, crying out as I came in a shower of glittering fireworks. My body shuddered and I slumped over him. 'Oh my god!' I gasped.

But he wasn't embracing me. His whole body was stiff and unyielding. 'Fucking hell, Layla.'

His words sliced apart my warm glow of satisfaction, and I sat back to look into his blazing eyes. 'What's wrong?'

'This is what's wrong, you stupid girl.' He lifted me off him and warm wetness trickled down my leg. I stared down at it, numb. 'I *told* you I was going to come, but you didn't listen. The last thing I need to deal with now is a fucking accidental pregnancy.'

The humiliation was thick, viscous. 'I'm sorry. But it felt so good. I couldn't stop.'

He threw me a dark look. 'You could try thinking about someone other than yourself.'

This stung. So far, everything we'd done had been geared towards his pleasure. Not to mention he'd practically said the same words to me after the first time we'd slept together. 'It wouldn't be a problem if we'd been using condoms,' I shot back.

'I'm a man, Layla, not some pimply teenager.'

I shrank beneath the sharpness of his words, imagining he was studying the pimple on my nose, thinking about how immature I was, and what a mistake he'd made getting involved with me.

'You'll have to get the morning-after pill tomorrow to make sure you don't get pregnant,' he said.

I gave him a horrified look. 'Where am I going to get it from? I can't go anywhere around here.' I'd done work experience at Glasswater Bay Pharmacy last year, and the resident pharmacist, Marjorie, had become a sort of mentor to me ever since. The idea of going to her with such a request was mortifying.

Scott gave a mocking laugh. 'You think no one in this town has ever gone to the chemist with something embarrassing? Have you ever heard Marjorie telling everyone in the pub about Pete's haemorrhoids or Mavis's bunions?'

My face went hot. 'Of course. You're right. I'll organise it.' But he still wasn't looking at me, and I needed him to look at me, to fill the void that kept getting bigger every day no matter how many times I told myself everything was going to be OK. 'Sorry, Scott. I didn't mean to cause any trouble.'

His eyes softened a little. 'You need to let me have control, Layla. It's too dangerous otherwise. You're so sexy that I can't help myself. Come here.'

He held out his arms and I moved into them with relief.

'It was so awesome to watch you come like that. You're an incredible woman, Layla.'

I buried my head in his chest. We were going to be OK. I squeezed him tight, tighter, as if I could absorb him into me so he could never leave.

*

Tilling Pharmacy was still closed when I pulled into the car park at 8.30 the next morning. I'd told Mum and Dad I needed to get to school early to finish off a group project, then I'd gone to the GP to get a prescription on my way to Tilling. I'd be late for school, but better that than waiting until afterwards.

After I'd left Scott last night, the reality of the situation had begun to press in on me. It was as if the theoretical embryo was already forming inside me, and the idea filled me with a creeping horror. Scott was right. It would be a disaster if I got pregnant.

Tilling was in the centre of Fleurieu Peninsula, halfway between Glasswater Bay and Victor Harbor, so I was unlikely to run into anyone I knew. There was a closed sign on the door of the pharmacy, but when I pressed my face up to the glass, I saw the staff moving around inside, setting up for the day. One of them, a middle-aged woman, kept glancing at me, but made no move to let me in, even though the store should've opened five minutes ago. Finally, she shuffled over, heaving an aluminium sign under one arm. She took her time unlocking the door.

'You're keen,' she said.

I held the door open for her so she could carry the sign out onto the pavement. 'I needed to get here before school.'

She eyed my school uniform. 'Couldn't go to the chemist in Glasswater Bay, then?' I didn't answer, and she followed me over to the dispensing counter. 'How can I help you?'

I held out the prescription to her and she was silent for a moment as she studied it.

'Ah.' She didn't move, as if waiting for me to give her an explanation. The longer the silence stretched out, the more pressure I felt to justify myself, but I remained stubbornly mute. 'Just a minute,' she said at last.

I waited, pretending to browse the shelves for several minutes before an elderly man in a white coat came out from behind the counter. 'You're the girl wanting the morning-after pill?' As if there were any other girls here. His voice dripped with disapproval.

'Yes, please.'

His pale eyes studied me. 'Do your parents know your situation?'

Anger simmered within me, but instead of sounding strong, my voice came out high-pitched and wavering. 'Can I have the pill, please?'

'I need you to answer a few questions for me first. Was this your first sexual experience?'

My face went hot. 'No.'

'How old are you?'

'Seventeen.' My voice became smaller with every answer.

'Hmm.' He tapped the box against his empty hand. 'How long have you been sexually active?'

I was so humiliated I couldn't meet his eyes. 'Couple of months.'

'And do you understand how to prevent a pregnancy?' His tone was cool, emotionless. No, not quite emotionless: judgemental. 'How many sexual partners have you had?'

'Please, can I just have the pill?' My voice was shaking so much now I could hardly get the words out. 'I need to get to school.'

He held the box out to me, but he didn't let go when my hand closed around it. 'Take it from me: none of these boys will think much of you once you've done the rounds. Try to keep yourself nice while you still can, hmm?'

I yanked the box out of his hand and returned to the counter. Tears of fury burned behind my eyes as I threw a note at the woman. She watched me, expressionless, as she took my money and handed me the change.

It was raining when I marched out of the store; the kind of stinging, sideways rain that felt personal. I ran to my car, the sobs already tearing from my body. I opened the box and popped the pill out of the blister pack. Fuck that guy. Fuck them both, with their judgement and their holier-than-thou opinions, treating me like a slut because I'd made one mistake. Blaming me, even though two of us had been involved. For the first time, I hated my body for what it could do, for putting me in this position. And I didn't need any more reasons to hate it.

I threw the pill into my mouth and tried to swallow it, but it stuck in my tear-clogged throat, so I got my drink bottle out of my bag and gulped down some water until it dislodged.

As I drove back towards Glasswater Bay, my righteous rage settled into something smaller, a slippery eel of shame that curled into a ball in my stomach and became part of me.

NOW

Layla could feel words dying in her throat when she woke. Her face was wet with tears. She tried to slow her breathing so she didn't wake up Cam, but it was too late. He shuffled close to her, hand on her shoulder. 'You were having a nightmare.'

It was such a comfort to be in contact with him again that she turned and put her arms around him. 'Sorry I woke you up.'

'It sounded bad. What was it about?'

'I can't remember now,' she lied.

It'd been a long time since she'd had that dream. Years, in fact. It had long ago lost its vividness; the visceral horror of what she'd been responsible for thinning out over the years until it was a stretched and pale version of the original. But now the full force of it hit her and it was as if she were still in the moment when she'd realised the chain of events she'd unleashed.

'You sounded really freaked out,' Cam said. 'You were saying something about losing control, and that you didn't mean to start it. Start what?'

Layla felt cornered. She released Cam and sat up, swinging

her legs over the side of the bed so she was facing away from him. 'I told you, I don't remember the dream.'

'If you don't remember, why are you getting so upset?' Her husband's hand landed in the middle of her back, tentative, unsure.

'I'm not upset!' She stood up and his hand fell away. She went to the ensuite and stared at her reflection in the mirror. Her freckles stood out on her naked, pale face, creased from sleep, her cheeks streaked with tears. Her eyes were red-rimmed. Her jawline looked spongy and loose. *Disgusting.* She splashed water on her face. She had to get this under control.

Cam was sitting up in bed when she returned, his brow furrowed. The bedside lamp was on, a small yellow glow in the darkness. The air felt too thin as Layla slid under the quilt and turned away from him. She knew there was a confrontation coming, but she suspended herself in the long silence, wondering how she was going to divert the conversation this time. Finally, he spoke. 'Is there something you want to tell me?'

She squeezed her eyes shut, unable to bear facing him. 'No, why?'

'Can you look at me? Please?'

Layla's head swam. She could start another argument, storm away, sleep on the couch, but how much longer could they hold on if she refused to speak to him? She rolled over to face him. Waited.

'I didn't want to force the issue. I guess part of me didn't want to know.' His face was naked, vulnerable. 'But now I need you to tell me.'

Dread clamped down on Layla's throat. 'Tell you what?'

His jaw worked, back and forth, back and forth, like he was chewing on his words, trying to decide whether he was going to spit them out or swallow them back down. 'Are you cheating on me?'

'What? No!' she cried with a mixture of shock and relief that she could answer this truthfully. 'Why would you think that?'

'I got another message from that Jodie Telford.' His chin quivered. 'She said to ask you about her husband.'

Layla couldn't speak, could only stare at her own husband, wishing this moment away so she'd never have to explain. He stared back at her, his eyes wretched.

'You hardly even look at me anymore,' he said. 'And as soon as I mentioned the husband you looked guilty. What am I supposed to think?'

'It's not that, you have to believe me,' she pleaded. 'I would never cheat on you. Never.'

'Then what?' He looked desperate. 'Why won't you tell me?'

Layla bit her lip and shook her head. 'I can't. I just can't.'

'Why do you keep shutting me out?' He stood up from the bed, his voice growing louder with each word.

Fresh tears squeezed from her eyes. 'Because I don't want you to hate me.'

He crossed his arms over his chest. 'What could be so bad that you can't share it with me?'

Layla pulled herself to a sitting position. This was it. She had to tell him, or everything in her life was going to fracture and she'd be left with nothing. She hugged her knees to her chest for a long time. When she finally spoke, her voice came out croaky and dry, as if she hadn't used it in days. 'Jodie's not involved in the reunion. That was just a coincidence.'

'So who is she?' His voice was softer now. Hopeful.

'When I was seventeen, I worked at a cafe that her husband owned.' She stopped, took a breath. 'We got involved.'

His gaze flickered just a little. 'You had an affair with him?'

She closed her eyes. 'I was young and stupid, and I thought he loved me. I thought he was going to leave her. I was such a fucking idiot that I actually believed a twenty-eight-year-old man was going to leave his family for a teenager.'

She felt the bed dip down with his weight, and his hand came to rest on her shoulder. 'You were just a kid.'

She looked up at him. 'But I wasn't blameless. I knew what I was doing, who I was hurting. He had little kids, Cam. But I did it anyway.'

'Why didn't you ever tell me?'

'Because I'm so ashamed. And because I know how you feel about cheating … the way you speak about that woman your father had the affair with. Your mum told me what you did to her car. You obviously hated her for what she did.'

He looked sheepish. 'I was angry, and she was the convenient person to blame. Otherwise, I'd have to face up to the fact that my dad was an arsehole.'

Layla dropped her gaze to the quilt. 'I thought you'd hate me.'

'I could never hate you.' He put his arm around her shoulders and she fell against him in relief. 'He was eleven years older than you, and he was your *boss*, for Christ's sake. He was in the wrong on so many levels. And I know you'd never hurt anyone intentionally.'

Layla was silent. Part of her wanted him to blame her, to punish her, because of course she *had* hurt someone. It may not have been intentional, but her actions had had consequences she'd never atoned for.

After a minute, Cam sat back from her. 'How did it end?'

Now she'd begun her confession, it was so tempting to let go and tell him the rest. But if he knew what she'd really done, he might not be so accepting. 'Not well. The relationship became toxic and I had to leave Glasswater to end it.'

He frowned. 'But your whole family moved to Adelaide, didn't they?'

She shouldn't have said that. Anxiety rose again. 'Yeah, Dad got a job in the city around the same time.'

He looked away, scratched his neck, looked back again. 'So did you leave because of his job or because of the affair?' There was curiosity in his eyes, and perhaps a little suspicion too.

Layla had the urge to curl up on the bed, clamp her hands over her ears, refuse to answer any more questions. No matter what she said, it only led to more half-truths, and she was so tired of maintaining the ever-changing story. She owed Cam the truth, and she realised now that she owed Jodie an hour of her time. Jodie was the only one who was truly blameless in this whole situation, and she'd been the one to shoulder most of the consequences. And if she really *had* seen what Layla had done, why hadn't she come forward years ago? She could've gone to the police and told them what she'd seen. There were no other witnesses as far as she knew.

'I think I'm going to go and see her,' she said.

'Who? This Jodie woman? Why?' If Cam noticed she'd ignored his previous question, he didn't push it.

'That's why she contacted me. She wants to have it out with me, I guess. And maybe I deserve to face up to what I did. Apologise, then come home so we can get on with the rest of our lives.'

'But *you* didn't cheat on her, her husband did.' He looked annoyed. 'And it's been twenty years! Who knows how many other affairs he's had since then?'

Layla knew the answer to that question. She avoided his eyes. 'But it's been eating away at me ever since she contacted me. And I've been taking it out on you and the kids. I want to put this behind me.'

Cam was silent for a moment, but then he nodded. 'If it's something you feel like you need to do, you should do it. When are you going to go?'

The image of the formal photo flitted into her mind again. Maybe it wasn't too late. Maybe it was possible to make amends for more than one mistake.

'I think I might go to the reunion after all.'

THEN

'Look at this one!' Shona spluttered, pushing the latest edition of *Dolly* across the table to Renee and me. It was raining, so we'd holed up in the library for lunchbreak and were ironically scouring the Dolly Doctor pages for funny stories. I'd never admit it out loud, but I had found considerable comfort reading the answers to those anonymous questions over the years.

Renee read aloud: '"My boyfriend and I want to have sex, but he doesn't want to use a condom. He says he's too big and they make him itchy. Is there anything else we could use? I can't go on the pill, my mum would kill me if she found out. *Very Horny, Perth*." Ha!'

'Bet she roots him anyway and gets pregnant,' Shona said. 'How stupid would you have to be to fall for the old "condoms don't fit me" line?'

My face grew hot as I tried to skim the response without being too obvious. I was one of those stupid people, but what was I supposed to do? I couldn't force him to wear a condom, and I wasn't on the pill, so I was hardly making an effort to be responsible either.

Then Renee's and Shona's attention shifted to a point over my shoulder, and I turned around to see Jason approaching our table. He shared his disarming smile with us as he sat down in the chair across from mine. 'How's it goin', girls?' He leant back in his chair and his eyes turned to me. 'Hey, Layla.'

'Hey yourself.'

'I was just wondering …' His brazen composure slipped a little and his eyes dropped to the table. 'Do you want to go to the formal with me?'

A curious detachment crept over me. Most of the girls in my year would've jumped at the chance to go to the formal with Jason, and a few months ago I would've been all aflutter with nerves at the very idea of his asking me. But now, his good looks and smooth attitude had zero effect on me. 'I'm seeing someone, actually. But thanks for asking.' And then I reached out and touched him lightly on the arm.

'Yeah, no worries.' He stood up, his too-cool-for-school mask back in place. 'See you girls around.'

We watched him walk away, then Renee gave me a solid thump on the arm. 'Are you *insane*?'

'Ow! I was just telling the truth. I *am* seeing someone.'

She gave an exasperated sigh. 'But Scott's obviously not going to take you to the formal now, is he?'

I stared down at the magazine in front of me. Somehow I hadn't even thought about that until now, but she was right, of course. For the first time, I felt a pang of regret at the things I would miss out on because of my relationship with Scott. Mostly, the benefits of being with an older man outweighed the negatives: his maturity, experience, the means to provide for us when he left his wife. But I wanted the normal high school experiences too. I wanted to get dressed up for the formal with my friends; kiss someone on the dance floor;

get drunk at the afterparty. And I wanted to share all of that with Scott.

'If he leaves his wife soon, maybe he will.'

I imagined how hot he'd look in a tux, how he'd probably be able to afford a limo to take us all to the venue, how he'd put his arms around me on the dance floor and hold me close, how he'd take me home afterwards and tell me he loved me.

Renee snorted. 'You're deluded.'

*

'When do you think we could have that weekend away?' I asked Scott that afternoon when I got to work. After what Renee had said earlier, I was determined to prove her wrong, to show her that our relationship was advancing.

He glanced at me with a distracted air. 'I dunno. I'd have to close the cafe on the Saturday. Could be hard to manage when I don't have a good excuse.'

I thought about it. 'Could you say you need to go to the city to get new crockery or something? I could tell my parents I'm spending the weekend at Renee's.'

He laughed. 'But I don't need new crockery. And even if I did, that'd be a half-day trip.'

'We can come up with something else.'

'It's not a good time now, Layla. Maybe down the track I'll be able to swing it.'

My doubt quickly translated into anger, and I threw down the tea towel I'd been using to dry the glasses. 'If you don't want to do it, just say so.'

I went through the kitchen and out to the lunch room, trying to hold back tears at my childish outburst. Picking a fight with Scott had been a stupid move. It wasn't his fault we were in this position, but it didn't make the disappointment any easier to bear. I'd been living on the promise of this weekend away for weeks, and now it seemed like it might never happen. I was stuck in limbo – I could neither share my high school experiences with him, nor do the adult stuff. But if I nagged him too much, he might not want me anymore.

The door swung open and Scott strode in. 'I didn't mean to be so abrupt. It's just hard to find an opportunity to get away for a whole night. We'll do it one day, I promise.'

My heart softened and I let him take me into his arms. 'I don't want to put any extra pressure on you, but I'm so tired of hiding away. I want you all to myself. I want to do normal couple stuff.'

He looked down at me, a gentle smile on his face. 'How about I take you to Victor on Sunday? We could go out for lunch together, where no one knows us.'

'Really? I'd love that.'

'Really.' He bent his head and kissed me briefly, and I was so grateful for this one small thing that I put my arms around his neck and pulled his head down to mine again.

'Jesus *Christ*,' came a voice from behind me, and we flew apart. Yumi stood, one hand on the doorframe, shock written across her face.

'Fuck,' Scott said.

'Sorry to interrupt. Your *wife* is here to see you.' She whirled around and stalked off.

'Fuck,' Scott said again.

He followed Yumi out without a backward glance, leaving me standing alone in the kitchen, my heart hammering. I waited in the lunch room for ages before returning to the cafe floor. There were no customers. Jodie had gone. Scott was cleaning tables; Yumi stood behind the counter.

'How long?' she said in a low voice when I came to stand beside her. I didn't answer her, and she turned to face me. 'How could you be so stupid?'

'It just … happened,' I said shakily. 'We're in love.'

She scoffed. 'Oh my god, you're such a child, Layla. I thought you were smarter than that.'

Rage bubbled inside me. 'Jealous, are you? I know you've always wanted him for yourself.'

'Oh, don't be ridiculous. Yeah, I thought he was good looking, but I'd never cross that line.'

I clenched my jaw. I wanted to hurt her for making everything feel wrong again right after I'd been so happy. 'Only because he'd never be interested in someone like you.'

Her eyes narrowed. 'Someone Asian, you mean? Racist much?'

'No, I mean a bitch,' I shot back.

'Wow.' Her mouth twisted into a sneer. 'Nice, Layla. What a charming stepmother you'll make to those little kids.'

'You don't have to be so judgemental,' I snapped. 'It's none of your business.'

'You're right, it's not.' She yanked off her apron, marched over to Scott and threw it at him. 'I quit.'

NOW

It was already over thirty degrees when Layla threw her bag on the passenger seat of the car and knelt in the driveway to hug the kids. It would be the first night she'd spent away from them, and Louis's face was already streaked with tears. Ella was cheerfully oblivious, while Cam hung back, his face inscrutable. Layla knew he didn't agree with her going to see Jodie, but while things were still tense between them, they'd been doing their best to reconnect over the last week.

Louis wrapped his arms around Layla's neck. 'Do you have to go?'

'It's only one night,' she said, kissing his forehead. 'And I've got a really important job for you while I'm gone.'

His big blue eyes widened. 'What?'

'Since you're going to be a big kindy boy in a couple of weeks, I'd like you to help Daddy look after Ella. Do you think you could do that?'

His face split into his brilliant smile that always sent a bolt of sunshine straight into Layla's heart. 'Yeah!' He turned to his sister. 'I'm the boss of you all weekend, Ella.'

'No you *not*!' Ella retorted.

'I am so!' he bellowed. 'You have to do whatever I tell you!'

Ella raised her arm to give Louis a smart slap on the top of his head just as Cam scooped her up in his arms. He and Layla shared a smile.

'Sorry,' Layla said, getting to her feet. 'I thought it might work.'

He shrugged. 'That's the problem with having strong-willed children with minds of their own.'

'If only they didn't have them in our general vicinity. Or each other's.'

He put Ella down and stepped forward to put his arms around her. 'I'll miss you.'

She hugged him around the middle. 'Me too.'

'Have fun at the reunion tonight.'

She made a face. 'Unlikely. But I'll try.'

He looked over her shoulder for a moment. 'Are you sure you still want to do this?'

'I'm sure.' Layla hugged him tighter. 'It's just a chat. I owe her that much.'

He snorted. 'You don't owe her anything after the way she's been threatening you. *He's* the one she should be punishing.'

Layla couldn't tell him that Scott had already received more than his fair share of punishment, so she turned away and opened the car door. 'I'll call you tomorrow.'

Cam put his hand on her arm. 'Wait, he's not going to be there, is he?' There was a stretched, vulnerable look on his face.

'Oh. I don't know.' She hadn't even considered the possibility. The thought was horrifying.

'But what if he tries to …' He didn't complete the thought. His eyes were wild as he fought with his own doubts and insecurities.

'You can trust me, Cam.' She took his hand and clasped it tightly. 'I'm there to see Jodie. I don't even know if he's still … on the scene.'

'OK.' He smiled at her, but he still looked worried. Layla knew he wouldn't stop worrying until she was safely back at home. Not that she could blame him, after she'd lied to him for all these years.

He bent to pick up Ella again, Louis standing at his feet, and Layla turned and got into the car.

'Say goodbye to Mummy,' Cam said, and the kids chorused an enthusiastic farewell.

'I love you,' she said out of the window to all three of them, but it was Cam's eyes that she sought out.

'We love you too,' he said, but she couldn't tell whether he was speaking for the kids or for himself.

She gave them a final wave as she backed out of the driveway. Though she was dreading her return to Glasswater Bay for a variety of reasons, there was also a sense of relief at the opportunity to escape for a while. Over the last few weeks, she'd assumed it was her own stress that had driven this wedge between Cam and her, but now she wondered whether it went deeper than that. Maybe they'd already been doomed and this was all part of the natural unravelling of their relationship.

As sprawling suburbia gave way to rolling hills covered in brown stubble, Layla's thoughts turned to her school friends. Shona would be fine, she was sure. While she'd mostly sided with Renee after the whole debacle, she'd never seemed to hold any lingering animosity for Layla. But without Renee to balance out their triangle, they'd drifted apart once they'd all started uni. Then Shona had gone off to London and it'd been too easy to lose contact altogether.

Renee would be another story. She'd seemed pleased to hear that Layla had changed her mind, and had immediately renewed her invitation to stay with her, but Layla knew it wouldn't be easy. She was going to have to face this head-on. Doing that in the same twenty-four hours they'd be going to their high school reunion, and staying at Renee's house – with her husband – would inevitably bring back all the painful memories. But amid the fear and dread this weekend represented, there was also a sliver of hope. Maybe it wasn't too late to revive their friendship.

THEN

I pulled my jacket tighter around me, shivering, as I waited in the rotunda in the park for Scott to pick me up. Sideways rain drilled in through the painted white beams, becoming rivulets on the wooden floorboards and joining the muddy puddle that was accumulating in the centre. I stepped further under cover to avoid getting wet. I'd told Mum and Dad I was going to see a movie with Renee and Shona in Victor, so Scott and I would have the whole afternoon together in glorious anonymity.

A navy-blue car pulled up at the edge of the park, glistening wet in the driving rain. I ran down the steps of the rotunda and across the sodden, yellowing grass. Scott seemed on edge when I swung into the car.

He pulled away quickly when I tried to kiss him. 'Careful. Don't want anyone to see us together.'

I settled in the passenger seat and clicked my seatbelt in place. 'I've been looking forward to this all weekend.'

He threw a nervous look out the window. 'Just be ready to duck your head in case we drive past anyone we know.'

It wasn't until we'd reached the outskirts of town and turned onto Range Road that he reached out and rested a hand on my thigh. I smiled at him. 'This is nice. Thanks for doing this for me.'

Within minutes, his fingers had crept up my thigh and he was stroking me through my jeans. I reached across to do the same for him, but he dashed my hand away. 'Jesus, Layla, the last thing I need is to have a crash with a seventeen-year-old in the car and a raging hard-on.'

'Looks like you've got one already,' I said with a laugh.

He glanced at me. 'I really want to fuck you right now.'

His language had become coarser lately, more abrasive, but maybe that was just what happened as a couple's sex life evolved. I'd read an article in *Dolly* that gave a tutorial of sorts on talking dirty, but the idea of actually doing it seemed ridiculous.

I'd been looking forward to having lunch together, doing things that normal couples did rather than only ever having sex, but when he turned off the highway into a rest stop, I didn't complain. He was taking this risk to be with me; it was the least I could do.

The rain had stopped by now, and he parked the car beside a wet picnic table. There were no other cars around. Scott got out and I followed suit. Wet twigs snapped under our feet as he led me behind the toilet block. Magpies warbled in the branches overhead. A gross smell emanated from the toilets and the rough bricks of the wall grazed my hands.

There was the crunch of tyres on gravel as we returned to Scott's car, and I kept my head down to avoid the curious stares I imagined were coming from the other car.

'Do you still want to go to Victor?' Scott said as we put our seatbelts back on.

I looked up at him. 'Of course I do. That was the whole point, that we'd go out for lunch together.'

'OK.' He smiled. 'Sure. Might have to be just coffee though. I have to be back by two.'

'Oh. OK.' I couldn't keep the disappointment from my voice.

*

We were silent for the rest of the drive across the peninsula, but when we reached Victor Harbor and got out of the car, Scott took my hand with a smile, and I couldn't help smiling back. Maybe this is what it would be like in Glasswater Bay one day, when we could be together for real.

Scott gestured to a cafe on the main street, and I followed him in. He ordered us both cappuccinos and we took a table near the back of the room. He held my hand under the table, and we chatted for a while: he told me about his plans to buy the vacant shop beside the cafe and knock down the internal wall so he could expand the business; I told him about applying to study pharmacy at uni, and how I was worried my grades weren't going to be good enough.

'So you'll be leaving Glasswater next year, then,' he said, his expression inscrutable. It was impossible to tell whether he was pleased or disappointed at the prospect.

'I could still live here and commute a few days a week, like Yumi does,' I said, but that must have reminded him of the scene in the cafe the other day, and he didn't respond. 'I can't believe school is almost over already,' I ventured after a while. 'It seemed like it was going to last forever.'

'Mmm.' Scott drained his coffee. 'Well, should we get back?'

'Scott.' I held my empty cup in both hands. 'My school formal is coming up in a month. I was wondering … do you want to go with me?'

He burst out laughing, then did a double take. 'Oh my god, you're actually serious, aren't you?'

My face went hot. 'I know it's lame, but—'

'I'm twenty-eight years old, Layla. I'm married. I'm not going to your fucking formal.' He shook his head, still laughing in disbelief.

Shame suffused me, hot and cloying. 'Of course, yeah. I guess I just thought … if you were going to leave Jodie anyway, maybe …'

His expression sobered. 'The time isn't right, Layla. And even if I did leave her now, do you really think it'd be a good look to take my seventeen-year-old mistress to her high school formal?'

I shook my head, the hurt and disappointment burrowing their way deeper and deeper inside me. I was such a child sometimes. No wonder he hadn't left his wife yet. 'No, you're right. It was a stupid idea.'

He took my hand again. 'It's not stupid. I understand why you want to go, but there's a far bigger world outside of high school. When you get out of that place you'll realise how meaningless all that stuff really is.'

'Yeah, I know.'

'You're so much more mature than your school friends, Layla. You really get it.'

His approval lit a tiny spark of pride within me, enough to keep my hope alive. Just enough.

Scott looked at his watch. 'We'd better go.'

We didn't hold hands as we walked back to his car. We didn't speak. Today was supposed to signify an advance in our relationship, but it felt like things had gone backwards. Instead, we'd had sex behind a toilet block (no, he'd *fucked* me), a rushed coffee and then he'd laughed at me for wanting what normal teenagers in normal relationships had. And now, barely an hour later, we were already on the road back to Glasswater Bay, where we'd have to go into hiding again, and I had no indication of when that status was likely to change. For the first time, I wished I'd never let myself fall for him, that I was still the girl I'd been a few months ago, awkward and unsure but without this constant, unrelenting doubt.

'You're not going to leave her, are you?' I asked quietly.

His eyes flicked to me, then back to the road. Just when I thought he was going to ignore my question, he put the indicator on and pulled over into a gravel car park that bordered a reserve on the outskirts of Tilling. He killed the engine. 'Walk with me for a minute?'

It wasn't raining, but a freezing wind whipped in from the coast, swirling my hair around my head as I got out of the car. The wet grass immediately soaked the hem of my jeans, water seeping into my boots, as Scott led me out into the reserve. We wandered around the border for a while before he came to a stop under a tree and took me in his arms.

'Layla, I want to marry you,' he said.

His glittering words cascaded over me. My heart soared with love, almost painful in its intensity. How could I have doubted him? How could I have wished this feeling away, even for a second?

'But you're not ready for that yet,' he went on. 'I think you know that.'

I gave him a tremulous smile. 'Yeah. You're right.'

Of course he was right! I was seventeen, still at school. Getting married now would be ridiculous. But all my childhood fantasies of fairytale weddings were already beginning to play in my head like music. He held my heart on a thread, waiting for the right time to draw me to him and bind us together forever. All I had to do was trust him.

'There's nothing left of my marriage,' he said. 'Jodie and I haven't had sex since you and I started sleeping together. It's over, and she knows it as well as I do, but it takes time to unpick a life, Layla. You have to understand that it's not as easy as just walking out on her and starting up with you. There are the kids to consider, and you and I would have to wait for a while – maybe a long time – before we could be out in the open. You need to know all of this, and you need to decide whether you're willing to wait however long it takes for us to be together.'

I bit my lip. His words made sense, and yet the idea of waiting still longer for him deflated my dreams.

He smiled gently. 'I understand if you can't deal with it. You're young, and you want to live your own life. I get that.'

My heart squeezed. He was trying to let me go, to release me from the complications of hiding our love. But I didn't want to be released. I wanted to go deeper and deeper with him, until there was nothing in the world that could pull us apart.

'I'm yours,' I said. 'I can deal with anything if it means we can be together.'

His eyes shone. 'I knew you'd understand. You're not like other girls, Layla. You see the big picture. That's why I love you.'

He kissed me and I closed my eyes, allowing him to sweep me away.

'Where's Jodie?' barked a woman's voice.

Startled, we leapt apart to see a middle-aged woman with curly hair standing a few metres away. She held the lead of a Jack Russell Terrier, who was jumping up and down and throwing his weight into his collar. I didn't recognise the woman, but from the way she was glaring at Scott, it seemed that she knew who he was.

'Who's Jodie?' Scott said, and there was something about his deadpan voice and expressionless face that sent a chill through me.

The woman turned away, the dog leaping around and huffing hoarsely. 'Disgusting!' she muttered as she stalked away.

'Let's go,' Scott said.

A gust of wind buffeted into us as we walked back to the car, but it wasn't enough to dispel the gloom that had descended.

'Who was that?' I asked when we were back on the road.

'An old friend of Jodie's mother.' His voice was curt. 'I've only met her once, at our wedding.'

'Do you think she'll tell her?'

His hands tightened on the steering wheel. 'How the hell should I know? I knew it was a mistake to go out in public.'

'Sorry,' I said in a small voice.

He was silent. This whole thing was my fault. If I hadn't pushed him to go out in the first place, this never would've happened. Somehow, I always managed to ruin everything.

It had started to rain again by the time we got back to Glasswater Bay, but Scott pulled over on the opposite side of the park to where I'd left my car.

'Thanks for taking me out today,' I said. 'Sorry it didn't end too well.'

He gave me a thin smile. 'You'd better go before anyone else sees us.'

I undid my seatbelt and opened the door a crack. Rain spattered the side of my face. 'I love you, Scott.'

He looked over his shoulder at the road behind us. 'I'll see you at work.'

I paused for a second longer, then got out. He drove off as soon as the door clicked shut again, sending a small wave of water over the kerb and onto my already sodden boots. Melancholy rose within me.

I walked slowly over to the rotunda, the rain drenching my hair until it hung in dripping snakes down the back of my neck. I wasn't expected at home for another hour, but I couldn't bear the thought of calling around to one of my friends' places to kill time. The way they'd look at me. The things they'd say when I told them what had happened.

I plodded up the steps into the rotunda and sat down on the bench that ran around the perimeter. The afternoon had taken me from happiness to hurt to ecstasy and to disappointment. I thought about the woman with the dog and cringed. Sometimes our love felt so perfect that it was easy to forget that there were other people involved. But now, for the first time, I imagined all the ugly words that would be hurled at me once this all got out.

Home wrecker. Slut. Whore.

Scott loved me. He wanted to marry me. That made it all worth it. Didn't it?

But no matter what magical things he said to me, nothing ever seemed to lift me up for long before my own misgivings dragged me down again. He hadn't slept with Jodie since we'd started sleeping together, but what about the month before that when we'd been doing all sorts of other things – had he still been having sex with her all that time? The idea of him touching her the way he touched me made my heart shrivel. If he really loved me, how could he carry on with her at the same time?

All the contradictory things he'd told me ran together in a loop around my mind.

I want to marry you, Layla. Don't get married young, Layla. It'll ruin your life. I love you, Layla. Love is a lie. It tells us stories that aren't true. You're so much more mature than your school friends, Layla. You're a bloody teenager.

My tears mingled with the rainwater on my face and dripped into my lap. I wished I was the little girl I'd once been, the one who still believed in true love, in happily ever afters. There'd been so many opportunities to get out of this before it had gone too far. But I loved him now. There was no going back.

NOW

Layla's optimism began to dissipate the closer she got to Glasswater Bay. The occasional glimpse of the ultramarine sea as she crested each rise along Main South Road was a sight that would lift anyone else's heart but only settled a greater weight on hers. A hundred times she fought the impulse to pull over, to turn the car around and drive home. Her limbs felt heavier and heavier as she slowed to turn right onto Bay Road, as if she were driving to her doom. The faded sign on the side of the road had been replaced with a new one since she'd left: a vivid coastal scene that looked like it'd been photographed from The Knob proclaimed: *Welcome to Glasswater Bay. Winner of Australia's Tidiest Town 2002 and 2004.*

Her stomach clenched as she passed the park. The rotunda still stood in the centre; it looked like it'd had a paint job or two over the years, but the structure remained the same. There were a few more picnic tables dotted around the park, and a fenced-off playground in bright plastic colours had sprung up near the main road. Before she realised what she was doing, she'd pulled over and got out of the car. A warm breeze sifted through her hair, smelling faintly of saltwater and seaweed, and the singed grass crunched under her feet as she crossed the park towards the rotunda.

A harried-looking young woman tried to herd her two small children out of the playground, but one of them threw herself down on the ground and started kicking and screaming. Layla masked a smile. She always found it comforting when other people's children misbehaved.

She continued over to the rotunda and up the steps. The bench still ran around the perimeter, but it was painted forest green now. Layla sat down in the same spot she had twenty years ago after the drive to Victor Harbor with Scott. How dramatic she'd been then; how big and hyper-real everything had seemed. Her life could have been so different if she'd ended things with him that day, instead of sitting here crying over the mixed messages he'd fed her and blaming herself for all that had happened.

But it had continued, and she was powerless to shut down the memories, especially now that she was back here where it had all begun. She'd arranged to go to Jodie's house tomorrow after the school reunion, and there was still the same creeping dread. But there was a sort of inevitability to it too. Twenty-four hours and it would all be over, and she could go home to her family and her life.

Before that though, she had to face Renee again. There would be no escaping the past with her, especially considering her husband would be in the same house.

She went back to her car. The address Renee had given her was burnt into her memory; she didn't need to look it up.

As she entered the main township, everything felt so familiar and yet so strange. There was Bob Keen's house on the corner. She wondered if he was still alive; if Keen's

Deli was still there. The blueprint of the streets still lived inside her brain, and she turned down Collins Street, hung a right at Lookout Drive then turned left down Angel Street. Number fifty-six. A modest, orange brick house, built in the seventies, with an immaculate green lawn and hydrangeas planted in tyres in front of the verandah. She recognised the house, had a vague memory of having been inside it as a young child, but she couldn't remember who had owned it.

The weight of the years pressed down on her shoulders as she parked the car at the kerb. It was still morning; the sun hadn't quite reached its peak in the sky, but it was already hot. She'd always hated summer in Glasswater Bay – all there was to do was lie on the beach or surf, and she'd never been a beach babe. Even a few streets back from the beach, the heat was as sticky and stifling as it was anywhere else. No trees lined the streets to offset the baking heat that radiated from the bitumen roads. There was no relief for a girl who would rather have been reading than cavorting in the waves.

She'd told Renee she'd be here at midday, but it was too hot to sit in the car and wait, so she got out and crossed the lawn to the front door. She could hardly breathe. Part of her wanted to turn around and run, but the other part was filled with a girlish yearning for the days of their innocence, before she had ruined everything.

The doorbell sang through the interior of the house, and footsteps approached from within. The door swung open. 'You're early! Hi.'

Her old friend's figure was still slight and graceful, but there were fine lines around her mouth and a few stray grey hairs were threaded through her red hair. She wore a loose white linen shirt and jeans. No make-up, but she carried the air of a woman who was comfortable in her own body. Layla felt suddenly self-conscious, with her full face of make-up and her smart clothes. She had no idea if her own hair was turning grey because she had a standing monthly appointment to have her roots touched up, a shade lighter than her natural colour. She didn't wear make-up to make herself feel good; she was a slave to it.

'Sorry, do you want me to come back?'

'No, don't be silly! Come in.' Renee stepped forward and they hugged awkwardly.

She still smelt the same. Layla hadn't expected that. Tears threatened behind her eyes.

Renee noticed Layla peering past her. 'He's not here. He's taken the boys surfing at Tor Beach. They'll be back later this arvo.'

The relief was instant but temporary. Putting off the inevitable confrontation only increased her nerves. Layla followed Renee into the living room and set her bag down on the floor beside one of the couches. She studied the photos that hung on the wall: Renee and her husband, their kids playing on the beach, family photos that had obviously been taken by a professional. 'I can't believe your kids are so big,' she said. 'Mine are only two and four.'

'Got any pics you can show me?'

This Layla could do. She got her phone out of her bag and flicked through her album to show Renee photos of Louis and Ella.

'They're so cute. They look like you.'

Layla raised her eyebrows. 'Poor things!'

Renee gave her a curious look. 'They're gorgeous, Layla. I miss that age when they're still all soft and squishy.'

Layla gave a strained smile at this oft-repeated sentiment. 'People keep telling me that, but it's not all it's cracked up to be. Some days I feel like I'm going insane.'

'Oh yeah, toddlers are a fucking shit show, no doubt about it.'

Layla burst out laughing, and the tension dissipated a little. This was the Renee she remembered. 'You're not wrong.'

'And I had two at once!' Renee looked wistful. 'But believe me, blink now and tomorrow they'll be starting high school, like my boys are about to. Do you want a coffee? Tea?'

'Tea would be great, thanks.'

The kitchen looked like it had recently been renovated. Layla pulled out one of the stools at the long charcoal bench and sat down. 'How's work? You're in Victor, right?'

'Actually, I'm about to open my own practice here in Glasswater Bay. Fuck knows there are enough clinically depressed people in this town.' She laughed self-consciously.

'Congratulations!' Layla said. Everyone had been surprised when Renee had changed her plans to study law and applied for psychology instead, but as soon as she'd made the decision, it had seemed right. 'I hope it goes well.'

Renee eyed Layla over the tea bag she was dunking in a mug. 'So what made you change your mind about the reunion?'

Layla's insides shrivelled. 'I guess I got sick of running. I feel like I haven't stopped since I left.' She looked down. 'I also wanted to make things right. Between us.'

Renee was silent. Layla wished she could take back what she'd said. She hadn't meant to be so honest; not this early anyway. It made her feel vulnerable, and she hated feeling vulnerable.

'I also want to see if Katrina's let herself go,' she added.

Renee laughed. 'She hasn't. Sarah Bennett is still in touch with her and apparently she still looks bangin'. But she's twice divorced and miserable, if that helps?'

'It doesn't really. I don't wish unhappiness on any of them. We're all different people from who we were then.'

Now it was Renee's turn to look away. She got the milk out of the fridge and added a splash to the tea, then pushed the mug across the bench to Layla. 'Yeah, about that.' Her eyes drifted to a photo of her husband and her in a silver frame beside the coffee machine. 'He's having trouble letting go. Just so you know.'

Layla swallowed. 'Would it be easier if I stayed somewhere else? I could find a B and B or something if it's going to cause trouble for you guys.'

'Nah.' Renee waved her hand in a careless gesture. 'I told him he'd have to deal with it. It's only one night.'

Layla clasped the mug, ignoring the scalding heat. Renee's husband had more than one reason to hate her, and she didn't blame him. It was because of him that she and Renee had never managed to repair their friendship after school; why the three girls had never got the share house together like they'd planned throughout their teenage years.

No, not him. It was because of *her*, and what she'd done.

'When's Shona coming around?' she asked to banish her self-reproach.

'Not until five. She's got a family thing this afternoon. This is the first time she's come back in five years, so they're all monopolising her time.'

'She still single?'

'Proudly. She always said she didn't need a man, didn't she?'

At once, Layla could've been squeezed into a change room with her friends again, trying on dresses and laughing at Shona's determination to go to the formal without a date. If only she could've frozen time and remained in that scene forever, when her friends had still believed in her, when she'd still had hope. Before she'd fucked it all up.

She set down her mug on the bench. 'Where's your bathroom? I might just freshen up.'

THEN

Out of the blue, Jodie started coming into the cafe more regularly. Scott insisted that she knew nothing about us, but after the incident in the reserve, my paranoia had reached peak levels.

At first I avoided her, but after a while my shame channelled into anger at her, and I started blatantly flirting with Scott in front of her. In response, he gave me fewer shifts, and some days even sent me home early, so we began to see a lot less of each other. He'd hired another girl to replace Yumi, a Year Eleven called Anna. She was prettier than I was, taller, curvier, and the jealousy was acid in my guts.

'Do you think about Anna when you're with me?' I asked him one night as he kissed my neck.

'Don't be ridiculous,' Scott said, his hand already in my bra. 'I think about you when I'm with you.'

'But her boobs are much bigger than mine.'

He sighed. 'I don't care about her tits, Layla.'

'So why's she getting all my old shifts, then?'

He stepped away from me, his mouth turning down at the sides. 'Maybe because she doesn't nag me all the bloody time like you do.'

I felt sick. 'I didn't mean it like that. I feel like I hardly see you anymore, and she's so much better looking than I am.'

'You're being paranoid. Anna's younger than you, so I don't have to pay her as much. That's all there is to it.'

I hated myself for my insecurity, but every time I was on a shift with Anna, I imagined he was staring at her chest, and that she was intentionally leaving her shirt unbuttoned low enough to show off her impressive cleavage. And I started to wonder why Scott only ever seemed to hire young, pretty girls and no boys. I became more daring, even touching him in front of the customers in a reckless attempt to keep his attention on me. He acted like he disapproved, but I knew he loved the danger of it … I could tell by his ferocity when we were alone. These were the only times I felt as though I had any control over him, even if the sex was becoming increasingly unenjoyable. If I could make him do anything I wanted, just with the power of my body, then surely, one day, that would be enough.

*

One Sunday night, I went for dinner with my family at the Rusty Anchor, only to discover Scott was there with Jodie and the kids. I knew he'd seen me, because his face flushed ever so slightly when we made eye contact across the room. But then he pointedly ignored me for the entire meal. Every time I looked over, he'd be laughing at something one of his kids had said, or eating his schnitzel, or leaning over to whisper in Jodie's ear. He looked utterly unattainable, and fury began to fizzle in my veins. He'd told me his marriage was over – he'd told me he wanted to marry *me* – and yet here he was, taunting me, parading his family in front of me while I sat at a table with my parents and my idiot brother like a stupid child.

'What are you looking at?' Mum said after a while, following my gaze. 'Oh, there's Scott and Jodie. Hi!' She waved at them across the room, and Jodie raised a hand in return. Scott didn't even lift his head. My blood burned. I'd show them I wasn't the good girl they thought I was. I'd show *him* what I was willing to do to keep him.

The next time he went to the bar, I got up too. 'Getting another lemonade,' I mumbled to my parents.

Scott shot me an annoyed look as I came to stand beside him.

'Enjoying your meal?' I said, resting my elbows on the bar.

'Sure.' His gaze darted from Barry, the bartender and owner of the pub, then back to me. 'You?'

'Well, the meals are as shithouse as always.'

'Oi,' protested Barry without any real conviction, handing Scott his beer.

'Can I get a lemonade, please?' I asked Barry.

'After what you said about my food?'

'Everyone says that about the food, Barry.'

He flashed me a grin as he moved up to the post-mix taps at the other end of the bar. I shuffled closer to Scott and lowered my voice. 'Go to the disabled bathroom. I'll follow you in a minute.'

'Don't be ridiculous.' He didn't look at me. 'My family is right there.'

Barry had poured my drink and was heading back towards us. The moment had almost passed. I had to do something.

'Well, if you don't want to fuck me, I guess I'll just have to go home and take care of myself.'

His breath came out hard. I turned away to pay Barry, and when I glanced back, Scott was already heading for the bathrooms. I took my lemonade over to the table where my family sat. 'Just going to the loo.'

Then I looked across the room, right at Jodie, and gave her a cruel little smile. My heart thundered in my chest as I followed Scott to the bathroom. I'd never been so direct, so daring. It was so easy to make him want me. I pushed open the door to the bathroom and Scott grabbed me. His fingernails raked across my skin as he ripped my jeans down and spun me around to face the mirror.

'You are a very bad girl, Layla,' he said.

There was no foreplay; he just forced his way inside me. It hurt, but I made eye contact with his reflection and said, 'Harder.'

His eyes were crazed with desire. 'You love being my little slut, don't you?'

'Harder,' I said again, clenching my teeth as my hips banged against the sink. He gave me a stinging slap on the behind. There was no love in his eyes, only hunger and something that looked very close to hatred. My brief triumph at snatching him from under the nose of his wife was swallowed by what I was letting him do to me.

After a minute, he came into the sink, then pulled up his jeans. 'I'd better get back out there.'

He slapped me on the bum again and walked out. He hadn't kissed me once; hadn't said anything other than demeaning dirty talk. And I'd let him degrade me. No, I'd encouraged him to. Humiliation leaked into every crevice, soaking me, drowning me. My eyes in the mirror were haunted and empty.

*

Over the following weeks, I tried harder to convince Scott that it was time for him to leave his wife, but he always had some excuse why he couldn't. His son was sick; Jodie was fighting with her mum; he was trying to save money to expand the cafe; I was in Year Twelve and needed to concentrate on school.

'I've been thinking,' I said to him one afternoon. 'Maybe I could defer uni next year and stay in Glasswater? I could work for you full-time and help you with the business.'

He gave a dismissive laugh. 'Don't be silly, Layla. You don't want to waste your life here with me. You've got a future.'

I felt miserable all the time, fluctuating between neglecting my school work and studying like a demon, always on the edge of crying.

'Oh, Layla, what's wrong?' Mum asked one night when she caught me huddled on the couch, tears sliding down my face, but I could only shake my head. She sat down beside me and put an arm around my shoulders. 'I know everything always feels so extreme when you're a teenager, but one day you'll look back at this and laugh.'

The tenderness of her touch juxtaposed wildly with Scott's; my hip bones still carried the ghosts of the bruises from the bathroom sink. It seemed like so long since anyone had touched me with love, and I longed to give into it. But the idea of her knowing how much of myself I was sacrificing to make him want me was horrifying. I threw her arm away and stood up abruptly.

Her hurt expression haunted me as I shut myself in my bedroom and buried my face in my pillow so she wouldn't hear me cry.

*

Renee, Shona and I loitered out the front of school one afternoon after the bell had gone, reluctant to go home but with no real motivation to do much more than enjoy the first warm day of spring. The sweet scent of jasmine flowers just bursting into bloom danced on the breeze from the vine that tumbled over the school fence. I didn't have a shift at the cafe this afternoon, and I felt lighter than I had in a long time.

We chatted about our final exams, which were now only a month away. School was almost over, and the rest of our lives yawned open, swallowing the shrinking year. Applications for uni closed in a couple of weeks, and we'd all been madly juggling our preferences to work out which direction we were going to take our lives. The possibilities consumed me. I'd barely spent any time with Scott over the last few weeks, and it was a curious relief. The prospect of leaving for uni next year seemed at once an escape and the loss of a dream.

'So, if Layla and I get our first preferences we'll both be at Uni SA,' Shona said. 'But your first preference is Adelaide Uni, right, Renee?'

Renee crossed her arms. 'Actually, I'm having second thoughts about law school.'

I bumped her with my elbow. 'Way to change your mind at the last minute. What are you thinking of changing to?'

She shrugged. 'I dunno. Psychology, maybe? Or I could defer for a year while I work out what I want to do.'

'No fucking way.' Shona shook her head firmly. 'We're all going to uni next year and we're gonna get a share house together, and when we've finished uni, we'll backpack around Europe, just like we planned.'

'Yeah, I guess.' Renee didn't look convinced.

I didn't comment. My suggestion to Scott that I could defer next year still hung over me, and I hadn't brought it up with my friends. If he asked me to stay, I'd do it, no question, but the idea of missing out on uni life with my friends left a little hollow feeling in my belly. And if I did end up marrying him, starting a life with him, the Europe trip might never happen either.

'Anyway, let's enjoy the rest of the year while we still can,' Shona said. 'So, who are we taking to the formal?'

My mood soured. 'We should all go without dates. You said it yourself, we don't need men.'

Renee's freckled face turned pink. 'Um, Shona. I've been meaning to tell you, but yesterday Daniel asked me to the formal.'

'Oh.' Shona looked taken aback. 'You're full of surprises today, girlfriend.'

'You don't mind?' Renee looked anxious.

'Nah, why would I? He's not my boyfriend anymore.'

'Thanks.' Renee was still flushed with shy excitement. 'It kind of came out of the blue. I hadn't really considered him in that way until he asked me, but now I can't stop thinking about him.'

'Oh! Oh!' Shona jumped up and down, pointing at Renee. 'When we went to Spiderbait, he kept, like, *staring* at you. Remember, Layla? I was super paranoid he was going to dump me for you.'

'What? No way,' Renee said, but she looked ever-so-slightly sheepish. 'OK, so maybe I kind of started liking him that night. But I never would've done anything about it while he was with you.'

They both darted a nervous glance at me.

'That's great, Renee.' I tried to sound enthusiastic. 'I'm really happy for you.'

'So, have you pashed him yet?' Shona asked.

'No, but we're going to see a movie on the weekend … I'm kind of nervous, isn't that weird?'

Despair welled up inside me again. I'd been so smug about being in a grown-up relationship, but now, with the formal coming up so soon, I was reminded at every turn how different my situation was from everyone else's. While my friends discussed Renee's upcoming date, my fingers found the bruises Scott had left on my wrists the other day.

'I'm going home,' I mumbled.

'Layla, wait,' Renee protested, but I kept my head down and walked away up the street. My mind was dark. I wanted to vanish.

But before I'd got far, Rasheed appeared, hands in his pockets. 'Hey, Layla.'

'Hi, Rasheed.' I had trouble disguising my impatience.

'I was wondering, do you want to go to the formal with me?'

He didn't seem as self-conscious as he used to. Faint surprise registered through my gloom as I realised that he looked as if he didn't really mind whether I said yes or no. 'Yeah, I don't think so.'

He shuffled his feet a little. 'I meant just as friends. I know you're seeing someone, but I thought it might be fun if we went together—'

My misery flashed into anger. I was so sick of hearing about the fucking formal, and the idea of going with strait-laced, geeky Rasheed was more than I could bear. I should've been going with the man who told me he wanted to marry me. And the fact that the last time I'd seen him, he'd pinned my wrists above my head and called me a dirty bitch – and that I'd let him – only deepened my self-contempt, made me want to lash out at the nearest person. 'And would your mum have to come as a chaperone, Rasheed?'

'No, I—'

'You know I'm with a real man now, don't you?' I took a step towards him. 'As if I'd want to go to the formal with a pathetic virgin loser like you.'

His expression cracked a little; he looked down at his feet. 'I guess that's a no, then?'

He started to turn away, but I wasn't done yet. I'd tasted blood and I wanted more.

'I keep remembering kissing you at the social and it makes me sick. It was like wrestling with a gigantic wet slug. It was *disgusting.*'

He looked back at me once. 'I get the idea, Layla.'

He walked away, and I looked around to find my friends staring at me in shock.

'That was really mean, Layla,' Renee said in a small voice.

The disappointment in her eyes was too much. 'And you can fuck off with your moralistic preaching, Renee.'

I ran all the way up the street to where my car was parked and got in, tears fogging my vision. What had I done? What kind of person treated their friends like that? I didn't deserve them. I didn't deserve happiness. I started the engine and roared away up the road, barely knowing where I was going until I'd pulled up outside the cafe.

'What are you doing here?' Scott said when I walked in. 'You're not working today.'

'Hi, Layla,' Anna said from behind the counter.

I could barely look at her, with her bright smile, her clear skin, her chest just about bursting out of her shirt. 'Could I talk to you about my shifts for next week?' I said to Scott. 'I need to swap a few.'

'Uh yeah, sure.' Scott followed me through the kitchen to the lunch room. 'What's up with you? You look weird.'

I wrapped my arms around his middle and pressed myself against him. 'I just needed to see you.'

'What's wrong?' He held me away from him.

I tried to pull his head down to kiss him. 'Tell me you love me.'

He craned his head away. 'What's going on? Has something happened?'

'Tell me you love me.' My tears began to fall. 'Tell me you want me.'

Scott took my hands and forced me away from him. 'Layla, stop! It's broad daylight, for fuck's sake, anyone could walk in here.'

'Then let them,' I sobbed. 'I'm sick of sneaking around. I want you for myself. Is that so selfish?'

'You need to snap out of it.' His eyes were hard. 'This is not the time or the place to talk about this. I'll see you tomorrow.'

'When are you going to leave her, Scott?'

He dropped my hands and gave an exasperated sigh. 'I get enough high-maintenance shit at home without coming into work and getting it from you.'

'You told me you were going to leave her soon. So when are you going to do it? When?'

His face twisted. 'You just won't get off my back, will you? I'm done with this. It's not worth it.'

'You don't mean that!' I flew at him, my hands on his chest. 'I can wait, Scott. I can wait. I've had a bad day, that's all. Sorry for being weird.'

He took me by the shoulders and shoved me away, and I bumped hard into the wall and almost fell. 'Look at you,' he sneered. 'You're a mess.'

I shrank beneath the contempt in his eyes. He'd hurt me before, but only ever during sex. This felt different. More shameful, somehow, in a way I couldn't articulate. 'Sorry, Scott. It won't happen again.'

'You can't come storming in here like this, Layla.' His voice was less angry now, but still there was no softness in his eyes. 'This is my life. I've got a business to run. Go home.'

And then he was gone, leaving me scraped out, empty. I'd come here seeking validation, but instead I'd come off desperate and pathetic. And now it was probably over.

When I went to the bathroom to clean myself up, my tear-streaked face was pale and grey under the fluoro lights, the whites of my eyes stained pink. My freckled nose, red from crying, seemed to dwarf my narrow face. No wonder Scott couldn't stand the sight of me. Why would anyone love a face like this?

NOW

It was almost a relief when the front door opened and Renee's husband and two boys walked in. Layla had been there for three hours and the four walls of the living room were beginning to press in on her. She and Renee had caught up on each other's lives and what all their old school acquaintances were doing, and they were running out of topics of conversation. They skirted around personal issues. Layla hadn't had the courage to bring up the reason she was here again. She almost welcomed the chance to get the confrontation out of the way.

'Hello, Layla,' he said. His voice was cool.

She tried to smile. 'How are you, Daniel?'

He didn't answer, just bent to kiss Renee. She looked up at him with a happy little smile, and something within Layla squeezed. They'd been looking at each other like that since they'd first got together in high school. Did Cam still look at her that way? Had he ever?

'How were the waves today?' Renee said as he straightened.

'Rubbish!' said one of the boys. His wetsuit was rolled down to his hips and he wore a white T-shirt. His shaggy auburn hair hung wet to his shoulders and his nose was scattered with freckles. His brother moved to stand beside him, looking curiously at Layla. They were identical, except that the second boy's hair was cut short around his ears. They looked so much like Renee had at the same age that Layla had to swallow the lump in her throat. She wondered what Daniel had told them about her, whether they were already judging her, just like everyone at school had.

Renee stood up and slung an arm around each of their shoulders. They were both already taller than she was. 'Boys, this is my old school friend, Layla. Layla, these are my handsome sons, Jonah and Henry.'

'Mum,' Jonah complained mildly. He tried to shrink away from his mother, but Renee pulled him back and gave him an exaggeratedly loud kiss on the cheek.

'Hi,' Henry said shyly.

'Lovely to meet you,' Layla said.

The boys mumbled barely intelligible excuses and made their escapes, leaving the adults alone together. A heavy silence pressed in before Daniel ran a hand through his wet hair and said, 'Going to have a shower.'

The two women watched him go. 'He's still the hottest guy from our year,' Renee said.

Layla laughed, then their eyes met as they both remembered, and the laughter died in her throat. She looked away.

'You don't have to keep feeling guilty about it, you know,' Renee said.

'There's a lot to feel guilty about, though, isn't there? And no doubt everyone will remind me of it tonight.'

'It was twenty years ago, Layla. No one cares about that now.'

'He does.' She waved her hand in the direction Daniel had disappeared.

There was a period of silence before Renee spoke again. 'Should I open a bottle of wine? I need to fortify myself for this thing.'

Layla raised her eyebrows. 'Pre-loading? Isn't that what got us into trouble twenty years ago?'

They went into the kitchen and Renee handed Layla a glass of white wine as they took seats opposite one another at the dining table. 'Bit more dignified than Jim Beam,' she said, taking a sip.

'God, that stuff was gross, wasn't it?'

They were both laughing when Daniel walked in. 'What's so funny?'

'Just reminiscing,' Renee said. 'Come and sit with us, babe. Have a wine.'

'Think I'll have a beer.' He turned away and stuck his head in the fridge before coming over to the dining table and sitting down beside Renee.

The conversation was stilted. Layla snuck the occasional glance at Daniel, but he didn't look at her at all. Renee was right: her first crush was still good looking, with his broad shoulders, open face and dark hair. And he was in great shape too, a slight thickening around his middle the only indication of age beginning to catch up with him. He was attentive to Renee, touching her arm occasionally and watching her when she spoke. Layla felt a pang of something – not quite jealousy, but a close relative. Until recently, her relationship with Cam had always felt on firm footing, but there was something about a love that had lasted from high school that left her with a tinge of envy.

Then Renee got up to go to the toilet, and Layla and Daniel were suddenly alone.

Daniel stared into his beer bottle for so long that Layla thought he might disappear into it. She fidgeted with her wineglass, then mustered up the courage to say, 'Looking forward to the reunion tonight?'

'Not really.' He glanced at her, then back to his beer. 'I'm only going because Renee wants me to. I don't see the point in hanging around with a bunch of people I never liked in the first place.'

Layla grimaced. 'Point taken.' She watched as he slowly started peeling the label off his beer bottle. 'I'm sorry about what I did … after the formal,' she said at last. 'It was … I was going through some shit. I know that's no excuse, but—'

He looked up at her now. 'You really think that's why I'm still angry?'

'I know it was more than that—'

'Jodie's my *cousin*, Layla. Life didn't stop for the rest of us when you left, you know. She's been through a lot.'

'I know.' Layla forced herself to meet his gaze. 'That's why I came back. To make amends. Or try to. I'm going to see her tomorrow.'

'You are?' Renee had walked in and was staring at Layla. 'You didn't tell me that.'

Layla tried to smile. 'Because she's not the only one I need to make things up to.'

There was a strained silence, then the doorbell rang and they all jumped.

'That'll be Shona,' Renee said unnecessarily. She disappeared again.

At last Daniel looked at Layla. 'I know you weren't entirely to blame. I mean, you were just a teenager. But everyone else has paid for it. Everyone except you.'

Sudden anger blazed inside Layla, hot and bright. 'You think I haven't paid? He ate away my self-worth when I was most vulnerable. For my entire twenties, I only went out with men who treated me like shit … I lived with a guy who hit me every week and threatened to kill me at least once a month. And I thought that was normal. So don't tell me I haven't *paid*, Daniel.'

His eyes widened. He opened and closed his mouth. Layla herself was in shock. She'd never told anyone about that period of her life; not Cam, not even her mother. But now there was no room left inside her to harbour it any longer. She looked up to see Renee and Shona standing in the doorway, looking shell-shocked.

'Oh my god, Layla.' Renee came over and put her arms around Layla, then Shona was there too, and the three of them were clinging to one another. Relief swathed Layla in a warm cocoon. Daniel sat at the table, cradling his beer and looking helpless. The beer label, wet with condensation, lay on the table like a carcass.

At last Shona stepped back and smiled through her tears. 'Trust Layla to bring the melodrama.'

'Ha! You were always the melodramatic one, as I recall,' Layla said.

Renee reached out and squeezed Daniel's shoulder. 'Babe, could you take the boys around to Mum's? We girls have some catching up to do.'

'Yep.' Daniel stood up and fled.

Shona watched him go. 'I've never seen anyone leave a room so quickly.'

Renee grinned. 'Men are pussies.'

'Well, what are we waiting for, bitches?' Shona spread her arms wide. 'Let's get ready to blow Glasswater to smithereens. Is fucking Katrina coming?'

THEN

Shona cranked the stereo in her car as soon as we got on the road to Adelaide, and we sang retro eighties songs at the tops of our lungs to cover the tension. Things were still tense between Renee and me since my blow-up at Rasheed last week.

It had been Shona's idea to go to Adelaide for the day to shop for our formal dresses. I wasn't really in the mood, but I couldn't not go to the formal, and I needed a dress. And besides, Scott hadn't rostered me on today, so it wasn't like I had anything else to do. Despite what he'd said to me that day about us being done, the next time I'd seen him he'd acted as if nothing had happened. My relief that he still wanted me mingled with confusion over his behaviour. When I referred to the way he'd shoved me into the wall, he gave a sort of puzzled chuckle, as if implying that the whole exchange existed only in my head.

When I'd told him where I was going today, he'd asked me to meet him up at The Knob tonight, and I wasn't sure whether I was looking forward to it or dreading it. It'd been ages since we'd done anything together outside the walls of the cafe kitchen, and that small spark of hope – the spark that

I kept buried deep inside, with a glow that diminished day by day – made me wonder whether this could be the turning point in our relationship. Maybe he was going to tell me he was finally leaving Jodie and we could be together.

On the other hand, the thought of what we'd do together made me feel numb and hopeless. I'd stopped faking orgasms, but he didn't seem to care. He'd pull my hair, graze my skin with his fingernails and his teeth, whisper dirty things in my ear. Sometimes he'd close a hand around my throat and I'd think, *He could kill me if he wanted to.*

'What's wrong?' Shona nudged my arm. 'I thought you loved this song?'

I flashed her a smile. 'Sorry. Just thinking about Scott.'

Renee groaned from the back seat. 'Seriously? When are you going to give up on that?'

Defiance flared in me, and I twisted around in my seat to look at her. 'Well, he asked me to marry him, so probably never.'

'Are you for real?' Shona shrieked.

'Yup.' The half-truth grew inside my head, and next thing I knew I'd outlined a whole wedding plan to them, until it was no longer a half-truth but a complete lie.

'So where's the ring?' Renee's voice was heavy with scepticism.

'We haven't got one yet. We're going to go to the city together to pick one out.' The more I spoke, the more I convinced myself that it was true. Well, it would be anyway. I just had to make it happen. Whatever it took, I'd make it happen.

'Did you know his wife is Daniel's cousin?' Renee said out of the blue.

My smile withered as she dragged me back to reality. 'What's that got to do with anything?'

'Apparently, their marriage is on the rocks.'

I smirked. 'I could've told you that.'

When Renee spoke again, there was no glee in her voice, only reluctance. 'And apparently, he's doing all he can to save it. Flowers, romantic dinners, the works.'

My throat constricted, my fragile dreams exploding inside me, leaving a tingling emptiness in their place. She was lying. She had to be lying, because how could that be true when he'd told me I was the one he wanted to be with? I didn't look at her, my voice wobbling as I spoke. 'I don't believe you.'

'I'm sorry.' There was real regret in Renee's voice now. 'I really am. But it's true. Daniel's parents were talking about it the other night. He's not going to marry you, Layla. He's just using you for sex.'

Her words floated above me, barely penetrating the thick fog of numbness that surrounded me. And from beneath that fog edged a sharper, darker truth: if it *was* true, what kind of person could do those things to me while still loving his wife? What kind of man had I fallen in love with, given myself up for?

'Hey, Layla?' Shona said, keeping her eyes on the road. 'I think Renee might be right. Maybe you should end this thing now, before you get hurt. You deserve a nice relationship with a nice guy.'

I nodded, biting down hard on my lip to hold back my tears. I didn't trust myself to speak, because I didn't know the words to tell her how deep the hurt had gone already, and that after what I'd done, who I'd become, a good relationship was the last thing I deserved.

*

Shona knew all the best shops to look in, and we spent a good hour squished into change rooms together, trying on dress after silky dress. None of us brought up Scott again, and I began to feel lighter and lighter. It seemed like years since I'd had good, simple fun like this. Despite Renee's revelation, I started to look forward to the formal, even though I wouldn't have a date and would no doubt be ribbed for it by Katrina and her minions.

'You need to get the blue one, Renee,' Shona announced. 'It looks shit hot with your hair and your complexion.'

'I didn't know there was a colour that went with freckles,' Renee grumbled, but she looked chuffed nevertheless. 'That one *was* my favourite.'

'You look beautiful in it,' I said. 'Daniel's gonna flip when he sees you.'

'Thanks.' Her eyes looked shiny. 'I know it's early days, but I really like him. And I think he likes me.'

'Of course he does. Who wouldn't?'

She grabbed me in a spontaneous hug. 'I love you guys.'

Shona joined in the hug. 'Those are the words of two chicks who want to get smashed tonight. My place when we get home?'

'Shit yeah,' Renee said.

I didn't want to spoil the moment by telling them that I'd already arranged to meet Scott tonight, so I just nodded and turned back to the pile of dresses. It'd been fun trying them on, but none had made me look anywhere near as good as my friends did. 'So which one am I gonna get?'

'The red,' Renee said. 'You'll clash with my hair, but you look hot in it.'

'I agree,' Shona said. 'Anyway, Renee'll be too busy pashing Daniel to worry about clashing with anyone's dress.'

'What about you?' I said.

Shona waved a hand dismissively. 'None of these are working for me. I think I'm gonna get a short dress.'

'Shona Porter, always bucking the trend,' Renee said.

'You'd better believe it, girlfriend. And speaking of bucking the trend, I'm not taking a date either.'

'You're not?' I said, surprised. 'Didn't Sam ask you last week?'

'I don't need a man to be fabulous. And Sam is a wanker anyway, as he's so fond of reminding everyone.' She slung an arm over my shoulder. 'So we can be fabulous together, Layla.'

We high-fived, and a flicker of light glimmered inside me. Maybe there could be a future without Scott in it, without the angst and the doubt and the shame. Maybe I *could* be fabulous.

*

By four o'clock we were on the road home, the back seat laden with dresses and shoes and make-up and a lot of other things we didn't need. I'd bought the new Magic Dirt album, which blasted from the car stereo while we all sang along.

'I'd change teams for Adalita, no question,' Renee said.

'She's a goddess,' I agreed. 'A rock goddess.'

'We should start our own band,' Shona said. 'How awesome would that be?'

'Um, Shona, none of us can sing or play any instruments,' I reminded her.

'Yeah, musical talent is kind of a prerequisite,' Renee said.

'Don't let reality get in the way of my dream, bitches,' Shona said.

We stopped in at Keen's on the way to Shona's place to order fish and chips, and my mood began to tank again as we passed the cafe. I walked on the other side of Renee and Shona, avoiding looking in through the windows. The idea of Scott knowing I was there made my insides feel cold and dark.

'Should we drop in at Daniel's?' Shona said when we were getting back in the car. 'We could see if his sister can get us some booze. My parents are out tonight.'

'Let's call him when we get to your place,' Renee said. 'He could bring some over later.'

We got back to Shona's and scoffed the fish and chips, and soon after Daniel arrived with the alcohol. He and Renee canoodled for a while before she pushed him towards the door. 'Off you go, we've got drinking to do.'

'Is that all the thanks I get for providing minors with alcohol?' Daniel laughed.

'Thank you,' Renee said sweetly, pulling him back to her and kissing him.

'Mmm,' he said, putting his arms around her. 'I could get used to that kind of gratitude.'

They gazed at each other with pathetic adoration, and jealousy swirled in my belly. Scott hadn't looked at me like that for such a long time.

Shona groaned. 'Get a room!'

When Daniel had left, Renee passed out the drinks, but I demurred. 'I can't. I have to drive later.'

'What?' Shona frowned. 'I thought you were staying here tonight.'

'I am.' I twisted the bottom of my T-shirt in my hands. 'I told Scott I'd meet him tonight. I thought I could come back here after … if you don't mind?'

Renee grimaced and threw her bottle top into the sink with a flick of her wrist. 'So I guess you're not going to end it, then?'

'I am.' But as the words left my mouth, I knew they were a lie. 'But it's already arranged.'

'So call the cafe now,' Shona said. 'Tell him you can't make it.'

I was torn. It would be an enormous weight off my shoulders to cancel the plans, to let loose with my friends instead.

'He makes you miserable, Lay,' Renee said. 'You've changed since you've been involved with him. The way you spoke to Rasheed the other day … that wasn't you.'

'I know.' Anguish rose inside me, and before I could prevent it, my face began to crumple. 'But I don't know how to stop.'

Together, they came over to me and each put an arm around me. I loved them so hard right then that it was almost too much to bear.

'We just want you to be happy,' Renee said.

Shona pressed the cordless phone into my hand. 'Call him now. Tell him it's over.'

I pressed my lips together and nodded. 'OK. OK.'

I took the phone into Shona's bedroom and closed the door. I knew the cafe number by heart, but still I stared at the phone in my hand for a long time before I had the courage to dial. One conversation and it would all be over. I could live a normal life again. I held my breath and keyed in the number.

'Telford's Cafe, Scott speaking.'

Somehow I hadn't expected him to answer, and now I was struck mute.

'Hello?'

'Sorry, hi. It's me. Layla.'

'Oh, hi.' The warmth in his voice immediately gave me second thoughts. 'It's been dead tonight, so I might be able to close early. I can't wait to ravish you later.'

I took a deep breath. 'That's why I'm calling actually. I won't be able to make it tonight.'

'Are you kidding? I've been looking forward to seeing you all day.'

'I know, me too,' I lied. 'But I'm at Shona's and we've had a couple of drinks. I don't think I'll be able to drive.'

'Shit, Layla.' He sighed. 'I thought we had a plan.'

'We did.' I squirmed. 'It's just … I feel like hanging out with my friends tonight, doing normal teenage stuff.'

'What are you saying, Layla?'

I hesitated, squeezing my eyes shut. Did I really have the courage to do this? Renee and Shona's chatter filtered under the closed door. If I got it over with, I could be back with them in minutes. I opened my eyes. 'I don't think I want to do this anymore.'

'What?' He sounded bewildered. 'Are you breaking it off with me? Over the *phone*?'

'No, I … Well, yeah. I think so.' With every word, I felt lighter. I was almost out. I was almost free. I hadn't known how badly I'd wanted it until now. 'I'll quit if you want, so it's not too weird.'

He gave a heavy sigh. 'Oh. Fuck. I had no idea this was coming.'

I sank lower on the bed, cradling the phone between my ear and shoulder. 'I'm sorry.'

'I can't believe you didn't have the decency to do this in person.' His voice was jagged, unsteady. I dug my fingernails into my forearm. 'Don't I deserve that much?'

I wanted to ask him whether I'd deserved to be called filthy names, to be thrown against the wall like a rag doll, but 'I'm sorry,' came out again instead. The brief euphoria I'd felt at being free drained out of me. I felt limp, like I had no bones.

'I guess that's what I get for falling in love with a teenager; you change your mind as often as your underwear,' he said bitterly. 'Last week you were throwing yourself at me and now you're telling me you're done. Good luck finding someone else who'll put up with your schizo shit.'

I clenched my arm harder. 'I'm sorry.' Tears came to my eyes. 'I did love you, but—'

'But what? It got too hard for you, so you gave up on me? I must've been wrong about you, Layla. I thought you were stronger than that.'

I couldn't speak.

'At least meet me tonight to talk things through like a grown-up,' Scott said. 'You owe me that much.'

My heart hurt. He sounded so sad and defeated. The least I could do was give him a proper explanation. I felt battered, flat, but could it really be any worse than the way he felt? Come to think of it, my friends were the ones who'd talked me into doing this in the first place. Everyone was always telling me what to do, what to think, how to act, and I was sick of it.

'OK,' I said at last. 'I'll come to the cafe after closing.'

'No, meet me at The Knob, just like we planned.'

My fingernails broke through the skin of my forearm. I winced but didn't let go. I knew if I went to The Knob, Scott would take control again, as he always did. But then the image of Renee and Daniel gazing adoringly at one another flitted across my mind, and a deep yearning swam in the pit of my belly. I needed to see that look in Scott's eyes again, to know I was loved. Just one more time, then I could let him go.

'OK.'

'OK. OK, great.' He sounded relieved. 'I'll close at ten tonight. See you there at ten thirty.'

I peeled my fingernails away from my skin to hang up the phone and stared down at the crescent shapes on my arm as they turned from white to pink to deep red.

*

'I can't *believe* you're still meeting him,' Renee said as I pulled on my jacket at ten twenty. 'You're not going to break it off, are you?'

'I am,' I insisted. 'But I owe him a face-to-face explanation. I couldn't break up with him over the phone.'

'You could've waited until your next shift.' She crossed her arms, her face pink. I knew she didn't believe I'd do it, but she hadn't heard the pain in his voice when I'd told him it was over. She didn't know how much I'd hurt him.

Shona saw me to the door. 'Be careful, OK? Stick to your guns.'

'I'm going to.'

'Are you going to come back here afterwards?'

I looked past her, but Renee hadn't followed us out. 'I think I kind of destroyed the vibe.'

She grimaced. 'She'll get over it. We're worried about you, that's all.'

I gave her a small smile. Maybe their friendship was enough to keep me strong, to carry me through this meeting. 'I'll see you at school on Monday.'

As soon as I left my friends, I felt the strength they'd lent me trickle away. They had their own lives; Renee had a boyfriend and no doubt Shona would have another one soon too. Like Scott said, who would be interested in going out with someone like me? It was only a matter of time before I reverted back to the pathetic sidekick.

I took the long way up to The Knob, and Scott's car was already waiting in the car park when I got there. He got out at the same time I did and we stopped a few paces away from each other. The moon was full and the silvery light shone on his face. One side of his mouth lifted in a half-smile and my heart did a little flip. 'I was worried you weren't going to come,' he said.

'Sorry I'm a bit late.'

He took a step towards me, then stopped. 'What happened, Layla? We've got a special connection. I know you feel it too. I don't understand why you want to end it.'

Did we have a connection? In the last few months, our connection had seemed little more than a series of quickies that had become increasingly base. Or maybe I was being naive and overly sentimental to think romance continued as a relationship progressed. He was watching me, waiting for the explanation I'd promised him, but now I could come up with nothing that sounded reasonable. All the lines I'd rehearsed on the way here had flown out of my head now that I was confronted with the naked hurt illuminated by the moonlight on his face.

'Renee has started going out with Jodie's cousin Daniel,' I said at last. 'He said you've been trying to patch up your relationship with her.'

He gave a rough laugh. 'So you believe what your friend says rather than giving me a chance to explain?'

'Well, no ... it's just—'

'So if Renee told you to climb up there,' he gestured to the giant granite outcropping, 'and jump into the sea, you'd do it, would you?'

I could feel him trying to turn it back on me, and I fought the urge to apologise again. 'I'm giving you the chance to explain now.'

His features softened. 'Jodie's dad has cancer. It's terminal. She's really upset about it, so I need to support her right now.'

'Oh. I'm sorry, I didn't know.'

'That's also why I can't leave her yet. But I don't want to lose you either, Layla.' He stepped closer, reached out and touched my cheek. My resolve stretched, twisted, sagged. 'I'm not ready to let you go.'

He came closer still, clasped my face in both hands, looked into my eyes with an expression that held all the meaning I'd been searching for from the start. I gulped it down with a thirst that felt like it could never be quenched. Maybe ... maybe if I gave it another chance, it would be better this time. It had to be better.

He bent his head and kissed me softly on the lips. I closed my eyes. This tenderness was what I'd been yearning for.

How could I turn my back on this? His hands were still on either side of my face; gentle, warm. If he could love me despite all the imperfections that I saw in the mirror every day, that bled out inside me, I couldn't let that go. I kissed him back, let my arms wind around his neck, let my body move in against his.

'I love you, Layla,' Scott said. 'Tell me you love me too.'

'I love you,' I breathed.

'Tell me you won't leave me.'

'I'll never leave you.'

NOW

Shona applied bright red lipstick and inspected her face in the mirror. 'Too much?' she said.

'Just enough,' Renee said. 'You look great.'

Layla eyed Shona's svelte figure with envy. She wore a short, yellow strapless dress that hugged a body that was as firm and toned as it had been when they were at school. Her hair was short and died various shades of purple, and her feet were clad in Doc Martens.

'You look amazing,' Layla said. 'You make me feel old and frumpy.'

Shona's reflection raised an eyebrow at her. 'Layla, there's nothing frumpy about you.'

'Well, things aren't as tight as they used to be.' She gestured to her hips and belly, which she'd covered in a black shift dress to disguise the soft, jiggly bits that she so despised.

'So?' Shona said. 'I'm thin because I don't sleep enough and I'm constantly stressed with my business, and when I'm stressed I go to the gym instead of sleeping, and the cycle continues. You guys pushed actual humans out of your clackers and still managed to have successful careers. I think that puts you in front.'

Layla couldn't help laughing.

'Yeah, but our clackers will never be the same,' Renee said wryly.

'Speaking of work, I can't believe you're starting your own practice,' Shona said. 'That's awesome. I always knew you'd be a great psychologist.'

'No, you didn't!' Renee laughed. 'You told me I was insane for not doing law.'

'Well, I was wrong. What about you, Layla? You always wanted to buy your own pharmacy, didn't you?'

Once, Layla had hoped to start her own business, but after having children, she had all but given up on her dream. Strange that she'd always been the brainy one when they'd been at school, the one most likely to succeed, and now her friends had overtaken her while she stagnated in the same job she'd been doing for ten years, bored yet too paralysed to take the leap into something new.

'I did. I do,' she corrected herself. 'But then we had kids and I put it off. Now I can't see a way of ever achieving it.'

'Work is really hard when you have little kids,' Renee said. 'But it does get easier once they're at school. The only reason I'm where I'm at now is because I had mine young. But I haven't forgotten that first year of being soaked in breast milk and despair while Daniel seemed to carry on as normal.'

'Cam is a great dad, but even now I hate him a little bit every time he goes to work and leaves me with them.' Admitting this felt like a betrayal to Cam, but Layla knew her old friends wouldn't judge her for it.

'Oh, I used to feel like ripping Daniel's nuts off whenever he headed out for a job at 7 am and left me with two screaming babies and no opportunity to have a shower for eight hours.' Renee laughed.

'You know, no one else has ever said anything like that to me,' Layla said. 'I thought I was the only one.'

Renee gave her a sympathetic smile. 'Because we've been conditioned not to say these things out loud. But I've had enough clients with PND to know what that does to a person.'

'I don't know how anyone does it.' Shona shook her head. 'Just the thought of it terrifies me.'

'So, while I've got my psychologist hat on, Layla …' Renee began, then paused. 'What you said earlier about the bad relationships you've had … Cam's not like that, is he?'

'No! God, no.' Layla rushed to defend her husband. 'He was the first person who made me feel worthwhile since school.'

Renee grimaced and looked down. 'I'm really sorry about the things I said to you after the formal. It's been haunting me for years. I should've been there for you, but I was too wrapped up in myself.'

Layla tried to smile, but the memory of Renee's words still cut like glass. *When did you turn into such a slut?* For years after that, she'd used hook-ups in place of true intimacy, her body as currency to make men like her.

On her second date with Cam, they'd gone out for dinner, and he'd been so sweet, and he'd kissed her for the first time in his car outside her flat, his lips so soft, but sensual. His restraint had surprised her. He hadn't tried to get in her pants, or convince him to invite him in; he'd held her face in his hands as his lips had played over hers, tasting her, savouring her. And, of course, Layla had blown it by trying to go down on him. He'd drawn in a sharp breath and gently held her away from him. 'Whoa, Layla, wait.'

She'd shrunk away from him, her face burning with embarrassment. 'Sorry, I thought … I thought you'd want me to. Sorry. I'm such an idiot.'

He'd given her a wry smile. 'I very much want you to, but I'd like us to get to know each other first. I'm hoping we'll have plenty of time for other stuff a bit later.'

At first, she'd assumed he was letting her down gently. All her life, men had valued her for her body, and she'd come to believe that was all she had to offer. This man was the first one who liked her, really liked her; the first one who'd thought her mind was worth knowing before her body. He'd been careful with her heart too. Though they'd never discussed it, on some level he must have known she was damaged, and he'd given her the space to rebuild herself. He reflected what he saw back at her, and somewhere along the way, she'd finally felt she deserved him.

She collected herself and touched Renee on the arm. 'We were teenagers; we were all shockingly self-absorbed.'

There was a knock on the bedroom door and Daniel called out, 'It's seven o'clock. Are you ready yet?'

'Coming!' Renee yelled.

*

It was like stepping into the past when they walked through the school gates. Renee and Daniel walked hand in hand in front of Layla and Shona.

'Still got a good arse, hasn't he?' Shona whispered in Layla's ear, gesturing at Daniel.

Layla laughed. 'I still remember you grabbing it at the social.'

Shona threw her head back. 'Oh man, that seems like a lifetime ago.'

'It was.'

'I can't believe our boys are starting at this hellhole in a couple of weeks,' Renee said. 'I feel about a million years old.'

'You look it too,' Daniel quipped, slapping her on the bum.

'Fuck off!' Renee pushed him, and he laughed and pulled her back to kiss her.

'Oh my god!' Shona hissed, pointing at the entrance of the gym where the reunion was being held. 'Is that Jason Stott?'

Layla's stomach dropped at the mention of his name. Jason's good looks had broadened; the sixpack all the girls had lusted over in high school had blown out into a round beer belly. A shaggy, untrimmed beard covered most of his face.

'He still lives here,' Renee said. 'After all that talk about becoming an actor, he only ever did a toothpaste commercial and couldn't get another gig, so he came back here to be a carpenter. He was the one who finally rebuilt the shops on the main street. They were vacant for years after the – wait, were you still here when all that happened, Layla? I can't remember.'

The blow swooped in and socked Layla in the stomach. Her heart threw itself against her chest. It was all she could do to prevent herself from turning around and running back to Renee's place, getting in her car, driving home and never returning.

'I don't know,' she said quickly, her voice shrill. 'Hey, before we go in, why don't we walk around the school, do some reminiscing?'

'Sure,' Renee said. 'Babe, why don't you go and talk to Jason while we check out all our old haunts?' she said to Daniel. 'We'll see you in there in a bit.'

'You're really going to make me go in there on my own?' he grumbled.

'It's not like you don't already know everyone. You'll live.'

They watched as Daniel went over to greet Jason, then turned and wandered across the quadrangle towards the main building.

'Do you think it'll be open?' Shona said.

'Yeah, they've opened up the whole school so nerds like us can see how much it's changed in twenty years,' Renee said. 'Which is not much, by the way.'

Layla pushed open the door and the competing smells came at her in a rush: sweaty socks, food that'd been left too long in lockers, the pine scent of floor cleaner. They walked up the corridor in silence, each entombed in their own memories of the place. There was no one else around. The walls seemed to breathe in and out on their own.

'The library,' Shona said as they reached the double glass doors.

The posters on the walls had changed and the shelving had been rearranged over the years, but the same white tables with red steel legs were scattered in the open areas, surrounded by the same mustard chairs. The three of them were drawn to one corner of the room to the table they used to sit at together. There was a wall of magazines beside it, stacked with some of the same publications they'd pored over as teenagers, like *Dolly* and *Girlfriend*, alongside newer ones like *Teen Breathe*.

'Remember how we used to giggle over the Dolly Doctor questions?' Layla said.

'"Can you get pregnant if a guy comes in your mouth?"' Shona said in a high-pitched voice, and they all laughed.

'Apparently, Dolly Doctor is online now,' Renee said. 'It was funny and all, but we learnt some shit from that, didn't we?'

They left the library and trudged up the stairs to the row of classrooms that ran along the balcony. 'Remember when Katrina threatened to throw Bruiser's Metallica CD over the balcony after we'd listened to 'Enter Sandman' on repeat for an entire double lesson?' Shona said to Layla, pointing out her old art classroom.

'Well, I didn't actually do art,' Layla said, but she did remember it, because she'd spent most of her free lessons in Shona's art class, chatting when she should've been studying.

'I wonder if Miss Grainger is still teaching,' Shona said dreamily.

'I wonder if she ever found out what a head job is,' Layla said.

They all giggled.

'I almost feel like a teenager again,' Renee said.

'I never stopped feeling like one,' Shona said. 'I keep wondering if there's this magical age when I'll start feeling like a real grown-up, but I'm almost thirty-eight and I'm not there yet.'

'I thought I was a grown-up when I was seventeen,' Layla said. 'I wish I'd known then not to be in such a hurry.'

'Didn't it suck when everyone told us our high school years would be the best years of our lives?' Renee said. 'And now I'm saying it to my own kids.'

They went down the steps and out onto the quadrangle. The white lines around the border had been repainted in bright blue, but the asphalt still looked as grey and rough as it had been when Layla had stacked it in front of her entire Year Nine class playing handball and grazed her knee. The scab had lingered all summer, breaking open again every time she bent her leg; a constant reminder of her mistake.

The sun sank towards the roof of the gym as they approached, shining directly into their eyes. Their steps slowed. Voices carried out through the open doors, the voices of their old classmates. Layla held onto the vivid feeling of nostalgia for a moment longer, then let it drain slowly out of her.

THEN

After that night at The Knob, I'd thought things might be different, and for a few days they were. But it didn't take long before Scott and I fell back into the same old pattern and I realised I'd made a mistake returning to him. I wished I'd never made him that stupid promise, but it was my own fault and now I had to deal with the consequences. The formal was coming up in a week. People at school talked of nothing else, but I was more worried about finding time to study for my final exams. Scott had gone back to rostering me on several nights a week, and I was barely getting any sleep around school, work and our increasingly rough sexual encounters. The idea of leaving for uni next year was starting to look like an oasis shimmering just beyond my reach.

'I've been thinking about your idea of working here full-time next year,' Scott said one night, twirling my hair around his finger as I sat on his lap. 'I think it could be good.'

I avoided his gaze. Renee, Shona and I had been spending our lunchbreaks in the computer room searching online for share houses for next year, and I was starting to get excited about it. 'But I'll be at uni. Assuming I get in, of course.

Even if I stayed here, I'd probably only be able to work on weekends.'

'What? I thought you were going to defer next year.'

'Maybe,' I said absently. 'I'm not sure yet.'

'I'm applying for a loan to buy the place next door. I was counting on your help to expand the business, like we talked about.'

'Oh. Sorry.' I was surprised. He'd never mentioned that I was an integral part of his plans. On the one hand, I was flattered, but on the other, the idea of being stuck in Glasswater Bay with him for another year was like being trapped underwater.

'You can't play with me like that, Layla.' His tone had become harder now. 'I thought we had a deal.'

'I'm sorry, I guess I misunderstood. I'll think about it.'

'And what am I supposed to do while you're *thinking about it*?' His fingers moved to the nape of my neck, pressing uncomfortably. 'One minute you tell me you're going to stay and the next you're going off to uni.'

I tried to shift so he'd let me go, but his fingers dug in deeper, and foreboding rippled over me. 'You told me not to waste my life here.'

He moved his hand to my throat. 'So I'm not good enough for you, then?'

'It's not like that!' I cried, but his hand tightened around my throat. 'Let me go.'

He drew closer, his face centimetres from mine, his breath hot on my face. 'Do you really think you're going to find someone else who cares about you the way I do? Look at you, your face is covered in pimples.' He gave my cheek a little slap with his free hand. 'You look like a pizza. None of the boys are going to look twice at you.'

I couldn't get enough air in, and the panic was building inside me. 'Scott, please, let me go,' I tried to say, but I couldn't get the words out.

The hard look in his eyes disappeared and he released me. I gasped, drinking the air back into my lungs, and got up from his lap. He stood up too and reached out for me, but I backed away from him, shaking my head.

'Sorry, Layla, but you scared me, talking about leaving me again,' he said. 'You promised me you wouldn't, didn't you?'

I didn't say anything. I'd told him I'd never leave him, and I'd meant it when I said it. But now ... that look in his eyes while he'd held my breath in his hand ...

'You can't blame me for being upset. You can't just change your mind on me like that.'

'I know, I'm sorry.' I had to pause to cough. 'I'll talk it over with my parents and see what they think.'

His lip curled a little and he looked like he was going to say something, but then he stepped closer and took me in his arms. 'I can't help how much I love you, Layla. Don't make me angry like that again, OK?'

He kissed me, and the gentleness of his lips against mine was such a relief. I melted into him, kissed him back, held him close. There was still time to fix this; he would keep loving me as long as I was the person he wanted me to be ... once I worked out who that actually was. Anyway, he was right: no one else would love me with a face like this. He was here, and I needed something to hold onto or I'd float away.

*

The door of the cafe had barely closed behind Anna the following night when Scott pulled me out to the kitchen. 'I'm going to fuck you so hard,' he hissed, already unbuckling his belt.

'Wait, Scott.' I raised my hands to stop him. 'I can't tonight. I really need to study.'

He sighed. 'Study, study, study. That's all you ever seem to have time for.'

'My final exams are in two weeks. I'm not going to get into my course if my grades aren't good.'

His mouth twisted into a smile. 'Don't worry, I can make it quick. You've been flaunting that arse of yours in my face all night. You can't leave me hanging like this.'

I hesitated. I didn't think I'd been flaunting anything … though there had been that moment as Dave was leaving earlier that I'd stepped backwards into Scott. But it had been an accident. He must've thought it was a message. It could be over within five minutes, but the idea of what he'd do to me made me feel dead inside. Mum had noticed the bruises on my throat this morning. I'd made some excuse about falling asleep wearing a necklace, but every lie I told her just embedded my self-loathing deeper and deeper inside me.

'I'm sorry. I really can't.' I backed away.

'Don't make me angry again, Layla.' His voice held a warning tone now, and sudden fear flared bright inside me.

'I have to go, sorry.'

I turned and walked out of the kitchen towards the cafe door. His footsteps echoed behind me as I fumbled with the key and opened the door, my steps quickening on the footpath.

The bell jangled over the door as he wrenched it open again. 'You can't walk away from me like this.'

'I'll see you after school tomorrow.' I got in my car, and as I started the engine, he locked the cafe door behind him and strode up the footpath towards his own car. My stomach fluttered. He'd left all the lights on in the cafe; we hadn't even balanced the till. My gaze flicked to my rear-view mirror as I drove. After a minute, a set of headlights appeared on the road behind me. I pressed the accelerator down a little harder. The lights got closer. I turned down a random street, but the car followed, getting closer all the time. I sped through the network of streets, turning this way and that. He was still following me. My heart pumped hard with adrenalin.

There were no other cars on Bay Road. Scott's car got closer and closer, until I thought it'd hit mine. I increased my speed and turned off the main road way too fast, and the back end of my car fishtailed out to the side for a second before I regained control. But still he stuck behind me. When I pulled up on my street, he drove up beside my car and lowered his window. I glanced at my house. It was dark, silent. Grudgingly, I wound down my own window.

'I told you I had to go home,' I said tremulously.

His face was desperate. 'I need you, Layla. I didn't mean to scare you, but I'm so lonely and I need to be with someone who loves me. You love me, don't you?'

Pity tugged at my heart. 'Of course I do, but I'm really stressed about school.'

'Just twenty minutes,' he pleaded. 'I'm so miserable at home. I want to die.'

His words filled me with horror. He looked broken, ravaged. How could I deny him comfort when he was feeling this awful?

'Twenty minutes,' I relented. 'Then I have to study.'

'Thank you, Layla,' he said. 'Thank you.'

His gratitude was warm in my belly as we drove in his car up to The Knob. But as he fucked me over the bonnet of his car, his fingers kneading my skin painfully, the blackness spread through my body until I wished I could disappear altogether.

*

Mum was waiting up for me when I got home, a cup of tea cradled in her hands. I itched to escape the room, mortified at what I'd just done.

'You're up late,' I said instead.

'Where have you been?' Her voice was calm.

'I was at work.' My fingers linked together, twisting and untwisting.

'Your car has been outside for the last hour.' She set her cup down, and I noticed her hand was shaking. 'I called the cafe, but there was no answer. Where have you been, Layla? Don't you dare lie to me.'

Fuck.

'I've been stressing about my exams. When I got home, I went for a walk to clear my head.'

'At ten pm? For an *hour*?'

'I've been doing nothing but working and studying for months,' I said desperately. 'I needed a break, and once I started I couldn't stop.'

Her features relaxed. She believed me. 'I don't like you walking on your own at night. If you need a break, come home and watch a movie or something.'

'OK.' I gestured towards my room. 'I'd better get back to the study.'

She smiled gently. 'Take the night off. You look exhausted. Get an early night and start again tomorrow.'

'I'm working again tomorrow night. I need to fit study in whenever I can.'

Her brow furrowed. 'I think maybe you should consider quitting your job. School is way more important than some casual job.'

Somehow, this option had never occurred to me. Starting uni next year had been my escape route all this time, but if I no longer worked at the cafe, it'd be harder for Scott to pressure me into doing things. I could be free. It could be a way out.

'I'll think about it,' I said.

*

'You're quitting?' Scott said in disbelief when I turned up for my shift the following night. 'You can't quit now. I told you, I need you to help me with the business.'

'I've decided not to defer next year. I'm probably going to move to Adelaide, so …' I could feel him staring at me, but I dared not meet his gaze. It was only the two of us behind the counter. There were no customers.

Scott's hand closed around my upper arm, his fingernails digging into my bare skin. 'Why did you lie to me?'

'I told you I'd think about it, and I decided to—'

283

'You uppity bitch. You think you're better than everyone in this town, but what do you reckon they'd think of you if they knew the things you did with me? If they knew how you loved being my little whore?'

I yanked my arm out of his grip. 'I don't like being choked or slapped or pinched.'

'What?' His mouth was smiling, but there was a dangerous hardness to it now, his eyes like flat pebbles at the bottom of a creek. 'You're always encouraging me. You practically beg me for it.'

'No. No, I don't.'

He advanced towards me. 'Yes, you do. I bet you'd blow me right here if I asked you to.'

I shook my head furiously, but before I could protest again, the bell over the door tinkled and a couple of kids from school came in. Scott took their orders and they sat down at a table near the window. While I was making the coffees, he sidled up to me again, his mouth close to my ear.

'If you didn't like it, you would've said something earlier. You're no good, Layla. You're depraved, like me. That's why we're so good together.'

I left the coffees half made and fled to the bathroom. I sat down on the lid of the toilet, my head in my hands. Was I bad because I let him do those things to me? Was there a part of me that liked being treated like that? Why *hadn't* I ever asked him to stop?

I opened the door of the cubicle and went back out to the cafe floor. Scott was unstacking the dishwasher. He didn't look up. 'You can't quit. We're not discussing this again.'

Impotent rage wormed into my limbs. 'You don't have a choice. This is my last shift. I'm done.'

He looked up at me with a bland smile. 'I'm not letting you go that easily. You're mine, Layla.'

My fingers began untying my apron, and I lifted it over my head and let it drop to the floor. 'Not anymore. I don't want to see you again.'

Before he had the chance to respond, the cafe door opened and Bob Keen walked in. 'Layla!' he boomed. 'Get us a long black, will ya, love?'

I stepped out from behind the counter. 'Sorry, Bob, I would, but I don't work here anymore.'

I didn't look back as I crossed the cafe floor to the door. With every step, I felt stronger. I'd done it. I was free.

NOW

The gym was dark as they stepped inside, out of the bright sunlight. Layla pushed her sunglasses onto the top of her head and hung behind Renee as she began to greet their old classmates. She didn't immediately recognise anyone, but if she looked closely enough, features began to embed themselves in her brain one by one, until she remembered. After a few minutes, she realised others were doing it to her too. She grabbed a handful of chips from a bowl on one of the tables.

'Layla?' A woman stood by her elbow, a glass of bubbly in one hand. She looked older, and it took Layla a second to remember they were the same age, which made her wonder what others were thinking about her. 'It is Layla, isn't it?'

'Yeah, hi …' Layla racked her brain to work out who she was without looking too obvious. 'I'm sorry, I have a terrible memory.'

'Jodie.'

Layla almost inhaled the chip she was eating. But no. She'd seen Jodie Telford's picture; this was definitely not her. With a rush of relief, she recognised the woman. 'Jodie Wilson, right?'

The woman smiled. 'Yep, still Jodie Wilson. What about you? Still Layla Flynn, or did you get married?'

Layla picked up another chip and popped it into her mouth. 'Both. I'm married with two kids, but I didn't change my name.'

'Oh, one of those, are you.' It was a statement rather than a question. 'How nice that you managed to find a husband of your *own*.' She gave a little titter.

Layla bit down on the urge to do something violent. 'Well, nice to see you again, Jodie. If you'll excuse me, I'm going to grab a drink.'

'Sure, Layla. Talk to you again later.'

'Not if I can help it,' Layla muttered under her breath. She found Shona and linked arms with her. 'I need a drink.'

'Fuck, me too. Over here.' She steered Layla across the room to the long table lined with empty glasses and bottles of wine. Shona picked up one of the bottles of red and studied it with distaste. 'Rawson's Retreat? Jesus Christ. I thought if I came back to South Australia I'd at least get some decent fucking wine.'

Layla laughed. 'What did you expect from Glasswater Bay?'

'Should've brought a hip flask.'

They poured themselves generous serves of the least offensive of the wines, then turned to survey the room. 'Jodie Wilson just called me *one of those* because I didn't change my name when I got married,' Layla said.

Shona threw her head back and barked with laughter. 'Let me guess, she's still single?'

'Well, yeah, but so are you,' Layla pointed out.

'Touché.' They clinked their glasses together.

They watched Renee as she moved from group to group, chatting and laughing. 'I still can't believe she moved back here after uni,' Layla said.

'For him.' Shona gestured to Daniel, who was never far from his wife's side. The two of them exchanged smiles from time to time.

'I'm glad it worked out between them,' Layla said.

Shona glanced at her. 'They were always going to end up together. Even when he was with me, it was always her he was looking at. Nothing anyone did was ever going to change that.'

Layla turned away to top up their drinks for the third time. 'At this rate, we're going to be sozzled before the food comes out.'

'With any luck.'

'I bet there'll be party pies.'

After a while, Jodie came over to stand with them, and Layla groaned inwardly.

'Having fun, girls?' Jodie trilled. 'It's so great to all be together again, isn't it?'

'Absolutely.' Shona raised an eyebrow at Layla, and Layla had to suppress a laugh.

'I must say, when I decided to organise this thing, I didn't expect you two to come,' Jodie said. 'You were both always so … sarcastic. I didn't think it would be your kind of thing.'

'*You* organised this?' Shona's voice rose an octave.

Jodie nodded proudly. 'I wasn't sure how to get in touch with you, but Renee told me she'd pass on the invitation.'

'So you're the one responsible for the Comic Sans on that invitation?' Shona's voice wobbled with barely contained laughter.

'And the typos,' Layla added.

'And this shithouse wine,' Shona said.

Layla lost the fight and laughed out loud. Jodie shot them both an annoyed look. 'At least one of us is making an effort,' she hissed. 'I must say, Layla, I'm surprised Renee's letting you stay at her house after your little performance at the party after the formal.'

Layla's amusement shrivelled.

'How would you know? You weren't even *at* the afterparty,' Shona said, an edge to her voice.

'It's all anyone talked about at school the next week.' Jodie smiled smugly. 'Everyone certainly kept their boyfriends close by their sides after that! Although I must say, it wasn't much of a surprise once we all found out you'd been carrying on with Scott Telford all that time.'

Layla's whole body was vibrating with anger, but she forced herself to keep leaning casually against the table. 'I must say, Jodie, do go and fuck yourself.'

Shona burst into laughter. Jodie's mouth opened and closed a couple of times. 'Wow, rude!'

'She turned into a bit of a cow, didn't she?' Shona remarked as Jodie stormed away. 'She was always so nice at school too.'

'Mmm.' Layla's mood had soured. How stupid of her to think her reputation wouldn't have stuck with her. 'I think I might go.'

'You're not going anywhere.' Shona grabbed her arm. 'Let's mingle.'

And Layla allowed herself to be swept up by Shona's outrageous vibe, as she always had back in high school. For an hour they circulated the room, chatting to their old classmates and catching up on what they'd all been doing for the last twenty years. Layla began to relax again, and when Shona nudged her and pointed out the trays of party pies and sausage rolls that were coming out, they laughed until tears streamed down their faces, and she realised she was actually enjoying herself. No one else said anything about the formal, or about Scott. No one else cared. She felt another load slip from her shoulders. She spoke to Katrina, and not even the school bully who had once taunted her had anything bad to say. In fact, she was quite nice.

She and Renee were in animated disagreement about which teacher they'd had for Maths in Year Ten when there was a tap on Layla's shoulder. She turned around to see a very good-looking and very tall man. 'Hello, Layla.'

She stared at his black hair and olive skin and the smooth angles of his face, and it took her several seconds before she realised who it was. 'Oh my god, Rasheed?'

'Dude, you got hot,' Renee said approvingly. She glanced across the room, where Jodie had bailed up Daniel. 'Uh-oh, I'd better go and rescue my husband.' She threaded away through the crowd.

Rasheed turned back to Layla. 'It's good to see you again. I didn't think you'd come.'

'Why does everyone keep saying that?' Layla was feeling a little tipsy and her usual filter had dissolved. 'Why wouldn't I come when I left such a great impression on everyone?'

He blushed a little. 'How are you? Got a family?'

'Uh, yeah, a husband and two kids.' She showed him photos on her phone. 'What about you? Are you married?'

'I am.' He got his own phone out and showed her the photo on the home screen. 'His name is Adam and he's a stockbroker. We live in Sydney and we're having a baby in May.'

Layla almost choked on her mouthful of wine. 'That's great. Congratulations.'

He grinned. 'Thanks.'

'So what made *you* come back? Most of these people weren't very nice to you either.' She looked down. 'Including me.'

He shrugged. 'Because they don't scare me anymore. And it doesn't matter now. You of all people should know that.'

She studied him for a moment. 'It still matters to me. For twenty years, it's mattered. But then, you didn't hurt people the way I did.'

He smiled sadly. 'If it helps, I never blamed you.'

She nodded. 'It does a bit. Thanks.'

They watched the crowd in silence for a few minutes.

'You were only seventeen, Layla,' he said eventually. 'You made mistakes. Maybe it's OK to let it go now?'

If he knew what she'd really done – the suffering she'd caused – he probably wouldn't be quite so generous, but Layla allowed herself a small smile. 'I'm glad you came, Rasheed.'

'Me too.'

Then the lame music that had been playing cut out abruptly, and they looked over to see Shona plugging her phone into the stereo.

'Hey!' Jodie cried. 'I spent hours putting that playlist together.'

'Well, it sucks arse!' Daniel yelled from the other side of the room, and everyone laughed.

'Yeah, let's listen to something decent,' someone else said.

'Dirty Jeans' by Magic Dirt began blasting from the stereo. Layla's eyes met Renee's, then Shona's, and she whooped and joined her old friends to sing and dance like they had when the song had first come out twenty years ago. Ten minutes later, almost everyone in the room was dancing to Shona's playlist of Australian indie music, their normal, serious, grown-up lives temporarily forgotten as they abandoned themselves to the music of their youth. Even Jodie joined in. And Layla felt happy. And for the moment, she allowed herself to believe that everything might be OK after all.

THEN

It was over. I didn't see or hear anything from Scott. I studied hard, I hung out with my friends, and I began to imagine what life would be like when we all moved to Adelaide together next year.

But then, the morning before the formal, when I got out of my car at school, there he was, leaning against his car, arms crossed. I shivered with apprehension. Given his previous aversion to us being seen in public together, I'd assumed he wouldn't try to get to me once I'd left the cafe, so it was a shock to see him here, in broad daylight, waiting for me. I hoisted my bag onto my shoulder. 'What are you doing here?'

He smiled sadly. 'I've missed you. I wanted to see you again.'

There was something about his vulnerable expression that slowed my blood. 'I have to get to school.'

He looked at his watch. 'It's only eight thirty. Surely you have time to talk for a few minutes?'

'I told you, I can't see you anymore.' I tried to walk past him quickly, but his arm flashed out and caught my hand. 'Let me go.'

'I'm not going to hurt you, Layla. I could never hurt you.'

'But you did.' I pulled my hand out of his and gestured at my arm. 'What do you think these bruises are from?'

His gaze darted to my arm, then back to my face. 'I hardly touched you. I was just upset because you said you were going to leave me.'

'I have to go.' But my feet had turned to lead, and I couldn't seem to walk away.

'Meet me tomorrow night,' he said. 'I want to make it up to you.'

'It's the formal tomorrow night. I'm getting ready at Renee's house.'

His mouth turned down at one side, as if I'd disappointed him. 'Those people don't care about you, Layla. Not the way I do.'

'They're my friends.' My voice was growing weaker by the second.

'And all they've done is try to get between us. You're better than them. You always have been. They're just girls; you're a real woman.' His voice was low and gentle and curiously hypnotic. The strange, leaden feeling was creeping up my legs, filling my belly, climbing up to my chest. It would be so easy to give in to him. The optimism I'd carried inside me for the last few days now seemed pointless. He was in my system, pulsing through my veins, beating inside my heart, poisoning me from the inside out. He'd been right. I was no good.

'Layla!' came Renee's voice from up the street, and the spell shattered. I broke my gaze with Scott to wave to her as she got out of her car.

'She's not going to be there for you when you need her, Layla.' Scott opened his car door. 'The sooner you realise that, the better.'

I ran. Even as his car pulled out from the kerb and drove away, I ran all the way to Renee.

She scowled. 'What was *he* doing here?'

'He wanted to see me, but I told him to go.' My voice shook with the half-truth.

'Well, good.' She glanced at me as we walked towards the school gates. 'I can't believe he had the hide to turn up at school. Are you OK?'

I gave her a sideways smile. 'Sure I am.'

After the adrenalin of seeing Scott again had drained out of my body, I felt as if I'd been run over by a truck. If Renee hadn't shown up, I didn't know what I would have done. I couldn't understand why I found it so impossible to say no to him, why he was always able to convince me that I needed him. Over the course of the day, I kept telling myself it was really over, but that dead feeling was still inside me, dragging me down.

*

Shona managed to sneak a sixpack of pineapple Bacardi Breezers in the bag of stuff she brought to Renee's, and we were already tipsy and giggling our heads off.

'What do you reckon Katrina's gonna wear?' Shona said.

'Something skimpy to show off her eating disorder,' Renee said, and we all laughed.

There was a knock on the bedroom door. 'Are you girls dressed yet? I want to take photos of you!'

'Not yet, Mum,' Renee called back, hastily draining the last of her bottle and stashing it under her bed.

'We'd better get going,' I said. 'Daniel's going to be here soon and we're all still in our underwear.'

'That'd fuel his wet dreams for months.' Shona winked at me.

Renee pushed her. 'Don't be gross. He's not like that.'

'Oh Daniel, my one true love!' Shona shrilled, crossing her hands over her heart.

'You joke, but one day you'll meet someone you're really into, and then you'll understand.'

'Me? Nah. I don't need a man.'

We zipped each other up and preened in front of the mirror. We'd all had our hair and make-up done that afternoon, and we looked like supercharged versions of ourselves. My hair hung over my shoulders in soft, Hollywood curls, Shona's was all bunched up on top of her head in an artfully messy bun held together with about a thousand bobby pins, while Renee's was done in fifties pin curls.

'We look hot,' Renee said.

'Totally,' I said.

And we really did – even me. I'd never had my make-up done before and I couldn't believe how different I looked – my freckles had disappeared under the even coat of foundation, my eyes looked even bluer against the dark, smoky eyeshadow, and my normally thin lips looked luscious and full. There was no sign of the pimples I hated. This was the first time since the early days with Scott that I'd felt sexy, and it was definitely the first time I could see it for myself. I couldn't stop staring at my reflection. Maybe if I could learn how to recreate this look myself, I wouldn't need Scott to feel good after all.

'We'd better go out so Mum can take a million photos of us.' Renee rolled her eyes, but I could tell she was looking forward to it.

We made sure we'd hidden the empty bottles properly and then emerged from the bedroom. Mrs Kennedy covered her mouth with both her hands when she saw us, her eyes bright with emotion. 'Oh, *girls*, you look so lovely! Derek? Derek! Get the camera, quick!'

We posed together and separately so Mrs Kennedy could take photos, promising to print extra copies for us and our parents. Daniel knocked on the door, and it was kind of cute to see how obviously bowled over he was by Renee's appearance and how shy he was with her parents. He kept sneaking looks at her as he shook her dad's hand, and blushed when her mum kissed him on the cheek.

When it was time to go, we piled into Daniel's car and waved goodbye to Renee's parents.

'I can't believe it's the formal already,' Renee said.

'I can't believe how amazing you look.' Daniel put his hand on her leg, and they exchanged a smile.

Shona looked at me and pretended to stick her finger down her throat, and we both giggled.

*

The dinner before the formal was fairly dull; obviously, there was no booze, and everyone was too keen to get to the main event to eat much. Renee and Daniel spent half the time snogging while the teachers weren't looking, and Shona and I casually riffed off each other until it was time to go.

'I bet you twenty bucks Jason and Katrina break up tonight,' I said.

'You're on. There's no way Katrina's gonna sully her precious high school memories with a break-up.'

'We'll see.'

The formal itself was mostly fun, though the music was terrible. Shona coughed up when Jason had a very public fight with Katrina on the dance floor and she stormed off, but my mood began to dip towards the end when the slower songs came on and all the couples started swaying together. How ridiculous I'd been to invite Scott to this. No wonder he'd laughed at me. And yet, watching my classmates made me realise that I still wanted it, that I could've had it if I hadn't kept on with Scott. Two boys had invited me and I'd thrown it back in their faces. Rasheed had come without a date too; he sat on the other side of the room by himself, watching everyone else like I was. I stood up and went over to him.

He looked startled when I approached his table. 'Hey, Layla. Having a good time?'

'Not really. Do you want to dance?'

He studied me, as if trying to decide whether I was playing a trick on him. Or maybe he wanted nothing to do with me after the way I'd treated him. 'OK.'

He stood up and we went out onto the dance floor. 'Eternal Flame' by The Bangles was playing, and I almost laughed out loud. If this was a high school drama, this would be the moment the two of us realised we liked each other, and we'd kiss for the first time. Except this was Rasheed, and we'd already kissed, and the last time I'd seen him I'd called him a pathetic virgin loser. He put his hands on my waist and I put mine on his shoulders. We avoided each other's eyes as we tried to find a rhythm that would maintain the distance between our bodies.

'Your boyfriend couldn't make it tonight?' he said eventually.

'We broke up.'

'Oh. I'm sorry to hear that.'

We danced for a bit longer, and it began to feel less awkward. His hands were warm on my waist, and I started to feel even worse about the way I'd treated him.

'Rasheed … I'm sorry about what I said the other week. It was nasty, and I didn't mean it. You're not a loser. You're a good guy.'

He smiled a little. 'It's OK.'

'No, it's not. I don't want you to think that's how I treat people.'

'I don't think that. You've always been nice to me. You're a good person too, Layla.'

His words gave me a rush of gratitude. After the last few months of Scott making me believe there was something wrong with me, to hear someone tell me I was good … well, it felt good. And I don't know, maybe it was the corny music, but I started to feel quite affectionate towards Rasheed. Maybe I could have my high-school-movie moment after all. I moved my hand to the back of his neck and pulled his head gently down to mine. His lips were soft and light and not at all like our last encounter. I moved in closer to him and opened my mouth a little, but he raised his head and took a step back, his hands still on my waist.

'I'm sorry, Layla.' His face coloured as he searched for the right words. 'I like you a lot, but I think we should just be friends.'

The embarrassment burned in my throat. My fall was complete. I'd been rejected by the geekiest guy in school, at the formal, no less. 'Sure, no worries. Probably a good idea. Um … I'm just going to …' I left the dance floor and went over to where Shona stood, talking to Jason. 'Are we going to Bruiser's party after this? I need to get wasted.'

NOW

'I can't believe Rasheed is gay,' Shona said as they walked down the centre of the road on the way back to Renee and Daniel's place.

'Must have been kissing Layla at the social that did it,' Daniel said.

Layla looked at him in surprise, but he was grinning, and she realised he was joking. 'Bugger off!' She laughed.

'Actually, I feel a bit guilty,' Daniel went on to no one in particular. 'I used to call him a poof. God, I was such a dickhead in high school.'

'We all were,' Shona said.

'There's no excuse for some of the things we said to him,' Layla said. 'But he seems really happy now. It didn't damage him.'

They walked in silence for a few minutes. The air was still and warm. It pressed in around them in a way that felt intimate rather than claustrophobic. Layla's mind felt still too. She was nervous about talking to Jodie in the morning, but there was no fear anymore. She could barely remember the last time she hadn't been afraid.

'We should go to the beach tomorrow,' Shona said after a while. 'When we've got over our hangovers.'

'I'm going to see Jodie in the morning,' Layla said. 'And then I'm going straight home from there.' She was surprised by the melancholy she felt at the thought of leaving Glasswater Bay so soon.

'Hey, why don't you stay another night?' Renee said. 'It'd be nice to catch up for a bit longer.'

'I don't want to ...' Layla glanced at Daniel, then away. 'Thank you, but I'd better get back.'

'No, Renee's right.' Daniel gave Layla a quick smile. 'You should stay another day.'

THEN

Bruiser wasn't the brightest kid in school – this was his third attempt at passing Year Twelve – but he was renowned for his parties, and being a couple of years older than the rest of us, they were always stocked with plenty of alcohol. There were kegs of beer, pre-mixes, spirits, even a few bottles of wine he'd probably raided from his parents' collection. The music was already pumping when we walked in, and my mood lifted.

'Let's peruse the menu.' Shona led me over to the drinks table. Renee and Daniel were already ensconced on the couch in the dining room, kissing.

'Let's have vodka,' I said. 'It's quicker.'

'Amen, sister.' Shona poured us both generous serves of vodka into plastic cups, then splashed in some Coke.

We drank and danced and chatted with our classmates. It seemed like the music was alive in my body; I couldn't stop dancing. Shona and I started shimmying up against each other, and there were cheers and wolf whistles from around the room. The guys who hadn't already coupled off drew closer. I felt as if I could have anyone in this room I wanted.

Anyone.

Jason stood nearby, watching us – no, watching *me* – and I crooked my finger at him. He came over and I put my arms around his neck and moved in close, pressing my body against his. He put an arm around my waist and drew me in tight. He'd stripped off his tuxedo jacket and I could feel the damp warmth of his body through his white shirt. The song ended and he murmured in my ear, 'I think you need another drink.'

By the time he came back, there were two other guys trying to take his place while I cavorted around them, but he muscled in and raised a yellow plastic shot glass to my lips. 'Black sambuca,' he said, and I threw my head back and let him tip it into my mouth. It burned down my throat like aniseed fire, sending a shot of energy straight to my heart. I coughed and laughed at once. He threw his own down then hurled the plastic cups across the room and bent his head to kiss me. His mouth tasted of aniseed; his tongue curled around mine. I closed my eyelids and lights still danced behind them. My head was spinning, but the effect was exhilarating, like I was flying. His hands closed around my buttocks. I could feel his erection pressing against me and I rubbed against it, teasing him, then moving away. After being used by Scott for so long, it was intoxicating to be in control. He'd do anything I wanted; I knew it.

We left the dance floor and downed another couple of shots before moving into the adjacent room. It was empty other than one other couple kissing enthusiastically on one of the couches. They didn't even look up when we walked in. There were no lights on, and the room was shadowy and dark. Jason led me over to the other couch and we half fell onto it, laughing. My vision had blurred; everything looked black and white, but my other senses seemed heightened. The music from the next room swirled inside me. We kissed for a long time, until it felt like we were joined. His hand was on my thigh, moving up, and I unbuttoned his pants and slipped my hand inside.

'Do you have a condom?' I asked as I stroked him. My head was swimming and I felt dizzy, but I wanted to conquer him.

'You want to do it here?' He looked bewildered, glanced over at the other couch where the couple were still locked in each other's embrace. But I could see his excitement too.

'Why not?' I said with a sardonic smile. 'We'll all be out of this town soon anyway.'

'I had no idea you were like this,' he said as I straddled his lap and covered us with my dress while he rolled the condom on.

He groaned as I lowered myself onto him, but there was a void inside me, and I felt nothing. I rode him hard, trying to make it feel real, but everything was numb now, like I was made of liquid and would wash away. The room was spinning so wildly I could hardly see his eyes as he held onto my waist. And I wanted to see his eyes; I wanted to see how I could make them change just with the power of my body.

And then it was over, and he was gasping into my ear, and suddenly his animal sounds repulsed me. I climbed off and plonked down on the couch beside him as he pulled the condom off and dropped it on the floor with a splat. I felt like I was going to throw up.

'That was awesome.'

I couldn't even look at him. I was sickened by what I'd just done. 'I need another drink.' I wriggled my knickers back up and returned to the other room. Someone was pouring out more shots of sambuca at the drinks table, and I downed two of them, one after the other. The alcohol dulled my senses further, providing a fuzzy cushion that suddenly made the whole episode seem incredibly funny.

'Hey, Layla, maybe you should slow down a bit.' Renee's face swam in front of my eyes.

'What? I'm totally fine!' I put an arm around her shoulders. 'Have a shot with me, bitch.'

'How about you have some water instead?'

I rested my head on her shoulder. 'You're so nice, Renee. So niiiiice.'

'And you smell like liquorice.' Her voice was amused. 'You're wasted, man. What've you been up to?'

I laughed. 'I totally just rooted Jason in the next room.'

Renee moved away from me and stared at me in shock. 'Are you serious? That's not like you.'

'Why does everyone keep saying that? It's not like I signed some contract promising to be the good girl forever. Why aren't I allowed to have some fun?'

But it was coming back again, that horrible feeling. Renee's brow was furrowed, and I followed her gaze to where Jason stood with a bunch of guys. They were all laughing and fist-bumping him and glancing over at me, and as I looked around, I realised the story was already rushing through the room like a bushfire. Eyes stared back at me, some baleful, some curious, some amused. Before I had the chance to react, Katrina was storming up to me, her pale face livid.

'We only *just* broke up and you're already screwing him?' she shouted. 'In front of everyone? What kind of person does that?'

The alcohol pumped through my bloodstream, fiery and hot, and my shame hardened, transformed into the meanness that had been coming out more and more regularly. All through high school, I'd been intimidated and taunted by this girl based only on a pointless hierarchy. But school was almost over and the hierarchy was bullshit. She didn't matter anymore; she never had. I brought my face up close to hers. 'You know I was the one he really wanted, right? He only asked you to the formal because I turned him down. It's not my fault you couldn't satisfy him.'

She glared at me, her icy-blue eyes wide. 'Slut!' she spat, then wheeled around and stalked away, teetering a little on her stilettos.

'Bitch!' I yelled after her. I turned back to Renee with a laugh, but she wasn't smiling now. She looked worried.

'Maybe come and sit down for a while,' she suggested. 'Sober up a bit.'

'Nah, think I'll go and dance again. Join me?'

'I really think you should have a break. You're not acting like yourself.'

I rolled my eyes. 'Go and be boring with your precious boyfriend, then.'

Her face fell, but I didn't wait around for more of her judgement, just strutted back onto the dance floor, waving my hands over my head. The girls who were there drew away from me with disdainful expressions, but the boys … the boys came in closer. I tipped my head back and smiled up at the ceiling as it spun over my head. There were hands on my body and I had no idea whose they were, but it didn't matter. They wanted me. They all wanted me.

Then someone's arms were around me and I tried to focus on his face, but everything was so blurry that I couldn't make out any features, and now he was kissing me and his hands were all over me, and I wasn't sure where he ended and I began. He took my hand and led me into that shadowy room and he lay me down on the couch and I couldn't see or feel anything and the world was spinning wildly and there was this vague feeling of wrongness in my head. Then his weight was pressing me into the couch and his fingers were inside me and his breath was foul on my face and I wanted to get up and run but I was so, so tired and I couldn't resist or fight or even move.

Then, 'Get off her!' came Shona's voice and the light came on and his weight disappeared. I lay on the couch, my dress up around my hips, blinking at the fuzzy shape of my friend. She helped me sit up and rubbed my back. 'What were you thinking going off with Bruiser? He's disgusting.'

'*Bruiser?*' I laughed, but beneath my amusement a tornado of horror was building inside me. 'That was Bruiser?'

'You didn't even know who it was?'

I giggled. 'I'm so drunk.'

'Come on.' She took my hand and pulled me to my feet. 'Let's get you some water and something to eat.'

'Eating's cheating, Porter.' I weaved behind her as she led me out of the room and into the dining room, where Daniel sat on a low brown couch against the wall.

'Where's Renee?' Shona said.

'In the bathroom.' Daniel gestured to me. 'What's going on with her?'

Shona sighed. 'She's fucking paro. Can you look after her for a minute while I go and get her some water?' She deposited me on the couch beside him and disappeared.

I rested my head on Daniel's shoulder. 'My feet are killing me.'

'Why don't you take your shoes off?' he said.

'Too tired.'

'So you're pretty trolleyed, hey?'

I looked up at him with a smile. 'How can you tell?'

He smiled back. 'Lucky guess.'

I snuggled back into his shoulder. He felt warm, solid, dependable. 'Sorry to hear about your uncle,' I said.

'What about my uncle?'

'The cancer. How long's he got left?'

He shifted away from me so I had to straighten to look at him. 'What are you talking about?'

'Jodie's dad. Scott told me he had terminal cancer and that's why he couldn't leave her—' I stopped abruptly. Of course. Of course. I was such an idiot. I covered my eyes with my hands. 'But he was lying to me, wasn't he? He's been lying to me all along.'

'Layla.' Daniel's hands were on my shoulders. 'What are you saying?'

What *was* I saying? The whole night had contracted into a thick fog, and there was a weird buzzing in my head. I needed to sleep, but the warmth of Daniel's hands seeped into my shoulders, and it was so nice to be touched by someone. He was the first boy I'd ever liked, the first one I'd pined over, and suddenly that felt really important. Why hadn't I made a move on him way back before I'd got involved with Scott?

I dropped my hands from my face. Daniel was looking at me with such intensity, and I needed something that was real and pure. I touched his chest and leant in to kiss him.

His expression changed to panic. He turned his head to the side and shrank away from me, and with a lightning bolt of shock I realised the unforgivable mistake I'd made. But it was too late, because Renee was in the room and the look on her face cut straight into my soul. I scrambled to my feet and my stomach lurched.

'Renee.' Daniel's voice was desperate. 'I didn't do anything, I swear. It was her. She—'

'I thought it was different with you,' Renee said. 'I thought you liked me.'

'I do.' He got up and tried to embrace her, but she backed out of his reach, holding up a hand.

'I can't look at you right now. Just go.'

He threw a bitter look at me. 'Skank!' he muttered under his breath as he left the room.

When I turned to Renee, there were tears in her eyes. Everything felt out of control. 'I'm sorry. I didn't know what I was doing.'

'Don't you dare use alcohol as an excuse.' Her voice wavered. 'I never thought you'd do something like this to me. When did you turn into such a slut?'

The events of the night closed in on me. 'I just wanted to feel something. I don't mean anything to anyone.'

'You meant something to me. You were my friend.'

'What do you mean were?'

'I really liked him, Layla. You've destroyed everything. Don't speak to me again.' She turned away.

I grabbed at her shoulder. 'Renee, please! I didn't mean it!'

She shrugged me off. 'Go home, Layla.'

And she walked out of the room. Shona stood in the doorway, looking at me in utter shock and dismay. After a second, she turned and followed Renee.

I wanted to cry, but there was nothing left inside me. The room wasn't spinning anymore. I was still drunk, but the euphoric feeling had disappeared. There was a sickening heaviness in my stomach and my ankles were burning from the blisters my shoes had rubbed into my skin. I bent to remove them, then wandered through the rooms of the house. Most people had left; I could make out Bruiser's hulking shape in one corner of the living room, fiddling with the stereo. A few of the guys still stood around the room, draining the last of the alcohol. I tried to slip out without anyone seeing me, but one of them glanced over and called out, 'How about a lap dance, Layla?' He mimed a lewd sexual act and the others all guffawed. I opened the front door and stepped out onto the verandah, the cold night air piercing the fog of drunkenness.

It seemed inevitable when I set off up the footpath, stumbling over the cracks in the pavement, that he was there, sitting in his car just up the street from Bruiser's house. The passenger window was open and he called out to me in a flat voice, 'Get in.'

I stopped, my eyes heavy. I'd planned to stay at Renee's tonight, but that obviously wasn't an option now. There was nowhere else to go. Nothing seemed to matter anymore. I opened the door and got in.

He didn't speak. My house was only a few streets away, but he directed the car onto the main road and then turned off into the small bitumen car park behind the Foodland. I wondered idly what he was going to do with me, but I couldn't muster up the energy to care.

'Everyone who came out of that party was talking about what you did.' He stared straight ahead, his hands still clenched around the steering wheel. 'Three guys, Layla — you fucked three different guys in one night?'

My disgrace was visceral. 'One,' I said in a small voice. 'It was only one.'

He finally looked at me. 'I always knew you had a bit of the wild girl in you, but I didn't think you were this fucked up.' He laughed mirthlessly. 'None of those guys are actually interested in you, you know. You're not even that attractive. You should hear what everyone was saying about you.'

A sob rose in my throat at the memory of Renee's face. 'My friends …'

'I was right, wasn't I? They weren't there for you when you needed them. I'm the only one who cares about you now.' He smiled cruelly. 'Get out of the car.'

I started. 'You're going to leave me here?'

'Get out.'

I opened the door and stepped out. The asphalt was rough and cold on my bare feet. I waited for him to start the engine and roar away, but instead he got out too and came up close, then wound his hand up into my hair. 'You're mine, Layla. No one else touches you, you understand? You're mine. You don't get to decide when this ends.'

NOW

The air in the room was stifling when Layla woke. She stretched out her legs, searching for a cool spot between the sheets, and her foot hit warm skin. She rolled over to find Shona's face on the pillow beside hers, and she started. Shona opened her eyes, blinked and groaned. 'What time is it?' she grumbled.

Layla glanced at the clock radio behind Shona's head. 'Eight thirty. I haven't slept this late in almost five years.'

Shona groaned again. 'Late? I guess that's why I never had kids.' Her eyes fluttered closed, and within seconds her breathing slowed and deepened into sleep again.

Layla lay still for another few minutes, but her head was pounding and sleep wouldn't come back to her. She got up and pulled on her jeans, then grabbed her bag and detoured into the bathroom to wash her face and put on enough make-up to cover her imperfections.

Shona had planned to go back to her parents' place last night, but when they'd got back to Renee's they'd all stayed up drinking for another two hours, and Layla and Shona had ended up sharing the bed in the spare room. Layla hadn't been this hungover in a long time.

The house was deathly silent when she went out to the kitchen. She was desperate for a coffee, but she dared not switch on the machine and risk waking anyone up. She poured a glass of water from the tap and took it out to the backyard. The morning was still cool, a welcome relief from the close heat within the house and the nausea that churned in her belly. There was a light breeze, but Layla knew from the sweltering summers of her childhood that it would soon give way to shimmering heat. She sat down at the table under the pergola and sipped at her glass of water. After the light feeling that had followed the reunion last night, the meeting with Jodie in a few hours began to weigh on her again. She'd held onto this secret for so long now that she ached right down to her soul. But she was tired of holding on. Rasheed's words from last night echoed in her head: *Maybe it's OK to let it go now?*

No matter what happened with Jodie today, she couldn't run anymore. She had to face up to what she'd done.

Her phone stared back at her from the table. Cam would already be up, herding the children and catering to their endless demands. He was the one she loved more than any other, and yet she'd been lying to him constantly lately, and, by omission, ever since she'd known him. If she wanted to save their faltering relationship – and she did, more than anything – she had to tell him the full story. She took another sip of water and dialled his number.

'Hey.' The warmth in his voice was like a bath; she sank into it gratefully. 'How was the reunion?'

'It was actually great. I had a really good time. I'm quite hungover this morning though.'

'That's great … that you had fun, not that you're hungover.' There was a smile in his voice. 'We really miss you.'

'I miss you too,' she said. 'But if you don't mind, I've decided to stay on for another day. I'd like to spend a bit more time with Renee and Shona.'

'Of course. We're doing fine.'

'And there's ... there's something else I need to do.'

'What's that?'

'I need to go to the police.'

Silence. Layla's heart stuttered as she waited for his response.

'*What?* What happened? Are you OK?'

'I didn't tell you everything about what happened when I was a teenager.'

He took in a deep breath, but when he didn't speak, she began to. She told him the whole story: what she'd done, what the consequences had been, the real reason Jodie wanted to see her. He remained silent throughout. Every now and then, she heard one of the kids shout in the background, but Cam didn't say a word.

'So that's why I'm going to the police,' she finished. 'I need to own what I did and face the consequences.'

When Cam finally spoke, his voice was thin and shaky. 'But what about us? What if you go to *jail*, Layla? Where does that leave us?'

Layla pressed her lips together to hold in the emotion. 'My mum will help you out if it comes to that.'

He laughed mirthlessly. 'For fuck's sake, Layla, do you know what you're saying? You want to take the fall now for something that happened twenty years ago?'

'Fuck*sake*!' came Ella's voice in the background.

'It didn't *happen*. I did it.'

'But it wasn't even intentional!' His voice was high, desperate. 'It won't change anything for them.'

Tears slid down Layla's cheeks. 'But it will for me. I can't live with this anymore, Cam. I understand if you want to leave me, but if I don't face up to what I did, it's going to kill me.' A sob escaped her.

Cam's breath whooshed out. 'Oh god, Layla, of course I don't want to leave you. Why would you think that?'

Layla grimaced, torn between relief at his words and dread at voicing the fears she'd been harbouring for weeks. 'Things have been difficult between us lately. I know you're not happy, and now this … well, I wouldn't blame you.'

'Is that what *you* want?'

'No!' she cried. 'No, I don't want to lose you. I love you.'

'Well, I'm glad.' His voice was a little warmer. 'I love you too. But I don't understand why you want to punish yourself for something that happened so long ago. What if she's bluffing? What if she doesn't know anything?'

'But *I* know.'

He sighed. 'You're really going to do this, aren't you?'

'I have to.'

'Do you want me to come? I could go with you.'

Layla was tempted. Maybe she could bear it more easily with her husband by her side. But the police would want to know her motive, and then she'd have to tell them how Scott had debased her, how she'd been driven mad with the need to find a way out. She couldn't bear for Cam to hear those details … both for his sake and because she didn't want him to think less of her once he knew what she'd let Scott do to her. 'No. Thank you, but this is something I need to do on my own.'

Cam sighed again. 'OK, if that's what you want. But please call me afterwards and let me know how it went.'

She promised him she would.

'Fuck*SAKE!*' Ella bellowed, and they both laughed nervously.

After she'd spoken to both the children, she was hanging up when she heard the hum of the sliding door. She looked up to see Daniel.

'Morning,' he said.

'Hi.' She swiped the back of her wrist across her eyes. 'Sorry, I was talking to the kids. I miss them.'

He nodded, shuffling his feet. 'Do you want a coffee?'

'Oh, yes. Thank you.'

He went back inside, giving Layla a chance to compose herself. When he returned with two steaming mugs of coffee and sat opposite her, she gave him a grateful smile. 'Thanks.'

He took a sip from his mug. 'Couldn't sleep?'

She shook her head ruefully. 'The kids have trained me to get up at six every morning. Eight thirty is a sleep-in.'

'I remember that stage. Don't worry, by the time they're teenagers you'll have to pry them out of bed with a crowbar.'

'Revenge.' She grinned.

'Layla.' He looked down into his cup. 'I'm sorry I told everyone at school about you and Scott.'

'I don't blame you. I ruined things for you and Renee.'

'But what I did made it impossible for you to stay here. Your whole family had to leave.'

She held his gaze for a moment. 'I didn't leave because of you, Daniel. In fact, that's part of the reason I came back. I was the one who—'

'How on earth are you guys even alive right now?' came Renee's voice from the doorway.

The unspoken confession hung in the air. Layla retreated. 'The power of coffee.'

'I'll make you one.' Daniel stood up.

'Thanks, babe.' Renee took his hand for a second as he passed her, then sat down in the chair beside Layla. 'When are you going to Jodie's?'

'Ten.'

'How are you feeling about it?'

Layla grimaced. 'Terrified. I can't possibly make it up to her. Ever.'

'I know you feel guilty about it, but he was the one who cheated. He's the one she should be punishing.'

Again, it was on the tip of Layla's tongue to tell her the truth. Until this morning, her mother was the only one who knew what had really happened that day, but now it felt like a tidal wave inside her, threatening to gush out over anyone who was in her way. She reined it back in. She owed Jodie the truth first, then the police. Everyone else could come after that.

Instead, she put her hand over Renee's. 'Thanks for inviting me. I'm really glad I came.'

'So am I. I've always felt bad that I let us drift apart. It all seems so insignificant now that we've got our own families.'

'You don't need to feel bad. I was the one who stuffed things up for you.'

Renee squeezed her hand. 'But that's the thing. You didn't. Daniel got an apprenticeship here when school finished. We would've had to break up at the end of the year anyway. And I know he didn't kiss you … we had a discussion about what to do, and decided we'd go our separate ways and see what happened when I finished uni.'

'And you came back.'

Renee smiled. 'I came back. And if I hadn't got the job in Victor, he would've come to Adelaide. Daniel and I, we were inevitable.'

'That's what Shona said,' Layla mused.

'What did Shona say?' Their friend appeared, coffee in hand, her eyes still bleary with sleep, and plonked into one of the chairs.

'About these two star-crossed lovers overcoming all obstacles to be together,' Layla said.

Shona stuck her finger in her mouth and pretended to gag. They all laughed. Then she clasped her hands behind her head and stretched languidly. 'So, Katrina was weirdly nice, wasn't she?'

'You sound disappointed,' Layla said.

'Well, you go through your life expecting some things to never change, and the next minute the school bully is lovely and the nice girl is a judgemental twat. When the hell did Glasswater Bay become so bloody unpredictable?'

'You're the one who's been off in London all these years and you haven't changed a bit,' Renee said.

'I'm choosing to take that as a compliment,' Shona said primly.

'So you should,' Layla said.

'Do you think you'll ever come back?' Renee asked.

Shona's usually brash expression slipped. 'You know, I love living in London, but this weekend is the closest I've ever come to considering moving back to Australia. I've got friends there, I've got a career, I've got an apartment. I've even got a friend with benefits who has an outside chance of becoming more than that.' Layla gave a low whistle and Shona grinned. 'But I've never had a connection with anyone there like I have with you guys. Our roots go deep. I miss that.'

'Me too,' Layla and Renee said together.

Daniel came back out with more coffee and gave a mock groan. 'Jesus, are you lot crying *again*?'

THEN

I kept my head down when I walked into school on Monday, but the laughs and the sneers and the taunts followed me everywhere. Even those who hadn't been at Bruiser's party had heard about my exploits by recess. No one spoke to me. Not even Shona. It was the last week of school before final exams started, but the idea of getting through five days of this was unbearable.

After Scott had finished with me on Saturday night, he'd dropped me home. I'd left all my stuff at Renee's, including my keys, so I'd snuck down the side of the house and in through the laundry, which Mum and Dad always left unlocked. Somewhere along the way I'd lost one of my shoes, and I clutched the remaining one as I tiptoed down the hallway. I'd almost made it when Mum appeared in the doorway of her bedroom. She'd switched on the hallway light and gasped as she took in my appearance.

'What happened?' she said. 'I thought you were spending the night at Renee's.'

Finally, the tears came. 'We had a huge fight. She hates me.'

'Oh, Layla.' Mum stepped forward and I fell against her. 'You're clearly quite drunk, and people have all sorts of arguments when they've been drinking. I'm sure everything will be OK by Monday.'

But it wasn't OK. When I'd tried to call Renee last night, she'd refused to come to the phone, and she hadn't even shown up at school today. Daniel was there, but the few times I'd caught glimpses of him, his face had been stony. When the bell went at the end of the day and I walked out of the school gates towards my car, small knots of students were standing around chatting. Those who spotted me whispered and laughed.

My car was parked down below the oval, and as I drew closer I saw three Year Eleven girls huddled around it. They didn't see me coming and so I was almost among them when one of the girls finished spraying *SLUT* across the windscreen of my car with shaving cream.

'Apparently, she had sex with three different guys on Saturday night!' one of them said. '*Three*, can you imagine?'

'I heard she's been doing it with Scott Telford for, like, months,' another said, and the other two shrieked.

Horror clenched in my chest. Was Renee taking revenge on me by telling everyone my deepest, darkest secret?

'You should write "home wrecker" on the back windscreen!'

I stepped forward and yanked the can of shaving cream out of the first girl's hand and hurled it onto the oval. 'Get the fuck away from my car.'

They all gasped with shocked laughter and backed away as I opened the car door and got in.

'Sucked any dicks today, Layla?' one of them yelled as I started the engine.

I blinked through the tears of useless, humiliated rage, trying to see past the back-to-front letters that branded the windscreen as I roared away.

*

I drove straight to Renee's place and knocked on her door, tears still running down my face. She mustn't have been expecting me, because she opened the door straightaway.

'Go away, Layla.'

'Can I talk to you?'

She crossed her arms over her chest. 'I've got nothing to say to you.'

'Seems like you had plenty to say to everyone at school though.' I gestured to my car on the street. The shaving-cream letters had run into one another in the wind, but there was no mistaking what they said.

Her expression wavered a little as she followed my gaze. 'Yeah, well. I didn't say anything to anyone. But what did you expect, Layla? You brought this on yourself.'

I wanted to bring up the boys she'd slept with over the last couple of years, ask why I was being punished for losing control once, ask why she hadn't been there when Bruiser had me on the couch, semi-conscious, but I knew all the reasons why already, and they all led back to my own stupid choices. 'Apparently, there's a rumour going around about me and Scott. You and Shona were the only ones who knew, so I guess I have you to thank for that.'

She blew out an exasperated breath. 'You told Daniel, you idiot. I guess he's still pissed off after you tried to jump his bones.'

I remembered my drunken rambling to Daniel and raised a hand to my mouth. She was right; I was an idiot.

'Anyway, it was only a matter of time before everyone found out about it,' Renee said. 'Small town and everything.'

I stared at my feet. 'So, you and Daniel are still together?'

'We broke up yesterday.'

'But he didn't do anything wrong,' I said. 'It was all my fault.'

She shrugged dispassionately. 'He's staying in Glasswater next year. I'm going to uni. So I guess you saved us the trouble of breaking up in a few months.'

'I'm sorry, Renee.'

She didn't say anything; just hugged herself tighter.

'Can I come in?'

'I told you, I don't want to see you anymore.'

Desolation rose within me. All through the horrible aftermath of the party and the school day, I'd been counting on being able to get her back. I'd thought our friendship could withstand anything, but she looked so cold now, as if we'd never meant anything to each other. 'But what about the share house next year? We had it all planned.'

She scoffed. 'You should've thought about that before you came onto my boyfriend.'

'I didn't mean to hurt you,' I said. 'Please don't hate me.'

'I have to go.' She bent to pick up my bag from the floor, then held it out to me. 'Here, take this.'

Then she stepped back and closed the door.

*

I trudged slowly towards the school gates the next morning. This was the last place I wanted to be, but I had nowhere else to go, nothing to do except study for exams next week. There was only blackness in my mind.

'Layla,' came his voice.

I stopped and ducked to look at him through his car window. 'What do you want?'

'Jodie knows about us.'

I turned this information over in my mind. He gestured to the passenger door. I knew I should ignore him, walk on, go to school and let the barrage of insults bounce off me until the day was over. But what was the point in even showing up? It was the last week. I wasn't going to learn anything new now. I slid into the car and dumped my school bag on the floor.

'How?'

'Because you left your fucking shoe in my car.'

'Oh. I was wondering where that got to.'

He shot me a filthy look and pulled out from the kerb. After a minute, I realised we were heading up to The Knob, and I started to wish I'd gone to school after all. The car park was, as usual, empty, the grassy expanse leading up to the granite outcropping deserted.

'Everyone's going to find out about this now,' he said.

'I don't care,' I said sullenly. 'I'm leaving Glasswater soon anyway.'

'But I'm not!' he shouted. 'How could you be so selfish? First you promised me you'd stay, then you change your mind and decide to destroy my marriage on your way out? You've ruined me.'

I gave a hysterical laugh. *'I've* ruined *you*?'

He lunged at me and pinned me against the car door, his hand around my throat. 'Are you laughing at me, bitch? I could kill you.'

His eyes were full of fury. I knew I should be afraid, but I couldn't make myself feel anything. 'Do it.' His hand had cut off my breath and my voice came out in a hoarse whisper. 'Go on.'

He released me and sat back, a shocked expression on his face. 'Jesus, Layla, don't say that. Don't ever say that.'

I remained hunched against the car door, coughing, as far away from him as possible. He watched me for a minute, then reached out and touched my face gently, and I cringed away from him.

'I'm sorry. You just make me so angry sometimes, pushing me away when all I want is to be with you.'

'You've been lying to me.' My voice was croaky. 'I know Jodie's father doesn't have cancer.'

'What?' He looked confused. 'I never said he did.'

I sat up straighter. 'You did. You said he had terminal cancer and that you needed to support her through it.'

He gave a bemused smile. 'I think you're getting confused. You must be studying too hard, not to mention frying your brain with all that booze the other night. I said Jodie was fighting with her mum, that's all.'

I frowned. 'I'm sure that's what you said. That night I met you up here, when I tried to break it off with you.'

He shook his head, tapped me lightly under my chin. 'No, I told you we had a special connection, remember?'

Self-doubt clouded my certainty. 'I remember that, but—'

'Now she knows about us, we can make it official. We can be together.'

'But …' I faltered. He was so confident, and my memory of the conversation seemed fuzzy and indistinct now. His eyes were soft and loving, and I began to wonder if I'd dreamed up the moment before; his hand around my throat. Maybe I was going crazy. Still, I resisted. 'I'm going to uni next year.'

'You know you're not going to find anyone else who loves you like I do. Who doesn't mind your acne and your big nose and small boobs.'

My heart withered. Gently, he drew me towards him and lay my head against his shoulder, and I let him do it.

'Stay,' he said softly. 'Stay here with me.'

My mind swung wildly between emotions as he stroked my hair back from my face, handling me with such sensitivity that I thought I might cry. He could be my last chance at real happiness, and after losing Renee, I needed to believe that happiness was still possible.

He tilted my chin up to look into my eyes. 'Please stay, Layla. I can give you everything.'

My soul ached to believe him. If it was all out in the open, if we did it right, maybe it could cancel out my mistakes and fill up this bottomless void inside me. Maybe everyone would stop hating me. Maybe everything really could be perfect.

*

My parents were still at work when I got home, but Zach was sitting in the kitchen scoffing down a packet of chips. He glared balefully at me as I got the Coke out of the fridge and gulped some from the bottle. 'Where were you all day?'

'At school, dipshit.' But I turned away to avoid his eyes. After Scott had gone to open the cafe, I'd spent the day sitting in the rotunda at the park, flicking through my textbooks and trying to burn the information onto my brain.

'No, you weren't.'

'What do you care anyway?'

'Everyone's talking about you, you know. Even the Year Eights.'

My face went hot. 'It's all lies. Just ignore it.'

'All of it?'

'Shut up, idiot.' I left the Coke open on the bench and went to walk out.

'I'll tell Mum!' he called out.

I raised my middle finger over my shoulder and went to my room. No sooner had I left Scott than I'd begun to question everything again. He hadn't said when he was going to leave Jodie and what the next step would be. And after Zach had reminded me of the rumours circulating the school – and probably the whole town by now – the idea of staying in Glasswater Bay was even more agonising. I'd split up a family. Even if we lived a respectable life together, people weren't going to forget that. And though the cafe had been an OK place to work through school and save a bit of money, I couldn't imagine spending every day there, balancing the till and ordering stock. I still wanted to be a pharmacist. I still wanted to move to Adelaide and live the uni lifestyle before I settled down. Besides, half the people my age were leaving next year. And how the hell was I going to tell my family?

I was still tying myself in knots when Mum got home. She came to my room and stood in the doorway. 'Something weird happened at work today.'

Foreboding twitched in my belly. The parade of residents who visited Glasswater's only dental surgery were always keen to gossip with the receptionist, so Mum was often one of the first to find out what was happening around town. I tried to make my voice sound casual. 'What's that?'

'Natalie Rogers came in with a broken crown, and when she was paying her bill, she told me I should keep a better eye on my daughter. Do you know what that's all about?'

I shrugged even as my heart raced. 'No idea.'

'And it wasn't just her. Bob Keen was in for a check-up later in the day and he said he was sorry to hear about what you've been up to. What on earth is going on?'

Panic leapt inside me. How was I going to talk my way out this time? 'OK, I didn't want to tell you this, but I kind of wagged school today.'

Mum frowned. 'That's not like you.'

I looked down at the crosshatch pattern of my bedspread. 'Renee and I are still fighting. She doesn't want to live together next year anymore.' I bit my lip.

Mum's head tilted to the side. 'Oh, Renee'll come around. You girls have been friends since kindy. I bet she'll change her mind when the time comes to go to the city.'

I dared to look up at her. 'I'm thinking about deferring next year. I could stay on here for a while, go back to work at the cafe and save up some money.'

'Don't be silly,' Mum said. 'We'll lend you the money if you need it. Don't put your future on hold because of a fight with Renee.'

She turned and walked out and I flopped onto my back on the bed. I wasn't sure which option was worse: staying here with Scott or moving to the city by myself, with no friends.

NOW

After breakfast, Layla had a shower and dressed in jeans and a loose shirt. She tried to keep her hands steady as she put on her make-up using the mirror above the dressing table in the spare room. With each layer she applied, she felt calmer, more in control.

Renee came into the room and perched on the edge of the spare bed. 'Contouring on a Sunday? You're keen.'

Their eyes met in the mirror, but Layla didn't say anything.

'I wanted to give you these.' Renee held something out towards her, and Layla turned to see the fan of glossy photos. 'Mum had extras printed for you. I've been holding on to them all these years.'

Layla's throat felt thick as she took the photos from Renee and studied them: the bright colours of their dresses, their smiles, their sparkling eyes, the love that shone between them. 'Thank you.'

'Sorry I never gave them to you. I was so selfish, letting one mistake come between us like that. You needed help, and I wasn't there for you.'

'You are now, and that matters.' Layla smiled at her, then looked back at the photos. 'God, I wish I'd known back then how good I looked. And now look at me.'

Renee was silent for a moment, and when Layla looked up at her, she was frowning.

'Layla … I know we haven't seen each other for a long time, and I don't want to overstep the mark here, but from what I've seen, you seem to have a difficult relationship with your body.'

Layla gave her a wry grin. 'Are you psychoanalysing me?'

Renee's expression didn't change. 'You bet I am.'

Layla turned back to the mirror and twisted the lid off her mascara. 'I'm getting close to forty. Don't we all have some body image issues at this age?'

'Sure.' Renee nodded. 'But being a bit down about our changing bodies is not the same as looking in the mirror every day and hating what you see.'

Layla started, and the mascara brush streaked across her cheek. She swore and rubbed at the black mark with one finger, avoiding Renee's eyes.

'When we walked to the reunion yesterday, you checked your reflection in every window we passed,' Renee went on. 'And you've made numerous negative comments about your looks since you got here. I know you had some self-esteem issues in high school, but this seems different. I think you might have depression or anxiety. Or maybe both. If you like, I can recommend a psychologist in Adelaide who might be able to help you.'

Layla was silent until she'd finished her make-up, trying to decide how much to tell Renee. She put down the mascara brush, turned around and leant against the dressing table.

'When I was seventeen, Scott used to tell me I was in my prime, and that my body was all I had to offer. He seemed to know exactly the things I was self-conscious about, and he'd pick at them like a scab until I was so insecure that I thought I didn't deserve to be loved. And it was no different when I started seeing other people. The guy I lived with – the one who abused me – he used to tell me I was ugly, and I believed him.'

Renee's eyes were soft with empathy. 'I'm sorry you had to go through that. You're not ugly, inside or out. You deserve love as much as anyone else does.'

'Cam is the sweetest man I've ever known.' Layla's voice shook. 'And he loves me. And yet we can't even have sex with the lights on because I don't want him to see my body. My own husband!'

Renee smiled sadly at her. 'I know it's easier said than done, but you don't have to live like this.'

'I just want to go one day without obsessing over how I look and what other people think of me. It'd be simple to blame Scott, but there must be some weakness inside me that makes me feel this way. That makes me so fucking self-indulgent.'

'It's not self-indulgent, Lay. It's mental illness.'

Everything within Layla resisted the term. She wasn't mentally ill; she was just inadequate. But maybe she didn't deserve to feel like this. Maybe it wasn't normal. Maybe she could be free of this constant, dragging burden. She turned back to the mirror and stared at her reflection, at the tears that had tracked rivulets of foundation down her cheeks. 'In a stroke of irony, now I've ruined my make-up and I have to leave in five minutes.'

'Wash it off,' Renee said. 'Go to Jodie's without it.'

'Wash it off?' Layla stared at her reflection. Even the thought of going out without it made her insides curl up with anxiety.

'She's not going to notice whether you're wearing make-up or not. To be perfectly blunt, she's not going to give a shit about how you look.'

Layla stood up straighter. 'No. She won't.'

Renee smiled. 'Try it for one day.'

She followed Layla into the bathroom and watched as she washed her face in the basin. They both stared at her scrubbed-clean face in the mirror.

'I look shiny,' Layla said.

'You look new,' Renee said.

'I can't do this every day.'

'You don't have to. I wear make-up too, you know. This isn't about being a puritan. It's about accepting yourself, and loving yourself.'

Layla nudged her. 'You've always been a bit in love with yourself, though, haven't you?'

Renee gestured to her face and her body. 'And why wouldn't I be? Honestly.'

They grinned at each other. Layla's face felt cool and fresh, as if she'd sloughed off an old skin.

'Are you ready for this?' Renee said.

Layla took in a deep breath and let it out slowly. 'Yeah. I'm ready.'

THEN

Scott stretched and then clutched at his back. 'Christ. I've been sleeping on the couch for the last few nights and I think I've put my back out.'

We were up at The Knob, sitting on the bonnet of his car. It was a balmy evening, and the ever-present wind was almost pleasant, the salty tang of the sea below dryer and sharper than usual. I was silent. This was the third time he'd indirectly referred to a change in his relationship with Jodie, but now that the thing I'd been waiting for all this time looked like it was finally in reach, I was no longer sure I wanted it. His touch was cloying, claustrophobic. I had to resist the urge to brush him away when he kissed my neck.

'Your arse is getting bigger,' he murmured, his hands up under my shirt. 'Pity your tits didn't catch up.'

I shrank away from him. 'You said you liked them this way.'

'Well, sometimes it'd be nice to have something to grab hold of.'

I pushed his hands away. 'Feel free to stop grabbing hold of them, then.'

He drew back, a look of disgust on his face. 'You don't

have to be so touchy. I've given up a lot for you, Layla. The least you could do is be appreciative.'

I had the urge to push him, to make him angry out of a dull curiosity to see what he'd do. 'I've given things up too,' I muttered.

'What?' His gaze was too piercing, and I had to look away. 'Nothing.'

'No, what did you say?' He put his hand on my cheek and turned my face to look at him.

'I said I've given things up too. My reputation in this town, for one thing. Maybe a career.'

He laughed. 'You ruined your own reputation with your behaviour after your school formal. That was nothing to do with me.'

'Are you going to bring that up every time you're angry with me?'

'It was only a week ago. And every time I think about some pimply teenage dickhead putting his hands on you, I want to …' He clenched his jaw, breathed out hard, then lunged at me.

I let him kiss me for a minute, but when he became more insistent, I pulled away. 'I don't really feel like it tonight. Sorry.'

He looked like he was trying his best not to appear exasperated. 'Are you worried about your exams next week?'

'Not really. I feel like I've studied as much as I can. I know the stuff back to front.'

He sighed. 'So what's the problem?'

'I'm just not in the mood.'

He nuzzled my ear, but I couldn't bear it, so I slipped down off the bonnet and walked over to stand beside The Knob.

I placed a hand on it. The stippled surface of the granite still held a hint of the day's heat. After a moment, Scott came to stand beside me, his bare arm almost touching mine. 'What's wrong, Layla? Why won't you let me touch you?'

I turned to face him. If I didn't tell him what was in my heart now, it might be too late to ever get out. 'I think we should end it.'

'What? Why?'

'I want to go to uni, Scott. I want to get out of this stupid town and live in Adelaide and get pissed in the uni bar and do all that stuff young people do.'

He stepped back, his face bitter. 'You want to fuck other people, then?'

I hesitated. 'That's not it. But I think maybe I should experience the world a bit, start a career, and yeah, have relationships with people my own age. If I stay here with you, I'll end up working in your cafe, having kids young, living someone else's life.'

He grabbed my arm and shook me roughly. 'And what's wrong with that life, you selfish bitch? You're only ever thinking of yourself. I've fucked up my marriage for you, do you understand that?'

'I'm sorry! I don't want to hurt you, but I want to be happy. I'm not happy here.'

He forced me back towards the cliff edge. 'You run hot and cold like a fucking tap, Layla. One minute you're a nympho and the next you're fucking frigid. It makes me so angry.'

The void yawned behind me, sucking me towards it. If he let me go now, I'd tumble over the cliff. My body would smash on the rocks, split open; the sea would swallow me whole. And in this moment, with his angry eyes up close, blazing at me, that seemed preferable to this constant uneasy feeling, of never knowing how he was going to react, of feeling like a madonna one minute and a whore the next.

He hauled me back from the edge and released me, his face anguished. 'I can't live without you, Layla. If you leave me, I'll kill myself.'

His words robbed my breath. He couldn't make me responsible for that. And yet … he looked so vulnerable now, the misery in his eyes so convincingly replacing the fury that had been there only seconds ago. I took a step towards him, touched his arm. 'Don't talk like that.'

He put his arms around me and buried his head in my shoulder. I embraced him in return because I wanted to comfort him, and what was the harm in that? And when he started kissing me again, I kissed him back, because I didn't want to hurt him, and what was the harm in that? And when, a few minutes later, he was inside me, murmuring, 'Your body's made for fucking, not for giving out medication to old people,' I let him do what he wanted with me, because this was all I was good for, and hoping for more had always been ridiculous.

*

We were halfway through dinner when the phone began to ring. Dad got up, still chewing. 'I'll get it.'

As soon as he left the room, Zach began eyeing off the remaining chops on his plate. Ever since we'd been kids, we'd always taken any opportunity to steal the fat from each other's lamb chops. The meat itself was chewy and unremarkable, but that little curl of fat was always the tastiest, slightly charred on the outside from the barbecue, melt-in-your-mouth sweet on the inside. Zach had just reached over to swipe one of them when Dad walked back in, grumbling, and he snatched his hand back.

'Who was it?' Mum said.

'Dunno, the bugger hung up as soon as I answered.'

'That's weird, that happened to me twice earlier.'

'Me too,' Zach piped up.

Dad grunted. 'Bloody kids, probably.'

I kept my eyes on my plate. Scott had wanted to catch up again this week, but I'd told him I'd be busy with exams. He'd been annoyed, as if I'd planned to go to my exams just to piss him off. I had no doubt that it was him calling, and he was hoping I'd answer so he could convince me to meet him, but the thought of giving myself to him again made me feel sick, like there was an illness inside me that only got worse the more I did it. Avoiding him was the only way I could stop the sick feeling, but now he was growing increasingly reckless. I had to shut him down before my family found out what was going on.

When the phone rang again ten minutes later, I jumped up. 'My turn.'

I took the cordless phone into my room before I answered it.

'Layla, thank god it's you,' his voice gushed out. 'I thought you were never going to pick up.'

'You can't call me here like this!' I hissed. 'My parents are getting suspicious.'

'Does it really matter anymore?' he said. 'We're going to be together soon anyway.'

My stomach clenched. 'I can't think about any of that until my exams are over. Can we talk after that?'

He sighed. 'I don't know why you're even bothering with exams if you're going to stay here anyway. I didn't finish Year Twelve and I'm doing all right.'

I had the perverse urge to laugh, but I reined it in. 'I have to go.'

'I need to see you. Can you sneak out tonight?'

I felt his tentacles reach out, clasp around my throat the way his hands did. 'I can't. I have to go.'

I hung up before he could try to convince me and hurried back to the kitchen. Mum looked curiously at me. 'They actually answered this time?'

'Nah.' I sat down and stabbed a piece of potato with my fork. 'Another hang-up. I just went to the loo.'

But Zach was looking at me with a dubious expression. 'Didn't hear the dunny flush.'

'That's because you're deaf, butthead.'

'Layla,' said Mum.

'So what are you and your friends going to do when your exams are over?' Dad said. 'You must have a big celebration planned.'

I shrugged and shovelled more food into my mouth so I didn't have to answer. Mum hadn't told Dad about the state I'd come home in after the formal, and he had no idea that Renee was refusing to speak to me and Shona hadn't given me much more than a hello on the few occasions we'd crossed paths. Everyone else was still giving me sideways looks and whispering behind their hands about Scott and me. I had no friends left and no one to celebrate with.

'When I finished school, my mates and I went up the coast and surfed for two months straight,' Dad said. 'Of course, I only went to Year Ten, so it doesn't quite measure up to your achievement.'

'It's not that big a deal, Dad. Pretty much everyone finishes Year Twelve these days.'

'Except that boy … Benjamin, isn't it?' Mum said. 'Hasn't he been trying for three years?'

Zach's eyes met mine across the table. He smirked. 'Bruiser's just there for the jail bait now.'

I choked on my mouthful.

'Zach! Don't be vulgar,' Mum said.

'Maybe we should go to the river shack for a week?' I said, desperate to cast that memory from my brain, desperate to avoid the inevitable confrontation with Scott when I'd run out of excuses not to see him.

'Your father and I can't get time off work at such short notice,' Mum said. 'And Zach's got school.'

'Why don't you and your friends go up?' Dad said. 'You're old enough to go away on your own now.'

I wanted to cry. A few weeks ago, I would've jumped at the chance, but now I'd lost everyone I cared about. 'Nah, that's OK.'

'You'll be the first one from our family to go to uni,' Dad said. 'That's worth celebrating. I'm very proud of you, Layla.'

Zach rolled his eyes, and I threw a pea at him.

*

He was waiting for me when I walked out of the town hall after my last exam. I was flushed with a curious combination of elation at finishing school and emptiness at the land of in-between I was now in, but the sight of him banished any sense of achievement, reminded me of the dead end that was ahead of me if I stayed. The other students goggled with delighted horror at the scandal, but none of them said anything to me. Even Renee turned away, shaking her head. No last goodbyes for Layla Flynn, the disgraced one.

'You shouldn't be here,' I said dully.

His eyes crinkled with that smile I'd fallen in love with, back when I'd thought real love was possible. 'I thought you might want to celebrate. You've finished school. That's amazing.'

'I don't feel like celebrating right now.'

I kept walking towards my car, but he followed. 'I thought we could go to the city for the afternoon.'

'I don't really want to, Scott.'

'Just to Victor, then. I'll buy you a proper lunch this time.'

I stopped and turned to face him, about to unleash my frustration, when Rasheed jogged up to us. 'Sorry, Layla, I almost forgot about that coffee we were going to get.'

I threw him a grateful smile. 'Oh yeah, me too. Sorry, Scott, I've already got plans. Shall we go, Rasheed?'

Scott fell back as Rasheed and I set off together. My heart was pounding. He was going to be furious. He'd want to punish me later. 'Thank you,' I said quietly to Rasheed.

'Anytime,' Rasheed said. 'Is it OK if we go in your car? My mum dropped me here.'

'Of course.'

'I guess going to Telford's is out of the question?' There was a smile in his voice, but I was too busy looking back at Scott to answer. He was watching us, his fists clenched by his

341

sides. 'But we don't have to go anywhere if you don't want to. It's cool if you just want to drop me home.'

We got in the car and I started the engine. 'We should go to Victor and get a proper drink before schoolies starts. You're eighteen, aren't you? We deserve to celebrate after this fucked-up year.'

He looked embarrassed. 'I'm a Muslim. I don't drink.'

'Right. Sorry.' I pulled out from the kerb and began to drive without knowing where I was going to go.

'So are you moving to Adelaide next year for uni?' Rasheed asked.

'I'm not sure yet.'

'You'll commute?'

'I don't know.' I gripped the steering wheel in both hands. 'Actually, do you mind if I drop you home? I think I just want to chill for a while.'

'Sure. I'm on Jones Avenue.'

We drove in silence until I pulled up outside his house. 'Thanks again for rescuing me back there.'

'That's OK.' He ran a hand through his hair. 'Listen, Layla … you're not the person they say you are. Stay safe, OK?'

I nodded, pressing my lips together to hold in the shame at everything I'd done. 'Might see you around.'

When he'd gone inside, I drove the few blocks home. The house was quiet and cool. I sat down at the kitchen table, and the absoluteness of this chapter in my life being over settled on me. It was crushing. I should've been out celebrating with my friends; we should've been booking our campsite for schoolies at the Victor Harbor Caravan Park, planning the booze we were going to sneak in. But instead,

I was sitting here alone, no friends left, being pushed in one direction by my parents and pulled back in the other by Scott. I no longer had any perspective on whether I wanted to stay or go.

I was staring out the window when there was loud knocking on the front door, and I started nervously. I'd left the door open to let the breeze in, but the security screen was locked. Scott stood on the verandah, his jaw working, his eyes hard.

'Did you fuck him?' he demanded.

'No,' I said.

'Did you suck his dick? Did he stick his fingers in you?' His mouth was twisted with rage.

Fear, shimmering like summer sun on a hot road. 'You need to leave.'

'Open the door,' he snapped. 'I want to talk to you.'

'Who's looking after the cafe while you're following me all around Glasswater?' I knew I was heading into dangerous territory, but it felt as if I'd been dancing on a knife's edge for so long that I wanted to make something happen, even if it meant provoking him for a response that'd give me a reason to end it for good.

'None of your fucking business. Let me in.'

There was no affection in his voice now, no attempt to soften his tone or turn on the charm. The danger rose from him like steam. He wasn't going to leave. 'I'll call the police if you won't go.'

He laughed. 'The *police*, Layla? Do you really think they're going to take you seriously? Everyone in this town knows what you're like now. All I'd have to do is tell them how obsessed you are with me, how determined you were to ruin my marriage, how I came around here to ask you to leave me alone, but you keep making up these lies like the dirty little slut that you are.'

Desperation flooded me. 'Why are you being like this?'

'Because *you're mine!*' He slammed both his hands against the screen door, making it rattle furiously.

My heart felt as though it would leap out of my chest. 'I was never yours. I never will be.'

His mouth twisted. 'You think you're so much better than everyone, but you're just a boring, ugly little bitch, and you belong in the gutter.'

And finally, I realised the truth. How had I kept giving him the benefit of the doubt when he'd given me so many demonstrations of the violence inside him? That look in his eyes … a man like that wasn't capable of love. And there was nothing I'd ever be able to do to change that. It wasn't my fault.

'I want you to leave.' My voice was shaking uncontrollably, but I had to get the words out; I had to make him understand that this was the end. 'I *never* want to see you again.'

'I won't give up, you know. Just when you think it's all over, I'll be there. *Pow!*' He punched the screen door level with my face. I jumped back in terror and slammed the door closed.

I waited there, in front of the door, holding my breath, until I heard his footsteps receding. After a minute, I went into Mum and Dad's room and peered through the curtains onto our front yard. Scott was stalking back down the path, alternately shaking his right hand and glancing down at his bloodied knuckles.

When he'd got in his car and driven away, and I was certain he wasn't coming back, I ran around the house to make sure all the windows and doors were locked. My breath was coming in gasps.

I went to my bedroom and sat on my bed, hugging my knees to my chest. There was one thing I was certain of: if I kept going back to him, one day he would kill me. If I wanted to be rid of him – really rid of him – I was going to have to take drastic action.

NOW

Layla sat in the car outside Jodie's house for a long time, until the air-conditioned interior of the car gave way to suffocating heat. But still she couldn't move. She'd never been inside the house, but she'd driven past it enough times as a lovesick teenager for it to be imprinted on her memory: cream brick, dark-brown tiled roof, two matching windows with lace curtains. The only difference was the ramp that now ran down the front of the house up to the door. The sight of it sent a shockwave over her. Somehow, she'd blocked out the reality of the situation, what she'd been responsible for, but seeing this, right in front of her eyes, changed the whole dynamic of her visit.

At ten past ten, one of the curtains twitched aside for a second, then the front door swung open to reveal the woman who had been stalking her dreams for the last month. She was still beautiful. Her high cheekbones preserved the look of youth that many younger women hungered after, and before she could prevent it, jealousy stabbed into Layla, followed by a wave of self-loathing. She was despicable. She unclicked her seatbelt and got out of the car, her shirt clinging to the sweat on her back.

Jodie crossed her arms as Layla approached. 'How long have you been sitting out here?'

'A while,' Layla admitted. She peered over Jodie's shoulder into the interior of the house.

Jodie glanced behind her, then back to Layla. 'Don't worry, he's not here. He's been in permanent care for a few months now.'

'Oh.' The relief almost knocked Layla to her knees. 'I'm sorry to hear that.'

'Oh, give me a break,' Jodie sneered. 'You wouldn't know how to be sorry.'

Layla wilted under her gaze, unable to respond.

Jodie shook her head. 'Well, come in, then.' She turned, and Layla followed her into the living room. 'Want a coffee?'

'Yes, please.' Though the gap in their ages had closed with time, Layla still felt like a schoolgirl in the presence of the latent anger that simmered within this woman. She sat down on the worn leather couch, wiping her sweaty palms on her jeans as Jodie disappeared to make the coffee.

'How do you take it?' Jodie called from the kitchen.

'White, no sugar, please.'

Layla fiddled with the strap of her handbag as the hiss of the kettle from the next room rose to a low roar. Too late she realised it was going to be instant coffee. She hadn't drunk instant in years and she didn't like it, but she'd look totally up herself if she changed her mind now. And Jodie's hostility had cast a pall of authority over the house that she didn't feel qualified to question. She could serve her a cup of cat piss and Layla would probably still drink it.

Jodie returned and handed her a steaming mug. It scalded Layla's hand, but she ignored the pain until she could take hold of the handle. 'Thanks.'

Jodie sat down opposite her and watched as she took a sip. 'Thanks for coming.'

'I'm sorry I put it off for so long.'

Her stern expression didn't falter. 'How was the reunion last night?'

Layla realised with a sense of surprise that, despite the resentment that emanated from her, Jodie was as nervous as she was. 'It was good, actually. I'm glad I went. I thought everyone was still going to hate me. But they didn't.'

Jodie gave a low laugh. 'Oh, things have changed around here over the years, believe me. You'd know that if you hadn't run off.'

'I went to uni,' Layla said in a small voice.

A sceptical sound escaped Jodie's lips. 'Oh, come on. Four months early, with your entire family? Right after you set fire to our cafe?'

So, it'd begun.

THEN

On Sunday morning, I drove into the main street and parked my car on the Esplanade. Most of the shops were closed today, other than Keen's, and that didn't open until eleven. The main street was dead, aside from the occasional person out walking their dog. I'd never returned my cafe key to Scott, so once I was sure no one was around, I unlocked the front door and slipped inside.

I only had the skeleton of a plan in my head. All I knew was that I needed to create a distraction big enough for Scott to forget about me, at least until I could get out of Glasswater Bay. The cafe was the only thing he seemed to care about, so that was the most logical thing to target. Nothing too serious. Nothing that would hurt anyone. I pushed through the door into the kitchen and assessed my options. It would have to look like an accident, or he – and the police – would come after me. I could switch on one of the gas burners, but it wasn't conceivable that Dave would've left it on, nor that no one would've noticed before closing last night. And if I left it on without igniting it, the whole kitchen would fill with gas, and when Dave got here on Monday morning and went to light the stove, the flames would blow up in his face. I couldn't do that to him.

My eyes fell on the sandwich press. On its own, it wouldn't be enough to start a fire, but if I left something lying over it … something that would catch alight if it was on for long enough … long enough for me to be far away. It would be a small fire, confined to the kitchen. The fire station was only around the corner. It wouldn't cause too much damage, but it'd be enough to keep Scott occupied dealing with insurance and repairs. No one would get hurt. No one would suspect me.

My finger hovered over the power point. For a second, I considered the possibility that Dave might be landed with the blame. He might lose his job. But my fear of Scott was greater, so I switched it on and opened it up. I began searching the shelves for something that would take a while to catch alight. I could lay the power cable over it, but that would probably trip the safety switch and the power would go out before the fire could start. Paper would catch too easily. Was plastic wrap flammable? That seemed like something I should've learnt at school.

After a moment, I got the loaf of bread down from the shelf and started to make a sandwich. I made it look legit: prosciutto, Jarlsberg, baby spinach. I left out the tomato for fear it'd make the sandwich too damp to burn. Then I placed the sandwich on the hot surface and locked the sandwich press closed. The minutes passed slowly as I waited until the smell of melting cheese began to waft out, then, before I could change my mind, I ran out of the kitchen, opened the front door and locked it behind me.

I walked rapidly back down the main street. A deep dread lay in the pit of my stomach. Across the other side of the Esplanade, I was passing a red Torana SLR parked on the wrong side of the road when a hand snaked out of the open window and caught my arm. I gasped in fright. Matty's face appeared, striking instant fear into me. A backpack sat on his lap, like he'd been about to get out. His face broke into a grin.

'I hear you're the town bike now, Laaaylaaa. How come I never got a ride?'

'Fuck off, Matty.' I pulled away from him, but he opened the car door and got out onto the footpath.

'So, you've been rooting Telford all this time? Not the good girl everyone thought you were, ay?' He came up close to me, and my stomach lurched at his scent of sweat and chemicals. 'Here's a bit of free advice for you: I'd stay away from that prick if I were you. He's trouble.' Then he chuckled. 'Anyway, you can tell him not to worry, I'll keep Jodie warm at night.'

Before I had a chance to react, he turned and strode away across the street. I watched him for a moment to make sure he didn't turn back, then sat on the same bench seat Renee, Shona and I had got pissed on months ago and stared out at the ocean. It'd taken me my whole life to recognise the irony of this infinite, open view that lay just out of reach of the claustrophobic clutches of this small town. Mostly, I'd been happy here, but in recent years the bonds of this place had tightened around me, and I wondered if escape would ever be truly possible. So many of Glasswater Bay's residents had lived here all their lives; their parents and grandparents too. Now, when I was on the verge of escape, my return seemed inevitable, even if only to visit my family. And when I did, Scott would still be here. Setting fire to his cafe wasn't going to change that. This wasn't the person I wanted to be.

I stood up and started to run.

NOW

Layla took refuge in the sweet, burnt taste of boiling water poured over coffee granules before she had the courage to speak. 'You wanted me to face up to what I did to your family. So tell me.'

Layla could sense the barely contained tension bubbling within Jodie. For a moment, the older woman stared down into her coffee, then she raised blazing blue eyes to meet Layla's. 'Can you imagine what it was like? Knowing your husband was sleeping with a teenager?'

Layla shook her head.

'Having to go into that cafe, seeing you, with your youth and your perfect body, touching my husband right under my nose. The way you used to *look* at me, like I was dog shit under your shoe.'

Layla hung her head at the memory of her own jealousy and insecurity, dressed up as blind arrogance.

'You made me feel old, and I hated you for that.' She spat out the words bitterly. 'I was twenty-eight years old and I already felt like my best years were behind me.'

'I'm so sorry,' Layla said.

'Then there was that night at the pub.' Her lips quivered with rage. 'You took him off and screwed him in the bathroom, then sent him back to the table with his little kids, smelling of you.'

Layla buried her head in her hands. 'I'm sorry, I was so awful. I've hated myself for years for the way I acted.'

'Well, so have I,' Jodie shot back. The angry silence boiled around them, thick and hot. 'But that's not the reason I've resented you for so long,' Jodie said at last, and Layla looked up. 'You know, I've never told anyone else this, but I was about to leave him. Oh, not because of you,' she added. 'Our relationship had been dead for years. But every time I tried to end it, he'd turn on the charm, organise romantic dinners, convince me we were meant to be together. Or he'd bring the kids into it, lay the guilt trip on me about what it'd do to them if we split up. He constantly made me question myself.'

'He did that to me too,' Layla said.

Jodie appraised her for a moment. 'So I guess you worked out that he wasn't the nice guy everyone thought he was.'

Layla had the urge to pour everything out to her, but she was here to listen to Jodie, not to tell her own story. She bit her lip and nodded instead.

'Well, I wasn't perfect either. I kind of got interested in someone else, but I hung around with Scott so I could save enough money to leave him and get custody of the kids. I was almost there, you know. I'd opened my own bank account and had been transferring small amounts of money for months. I had a whole plan set in place when you started that fire and he ended up permanently disabled. I couldn't leave him then, could I?'

A mix of guilt and sorrow churned inside Layla. If only she hadn't made this woman an enemy when she'd only ever been another flawed human, struggling with many of the same uncertainties Scott had put her through. Jodie had wasted all those years tied to a man she hadn't loved since she was practically a teenager herself, sacrificing her own happiness, her own future, to do the right thing.

Jodie gestured expansively. 'They all thought I was a bloody saint. Of course, they worked it out eventually, but it's too late now.'

'I'm so sorry,' Layla said again. 'I never wanted any of that to happen. I was desperate. He used to hurt me … I just wanted to make it stop.'

'You could have gone to the police. But burning down the cafe? What was that supposed to achieve?'

'I don't know. I wasn't thinking. He told me if I went to the police, he'd tell them I was crazy, that I was obsessed with him.' Layla wrung her hands. 'And I believed him. I believed that my reputation would be enough to exonerate him.'

For the first time, a hint of sympathy lit in Jodie's eyes. 'The police are always ready to blame the woman. Or the girl, in your case.'

Regret filled Layla to the brim. After all this time, she'd never expected compassion. It was too much. 'You're right,' she said. 'I did cause the fire, but it was never supposed to hurt anyone. It was only ever meant to cause a bit of damage to the kitchen, enough to take his attention off me for a while.' She hesitated. 'There was someone across the other side of the street when I came out of the cafe. It was you, wasn't it?'

Jodie nodded. 'I was on my way to the bank to withdraw the last lot of money I needed, then I was going to go home and tell him I was leaving him.' She gave a bitter laugh. 'But of course he wasn't there.'

'I changed my mind. I couldn't go through with it. When you saw me, I'd gone back to turn off the sandwich press. But it was too late. It must have still been hot enough to start the fire, or maybe something fell on top of it. I don't know.'

Confusion crossed Jodie's face. 'Sandwich press?'

'That's how it started. I put a sandwich in there and left it on.'

Jodie leant forward, her hands on her knees. 'What are you talking about? The fire originated in the storeroom. The police found residues of kerosene.'

THEN

There was still no one on the street when I rushed back into the cafe and through to the kitchen. The sandwich was sizzling furiously; the room was infused with the smell of burnt cheese. I switched off the sandwich press at the power point, then unplugged it for good measure. The sandwich was a blackened mess and I had to lever it off with a spatula so I could dump it into the bin.

My breathing began to slow as I scrubbed off the burnt cheese with paper towel. It was hard to believe now, in this moment of calm, that I'd ever had such a stupid idea. I'd been scared, that was all. But he couldn't hurt me now. I'd be out of this town soon, and he'd forget about me, and I'd never have to worry about him again.

I'd just walked out of the kitchen when I heard a thud from behind me, as if something had fallen off a shelf. My heart leapt. I poked my head back into the kitchen, but it was empty.

I slipped back outside onto the footpath. Too late, I noticed a figure across the street, but I ducked my head and kept going, as if it were perfectly normal to walk out of a closed business on a Sunday. Everyone knew I used to work here;

if anyone asked, it'd be easy to say that I'd gone back to pick up something I'd left. And the disaster I'd almost created was averted, so there'd be no reason for anyone to ask anyway.

The sun was warm on my shoulders, seeping into my skin like disinfectant, washing away my wrongdoings. By the time I reached the Esplanade again, there was such a deep sense of peace inside me that I wasn't ready to go home. I slipped off my thongs and left them on the top of the stone steps that led down onto the beach.

Renee and Shona had always joked that it was a waste that I'd grown up in a quaint seaside town when I hated the beach, but sometimes, on mornings like this when there was no one around, I liked being down here. The sand was cool and smooth under my feet and the breeze tossed my hair. The beach curved around the bay like a crescent moon. At this time of day, the water was as still as the town's namesake, and calm enough to keep the legion of surfers away. With every step, my worries lifted and floated above me. Maybe there *could* be a life after Glasswater Bay, where I could start fresh, without the reputation I'd earned here. I felt like I could walk forever.

When I reached the end of the bay, I turned around to walk back. The wind had picked up now and I was heading into it; it streamed over my face and whistled in my ears. Soon the surf would rise and the men and women, teenagers and kids, locals and tourists alike, would show up in their wetsuits, surfboards tucked under their arms, to launch themselves into the sea and take on the waves. But for now, the beach was just for me. The faint sound of a siren started up in the distance.

I began to formulate a plan to get Renee to forgive me for what I'd done at the formal afterparty. Mum was right: we'd been friends all our lives; we were beyond the stale cliché of letting a boy come between us. And anyway, she and Daniel had broken up. We'd both be in Adelaide next year. There'd be plenty of time to reconnect and become friends again.

It was only as I reached the concrete steps that I realised the sirens had grown louder, and that others had joined them. They sounded close. Foreboding sprouted inside me. Mavis Johnson passed me on the steps, her little white Maltese Shih tzu straining at the end of the lead. She paused and looked back. 'There must be a fire nearby. Look at that smoke.'

I followed her gaze. Black smoke belched above the buildings of the main street, staining the perfect blue expanse of the sky. Still more sirens joined the others. The bottom of my stomach dropped out. I shoved my feet back into my thongs and ran across the Esplanade. Five fire trucks had colonised the main street; the firefighters in their white helmets and heavy uniforms shouted orders as they unfurled the giant fire hoses. My heart leapt as I took in the flames that burned bright behind the cafe windows. How could this have happened? I was so sure I'd turned off that sandwich press. The brief pocket of peace I'd found on the beach was drowned by the dull roar that was coming from inside.

'Stand back, love!' one of the firefighters called out to me, and I fell back to the other side of the street with the small knot of curious locals that had accumulated there. It looked like the flames had spread to the vacant shop next door, the one Scott had talked about buying.

Then a car screeched to a halt nearby. Scott threw himself out, a look of anguish on his face. Before anyone could stop him, he'd run across the street and through the cafe door.

'You can't go in there, you bloody idiot!' one of the firefighters shouted.

'Someone call an ambulance!' another shouted across at us.

Paul Potts announced with somewhat inappropriate pride, considering the situation, that he had a mobile phone, and he called triple zero while the rest of us watched with mute horror as the firefighters poured into the building. My heart pounded painfully against my chest. I had the urge to flee, but I couldn't tear myself away while Scott was in there. No one was supposed to get hurt. There wasn't even supposed to *be* a fire. What had I done?

Then there was a cracking sound from inside, followed by a crash. 'The beam's come down!' came a muffled shout. One of the firefighters ran out and pulled up his visor. 'Has someone called that ambulance?' The edge of desperation in his voice clamped my throat with sickening terror.

At last more sirens approached. An ambulance pulled up and two paramedics leapt out. The firefighter who'd yelled out at us was talking to them as they got a stretcher out of the back of the ambulance, his words just loud enough for us to hear from across the street. 'I think it's a spinal injury. The beam fell on his neck so we couldn't move him.'

A few people around me gasped. 'We should let Jodie know,' someone said, and there were murmurs of assent.

'Maybe you should go home, love?' A gentle hand landed on my shoulder, and I looked up to see Bob Keen's kindly face. 'This is no place for a young girl like you.'

His words sent sensation back into my limbs. I nodded. 'OK. Yeah.'

I jogged down the street towards the Esplanade. When I looked back, the paramedics were carrying the stretcher back to the ambulance. Scott lay motionless on it, a brace around his neck.

NOW

Layla stared at Jodie. 'Kerosene?' she repeated.

Jodie's eyes widened. 'You mean that wasn't you?'

Layla shook her head.

'The police found the empty tins in the dumpster in the alley, but there were no fingerprints,' Jodie said. 'Scott was never charged because they couldn't prove anything, and it didn't make sense that he'd run into a burning building that he'd set alight himself.'

An enormous wave of relief washed over Layla, almost taking her breath away. She hadn't been responsible. All this time she'd punished herself, and she hadn't caused the fire after all. She felt like dancing in the street, but she'd promised Jodie she'd listen to what she had to say. 'Why *did* he go in?'

She shrugged. 'He never told me. Maybe he kept a stash of money in there so he could leave *me*, who knows?' She gave a barking sort of laugh. 'Regardless, we lost everything. Insurance wouldn't pay out because they claimed it was arson. We could've fought them on it, but we were all in such a state of shock after the accident. Then there was rehabilitation, and therapy, and I had to give up my job to care for him. The money we had ran out pretty quickly.'

Layla took a sip of her coffee, but it had gone cold now, so she placed the cup down on the coffee table. 'You've cared for him yourself all these years?'

Jodie nodded. All the anger seemed to have drained out of her now. 'For a while, there was hope that he might walk again, but that didn't happen. Then a few months ago, I put my back out and I couldn't lift him anymore. Claire – my daughter – helped out where she could, but then she got pregnant and I couldn't ask her to do it either. And he's started having some heart problems, so he needs constant care. At least I was able to get a job again, but it's only part-time, and most of his disability pension goes to the nursing home. I do get a bit of extra help, but there's not much left over after the mortgage and bills.'

At last, Layla understood. She may not have been responsible for the fire or Scott's accident, but Jodie still wanted her to know how it had felt to see Layla escape Glasswater Bay while she'd had her chance at happiness plucked away from her at the very last minute, leaving her living a life she didn't want for twenty years. Guilty tears came to her eyes. 'I'm sorry.'

Jodie laughed again. 'Well, it turns out it wasn't your fault after all, was it?'

'But all this time you thought it was. Why didn't you tell the police you'd seen me come out of the cafe? Why didn't you come after me earlier?'

She shrugged. 'Honestly? I don't know. I guess in a way I didn't actually blame you for what I thought you'd done. I know what he was like – I figured he must have messed you up pretty bad for you to do something like that. You'd always been such a good, responsible girl. Well, up to a point, anyway.'

Layla allowed herself a small smile.

'It was only after he'd moved into the home and I could finally think about myself again that all that anger caught up with me. I wanted to punish someone, and when I found you, with your perfect life and your perfect family, I wanted to hurt you.'

'How *did* you find me? And how did you know about Cam?'

Jodie looked sheepish. 'I asked Renee. She said you'd lost contact years ago, but she told me you had a husband and kids. It didn't take long to track him down.'

'Jodie, I'm sorry,' Layla said. 'I really am. Scott may have manipulated me, but I was old enough to know I was doing the wrong thing. And I did it anyway.'

Jodie gave her a strained smile. 'He was a narcissist who exploited your youth and used his position of authority to get in your pants. Part of me has always felt bad that I didn't try to … I don't know, warn you or something. But at the time, it was kind of a relief when he stopped constantly pawing at me. He was a lousy shag.'

Layla laughed out loud. 'That I can agree with.'

Jodie's eyes twinkled. 'The man wouldn't go down if his life depended on it.'

They both laughed now. Layla felt lighter than she had in years. She wasn't to blame. The relief was dizzying. She dragged her attention back to Jodie. 'Are you … happy?'

Jodie's expression cracked a little. 'I've found some happiness. My first grandkid is on the way. I've even got a man.'

Layla raised her eyebrows. 'And what do the good people of Glasswater Bay think about that?'

'Like I said, things have changed around here. And anyway, most of our so-called friends drifted away after the accident, so they're hardly in a position to judge.'

Layla looked up as footsteps approached from outside and a key slid into the lock.

'Oh, that'll be him now,' Jodie said.

The door swung open and shock bolted into Layla. She scrambled backwards on the couch, her heart beating wildly. 'What is this? What's he doing here?'

THEN

I sped all the way home, my breath coming in panicked gasps. When I reached my house, I was relieved to see Dad's car wasn't there. He and Zach must still be at basketball. Mum was the tough one in the family; she was the one I needed now. I ran inside, slamming the front door behind me.

'Where have you been?' Mum called from the kitchen.

As soon as I rounded the corner and she turned away from the sink to face me, her hands dripping with soap suds, the full realisation of what I'd done hit me, and I crumpled to the ground. Mum rushed over to crouch beside me, her wet hands clasping my face.

'Layla, what's wrong? What happened?'

'I've done something bad,' I sobbed. 'Something really bad.'

'What? What did you do?'

But I couldn't answer, could only fall against her, gasping for air as the image of Scott on that stretcher flashed across my mind again. I'd wanted to escape from him, but not like this. Mum held me to her tightly as I hyperventilated into her shoulder, my head spinning with terror. Finally, she held me away from her, her brow furrowed.

'Layla, please tell me what happened.'

'There was a fire at the cafe,' I said. 'And I think I ... I started it. It was my fault.'

Mum's frown deepened. 'But you haven't worked in the cafe in weeks. Why would you ... Oh.' Her face transformed as she put it together. 'Oh, *Layla*!'

The disgrace almost knocked me to the floor again. 'I'm sorry,' was all I could get out between sobs.

'So *that's* why everyone's been looking sideways at me lately. Fucking cowards couldn't tell me to my face.'

I'd never heard Mum swear before, and it jolted me out of my self-absorption. 'I've been so stupid. He told me he loved me.'

'Have you slept with him?' she asked. I bit my lip and nodded. 'Christ, Layla.'

'I'm sorry,' I said again. It seemed I'd been saying those words over and over for the last six months, and I was so, so tired of saying them. 'Please don't tell Dad.'

'Why?' she asked desperately. 'Why would you start a fire?'

I clutched at her arms. 'He said he was going to leave Jodie, but then he changed. Things got out of control. He started hurting me and he ... he told me he'd kill me if I left him. I didn't know what else to do! I didn't mean to start it ... I went back to try to undo it, but I was too late.'

Her face began to crumple, and she pulled me into her arms again. 'Oh, my Layla.'

I'd expected her to be furious with me for my stupid actions, and it was so good to be held by her again. I clung to her for precious minutes before I managed to compose myself enough to speak again. 'There's more ... Scott turned up after the fire started and ran into the cafe. A beam fell on him … I think he's broken his neck. I think I … I think I might've killed him.' I broke down into sobs once again.

Mum's hand rose to her mouth, her eyes darting from side to side as she thought. 'Did anyone see you?'

I hesitated, remembering the figure across the street when I'd left the cafe for the second time. I hadn't even checked to see who it was. I knew I should tell her everything, but I felt so horrible about what I'd done that I didn't want her to know I'd been so careless. All I could think about was how badly I wanted her to take over the situation and make it go away. 'Not until the fire trucks were already there. I saw Mavis down at the beach and she pointed out the fire. By the time I got up the street, there was already a group there.'

'How did you start it?'

'I put a sandwich in the sandwich press and left it on. But I went back ten minutes later and turned it off. I don't know what happened … it must have still been too hot.'

'OK, OK.' She tapped her finger against her chin. 'That's good. Even if they trace it back to the sandwich press, it'll look like an accident.'

'You don't think we should go to the police?' I wasn't sure whether to be relieved or more worried.

Mum was silent for a minute. 'Of course we *should*, but it was an accident. He's the one who ran into a burning building. And after what he's done to you …' Her jaw worked. 'But to be sure, I think we should leave. Move to town or something.'

I stared at her. 'Really?'

'After the way people have been acting lately, not telling me when my own daughter is in trouble, I don't have much love left for this town. And you'll need somewhere to live when you start uni next year anyway.'

'But ... but what about Dad and Zach? How will you convince them? You're not going to tell Dad, are you?'

She pressed her lips together. 'Leave Dad to me. Now you go and get yourself cleaned up before they get home. I'll think about how to handle this.'

NOW

Jodie glanced at Layla. 'What's wrong? You remember Matty, don't you?'

Layla stared at her in disbelief. '*He's* the one you're with?'

Jodie gave her an accusing look. '*You're* going to judge me now? Really?'

But Layla's heart was beating hard at the memory of her confrontations with Matty all those years ago. She raised reluctant eyes to look at her attacker. The years had not been kind to Matty. His face was red, whether from sunburn or habitual drinking Layla couldn't tell. His belly was rounded, his jeans hanging low on his arse, his beard scraggly. He appraised Layla with watery eyes.

'Laaaylaaa's all grown up,' he murmured with a half-smile.

'Oh shut up, you dodgy old bugger,' Jodie said. 'Make us more coffee, will you?'

His face changed when she spoke to him. He ducked his head, a look of momentary embarrassment on his face, and disappeared straight into the kitchen. The kettle started up again before Layla had the chance to turn down a second unwanted coffee. Her hands were still trembling just from being in his presence.

Jodie was watching her with a curious expression. 'I know he's a bit rough around the edges, but somehow it works. He's been good to me. He helps me out with money sometimes.'

But all Layla could think about was how it had felt to be cornered in that alley.

Jodie frowned. 'Are you OK? You seem kind of freaked out.'

Layla met her gaze. 'Matty groped me once in the cafe. And then he bailed me up a couple of times when no one else was around.' Her voice dropped to a whisper. 'He threatened me … I thought he was going to …' She couldn't finish her sentence.

Jodie's face contorted with understanding. 'Oh. I'm sorry. Matty wasn't such a good guy back then. I don't think he would've actually hurt you; he just liked throwing his weight around a bit, intimidating people. I'll tear him a new one if you want.'

But Layla couldn't answer. There was something about this situation that nudged at the edge of her mind, but no matter how hard she tried to grasp at what it was, it kept sliding away.

'He changed after the accident,' Jodie went on. 'Grew up a bit. I guess that doesn't really help you, though. It never really goes away, does it?'

Layla recognised something in Jodie's eyes that lived inside her as well. So many women. It was a wonder the human race continued when there were so many reasons to be distrustful and afraid.

Matty returned to the room with the coffees and handed one to Layla. As soon as he sat down beside Jodie, she punched him on the arm. 'Ow!' he exclaimed. 'What was that for?'

'You attacked her.' Jodie gestured to Layla. 'When she was *seventeen*!'

Matty rubbed his arm, raised guilty eyes to meet Layla's. 'Yeah, sorry about that. I was so far up meself back then I thought I could do anything. I wasn't gonna … you know.'

Angry heat rushed to Layla's face. 'How was I supposed to know that? I still remember your exact words – *I could do whatever I fucken wanted to you right now, and there's no one around to hear.* I thought you were going to rape me.'

'Fuck. Yeah, OK. Sorry.' He hung his head.

Layla didn't trust herself to speak. She gulped some of her coffee, trying to swallow down her fury along with it.

'I was pissed as a maggot that night, and … actually, probably the other times too. I seemed to be pissed all the time back then.' He scrubbed at his eyes with the heels of his hands. 'Fucken hell. Sorry.'

Layla stared in astonishment as Matty dropped his head into his hands, his shoulders shaking. His whole body seemed smaller, diminished. This was not the same man she'd once been afraid of. She couldn't let it go, couldn't forgive him, not yet, but a tiny spark of sympathy glowed deep within her as Jodie's hand found his and he clasped it tightly.

'He stopped drinking after the accident,' Jodie said. 'With all the shit I had to deal with, I told him he'd have to give up the grog if he wanted to keep seeing me.'

Matty looked up, his eyes wet. 'And I did,' he said proudly. 'Haven't had a drink in twenty years.'

Layla's mind stumbled, whirred. 'What do you mean, *keep seeing you?*'

Jodie winced. 'Matty was the one I was going to leave Scott for. But it was complicated. The three of us … we had a history.'

The image of Matty getting out of the Torana on the Esplanade flitted through Layla's mind. The backpack he'd slung over his shoulder. The smug smile on his face. *Tell him not to worry, I'll keep Jodie warm at night.* The chemical smell that had emanated from him, as if he'd spilt petrol on his clothes. The sound she'd heard just before she'd left the cafe. These individual elements hovered before her for a moment before coming together in a clear image. She stood up from the couch and moved away from them, hand over her mouth.

'It was you!'

'What?' Jodie sounded bewildered. 'What was him?'

'Don't you give me the innocent act after you hauled me all the way here,' Layla snapped. '*You* were there in the main street right after he was. You're the one who made him start the fire and then you let me believe all these years that it was my fault.'

Jodie stood up too, her eyes wide. 'I don't *know* who started the fire! I always thought it was you. I had nothing to do with it, and Matty would never …' She glanced back at her lover, and stopped dead. 'Oh, fucking hell, Matty, you didn't?'

He seemed to shrink as he gazed up at her from the couch. 'I just wanted to punish him after he hit you that night. I couldn't let him get away with treating you like that. I fucken loved you … I would've done anything for you.'

A long, anguished look passed between them.

'Tell me you weren't trying to kill him,' Jodie pleaded.

'No!' Matty stood up, his eyes wild. 'I hated that fucker, but I wouldn't have *killed* him. After he knocked you around, I wanted to take something away from him. How was I supposed to know he'd go *in* there?'

Jodie flew at him and slapped at his chest with both hands. 'Jesus Christ, Matty! We were so close, you fucking idiot!'

He tried to take her into his arms, but she pushed him away. 'I'm sorry.' His voice was wobbly; his shoulders slumped in defeat. 'I've tried to make up for it … I never meant for that to happen.'

Jodie crossed her arms over her chest and turned away, hugging herself. There were tears in her eyes. Matty was sobbing now. Any last resemblance to the arrogant twenty-something he'd once been disintegrated. He looked old. He looked defeated. Layla could hardly bear to look at him. She no longer knew how to feel about anything. Everything she'd believed for more than half her life had exploded into this wild confetti of nuance.

'Don't hate me, Jodes,' Matty begged, his voice cracking.

Jodie turned back to him, tears streaking her cheeks, and wrapped her arms around his middle. He held her close, resting his cheek on top of her head. The intimacy between them made Layla long to be with Cam. He'd be so happy to find out the truth. And her mother – maybe they could finally bridge the awkward gap that had grown between them for so long.

After a minute, the two of them moved apart and Jodie's eyes found Layla's. 'I suppose you'll want to go to the police now.'

Layla was silent. The rule-following good girl she'd been as a teenager still lived there inside her. Telling the police what had really happened would be the right thing to do. She'd be able to move ahead with her life, her conscience clear that she'd done all she could to right the wrong that she'd thought was hers all these years. But at the same time, it wouldn't change anything. Scott would still be in a nursing home for the rest of his life. And the fragile happiness Jodie had found would once again be shattered. Matty might end up in jail, and she'd lose the man that she loved in spite of his faults; she'd lose the financial help he gave her. She'd be broke and alone and still tied to the man she'd lost the chance to escape from years ago. Layla had found closure, but Jodie's wound had been reopened with the discovery that it had been her own lover who'd been responsible for tearing it apart in the first place.

And as for Matty, he might have been an arsehole once, but he'd turned his life around. Regardless of how she'd despised him at the time, he'd acted out of love – had, in fact, done the exact thing Layla herself had been planning to do before she'd changed her mind. There was nothing to be gained by punishing him further when he'd done his best to make it right ever since. If it hadn't been for the part she'd played in the whole mess, none of this might have happened.

'No,' she said. 'I don't think I need to do that.'

THEN

Zach and I got in the back of the car and buckled our seatbelts, while Dad slotted the last of the boxes into the boot of the station wagon. The boxes of crockery, meticulously wrapped in newspaper, were stacked on the seat in between us, held steady by the press of our bodies. Mum locked the front door of the house and she and Dad stood for a moment, looking at the *For Sale* sign planted in the lawn.

Zach's sullen eyes met mine over the boxes. 'I hate you for this.'

'I'm sorry,' I whispered.

'Bitch!' he muttered, turning to look out of his window.

I blinked back tears. Zach had been furious when Mum and Dad had told him we were moving to Adelaide. He had a solid group of friends here; he'd been looking forward to going into Year Nine next year and no longer being in the youngest group at high school. He'd have to start again at a new, bigger high school, where he wouldn't know anyone, where he'd have to navigate a public transport system to get there every day, where he'd be the new kid. And it was all because of me.

I didn't know what Mum had told Dad, because we never spoke about it directly. But from the way he kept giving me spontaneous hugs, and from the way he sat with his head in his hands when he didn't know I was watching, and from the way his eyes slid away from mine, I knew that she'd at least told him about my relationship with Scott. He'd called in a favour and managed to score a job at his cousin's garage in Port Adelaide, and Mum had been applying for receptionist jobs. They'd found a rental in Croydon Park and Zach would start at Adelaide High in the new year. Everything was arranged. I hadn't had to do anything, other than cry and feel guilty.

Mum had made a few discreet enquiries and discovered that Scott was in a serious but stable condition. The beam had fractured one of his cervical vertebrae, causing paralysis. It was likely he'd never walk again. The spectre of horror he'd represented had shrivelled to nothing.

Mum and Dad got into the car. 'Ready to go, kids?' Dad said with false cheer. None of us answered.

I stared out the window as we drove through the knot of streets where I'd lived all my life. I'd tried to call Renee last night, but she'd refused to come to the phone, so I'd gone around to Shona's instead to tell her I was leaving. It was an awkward exchange, but she'd hugged me before I left and promised to pass on the news to Renee. 'Don't be a stranger next year, OK?' she'd said as she waved from her front door.

On the side of the road up ahead was the sign announcing that we were leaving Glasswater. *Thank you for visiting Glasswater Bay*, proclaimed a cartoon tugboat in faded multi-coloured lettering. *Please come again soon!* Tears slipped out onto my cheeks as I thought about how many times I'd passed that lame sign. This town had been my home for my whole life, and for half of that I'd been thinking about leaving it.

I'd never imagined fleeing in such circumstances, taking all my earthly ties with me. No family home, no friends. No reason to ever come back.

The sign flashed by and I turned my eyes to the open road ahead. A new life awaited me in Adelaide; a new life where I could reinvent myself, be whoever I wanted to be, find new friends, a career, and maybe, one day, happiness. I wound down the window and the wind whipped my hair around my face, lifted my heart, caught up all my torments in a flurry and tossed them out of the window.

NOW

The first thing Layla noticed when she got out of her car at The Knob was the stillness. She inhaled it: the salty tang of the sea; the dry, herbaceous scent of the shrubs that grew along the border of the car park. The air expanded her lungs. It was the first time she'd been here that there was no wind. It felt like a sign.

Then her gaze shifted to the giant granite outcropping, its contours familiar but removed, in the way a dream left a shadowy memory on the mind. There was a fence around it now: solid wooden posts with tightly strained, braided wire stretched between them. The fence extended along the cliff to a raised decking area with a sign above it: Tor Lookout. She wandered over to the deck and stood, grasping the top wire with both hands, looking down on the curve of the bay far below. For the first time she saw its true beauty, unclouded by the angsty veil of adolescence.

She'd come here to call Cam, but now she found herself reluctant to break the spell that her return to her home town had cast over her. Dragging her mind back to her life at home seemed impossible. Finally, she got her phone out and dialled her mother's number instead.

'Layla?' There was an edge of anxiety in Angela's voice. 'Is everything OK?'

Tears came to Layla's eyes. 'I didn't do it, Mum.'

'Didn't do what? What do you mean? Layla?'

But Layla couldn't get the words out. She'd called her mother to share her relief, but now it occurred to her that the truth might not be as comforting to Angela as it had been to her. Layla's mistake had uprooted her family and, ultimately, split them apart. Leaving had never been necessary.

'I didn't start the fire,' she said. 'Scott's accident ... it wasn't my fault.'

Layla waited, but there was silence from the other end of the line. Then Angela took a deep, hitching breath, and Layla realised she was crying. Tears came to her own eyes.

'I'm so sorry, Mum,' she said. 'I made everyone change their lives, and it was all for nothing.'

'Oh, Layla,' came Angela's jagged voice. 'I'm so happy.'

'You're not angry?'

'Of course I'm not angry! I know how much you've suffered over this. I never blamed you ... I've only ever wanted you to be happy.'

Sweet relief washed over Layla. She told her mother all about the meeting with Jodie, and about the school reunion, and passed on the scant information about the Glasswater Bay residents that she'd gleaned from Renee. And by the time they hung up, there was a tentative warmth between them that Layla clung to with both hands.

As for Cam, he was overjoyed to hear the news, but when she'd got to the end of the story, there was still an unresolved feeling in the pit of Layla's belly. All this time, she'd taken it for granted that their problems were tied to the things she'd kept from him, but now that barrier had gone, she realised there was a deeper dysfunction there. And it had always been there; she'd just been too tied up with guilt and shame to see it.

'I'm so glad that's over with,' Cam said. 'Now we can forget about all this and get on with our lives.'

'But …' Layla hesitated, unsure how to articulate the strange uncertainty inside her. 'I don't know if I want to forget about it. It's part of who I am.'

Cam gave a short laugh. 'But it doesn't have to be. What you've thought all this time … it was never the case.'

'It's not that. The things I did … I may have been wrong about the fire, but I'm still the *bitch who ripped a family apart*, as you put it.' The words tasted bitter in her mouth.

'God, Layla, I wasn't talking about *you*.'

'But you may as well have been. I know it's partly because of what happened with your dad, but sometimes your attitudes about women make me uncomfortable.'

'What do you mean? You know I have nothing but respect for women!'

'Yeah, if they fit your view of what a woman should be,' Layla said carefully.

'That's not fair, Layla. I've never expected you to be anything you're not.'

She sighed. 'But you've chosen to believe things about me that fit with what you want to see. The fact is, I slept with a *lot* of men before I met you.'

Layla imagined him cringing away from her words, not wanting to believe them.

'You were probably traumatised because of what that bastard did to you,' he said.

Layla blew out an exasperated breath. 'But that's just it! It doesn't matter *why* I did it. I don't want to feel like I need to keep parts of me hidden from you anymore. Can you understand that?'

Cam didn't speak straightaway, and when he did, his voice was shaking. 'You're right. I'm sorry. I should never have made you feel that way.'

'I love you, and I want to be with you. But there are obviously some bigger problems between us than either of us realised. I think we should consider having relationship counselling so we can solve them together.'

There was a long silence, and Layla held her breath and clutched the phone tight. Maybe it was too late to mend their relationship. Maybe they were both too damaged.

'I think that's a good idea,' he said at last. 'I don't want to lose you.'

She let out her breath in a gust of relief. 'Thank you.'

'Are we going to get through this?'

'I think we will, if we do it together.'

*

Layla, Renee and Shona picked their way down the stone steps and did the classic Glasswater summer quick-step across the searing sand to the shade under the jetty. Renee spread out the picnic rug in a spot that hadn't already been taken, and they sat down on it as Jonah and Henry ran to the water. Daniel gave them a small wave and sauntered off after the boys.

When Layla had got back to Renee's place, it'd been on the tip of her tongue to tell her friends what she'd discovered, but then she'd decided it wasn't her secret to share. The realisation gave her a heady sense of freedom. She could let the knowledge slip through her fingers and take flight on the air. Now it was Jodie and Matty's secret to keep.

'Fancy a wine?' Renee produced a bottle of riesling from the refrigerated bag she'd brought.

'Hell yes.'

'Ah, shit,' Renee said, her head in the bag.

'What's wrong?'

'I forgot to bring the bloody glasses.'

'Pfft.' Shona plucked up the bottle and twisted off the screw cap. 'Did you learn nothing from our high school days?'

She took a swig from the bottle and passed it to Layla. They laughed as they passed the bottle back and forth between them, watching Renee's sons thrashing around in the water, splashing each other and laughing with the friends they'd run into.

'Uh-oh,' Shona said. 'Look who's coming over.'

They looked up to see Jodie Wilson picking her way between the towels spread out on the sand, her wet hair straggled over her shoulders. She eyed the almost-empty bottle in Layla's hand. 'Liquid lunch, girls?' she trilled.

Shona scowled at her. 'There's solid lunch in there too. We just haven't got to it yet.'

Jodie twisted the corner of the towel that hung around her neck in one hand. 'I wanted to apologise for the things I said to you last night, Layla. I guess I was jealous. I haven't really done anything interesting since high school, and you guys are all successful, so ...'

Surprise fluttered through Layla. It seemed that she'd been closed off from everyone for years, and nothing she'd thought about anyone was concrete. People's capacity to surprise was consistently dazzling. She smiled up at Jodie. 'Well, I had a great time. You did a good job organising it.'

Jodie blushed. 'Thank you.'

'Apart from the music,' Shona added.

'Do you want to join us?' Renee patted the rug.

'We've almost finished the wine though,' Layla said.

'Don't worry, I brought two,' Renee grinned.

'Thanks, but I was just heading home,' Jodie said. 'Thanks for coming last night. It meant a lot to me.'

They waved as she continued up towards the Esplanade, hot-footing it across the sand.

'I'm going for a swim,' Shona announced.

Layla and Renee watched as she took off her white shirt and jogged down towards the water in her hot-pink bikini.

'I can't believe how great she still looks,' Layla said enviously.

Renee looked sideways at her. 'You'd look great too if you were out there in a bikini.'

Layla shifted uncomfortably. Renee had lent her some bathers, but she knew she wouldn't have the courage to strip off her clothes and expose herself to all these people. She stretched out her legs and curled her bare toes into the sand. 'Well, if there's one thing that hasn't changed, it's that I still fucking hate the beach. What's with sand? It's all kind of greasy, but it also makes my skin feel dry and gross, and I'll still be brushing it off myself in two days' time. You can wash it off in the water, but then you have to cross the bloody sand again to get out of here, so you're destined to be fucking covered in the stuff permanently. And what the hell is the point of going to the beach to cool off when you're just as hot by the time you get back to your car? And even if you don't dry yourself at all so you can retain some semblance of coolness, your car is like a bloody oven when you get back to it, so by the time you get home you're sweating like a pig again. I just don't get it.'

Renee chuckled. 'You were always wasted in this town.'

'Still am.'

'Are you going to be OK?'

Layla met her gaze. 'Yeah, I think I am.'

Renee's smile of genuine pleasure was so delicious that Layla had the urge to hug her.

'Will you come back to visit us again?'

'I'd like that. And you should come to Adelaide sometime too.'

'I will.'

They sat in silence for a while, polishing off the bottle of wine.

'Come on.' Renee stood up decisively and pulled Layla to her feet. 'We're going for a swim.'

'Oh no, Renee, I can't,' Layla protested.

'C'mon, Lay.' Renee gestured around her. 'What do you care what these people think? They're all here to have fun. No one's looking at you, and even if they did, what does it matter?'

The slippery eel of shame that had lived within Layla for so long twisted and cringed. The idea of revealing so much of herself with all these people around was like contemplating her own death. She couldn't do it. She wouldn't do it. Renee waited. Then Layla looked around at the people who surrounded them, and realised Renee was right. None of them were paying the slightest bit of attention to her. There was a man not far from them with a huge hairy belly. A teenage girl, her thighs dimpled with cellulite. An old woman, her bathers still wet, every inch of her skin deeply wrinkled. All of them were smiling. There was something exhilarating about their lack of self-consciousness. None of them were grotesque, as she had always considered herself: they were beautiful. Maybe she could be too.

'OK,' she said.

Before she could change her mind, she pulled off her clothes, shrinking inside Renee's bronze one-piece. She felt vulnerable, exposed, as she followed Renee down to the water's edge. But no one looked at her. Everyone was absorbed in their own fun. The foaming water pulled at her feet; the wet sand sucked them down as if trying to swallow her whole. Renee looked back and smiled at her once, then dived under a small wave and came up, laughing.

Layla hesitated a moment longer, then waded out further and plunged in. The water was shockingly cold, but she felt her body come alive. She began to swim, striking out towards the open sea. After a few minutes, she stopped and treaded water, watching the families splashing around in the shallows, watching Renee and Daniel kissing like the young couple they'd once been. Exaltation swelled inside her. Now the fear had lifted, she could imagine bringing her own family here for a visit. She pictured Cam carrying Ella on his shoulders; Layla teaching Louis how to swim in the salt-stung surf. The time away from them had made her appreciate what she had, what she could have lost. When she got home tomorrow, she was going to focus on them, on her relationship with Cam. She was going to make it work.

But for today – just for today – she was going to enjoy this crystalline moment of happiness, this brief flash of clarity, when she could imagine what life might have been if she'd never left.

ACKNOWLEDGEMENTS

This book would not be what it is today without the people who supported and encouraged me along the way.

Thank you to my long-time friend and fellow author, Rebekah Turner, for always being the first to hear my unformed ideas and encouraging me to pursue them. It was your idea to throw in a school reunion that got the story back on track when it was faltering. Thanks for coming on retreat with me when I was writing the first draft, for always giving honest feedback on my terrible drafts, and for the many high school memories (especially from our art classes – I still sometimes wonder whether Ms Parsons ever found out what a head job was) that made their way into this book. You are a good egg.

Thank you to the whole team at Pantera Press for bringing my writing out into the world. As always, thanks to my editor, Lucy Bell, for your enthusiasm for this book from the first time I pitched the idea right through to the finished product. You always get exactly what I'm trying to do, and your guidance makes me push myself to be a better writer. Thank you also to Lex Hirst for your thoughtful feedback, which helped me to lift this story just that little bit more.

Thanks to two women for the wine-fuelled conversation that evening when we shared our stories of the men who used our youth, our roles, our bodies, as weapons against us. It was that conversation that convinced me I needed to write this book. Time's fucking up.

When I started writing this story, I didn't realise its backbone would be female friendship, but now it makes sense, because the small group of extraordinary women I'm lucky enough to call my friends are a constant joy in my life. Whether we've known each other for two years or thirty, catch up once a year or often enough to know one another's menstrual cycles, thanks for the laughs, the drinks, the debates, the advice, and for always being there.

Finally, thanks, of course, to my family ... My husband, George, for always listening and making the effort to understand the female experience, and for helping to facilitate writing time when it seems impossible among the relentless demands of work and a young family. And my kids, Finn, Cael and Lata, for providing endless creative material ... and I'm sorry, Cael the Chaos Demon, for accidentally writing you into this book.

ABOUT REBECCA FREEBORN

Rebecca Freeborn lives in the Adelaide Hills with a husband, three kids, a cat, a horse, more books than she can fit in her bookcase and an ever-diminishing wine collection.

She works as a communications and content editor for the South Australian Government, where she screams into the void against passive voice and unnecessary capitalisation. She writes before the sun comes up and thrives on unrealistic deadlines.

Rebecca is also the author of *Hot Pursuit* (2018) and *Misconception* (2019).

BOOK CLUB QUESTIONS

1. Discuss the significance of the Hannah Gadsby quote: 'A seventeen-year-old girl is just never, ever in her prime. Ever.'

2. One of the main themes in the novel is the issue of consent. Do you think consent is more complex than an age and a simple yes or no? Should the power differential also be a consideration?

3. Which character did you connect with the most?

4. In what ways does Layla's past affect her in the present?

5. How would you describe Shona, Renee and Layla's friendship? Discuss the importance of female friendship in this story.

6. How would you describe Scott's behaviour towards Layla?

7. Why do you think Layla felt like she couldn't share her past with Cam? Do you think it's better to know about your partner's past relationship history or not?

8. How do you feel about the resolution between Layla and Cam? Do you think their relationship will survive?

9. What role do you think Matty played in the story?

10. Do you think Jodie was justified in seeking Layla out? How did their confrontation leave you feeling?

11. What similarities did Layla share with Jodie?

12. How was Layla's relationship with her mother impacted by the affair with Scott?

Also by Rebecca Freeborn

Available in all good bookstores or from www.panterapress.com